A S......... L
KILLS NINE...

THE STITCHIN

MARK LAKERAM

ISBN: 978 0 9957929 4 4

To Stephen

CHAPTER 1
DAY 1

Samuel Yates jolted himself upright and rubbed his weary eyes. His heart was beating faster than normal. He started to think calming thoughts to bring his heart rate to a regular pace. Soon, he was calm, not because he had many peaceful memories, but because this was his daily ritual. He took a sip of water from the glass on the table next to the bed, then looked at the green-blue glow from the alarm clock next to it. The machine displayed 14:14. *At least, I made it to a couple of hours past midnight tonight*, he thought.

For a moment, he considered setting the clock to display the correct time but didn't. Instead, he threw his head back, pressed his skull into the pillow, shut his eyes and waited for sleep to take hold. As he lay there trying not to think, he realised what day it was. A wry smile crossed his face. Instantly, he tried to stop thinking about it, but actively trying to do so made it harder. One thing he had learnt was not to count the night away by staring at the clock every ten to twenty minutes. He knew from past experience that doing so just made sleep stay away longer.

Some time later—he wasn't aware how long it had been—he felt something near his feet. He realised that it was someone bouncing up and down at the foot of his bed. 'Wake up, little brother. It's your birthday.' The sleep assailant was moving towards his head. 'You can't stay in bed all day.'

Sam groaned. 'What time is it?'

'Your clock says two a.m.'

'That means two p.m. The twenty-four-hour clock setting needs to be adjusted.'

'You've missed breakfast and lunch.'

'Were you here for them? I only just heard you come in,' Sam lied.

The bed-bouncer looked sheepishly at his younger brother. 'No; I got lucky.' He winked, dived down on the bed and ruffled Sam's hair.

'I hope you had a shower afterwards.' Sam grimaced playfully.

'It was in a hotel room, so I definitely made sure I used all the amenities.'

'A hotel—sounds interesting. Go on then, tell me all about it.'

'Now that you're seventeen, you must stop living vicariously through me and go out and do it for yourself. Actually, scrap that, just continue to be you. You have to be the brains of the family, so just continue studying; fun will come later. Why don't you get up and get ready? I can give you your birthday present, and we can go out and get a late lunch—with our lunch talk being all the gory details of last night and the highlights, including her being northern, older and with no inhibitions whatsoever.'

'Yes, sir, Mitchell, sir.'

Sam noticed his brother very quickly glancing around the room. 'I'm sorry; they aren't around. You know that both Mum and Dad would have been very proud of you.'

'Thanks,' he responded. *I presume that's what I'm meant to say and what Mitch wants to hear.* 'I'll see you downstairs in a bit.'

'Hurry up. And don't wear trackies; jeans and a loose T-shirt will do.' Mitch placed his hand on Sam's forehead and kissed it, jumped up and raced out of the room that used to belong to their parents.

Twenty-four minutes later, Sam joined Mitch in the kitchen. On the counter, Sam saw a chocolate cake with one candle on it. 'You shouldn't have. I told you I don't want any fuss, especially with all the crap that has been going on lately.'

'It's for me,' Mitch said, lighting the candle. 'Blow it out and make a wish; that way, I won't sing.'

'I thought you said it was for you.'

'Please, just humour me.'

Sam blew out the little flame. He briefly thought about his parents. *Why bother? This year won't be any different, it will just be like the rest. No wonder I am emotionally stunted.* 'I wished for world peace.'

'Don't tell me or it won't happen.'

'I don't think that's on course to happen anyway.'

'Okay, Mr Cynical. Just open this.' Mitch handed him a wrapped present. 'Don't worry; it's not at all fussy and cost me zero pounds.'

Sam resolved to try to stop coming across as a brat and to just appreciate the effort his brother had gone to. *It should be easy to fake happiness—fate has made us both professional liars.* He opened the gift, prepared to say it was the best thing ever, regardless. 'You're a

3

twat.' He couldn't help but grin away. He looked up at Mitch, who had a grin on his face to match that of his brother. 'I'm not giving this back.'

'That's the point of a present...' He stopped as Sam started to put on the leather jacket. 'It's yours to keep.'

'Thank you. I've wanted this ever since I first saw you wearing it. Gosh, I must have been ten years old.'

'You were nine. I got it for my seventeenth birthday too. Now I'm passing it down, as I'm super-athletic, muscled and toned, and it's built for someone scrawny like you.'

Sam hugged his brother because the gesture made the day not so bad, and if he had looked at him in the face, he might have cried. 'I'm in better shape than you.'

'I guess you were too young to remember why I first got the jacket.'

'You were rebelling. I remember you and them arguing a lot around that time.'

'Something like that, but I got it to protect myself.' Mitch grinned. 'Let me show you what I mean.'

He led the way outside, with Sam following him. In the driveway stood two motorbikes. Given the size of the driveway, they looked small. Sam only appreciated the actual size once he was close enough to touch the bikes. 'How did you afford these?'

'Relax; they are just hired for the day. When I was seventeen, I bought and learned to ride a motorbike. Dad hated it and told me to get rid of it, hence, all the arguing. Not sure if you remember it? Mum seemed to not mind but had to agree with Dad.'

Sam noticed his brother pause and look spaced out. He's probably wondering if mentioning them still upsets me. 'What did you do with the bike? I remember you riding it but it wasn't kept here.'

'I had to store it at Ellen's place, that bookish girl whom I was seeing at the time.' Mitch smiled, looking a million miles away.

'The one who used to do all your homework?'

Mitch blinked and returned to the moment. 'I'm glad you remember all my words of wisdom. She loved a bad boy, and the bike just sealed the deal. Clever girls are wild, but you won't find that out. As you're super-smart, you'll always attract the pretty but simple ones.'

'Thanks for the worldly advice, but I'm not sure if that was a compliment.'

He laughed. 'Anyway, back to the beauties in front of us. Mine is the Honda African Twin. I used to have an XRV, but it isn't made anymore, and I couldn't find one for today. This one is the newer version; it's still a sports bike but with more technology. Yours is sporty and nimble; let me introduce you to the Kawasaki Versys-X. Hop on and I'll show you the basics; the controls, balance and riding techniques.'

Sam lapped up the knowledge being passed down to him. Moments like this made him feel like a normal teenager, one leading a regular life, with just standard teenage-angst to deal with. No abandonment issues, daily lying to teachers and friends, living the pretence of having a reliable nuclear family. He was a quick study and wanted to impress his older brother, who was his idol and not just his surrogate parent. After the thirty-minute crash course, they were ready to go.

'I'm going to ride next to you. We will go slowly at first and head to the warehouse area. Once there, we can go faster. If you need to stop at any point, signal to me and pull over. Keep your helmet on and visor down.'

The bikes were brought to life, and the brothers began the birthday ride, with Mitch slowly leading the way out of the drive and the family home. Sam followed; the adrenaline had kicked in and he was loving every moment. He wanted to get to the warehouse area as quickly as possible so that he could unleash the potential of the machine and impress his brother. But he decided to respect Mitch's instructions until he was more road-savvy.

As they hit the public road and Sam passed the front entrance to their neighbour's driveway, he felt sad. Sam quickly looked away from that house and decided to concentrate on the road. Where they lived was a no-passing-through traffic area, which made it relatively secluded. Once they hit the main roads, there would be more vehicles, people to judge him and proper driving challenges.

Mitch gave his little brother a thumbs-up, and Sam quickly returned the gesture. He didn't want to keep his hands off the grip for long. After a few minutes, concentrating on the road became second nature and a passive act. He felt a sense of jubilation. Now, he could take in all his surroundings and enjoy the newfound liberation that the bike gifted him with. Sam wondered if

Mitch felt as free as he did, and for a fleeting moment he hoped that his older brother wouldn't feel so free that he would just drive off and never come back. Honestly, Sam wouldn't have blamed him; and if their ages were reversed, he himself might have done just that.

More cars were on the road now, so more control and attention were needed. Sam looked around; Mitch was to the side in front of him. Sam wondered why all the Land Rovers and similar types of vehicles were out in force. It was the school holidays, so the soccer mums and their offspring would be in Southern Europe sunning themselves, just like he and his lot used to do. The convoy sped off.

'Must be Victoria's fortieth or a tea party for young Willoughby,' Sam said aloud. Not that anyone could hear him; he had started to give a commentary on the bike ride for his own amusement. 'We won't be seeing them again. They will be giving the unsavoury land up ahead a wide berth. We, on the other hand, are daredevil explorers and must traverse the zone to get to the warehouses and land-a-plenty. Once there, my cheetah, I will unleash your super-cat speed.'

Mitch stopped at the red light and signalled right. Sam copied. Mitch put up his visor. 'Not quite the open road, but isn't this just the best feeling ever?' He did the thumbs-up sign again as he realised he couldn't be heard. Sam saw the pure joy on his brother's face and made the same gesture to say he was enjoying himself. He was, his heart was beating faster, but not in the same way when he woke up during the night; this was an

7

excited elation. Maybe everything would be alright; after all, all he had to do was survive one more year, and then he would legally be an adult.

'Big brother is going faster on the African Twin now—maybe because he wants to get out of this area as fast as he can, as he never liked them. Didn't he use to get into skirmishes with them. They were always spoiling for a fight with the locals. Or maybe it is simply that he is enjoying being on a bike again. I'm loving it and it's only my first time. Maybe, I was born to ride. As for the area, it doesn't bother me. They have an amazing sense of family, something I only know about through Mitch, maybe I am jealous of them. There are fewer cars around.' His bike shook. 'We can actually go faster without worrying so much. But that has become second nature; I've only been on the bike for a short while and it is all becoming instinctive. I want to go so fast that the wind will make my new-old jacket flap around.'

They stopped at a red light, Sam looked around to take in the surroundings. On the kerb, he couldn't help but notice two teenage girls. They were probably slightly younger than he was, but he couldn't tell because they were wearing lots of makeup. They were hugging each other as if to offer the other comfort. When Sam looked closer, he saw that one of them had ripped tights and her hair seemed out of place, like she had just awakened. The most suitable description he could come up with was 'dishevelled.' He glanced over to Mitch to see if he had noticed the girls, but he couldn't tell, as his brother had his helmet on with the visor down. The light changed to green, and his brother moved off, so Sam followed.

After less than a minute of driving. Sam saw more people and a group huddled on the pavement. One of the women in the group looked up at him, and that's when he noticed blood on her face. As she moved her position to look at the riders, she broke the circle of the group. Sam saw a couple of young children in the middle, but he hadn't had enough interaction with little children to guess their ages. He could see, though, that they were less than half the height of the adults. From the way they held their bodies they both appeared injured. The boy looked dirty, like he had rolled over on the floor for a good hour. The only clean part of him were the streaks from his eyes to the bottom of his face, where his tears had cleared a path through the grime. The girl had blood on her face. The woman closed the circle again, pulled at her own sleeve and moved it towards the red on the little girl's face.

Mitch rode off, Sam followed. Ahead, in the middle of the road, was a mob. The two brothers had no choice but to stop and look. Men of different ages were pushing and shoving each other, in headlocks with one another. Some were going head-to-head and throwing punches at each other. Two on one, three on one. In the periphery of the fighting, there were people lying on the ground, holding parts of their bodies.

'What's going on here? What have we stumbled across?' Sam started to feel very apprehensive. He shivered as a cold sensation ran down from his neck to his spine. He didn't know what was going on; all he wanted to do was turn around and go home. People in his school said the locals of this area behaved like this, but he'd never really believed it. Mitch grabbed the hand grip on the Kawasaki to get Sam's attention and motioned that they should head right and down a side road. He let Sam go first and brought up the rear. Sam went faster than before because he wanted to get away from the sight ahead of him. He raced towards the escape route. He wasn't far down the side road when he encountered a further commotion. Numerous people were sitting on the kerb and in the middle of the road, nursing cuts and bruises. This time, the source of the misery seemed obvious to Sam.

Part of a building had collapsed, and people were pointing at it and screaming. Others were scrambling on top of the debris and throwing rubble from the mass, trying to find anyone trapped. It was carnage; it resembled some war-torn country that had just suffered a bombing. The victims appeared disorientated, they were dirty, bloodied, injured, and they were broken. Their emotions and behaviours ranged from utter disbelief to frantic scrambling around desperately searching for a loved one.

Even though Sam wore his helmet, the screams and sobs penetrated his brain. It was like his hearing had suddenly become super-sensitive because he could hear everything. *We need to help these people, get the bricks off them and get them to a hospital.* He felt light-headed. He forgot himself, where he was and what he was doing.

He felt a dull ache all over his body—his chest and legs were hurting. He realised that somehow, he had come off his bike and had hit the ground. Sam turned his head to the side and lying a couple of metres away from him was someone who was staring at him with eyes wide open and with his mouth open like he wanted to speak. Sam wanted to take off his helmet so that the guy could also see his eyes, but he knew there would be no point, as behind the man's expression, there was nothing. Sam put out his arm, about to crawl over to the body to make sure, but someone else threw a coat over the face of the empty shell that had been staring at him.

CHAPTER 2
DAY 1

'What took you so long to answer?' Her sister asked in a panicked voice.

'I was having a nap.' Sarah responded.

'At three in the afternoon? Please tell me you aren't working yourself silly.'

'No. I had a long night, but for other reasons.'

'Sarah, I am worried about you.'

'Don't be ridiculous. You have nothing to worry about.'

'After everything that happened to you, you should not be working and then you moved away? You should have stayed with us, spent some time with family. Your nieces miss you.'

'I miss the girls too, and of course, you, Clare. But you know that I was needed here.'

'It's wrong; it's too soon after that—' Clare took a long pause, thinking of her next word very carefully, '— incident.'

Sarah carefully deliberated her response because she wanted to pacify her older sister. 'I chose to come here; it's where I'm needed. Plus, you know nothing can harm me; I'm made of silver.'

'Sarah Silver, you are and always will be a force to reckon with. But am I not allowed to worry about my baby sister moving halfway around the country?'

'We Silvers are tough, so you'll be fine, and so will I.'

'I'm not a Silver anymore—'

'You should have never taken his name. I love Phil as a brother but come on—you gave up Silver for Long.'

'In love, you have to make sacrifices. I took his name because I knew that when we had children, I wanted us all to have the same surname.'

'You could have all been Silvers.'

Clare changed the subject. 'Why was it a long night? Are you having trouble sleeping?'

Sarah knew exactly what Clare was doing. She wasn't avoiding a feminist debate, but mainly by bringing this subject up now as opposed to when it was first mentioned, she was hoping for an honest answer to her original question.

'I sleep fine when I'm alone, but last night, I had company. He is like your Phil in that he is long, but not in name. He kept me up all night.' Sarah smirked at the phone, hoping that her sister would be blushing.

'Oh. Is he still there?'

'Yes, he's next to me. Do you want to say hello? I think this one is going to be your new brother-in-law.'

'That's awesome! I'll tell the girls, and we can start shopping for dresses. As Steph is the youngest, I presume you'll want her to be the flower girl.'

Sarah was surprised that Clare's sarcastic response was so quick. 'You know that I'm just messing with you.'

'Obviously; you gave it away by the marriage implication. But seriously, it wouldn't hurt for you to settle down. Okay, not settle down but get a good man,

13

have someone to take care of you. At least see this guy again.'

'How do you know we aren't dating?'

'I know you. Promise me you will give love a chance.'

'Yes, Mum.'

'Next time we speak, I want to hear all about a real date. And it had better be romantic. I love you; let others do the same.'

'I love you too, Clare. Kiss Steph and Sabrina for me, and Mr Long.' She emphasised the last word and smirked to herself. That could have been a long-drawn-out call about her moving to London, which her family didn't think was a great place for her as they were worried about her, but it ended abruptly. She had played her sister well; she always could, even when they were little. *It was for her own good. Anyway, it isn't like it was a complete lie; I did have sex last night and it was great.* At that thought, Sarah stretched out and smiled to herself as she reminisced. *Perhaps I will call him, but it will just be for more of the same.*

The phone rang again. It was a different ringtone, not the one reserved for Sarah's special contacts in her phonebook. Few people had her number; she never used it for any forms, so she never got unsolicited calls. This was work; instantly, she woke up and automatically switched her mind to professional mode.

'Hello, Sarah Silver.'

'Hello, Tanner.' She didn't need to pause; the sound of his voice was immediately recognisable to her.

'You don't work with me, so you can call me Pete.'

'That wouldn't sound right, and I used to work for you.'

'How is the South? Have you settled in?'

'Small talk doesn't sound right either.' She thought about the face at the other end of the line, particularly those striking blue eyes, that had a depth behind them that would make anyone confess anything.

'Always the professional; it warms my heart that you haven't changed a bit. I have a job for you, and to be honest, it's not just because it's on your new doorstep. From what I've read and seen, you are the only person who will be able to solve this case.'

You don't need to play to my vanity, Pete.

'I have emailed you everything I've seen; it's not much. And I've spoken to your future new boss and greased the wheel so you can start work early on this. I don't want to stitch you up. This isn't a priority for the department, for anyone really. But it is for me.'

'What's the case, Tanner?'

'Missing girl, well, teenager. Find Megan North.'

'That's not my area of expertise.'

'I know, Silver. Solve the case for me, for you.'

'What does that mean? And why do you care about this girl?'

'She's just a traveller girl. No one cares about her, that's the deal. Someone has to care; someone has to find her. You have to find her.'

'But—'

'I have to take another call. I believe in you, Sarah Silver. Good luck.'

'Tanner, Tanner—' The line was dead.

She got out of bed, traversed the multiple storage boxes and walked into the lounge and to her laptop and switched it on. It was the only thing she had made a conscious effort to get unpacked and set up. She spoke to the computer as to a confidante. 'Nothing is ever really normal with that man, but that was a stranger-than-usual conversation. The language he used did not seem quite like his, and since when was he bothered by a missing teenager? What is he involved with, and why did he call me and tell me nothing—no real details, no analysis, why it matters? He's been in this game too long to care "because someone should"; he's not a new officer but a seasoned professional.'

Sarah logged in to her police account before realising that her old details wouldn't work as she had left the Greater Manchester Police Force and hadn't been set up yet at her new job at the Metropolitan Police. She checked her personal email account, but there was nothing. She would have to go to the office in person and get set up a lot sooner than she had planned.

Sarah felt the emptiness of the room she stood in. It was cold and sterile, but she liked it. It was originally one of the briefing rooms, BR-4, used for cases where a big team wasn't necessary, because they either had to be very discreet within the department or the case wasn't deemed important enough. They were going to convert the room into more office space and had removed most of the furniture. She had been allowed to use the room for two weeks until she was scheduled to officially start.

Two weeks to solve a non-case, she thought, glancing around her new work home. The actual Metropolitan Police building was nowhere near as dead as this room. Theirs was a twenty-four-hour operation, but the evenings had fewer people; so, when she arrived after six in the evening, there was only a skeleton crew around. That suited her fine; she didn't want to mingle. She would not get close to anyone at work; she didn't need friends or anything else. And by now, they would all have known that she would join them soon and the rumours or even the truth would have spread already. At a minimum, there would be some resentment of her, while others—probably the majority—would hate her.

When she first entered the building, Doughty, her new boss, came to meet her and got her past security. It was like he had been expecting her. He checked her out, as she did him. He was larger than life, standing over six feet tall, and had a booming voice that commanded attention. It had been just them in his office; he wasn't shouting, but every word reverberated. He was pleasant enough to her, welcoming her to the team, but he didn't mention the other business. Now, he went straight to the point.

'Pete contacted me this afternoon and asked me to set you up immediately. He had heard of a case in this jurisdiction that he knew was you. His words, not mine. He said it wasn't something this division would be interested in. If you were to solve it, you would be doing everyone a favour. I read it; he's right, it's not something we would ever waste resources on. Missing eighteen-year-old traveller girl. Probably wanted to get away from the community, met a non-traveller and buggered off. Hardly something requiring the attention of a special branch. What is Pete Tanner's interest in this?'

'I don't know, sir. I haven't read the case file. Sir, how do you and Tanner know each other?'

'We go way back, trained together. I owe him a favour, which he's now used up with you and this case. You haven't officially started here, you're still being paid by Manchester for the next two weeks, so you can help him if you want. I pulled some strings and got you a temporary badge and computer access. Our relations with the traveller community would benefit from our presence and from our looking like we are taking their concerns seriously. I can even spare you a junior helper.'

'That's not necessary, sir.'

'It is.'

'Of course.'

'There is some ongoing remodelling work throughout the building, so I don't have a desk for you now. But make yourself at home in BR-4; it has just been cleared out. It's out of the way; you will have privacy there, so it should suit your needs. I'll walk you to the room. We'll go via IT and get you a computer and all that.'

'Thanks, sir.'

'If you have any problems, or if you find out that anything untoward is going on, come to me. We don't need a situation like that in Manchester blowing up in this constabulary. I prefer to maintain order in my own house. Are we clear?'

'Crystal.'

She had been sitting on the floor of BR-4 for a couple of hours, reading the case file. There was not much to it, so she re-read it a few times.

This doesn't seem to be a typical missing person case; it sounds like a case of a teenage girl running away, as Doughty said. There is nothing to make the case special or to warrant my involvement. Why does Tanner care about this? What am I missing?

Sarah had a full-sized photo of Megan on the screen; the astute detective looked at it closely. Sarah examined the face; it was made up like that of any teenage girl on a night out. The picture showed the girl's big blue eyes enhanced with smoky make-up and fake lashes, thick eyebrows, high cheekbones and full, pouty lips. But there was something else there. Underneath it all, Megan was hauntingly beautiful. It was not a face people would forget but one that looked like it enjoyed toying with trouble. Sarah continued absorbing the picture as the younger woman held her own and just stared back, daring the seasoned professional to find her.

Doughty had printed out the report for her. She took it out and stood up. She walked over to the clear freestanding Perspex board, the only piece of furniture left in the room, and stuck the photograph right in the middle. 'Megan North, I bet all the boys and maybe some girls loved you, but it's a fine line—did you cross it? Did you run away, or did something happen to you? Why does Pete Tanner want me to help you? What is the connection between you?' She wanted to write down her initial thoughts but there were no pens, so she walked out of the room and headed to another briefing room to get some.

She needed to write down the thoughts that were forming in her head. There was not a lot of information to go on, these were more avenues along which to start the investigation. Sarah walked out of the room and started to walk around the building looking for the main debriefing room. She had decided to swipe some of their marker pens. Glancing at her watch, she realised that she had been in that room for three hours. Becoming absorbed in a case was an occupational hazard. It gets you—no matter what the case, it gets you. The walk was doing her body good. She didn't realise that she'd needed to stretch and get her blood flowing again.

BR-1 was a lot bigger than the room she had been working in. It was set up more like a lecture theatre with staggered seating. She was at the front of the room, acquiring the pens, when she heard a sound outside the room. It was getting louder. Six doors, three on each side and at different levels, were simultaneously yanked open. Her peers started rushing into the room. She stared at them. Some looked like they were at the end of their shift and others looked like they had recently awoken.

Of course, they stared back at her. *It must look like I am about to brief them.* Silence then engulfed the room; and to her relief, she realised that Doughty was standing next to her. The respect he commanded was impressive. You could actually hear a pin drop. Even those officers still coming in and sitting down were doing so incredibly stealthily.

'This is Sarah Silver. She joined us early to work on a special case. I am sure you will all welcome her and show her the respect afforded to any senior detective.'

'Sarah Silver.' *Should I curtsey for them or do a little dance on the stage?* She could hear her name being whispered. She could see the officers leaning over and covering their mouths as they discussed her, telling those who didn't know about her their own version of what they thought they knew. She felt every eye in the room penetrate her. Not one person smiled or showed any warmth. The whispering was getting louder, but she didn't want to hear what they were saying.

'Thank you, Sarah,' Doughty said.

She took it as her cue to leave.

A lesser woman would have run out of there but she calmly walked out and, at the door, turned to look at the people in the room. 'Let me know if you need a hand,' she said confidently to no one in particular before heading out of the room and towards the nearest toilet.

Something serious must have happened, I wonder what? Surely, it would be a better use of my time to help them with whatever is going on?

She wanted to splash some cold water on her face and compose herself. She walked past the ladies and then the gents and went into the toilet for the disabled. She locked the door behind her and switched on the lights. She looked at herself in the mirror. 'Well, that could have been worse. You knew it would be difficult, but at least half the force saw you and can get it out of their system.' As she gave herself the pep talk, after saying the words out loud, she became tense. *Saw you.* She examined herself closer in the mirror. She had been in the BR-4 for a long time, with her hands in her hair while she had been thinking.

Her hair was all over the place. 'I know what to look for. Am I being too critical of myself? Surely, they thought I looked like a mess. It's night-time; most of them just rolled out of bed for whatever emergency had called them in.' *Or do they know more about me than they should? Did my mask fall?* She massaged her temples. Then she pushed the fingers of her right hand towards her hairline. Her left hand joined her right and she slowly tugged at her hair. She looked in the mirror; her expression was now that of a cold, hard detective. She saw a different face to what people looking at her saw. She saw the truth: no make-up, beauty routines, smart clothes or perfectly coiffured hair could hide her true self from the person who knew her best. *If only the world saw the real me they would all run a mile.*

She slowly pulled off the wig she had been wearing to see how strong it was, and she continued to stare at her now bald head and the many scars that were now visible.

CHAPTER 3
DAY 1

'Sam, Sam, are you okay? Does anywhere hurt bad? Can you move? If you can, we have to go.'

Sam heard Mitch's voice, but the dead man's eyes had transfixed him. Even though the man was now covered, it didn't matter—he could still see the face and the haunting, pleading expression. He realised that he would always be able to see it now whenever he closed his eyes. With that thought, he wanted to get as far away from the place as possible. He started to move. His chest hurt the most because that is what he landed on. It had winded him. Now, it felt like the after-effect of someone slapping him hard across his chest. His breathing was fine, but he felt claustrophobic wearing the helmet. He considered removing it for a second but decided against it, as he liked having the barrier up, protecting his face from the chaos unfolding in front of him.

Sam was now up on his knees when he looked up and saw Mitch. His older brother had taken off his helmet. He was staring down at Sam while helping his little brother to get up. 'Are you injured?' Suddenly, there was a loud bang, and the rest of the building collapsed. A massive plume of dust and wind smacked the brothers and sent them both to the ground.

Once the initial shock had passed, Sam quickly got up. He looked Mitch over to make sure he was also okay, and to his relief, he saw that his brother had already gotten up and was currently spitting out dust from his mouth. 'Mitchell, do you think we can help?' The screaming, shouting and general chaos already told Sam the answer.

'There is nothing we can do here. They need medical assistance and the fire brigade.' Mitch stopped to cough and spit. 'I'm sure the emergency services are on their way, which also means the police. We don't want to stick around for questioning. Let's go.' He picked up Sam's bike, set it upright and started walking with it to his Honda. 'Come on.'

When the bikes were side by side, Mitch hopped onto his. He wiped the dirt off the seat of the Kawasaki. Once Sam was seated and started his engine, Mitch held the hang grip on the Versys-X with his left hand and led them away from the carnage. He slowly took the first side street on the right. As they were turning down the new road, Sam took one last look. He saw a car enter the street they were just on. It was a black SUV. He thought he saw an identical vehicle behind that one but couldn't be sure, as they had moved off. Mitch was taking them down multiple roads; every chance there was to make a turn, he was taking it. Each turn was moving them away from the direction of the earlier fighting mob and the carnage of the collapsed building.

After continuing like this for about twenty minutes, Mitch let go of his brother's bike. 'Can you handle it from here?'

Sam made the thumbs-up motion, as he was still wearing the helmet; he dusted himself off and as before, he let his brother lead the way. He did not think about the events they had witnessed. He just concentrated on the road partly because he did not want to be thrown from the motorbike again but mainly because if he dwelt on the past hour, he might not have been able to keep it together.

Mitch stopped. Sam came to a gentle halt and took off his helmet so that they could talk. 'I have no idea where we are now.'

'I got lost when we entered the traveller area.'

'We are out of their territory, but I don't know where we are exactly. Do you have your phone with you?'

'Nope. In all the excitement of heading outside to see the surprise, I didn't pick it up.'

'Mine is out of battery after I stayed out last night.'

'Any opportunity to mention your conquest?' Sam laughed, trying to bring some light-hearted relief to their current situation.

His brother appeared to play along. 'I still have to tell you all about her. It's not a problem. If we just head west, we will end up somewhere that one of us will recognise.'

'Before that weirdness, I was really enjoying myself. And now that it's behind us, I'm actually enjoying the riding again.'

'It's awesome, isn't it? I promise that for your eighteenth, I'll get you your own bike.'

'I forgot it was my birthday. It's definitely going to be a memorable one. What a day!'

'We saw some crazy stuff, but let's not talk about it until later. We don't want to ruin the day because some gypsies were fighting over a dodgy build they had created.'

'Is that what you think it was?'

'Who knows? Come on, let's go. Switch on the lights as it's dark now and follow me.'

The brothers kept on riding, heading in the direction that should lead them to a familiar place; more importantly, it was taking them away from dead bodies, falling buildings and the disturbance.

Mitch pulled up, so Sam stopped and lifted his visor. 'See, over there is a warehouse,' Mitch pointed as he spoke. 'If we head that way, it should take us to other warehouses and the docks. From there, we can easily follow the river back to town and then home.'

'Okay. Let's go.' They rode over to what Sam thought was their newfound sanctuary. He was relieved to be getting away from the earlier chaos and that they could now find their way home. As they approached the building, they found that it was deserted, and no lights were on. It looked derelict, with overgrown foliage all around and smashed-in windows.

'We should cut through this warehouse. The ones on the outskirts are all like this—abandoned due to their proximity to the gypsies. But as we get further away, the place becomes nice again. High-end goods, tight security and open paths for riding free. I'll go first; make sure the door is open. Hopefully, it will just be a straight line to the other end. Once I've checked, we can exit through the other end. I'll flash my lights and you can follow.

Watch me as I go through and try to follow the same path I take.'

Sam watched as Mitch went up to the battered-looking shutters and tried to pull them up. He found that they weren't locked but wouldn't open smoothly. The mechanism wasn't working properly. He heaved at the door and put in a bit more effort, and the metallic door jerked open enough that they could pass through if they ducked down on their respective machines. Sam knelt next to his bike and watched as Mitch and his machine disappeared under the shutter.

Sam followed the light from his brother's bike; it moved in a straight line. He watched as the light became smaller and smaller until it stayed the same size. Mitch stopped. Sam guessed he was anywhere from fifty to a hundred metres away. Sam heard the echo of a metallic sound. Even though it was distorted, he recognised it as that of his brother opening the door at the other end. Success—Mitch was standing silhouetted against the fully open door at the other end of the warehouse. His arm was held up and it looked to Sam that he was motioning for him to come through.

He got on his bike, ducked and went under the shutter. As soon as he passed it, he sat upright. *Just a straight line*, he thought to himself repeatedly. The musky smell of the place gave him a dry cough. It reminded him of a time when a package was delivered and left out in the rain, and the box had gotten wet and had become merely damp cardboard boxes. Sam glanced from side to side to see if there was anything in the warehouse. There were objects scattered around, but given the current conditions, he couldn't make them out. He went back to concentrating on his brother up ahead, who was now back on the Honda.

His own light showed him it was a simple linear route, so he went faster to escape the smell and to put a greater distance between him and the earlier horrors. Because of his speed, he had gone past Mitchell and the door by the time he stopped.

'Alright, Evel Knievel. I knew you would love riding. I had a quick look-see up ahead while waiting for you. It seems like another warehouse. Let's do the same thing; that should put us back on familiar ground, and then, we can just go around the buildings in the future,' Mitch instructed Sam.

'I'm cool with that.'

They approached the outside boundary of the warehouse that they had just been in, which adjoined the warehouse with the one that they were planning to go through. The difference between this new warehouse from the previous one was immediately noticeable from the ground. Nothing was overgrown; actually, there was no plant life, not even a blade of grass that Sam could see with the lights from the bikes and the evening sky. If he had to describe this building, he would have called it modern, clean-looking and to some extent, clinical. 'This warehouse looks different from the other one. It seems to have more expensive stuff inside. I think we should go around.'

'I can't see any security guards or cameras. How about we try the door? If we can open it, we will take the shortcut. If not, then we can see if there is a way around.'

'If you are sure.' As Sam was speaking, Mitch had already made his way to what appeared to be the main door and was about to open it. Sam noticed the number fourteen stencilled on it.

It opened with ease. There was no sound and no straining; it just opened. It behaved like it was fully automated. 'See, nothing to it. Same thing as last time. I'll go first. You watch and see my route and then just follow,' Mitch said as he kicked his bike into gear and headed onwards.

Sam watched as his brother went into the warehouse. He followed the light from the African Twin, then it cut out. There was nothing from the bike, no brake light, nothing. Nothing from Mitchell. Ahead of Sam was pure darkness.

'Very funny. You can switch on the light now, Mitch.' *He's just messing with me because I didn't want to come in here.* 'Mitchell. I know you are just teasing me. I am coming in.'

Sam thought his brother was fooling around; well, that is what he hoped. However, because of the way the bike suddenly disappeared, he was worried that Mitch had an accident, like if he had fallen down a hole. *But then there would have been some noise, like a crash or bang.* He considered just walking in, in case there was a large hole up ahead, but he realised that he needed the headlight from the Kawasaki. He dismounted from the motorbike and pushed it along, using the handlebars to move it and swivel it as necessary like the elaborate torch that it had become. Sam had cleared the door and was trying to see where Mitch was, still holding on to the hope that he was being pranked. But he had a feeling that something was wrong.

Suddenly, the minimal illumination from behind him grew darker. When he realised what was happening, he turned around and caught sight of the door marked fourteen silently shutting completely. He left the bike and went back to the door, he tried to lift it from the bottom, but he couldn't. A panic started to grip him. He searched around the door for some sort of electronic control, a keyhole, a window—anything to help. Still searching for something to help him, he called out in desperation. 'Mitch! Mitchell! Can you hear me? The door we came through has closed and I can't open it. Are you okay?'

He turned around and went back to the bike. He had decided to just go forward. He needed to find his big brother. It was now obvious to him that this wasn't a game. Mitch could be in trouble. He walked with the bike using the headlight, searching for anything. He had walked about three metres when the motorbike just stopped working. The light, the power, everything on it just cut out. He tried to start the ignition, but nothing happened. He was about to try again, but he realised that if the same thing had happened to his brother on his

Honda, he might have been thrown off and be really hurt.

Sam wanted to run, but the place was in total darkness. He could not even see his own hand in front of his face. He shouted out for Mitch constantly, not caring if a security guard or anyone else heard him. He wanted another person to be there. A feeling of isolation started to grip him. Besides his shouts, there was no sound. When he wasn't shouting, he could hear his own loud breathing. He tried to move quickly; he held both his arms out in front of him, with the palms open, so that they would come in contact with anything first. But then every few seconds, he would stop and sweep his leg out in front of him to make sure there was nothing on the ground in front that he could trip on. Part of him was hoping to find Mitch on the floor, fallen off his bike but unhurt.

He knew his search technique was cumbersome, as he really couldn't see and his leg sweeping was becoming awkward. He stopped and shouted, 'Mitch, can you hear me?' No response. 'I am going to turn around and head back to the door we came in through. I am not going to leave this place without you, but I have an idea.' He hurried back to the door, keeping in a straight line. Once he had stumbled past his abandoned bike, he ran to the door. His palms hit door fourteen. He made another attempt to try to find a way to open the door. When he couldn't, he kicked the door a few times and charged at it. A small part of him hoped he could break it down, but he knew it was futile and he mainly did it to vent his frustration.

'Mitch, I am at the door. I can't open it, but I'll try to find another door with a light switch or something that I can use. If I find a window, I can break it, just to get some light in here. Once I can see, I will get you and we can both get out.' Sam placed his right hand against the wall and started to run. He kept his hand against the brick, partly to stabilise himself, as running in the dark was very disorientating, but mainly to find another exit. His idea was that there would be another door or a window somewhere in the warehouse. It would obviously be on a wall. If he touched all the walls, he would eventually come across it.

He ran, going anticlockwise, to keep his stronger right hand against the surfaces. He knew something could trip him, but he now had something to hold on to. He came to the first corner quite quickly—he was expecting it. From there, he ran more quickly, right hand touching the wall, seeking out any change in texture. His left hand was out in front of him, with the palm up to stop him from faceplanting if he should fall or if he came across the next corner.

He ran until he came to the end of the wall. He hadn't come across another potential access to the building. He was out of breath. It was still pitch-black, but he felt relieved because now, he should be at the back of the warehouse. He called out for Mitch again. Nothing. Sam rested for ten seconds, then started to run again. Staying in contact with what he presumed was the back of the warehouse, he hoped to find the opposite of door fourteen. It wasn't where he thought it should be, but he knew he couldn't fully trust his senses, as it was dark and silent, plus he was tired and hungry. Before he knew it, his left palm smacked the wall, rebounded and hit him in his face. He had reached the third corner and still found nothing. 'Mitch, please, where are you?'

This was not going according to plan. Sam was feeling the strain. He wanted to stop but knew he couldn't. He started running again, calling out to his brother every now and again. He reached the fourth corner without finding anything. *I am sure I was running straight; it felt like a rectangle. Screw this—I will go back to door fourteen and do whatever it takes to break it.* He reached the corner without finding the door. Now he just ran because he didn't know what else to do. When he was breathless, he would stop and have a rest and call out for Mitch. He kept going; he counted sixteen 'corners', meaning in his mind, he had gone around four times. Running changed to jogging and now, to a brisk walk. Each time, he moved his right hand either higher or lower in case he had missed something. One time, he went around clockwise using his left hand. He had nothing left to do, but he couldn't give up. He told himself he would just keep going around and around until the morning if he had to.

Immediately after Sam passed his seventeenth corner, his right hand came in contact with nothing, causing him to stumble and fall over. There was no way this was here before. *I couldn't have missed it.* He investigated the alcove in the wall as best as he could without seeing anything. He determined that it came up only to his waist, but it was wide. He started to crawl through. After a metre, he encountered a wall, but he soon realised that he could easily push it. It moved forward with ease. There was still no light or sound, but now, he had something to do; he had hope. The wall became unmovable, but there was some sort of opening to his right. It was a tighter space. He had to go down lower to crawl through it. Which he did. After a while, he stretched out his left leg behind him and came up against resistance. Something had closed off the route he had taken.

He had no choice but to keep crawling forward; he couldn't go back. As he pushed onwards the space kept getting smaller and smaller. Soon the width and height became tighter and tighter barely able to accommodate his frame. He felt scared but could do nothing but push on.

CHAPTER 4
DAY 2

Sarah drove the inconspicuous hired car towards the traveller site but thought better against taking it directly onsite. She needed to be discreet and to win the trust of the community. That would be hard enough to do without flashing a new motor in front of them. Ideally, she would not have come today, as the place would be crawling with police dealing with the other matter and it would be harder to get anyone to talk to her, but she had already lost too much time on this case. *For any missing person, the first 72 hours are the crucial stage and I am way past that. Maybe, the devastation of the other day might be something I can use to my advantage. They would be vulnerable and might just open up to me.* The tragedy of a building collapsing on many travellers and killing them could just give her the in she needed from this closed community to complete her mission.

She pulled up the car and parked it away from the cordoned-off zone and near some warehouses. This area was new to her, so beforehand she had studied the maps online and had determined the most suitable route for walking. As she started the journey on foot, she estimated that it would be twenty minutes long, at the brisk pace at which she walked. That worked for her, because she wanted to get a sense of the wider environment, and that was best achieved by soaking in the smells and the atmosphere and by getting to know the bumps on the road.

As she approached the traveller site it started to rain, but not heavily enough to cause her any concerns regarding her artificial hair. Sarah turned the corner and was met by five police cars with their lights silently flashing. Her lesser peers were milling around the entrance to the traveller site. The rain, clouds and on-off blue lights gave the area a certain bleakness, no doubt befitting the current mood of the people affected.

'Detective Silver,' she said, holding out her badge to the first officer she encountered.

He ushered her onwards. 'The others are all over the site, ma'am. We have mapped the area as best as we can, identifying those who bothered to give us a name. Are you looking for anyone in particular?'

'The Norths.' She watched as the young man searched his list.

'No Norths, ma'am. I can radio ahead and see if anyone else has found them.'

'That's not necessary. I will look around. Thank you for your help.'

'The team is on frequency Charlie-3. May I suggest that you start where no other officers are? That way, if anyone updates me with having spoken to any Norths, I can let you know.'

'What's your name?'

'PC Barranger.'

'First name, Barranger?'

'Dougie.' He started to blush. 'I mean Doug. My friends call me Dougie.'

She brushed some wet hair from her face. 'Okay, Doug.' She pegged him as a newbie because of his rank and manner, but mainly because he seemed to have no idea who she was as he was helping her and not recoiling at the mere mention of her name.

'Ma'am, do you want my umbrella? I have a spare one.'

She shook her head. 'No, thanks.' She smiled at him and walked off. She planned to follow his advice and avoid the other officers because they would be questioning and delivering bad news to other people, not to the family she was interested in. She headed to the location where the report said their caravan was. When she got there, it was obvious to her which one was the North's caravan. It was the one that should have stood where the big empty gap currently was.

I guess I had better start with the neighbours. She headed to the caravan to the left of the gap because she had noticed the curtain twitching since she stood in front of the space. She knocked on the door and waited. *If this were Dougie, his heart rate would be racing now, exhilarated by the hunt and the unknown.*

'What do you want?'

'Your name, for starters? I'm Detective Sarah Silver.' She showed her badge to the woman standing in front of her. 'May I ask you some questions?'

'I can tell you're gavver. I've been waiting for yous. How many people died? Whose fault was it?'

'Actually, this isn't about that. I'm looking for the Norths: Naomi and Michael.'

'They've gone. Why do you want them?'

'I'm following up regarding their daughter. Do you know where they have gone to?'

'No.'

'How long ago did they move?'

'I don't know.'

'What do you know?'

'I know that building weren't put up by our kind. They gonna say it was and blame us. Everyone here is saying it wasn't our work. Why would we build something shoddy that could put our own at risk?'

Sarah took out a notepad and wrote that down to humour the woman. 'I'll make sure I pass that information on, Mrs...?'

'I don't do business with other people's business. Leave me outta this.'

'Megan then. Did you know her?'

'I saw her around. Didn't speak to her; my generation don't speak to her generation unless they need a tellin' orf.'

'This is my card. If you think of anything, please call me. Thank you.' Sarah smiled and handed the woman the piece of paper.

The door to the right caravan opened as Sarah approached it, before she got the chance to knock on it. No one was standing in front of the area; she wondered if this was an invitation or a trap. It would be silly to start anything with so many officers on the site. She pulled out her radio and pretended to speak into it. 'I am just finishing off where the North caravan was, then I will join the rest of you.' That way, the occupier(s) would know she was not alone. She checked the weapon around her waist and entered the home. She immediately moved away from the door after making sure there was no one obviously in the space behind her.

The door was swiftly shut and standing behind it, Sarah saw a teenager. 'You looking for Megan?'

'Yes. How many people are in this caravan?'

'Just me. I shouldn't speak to you. We ain't meant to speak to gorgers, especially not gavvers. But she was my friend.'

Sarah examined the girl. She was probably the same age as Megan, but it was hard to tell. This girl wore a lot of makeup on, especially pink blush, which hid any natural beauty. She was on the large side by a good hundred pounds, which also made it harder to ascertain her age. 'What's your name? I am Sarah.'

'Rosie. The old biddy Flanagan is probably standing outside if she saw you come in after you spoke to her, or she be calling me Ma. I am going to make a show of it and kick you out. But we need to speak. Give me your car keys and I'll go wait for you in your car.'

Nice try. 'My car isn't here. I came in a patrol car with the other officers. Is there somewhere else we can go to talk?'

'Not here. Everyone knows everyone else's business. The grass has ears. You've already spent too much time in here.'

'Take my number and call me when you can talk. I can call you back.'

'No. No. They will find it; my phone is checked. Give me some money and I'll sneak out and meet you tonight. I don't have a car and we can't go local because I ain't being seen with you. There's a gorger pub, "The Black Sheep", opposite the train station in town. We can go there. But I need money.'

'You're wasting my time and Megan's. If you really want to help your friend, you would just talk to me.'

'Rosemary! Rosemary!' someone shouted.

'That's Mikey, brother. Get out, get out.' Rosie opened the door and grabbed the collar of the detective's coat to usher her out of the caravan. 'Look, I told you I barely knew the Norths. You'd better not bother me again. Brother, this gavver is just going.'

Sarah looked at the man who was now standing right outside. He was the complete opposite of his sister. He was not soft-looking, nor did he carry any extra fat. Here was a man who was built of solid muscle. He looked like a fighting machine. Mrs Flanagan was also outside her place and another man, probably the same age as Rosie's brother, was standing next to her, guarding her from the 'evil' police. 'You heard my sister. Get away from us!' he shouted.

'Mikey, it's fine. She wanted to know about Megan. I've told her we don't know the gal and to not bother us.'

'I'm just doing my job,' Sarah said as she grabbed Rosie's hand that was holding her coat and palmed a twenty into it as she brushed it off. 'I am here to help. If your sister or daughter went missing, wouldn't you want to know where they were?' She looked at Mrs Flanagan and then Mikey as she spoke. Her last statement seemed to get his attention. 'Mikey, do you know Megan? I bet an attractive man like you knows all the girls.'

'I know what you're doing; it's not gonna work. Get the F out of here.'

Sarah placed her hands on her hips, opening the long Mackintosh she was wearing, partly to look seductive but mainly so they could all see she was armed, then she moved a few steps so that she was standing directly in front of Mikey. He was a good six inches taller than she. Hands still on her hips, to give off a certain level of femininity, she invaded his personal space. He smelt like oil and petrol, with some cheap deodorant masking the smell of a car garage. She leant upwards so she could whisper to him, 'I know you know something; you have an obvious tell.' She stepped back and stared at him. He was obviously seething; she watched as he clenched his right fist, which was shaking.

A crackling noise broke the standoff, then a group of policemen on their radios came around the corner. 'We have some questions about the collapsed building.'

Mrs Flanagan and the man next to her went back into her caravan. Mikey motioned for Rosie to go inside, and he followed suit. As he left, he muttered, 'You'll keep.'

'We'll speak soon, Mikey.' She wrapped her coat back around herself and walked off, heading back to her car. *There was something about his facial expression whenever Megan's name was mentioned and his body language which was overly defensive—he knows something and is lying.* She thought it best to call it a

41

day so as not to scare off her only potential lead. Back in the car, she felt pumped. The thrill of the case, the intricacies of the players, the peril of the victim and she, Sarah Silver, the one to solve it and bring harmony to the situation is why she got up in the mornings. She checked her wig and used a towel in the back seat to take the rain off it. It wasn't like natural hair that absorbed water; it was more like material that repelled the liquid until it became too much. She looked presentable enough—she plugged in the name of the pub into the satellite navigation and took off.

Sarah had been sitting in the Black Sheep since leaving the site. To kill time, she slowly ate her dinner: fish and chips. The pub seemed overpriced for what it was, but then again, she was used to northern prices. She wasn't sure when Rosie would arrive, as she knew she would need to sneak off. This was of course based on the assumption that Rosie would show up. Her gut told her the girl wanted to. Her head told her it was a scam. She got up to get another drink and, standing at the bar waiting to be served, she scanned the room. The people in the pub were a mixed bunch—office and retail workers in for post-work drinks, from what she could tell. Definitely not a traveller hangout.

'Do you want another juice?' Asked the young man working behind the bar.

'No, I'll have wine spritzer this time. So have you worked here long?'

'You can come up with a better line than that.'

'I wasn't chatting you up; I was asking because I want to know if you might recognise my friend. I'm meant to meet her here tonight but I'm not sure if I'm in the right pub. Her phone is off and she's an hour late.' Sarah held up her phone and showed a picture of Megan, which she had snapped from the case file.

The bartender stared at it. 'Is she single? She's gorgeous. Almost as gorgeous as you.'

'Is that all you think about?'

'Occupational hazard. Alas, she's never been in here while I've been working, or I would have remembered hitting on her.'

Sarah looked at the glasses on the shelves and saw in the reflection someone approaching her. She spun around to see Rosie. 'I'll have the same as her,' the young woman said, smiling at the barman. He smiled back. Sarah detected a hint of disappointment that it was not the girl from the picture, before he left to go get the second drink.

'Thanks for coming. Grab that table over there and I'll bring the drinks over.' Sarah nodded towards an empty table in the corner.

Before the detective had a chance to sit down, Rosie said, 'I used all that money and more to get here; you'll need to give me more.'

Sarah took a sip on her drink, sat down and coolly stared at the girl opposite her. 'I'll make sure you get home okay.'

'I don't want to go home. I'm going to get in big trouble by just speaking to you. I want to run away. Me and Megan were meant to go together. That's why I know something isn't right. She wouldn't have gone anywhere without me.'

'Do travellers usually involve the police in their business?'

'No.'

'Why did her mother, Naomi, report her missing to us? Help me out here.'

'She must have been scared for her.'

'She thought other travellers were involved. That's why she involved us.'

'I don't know, guess she was worried for her. Megan wasn't a typical traveller gal. So maybe she thought a non-traditional solution would be best. But you need to ask her this yourself.'

'When did you last speak to Megan?'

'The day before she disappeared. Look, they're gonna say it was us, but no traveller would have done anything. Her family is well respected, so that gave her a status. Plus, everyone who meets her loves her.'

'How did the rest of the community deal with her non-traditional values? Like your brother, Mikey.'

Rosie started laughing, then knocked back her drink. 'He ain't actually my brother. We grew up together; I'm like a sister to him. His actual sister is my best friend.'

'Megan?'

'Yes. He stuck around after the family left. He's been looking for his sister here; the family is searching for her all over the country.'

'I need to speak to him. We are both trying to find Megan and make sure she is safe.'

'He don't know much about her. I know everything. She had a job in a posh bar. Not like this place. Proper classy. Like I said, she isn't like the other girls in our community.'

'Do you know its name? Or where it was?'

'It's in town. All money. Guys would shower gifts and money on her. She was getting the money together that we were going to run away with.'

'Rosie, if you can't remember the name can you take me there? Do you remember the names of anyone she mentioned to you? Perhaps an overly friendly customer or someone she was wary of. What work did she exactly do?'

'She was just a waitress, but people just tipped her well. They all fall in love with Megan. It ain't what you're thinking; she isn't like that. She had a boyfriend, a gorger. It was proper love. I think they met at the bar. He had lots of money.'

'Don't you think she may have left with this boyfriend or some other rich guy she met through work. Sounds like she wanted out from your way of life.'

'She wasn't a slag, she wouldn't just go with anyone. We were more than mates, we were like sisters. She would have told me if she was going. Even if she wasn't going to take me with her, she would have said.' Rosie dabbed at her eyes. 'But she would have taken me, she swore she would.'

'What do you know about the boyfriend, his name?'

'Tom Denton.'

She replied a little too quickly. 'Do you know where I can find him?'

'Yes. But listen; he was a wrong 'un. He led her astray. He didn't like it that she was, you know, a traveller. Our lot wouldn't have liked him; they would've sorted him out. But only I knew about him.'

'Where is he? Megan is most likely with him; they could be on holiday together.'

'That's the thing; she isn't. A week before she disappeared, I went with her to his funeral. He's dead.

CHAPTER 5
DAY 3

The cold air roused Sam. His head felt groggy, but he realised that he needed to open his eyes. Every time he tried, they shut themselves. After attempting this for about a minute, he managed to open them and keep them open. He realised he was lying somewhere outside and a sense of relief washed over his whole body. The last thing he could remember was crawling around the pitch-black tunnels that were decreasing in size and that had given him an awful sense of claustrophobia. He stretched out both his arms as fully as he could. In that moment, he promised himself to never take the small things in life for granted. His primary thought was, *it's over*. But what exactly was it? All he could remember was the crawling and his fear. He had no memories after that and had no idea how he got to where he now was.

Where am I? Now that he was more awake, he could start thinking rationally. He brought his arms together underneath his body and pushed himself to sit up. He felt achy, his chest hurt, his palms and knees felt like the skin had been scraped off. He glanced around and knew immediately where he was. Better still, he could see Mitch also lying down.

'Mitch! Mitch! You okay?'

There was no response.

He got up, ignored the pain in his body and mind, and moved over to his brother. He kept calling his name as he shook him. Then Mitch started to stir. The feeling of relief he had felt before was nothing to how Sam felt now. The strange night was over and they were both fine, and now he could get answers.

'Sam?' Mitch croaked.

'Yeah, I'm here. Are you okay?'

'Banging headache, but I feel fine. You? What happened? Where are we?'

'My head feels weird too.' *Not physically but since crawling through whatever it was I just have a sense of dread.* 'I can't remember much but I need to know what happened. I was hoping you could tell me. We're outside our house, in our driveway.' Sam watched as his brother vaguely came to and surveyed the surroundings.

'How did you get us here? Where are the bikes?'

'I didn't get us here,' he paused as the realisation started to grip him. 'Something bizarre has happened.'

'What?'

'That's the thing—I don't know. One moment it was night-time, we were in some warehouse, you disappeared, and then I got trapped. Then we both wake up back in our drive. What about the bikes? One moment they were working then they weren't. Also, I can't see them here. I'll check the road. Then we can go inside and call the police.'

'Mitch, I couldn't see the bikes,' Sam said as his brother was flicking through the various news channels.

'We can't call the police. They'd ask too many questions about our situation. Forgetting last night, questions that will get us into big trouble. Then if we include last night, what are we going to tell them? That we broke into a warehouse and lost some bikes we hired?'

'We can tell them that our bikes were stolen. We witnessed that building collapsing, that we can't remember anything from the night. And that it was all just weird.'

'They'll think you're high.'

'What about those bodies?'

'I can't find anything about it on the news. I bet some shoddy gypsies were hired to do some building work and they did a substandard job. I noticed lots of them around. Look, I'm freaked out too, but we can work it out.'

'What happened to you?'

'I was riding the bike, then you woke me up outside.'

'Did you fall and come off the bike? Was anyone else there? Did you get trapped, like down a narrow corridor?'

'No, not that I know of. I guess I was tired, fell asleep and presumed you got us back here. What happened to you?'

Sam could tell his brother was downplaying whatever had happened to him and how he was feeling, trying to be the hero and not cause a panic. He explained to Mitch as best as he could his version of the events. He left out how it made him feel, though. That when he was crawling around, he felt sick to his stomach, that he thought he was going to die, that as the space got tighter he could barely move. *I felt like I was in my own coffin, unable to move, unable to breathe. It got so bad that there were moments that I thought death would be better. It got so bad that I think I passed out.*

'That's messed up. Why don't we go back to see if we can find the bikes? It might also help jog both our memories. Plus seeing the place in daylight, we can see where you ended up. Bet it was something silly, like you ended up crawling up the post or the laundry chute. You'll see, it'll all be something straightforward.'

'Yeah, you're right. I'll just have a shower and then we can go.'

'Okay. I'll make us some sandwiches. I'm starving.'

As Sam walked upstairs, he felt a tingle at the top of his left leg. It was a different sensation compared to a normal itch. *Maybe, I bashed it when I was crawling around.* When he got to his bedroom, he stripped off his clothes and looked at his naked body in the mirror. His mixed green-grey-brown eyes surveyed the sight on the mirror. There were no obvious bruises. He had generally lost weight over these past weeks, which he didn't like. Where he was once quite athletic-looking because he was on the school swimming team, he was now slimmer and losing his once-toned body. He knew that due to his lack of sleep, he appeared like death, and last night certainly didn't do anything to help him overcome that. He now turned his attention to the top of his leg, to the place that had tingled. There was something unusual there. He traced his fingers over the area. 'What?'

He quickly dashed to switch on the light and grabbed his phone, to use the torch. He ignored the few messages and used it as a tool. He stared, his eyes dilated, the brown becoming the prominent colour as he searched for an answer. With his free hand, he kept touching the new thing. There at the top of the left leg on the inguinal crease, the part where the band of a fancy pair of boxers sits, was a one-inch long line. The cut was precise and very straight; it was surgical. It wasn't open or bleeding, as there were three extremely neat and tiny stitches across it.

Sam just remained in a state of shock, his mind trying to process what was happening. This was hard, as various incohesive thoughts just ran through his brain. *Did I have surgery? Was I abducted by aliens? This is small. What will I say if people ask me about this? What is this? Am I scarred for life? Who did this? Will a tattoo cover this?* But he kept ending up with the only thought that mattered: *What the hell is it?*

He put his underwear and T-shirt back on and headed back downstairs to tell his brother. The kitchen door was ajar, and as Sam approached it, he saw Mitch holding his own T-shirt up under his chin. His flies were undone, and his jeans were pulled down slightly, and his boxers were yanked down on the left side. Sam realised that his brother must have one too. For a fleeting moment, this gave him comfort, as it wasn't just him, then he felt guilty for feeling this way. He entered the room, deliberately making a noise so that his brother would be prepared for him. 'What are you doing?'

'I've got something on my hip; it feels itchy. I thought it was a scratch, but it looks almost surgical.' Mitch couldn't hide the panic in his voice.

'Can I see?' Sam examined the mark on his brother's leg. 'It's exactly the same as mine. Same position, same size and same appearance,' he stated as he showed Mitch the matching score.

Mitch stared at the similar impression adorning his brother, in complete bewilderment. 'I'm sorry.'

'Why are you sorry?'

'The bikes, the warehouse—they were my idea. I insisted.'

Sam sensed his brother was about to ramble on, but he didn't want him to feel guilty about something that really had nothing to do with him. He knew Mitch would take responsibility and could end up going to that dark place. He had to stop that from happening, so he lied as best as he could. 'Look we aren't dead.' *I don't think we are.* 'So it could have been worse, don't worry about it; there's bound to be a funny story, one I'll recount for years to come. I'm going to change my clothes and then we can go and find out the truth. Twenty pounds says that this time tomorrow, we will be laughing at this.'

They walked out the leafy cul-de-sac to the nearest bus stop, which was sixteen minutes away, then they took three different buses to get them as close as possible. Then they had to retrace their steps as best as they could. Strangely, there was no evidence of the accident—no cordoned-off areas, no emergency service vehicles in the area, nothing. Sam figured that his brother had avoided the accident area, but as they walked around, he could have sworn that it was the same place, as it looked so familiar. At that moment, the image of the guy who had died staring at Sam popped into his head. The phantom face was about to say something to him, but he quickly cleared it from his mind. Then the dead man's face popped back in Sam's mind, this time managing to speak. 'Help me.' *Compartmentalise, compartmentalise.*

When they eventually found their way, they realised that the warehouse was a good thirty-minute walk away. Sam's body still throbbed but he didn't mention it. They walked in silence. As they got closer to the warehouse, he realised that he was sweating. His heart was racing fast. He started to feel dizzy. He did not want to be there but he needed answers. Both he and his brother needed the normality they were used to, to return to their lives, and the night before was anything but clear-cut. *If Mum and Dad were here, they would have easily sorted this out for us. In fact, we would never have gotten into this situation.*

'Sam, we have to be cool. Whatever or whoever we find, we have to be calm. The best way to find out anything is to gain people's trust. We can't go in all guns blazing. We need to be subtle. Follow my lead,' Mitch said with a frown while touching his hip. 'But look, if anything untoward does happen, I will make sure they pay.'

As they approached the warehouse, it seemed anything but extraordinary. There were vehicles in the car park and people all around. His gut instinct told him it was the right place, but seeing it like this in the cold light of day he was uncertain and had to ask. 'Are you sure this is the right one?'

'Yeah, fairly certain. It does look so unassuming. Excuse me, mate. What do you guys do here?' Mitch asked the first person they were in earshot of.

The man looked them up and down. 'Computer parts.'

'Do you know if there are any jobs going?'

'You'll have to ask the boss, Alton. The big, black guy inside. You can't miss him.'

'Cheers, mate.' As they walked in, they saw no empty floor space. The place was littered with machines all around. They would not have been able to ride any distance on their bikes. From what Sam could tell, it looked like microchips, motherboards and the inner parts of computers being sorted and packaged. The workers appeared to be average men and women, no one out of the ordinary. They were doing their jobs while chatting with one another. They didn't even give the brothers a second glance. 'Over there—that must be Alton. I'll speak to him. See if you can discreetly find out anything else from anyone willing to chat with you, or any signs that we were here last night.'

Sam watched his brother go over to the foreman. It seemed apparent that they did not know each other. Sam looked around for any clues; tyre marks, a hole, anything but he saw nothing. *It can't be the same place.* All he could do was look at the workers going about their daily routines. He wanted to see something out of the ordinary, anything that might give him evidence to the events of the previous night.

Then he saw it.

On the wall was an 'In case of emergency' sign. He stared at the building plan. There were no other rooms or annexes apart from this one. It was just one large rectangular warehouse. According to the map, there were no corridors, no place from him to have gotten lost. He placed his hand on the wall next to the sign while he was thinking of what to do next. The moment his fingers and palm connected with the surface, it was like a shockwave went through his body and turned him into ice. He was frozen.

While one wall may seem pretty much like another to most people, including Sam, after spending hours desperately touching and groping the walls all night, he knew it was the same place. Paralysis gripped him; he wanted to run away, to shout out, but he couldn't. It was like an invisible entity had tightly wrapped its arms around him and prevented him from moving. Only his free hand, the one not stuck to the wall, started to shake by his side. He gasped for oxygen, the claustrophobic effect of the previous night taking hold of him.

'What's wrong? Have you found out anything?'

Sam looked at his brother who was standing right in front of him. Somehow, he had gotten there without Sam noticing. But the sound and sight of the familiar broke the spell. 'This is definitely the same place, but how can it be?'

'I don't think it is,' Mitch countered. 'The foreman said there are packing and quality control jobs going as they are very busy. They have various shifts throughout, including a night shift. It pays more obviously because of the unsocial hours. There is really no security, as the place is always busy and the goods aren't expensive.'

'He's lying,' Sam spat out angrily.

'I didn't get that vibe, but let's discuss this outside. You can tell me there what you found out. Remember, play it cool. Alton is at the other end of the building. I said we would stop by and let him know what shifts we want and collect the paperwork to be filled in. I'm Richard, you're Ben. Just pretend we want work and then we'll never see him again. Take a last look around; you'll see this isn't the place.'

Sam managed to disconnect his hand from the wall. *I just need a good night's sleep.* As they walked towards the other end, he tried to take in as much as he could as they moved—the conversations taking place, the tasks being done, the sights and smells, but none of it helped him. He shook Alton's hand and zoned out while his brother continued blagging the situation. There was a silence. Mitch had stopped talking. *Had they asked a question that he was meant to answer?*

Sam looked at his brother for a clue, but his brother was staring off, his eyes fixed on the open back shutter. Mitch quickly darted off, heading in the direction that had him transfixed.

'We'll be right back,' Sam told Alton and followed his brother. He couldn't see what had caught his brother's attention, as Mitch was in his line of sight. Mitch stopped shortly after reaching the outside. Sam moved to the left so he could see his brother and what was in front of him. Now he knew what his brother had seen, and in his mind, it confirmed that this was the mysterious building from last night.

The Kawasaki and African Twin stood there, appearing clean and unmarked, just as Sam remembered them when he first saw them. 'I haven't got all day, boys,' said a man standing next to the bikes.

Mitch started moving towards the stranger, and Sam followed. The short, round middle-aged man had a nose too big for his face and a bald head, he had a few wrinkles around his eyes and on his forehead. He had a tan giving him a sun-kissed glow. He did not seem threatening or dangerous, but the way he spoke gave him a sense of authority. He was dressed in all white: a white suit with a white shirt and dress shoes. Sam couldn't tell if they were expensive or not. He ran the last bit to catch up with Mitch, whom he noted had clenched his fists.

The man put both his hands in the air, as if to say 'I am unarmed and harmless,' and smiled. 'Welcome to the Stitchin.'

The outside of the Denton residence seemed to confirm that the place was empty. The front garden was not maintained. In a postcode like this, it should have been immaculate. There was no car or cars in the driveway. Sarah scanned the mail that she had taken from the box attached to the front gate. The post all appeared to be junk, but she kept them in her gloved hands as she rang the bell. Still no answer, just like when she tried the front gate, before she decided to jump over it five minutes ago. Now she deliberated whether to break into the house. Even though she was going through the motions of rationalising her decision, her mind had been made up earlier, when she scaled the front. She pulled out her special kit from her jacket pocket, looked over her shoulder and got to work picking the lock.

I've only been in the city for a few days and already I am breaking the law, must be a new first for me. The girl who put me on this course of action isn't playing me. I can tell there was a genuineness to our conversation and an innocence to her. I can read people well, but then she might be a scam artist. She didn't just read his name in the newspaper and use it for some perverse game she's playing with me.

His car wasn't in the driveway, but then his parents could have taken it. What if it didn't exist? What did she say? 'Megan drove me to the funeral in the car he gave her. She insisted I accompany her as she needed the moral support. We had to watch the whole thing from afar.' When I enquired further, she described the vehicle right down to the personalised licence plate. She wouldn't have known that unless she was telling the truth. But Megan having a car means she could be anywhere in the country. Maybe now that I have flagged the vehicle as being of interest some traffic camera will pick it up and I'll find the runaway.

She managed to complete the task in under two minutes. *I must be rusty.* As she entered the house, she heard successive beeps. She looked around for the control panel and source of the noise, walked over to it and tapped in 0307: Tom's birthday. The beeps stopped; she walked back over to the door and closed it, leaving the mail on a little table nearby. She had determined from the neighbours that the family was still in mourning over the tragic suicide of their beloved only son, hence her guess of the alarm code. If she hadn't been able to disarm it, she would have called the company and given her badge number and gotten it switched off remotely. Even though highly illegal, this way was easier—fewer questions, which she preferred.

Apparently, his parents couldn't understand why he had taken his own life. He had everything going for him. He was popular, good-looking, both physically and mentally healthy, had gotten a first-class degree and had great prospects. On paper, his was definitely not a typical suicide case. Mr and Mrs Denton had left the country to stay at their South of France residence, as their coping mechanism. That particular neighbour was trying to be subtle but implied that they had a lot of money, and money meant you didn't commit suicide. *Maybe they needed to reassure themselves that that was the case.*

She started wandering around the house while taking pictures with her phone. She looked around the entire downstairs; there wasn't anything interesting related to her investigation. She got to the stairs and headed up. There were numerous pictures on the wall along the staircase. *Very American.* She scanned them. It was mainly Tom and his parents in various stages of his life. The description given by the neighbours seemed accurate: 'A happy lad'. The family dog featured a lot. There were no pictures with Tom and Megan. *I'm guessing the traveller girl didn't make the cut. That is, if Rosie was telling the truth and they were dating. There is just something about all of this that doesn't quite add up.*

But some other girl did. She did not look like a relative but an actual girlfriend. The photos included some with them on holiday together, feeding each other at fancy restaurants and at family occasions with his parents. Judging by the time span of the photographs, it looked like they had dated for many years. *Then an affair with a girl from the wrong side of the tracks suddenly becomes more plausible.*

In autopilot mode, Sarah calculated various possible scenarios: his life was complicated and he took the easy option; he was in a love triangle and couldn't cope; both girls found out and dumped him so he ended it; it wasn't a suicide and one of the girls killed him—if Megan killed him in a jealous rage, it would explain why she took off, or someone else did it, like the parents or angry travellers. 'Was I drawn into the investigation of missing Megan to find out what happened to this man. His family seem more likely to have the pull to get Tanner involved.'

When she entered his bedroom, she was surprised. It was like he had gone out for the day. The bed wasn't made; there were two magazines on the floor, the laundry basket had some dirty clothes next to it, and the wardrobe was open. Tom's parents had obviously left the room as he had, and he hadn't left it in a state like he was preparing to take his own life. Sarah had seen enough suicide cases to know something was not adding up here. The planned deliberation to take your own life was missing here, in the chaos of this young man's bedroom. This was suspicious. Her alternative scenarios seemed more likely now. *I can second-guess myself all day: I need to find proof of Tom and Megan.*

She had to desecrate this sanctuary to look for clues. Her younger self would have felt bad, but the years of experience had weathered her. *I'll search the bedroom first then his bathroom.* She walked over to his bed; his bedside drawers had regular items and included an open pack of condoms, some random medals—five- and ten-kilometre runs and some for gymnastics; a Swiss army knife; a mini-torch; cufflinks; and headphones.

Next, she searched his bed, checking underneath it, under the mattress and pulling off all the sheets.

Nothing. She moved on to his bookcase, which had psychology textbooks from his degree, some fiction books he seemed to like science fiction and some comics. Sarah picked up each item and flicked through everyone, looking for any messages and loose bits of paper. She moved over to his window, breaking the stream of dust to better read the annotations in the textbooks; they were just academic notes. The window was large and it let a lot of light into the room. She noted that it provided, even though it was some distance, a clear line to one of the neighbouring house's bedrooms. Currently, the curtains were drawn.

Tom's clothes were different brands, including A&F, Ralph Lauren and Supreme. All the pockets were empty. Sarah checked the wardrobe, drawers and laundry basket. Next, she moved to the desk. He had a 49-inch curved Samsung television and PlayStation 5. There was a framed photo of him and the girl from the pictures on the stairs; she was in a cheerleader's outfit. Sarah opened the back cover but there was nothing else hiding in there. She noticed that there was a laptop charger on the desk, but she hadn't found a laptop. It wasn't downstairs. *Maybe the parents took it with them or maybe I'll find it when I check out the rest of the house, but I doubt that.* She powered up the PS5 and switched it on; there was no game inside. She scanned the online history before thumbing through his game collection, opening each case and checking for anything.

Then, she found it.

Hidden away in the Red Dead Redemption II sleeve was her first physical piece of evidence. There were only two photo booth pictures—someone else must have the other two—but there it was: Tom and Megan hugging each other, both looking deliriously happy.

Back outside, Sarah moved on, deciding to canvass the neighbours she hadn't yet spoken to or try to see if they were in. Most people weren't around, which was not surprising given the time of day and year. They were either working or holidaying, probably the latter, given the area. The two people she did talk to confirmed what she had already found out from Rosie, the Denton family's very limited social media and her investigation.

The current house she stood outside was the one next to the Denton's. The properties weren't joined and none of them on the road were terraced or even semi-detached, but they had all obviously been designed and built by the same company. *No one on the road deviated from the external design of the other properties. I guess that would have gotten them ostracised.*

The front garden and driveway were tidier than the Denton's, but it was in no way immaculate, like the rest of the cul-de-sac. There were no cars here, so Sarah didn't hold out much hope of anyone being in. She rang the bell and waited. No response. She rang again, waited impatiently, turned around and started to walk away.

'Can I help you?'

She turned around and saw a teenager who looked like he had just woken up. He was wearing grey

Superdry tracksuit bottoms and a blue Hollister hoodie with the zip half done up and the sleeves pulled down over his hands. His feet were bare. He had a white T-shirt on; she could not make out any logo. He had dirty-blonde hair and kind eyes that were in desperate need of a good night's sleep. He came across like he had been partying all night and could do with a good meal.

'Sorry for disturbing you,' she smiled. 'My name is Sarah Silver. I am a police officer.' The lad looked uncomfortable. *Most people always do when they see the police on their doorstep.* 'I have a few questions about the family that lives next door. I won't take much of your time, I promise.' He seemed nervous to Sarah. 'What's your name?'

'Erm… Sam. Samuel Yates.'

'Pleased to meet you, Sam. May I call you Sam?' She watched as he nodded; he seemed to be taking the opportunity to size her up. 'Are your parents in? Anyone else in the house?'

'No, it's just me. My folks are at work.'

'How well do you know the Dentons?'

'Are they in trouble?'

'Not at all. This is just a routine follow-up after their tragic loss.' She watched as he grabbed his left elbow with his right hand in a defensive stance.

'Okay. I've known them for a while. Since we've been living here but I haven't seen them since Tom's funeral. They always seemed like a close-knit family, always there for each other. I guess what happened was tough on them.'

'Did you know Tom well?'

'Well, yes. He is, was, my neighbour and we went to the same school. He was a few years above me, so finished years ago.'

Sarah noted to herself that he seemed to be calmer, probably because he knew he was not in trouble for anything. To her, he did not appear to be lying and seemed legitimately upset at the unexpected loss of someone he knew. 'Were you friends outside of school? Did you hang out together?'

'Not really. I mean, when we were younger, like when I was nine, we would play computer games together. But not in recent years. I guess it is not cool to hang out with someone younger. We had different interests and circles of friends. But he was a good guy.'

'Do you know the names of his friends? Did he have a girlfriend?'

'He was on the gymnastics team at school, had the potential to make it to Team GB, they used to say. Check out the other gymnasts, they were his mates. I don't know anything about a girlfriend. Sorry.'

'Did he seem happy?'

'I honestly can't say. Like I mentioned, we weren't close.' As he spoke, she noted he broke eye contact. He ran his hand through his hair, which caused the sleeve on his hoodie to pull up. Sarah noticed the mark on the back of his hand. He must have caught her looking because he promptly pulled the sleeve back down. 'I went clubbing last night.'

He's lying about something. It is probably that he is simply underage, that's why he is acting bashful. 'Don't worry, I was young once. It's an interesting stamp. Which club was it?'

'Umm... It's called the Falcon.'

'What about bars in the area—do you know the best ones? Did Tom ever mention liking any bar in particular?'

'That was the first time I had been to a club or bar. It was my birthday, so a group of my mates took me. We were lucky to get in; I guess it wasn't a busy night. I don't know the names of other places. My friends sorted it all.'

'Ahh, happy birthday.' Sarah paused, to make it appear like she meant it. 'Did you notice any of the kids from the other side of town at the club?'

'Do you mean the travellers?' His voice went higher as he said the last word.

'Yes. Do you know what they look like?'

'Sure. I have seen them around and off television shows.'

'Were they at the Falcon?'

'I doubt it. I mean, I don't know any of them, so can't be certain, but I wouldn't have thought it is their sort of place. It is very expensive.'

'Do they tend to hang out with the local kids?'

'They definitely don't go to my school and I don't really see them around town. I'm not sure how the people who grow up here would get to be friends with them. I doubt either side has much in common.'

'Do you like them?'

'I don't know them.'

Very diplomatic, Sam. 'Do they ever come to this neighbourhood, say, looking for work, offering to do jobs, selling anything?'

'Not that I know of. To be honest, people here pay a premium for everything, so I doubt they're the travellers' target audience.'

'That's true. How about Tom—did you ever see him with any of them?'

He paused, like he was thinking. 'You should check with his friends. They would know better than I do. I would say no if I had to guess.'

'Do you know a Megan North?'

He didn't respond.

Sarah pulled out a picture. 'This is Megan; take a look and see if you recognise her. Have you ever seen her with Tom, hanging around at the Denton's?' She watched as Sam stared at the picture. He held it in his hands and became mesmerised by the beauty of the woman. He just shook his head. Sarah was about to ask another question when her phone started ringing. She glanced at the identity. HOMEBASE. She answered. 'Sarah Silver here.'

'Hello, Detective Silver. This is Angelique from Vehicle Recovery. You wanted to know about a silver Range Rover Sport HST, with vehicle registration plate Dent 03?'

She walked away from Sam. 'Yes. Has it been spotted?'

'Not spotted per se. But we have found it.'

'Is it impounded?'

'No. The car was found by a couple of windsurfers in Wilson Lake.'

'Where is Wilson Lake?'

'Wilson Lake is local ma'am. It's a water supply reservoir between the docklands and the Colwood Farm camp, you know, the traveller settlement. It's used for some water sports by people who don't know better. One man filming his girlfriend dropped the camera in the water. It is waterproof and kept relaying video back to their computer. It picked up the vehicle and number plate as clear as day. That's when they called us. The system flagged me to contact you, so I am. The Recovery Team was notified first and they are already onsite, preparing to bring it up.'

'Thank you, Angelique. Can you send the exact location to my phone and any other details you have, like the vehicle history and the name of the officer in charge onsite? In fact, can you patch me through to the team?'

'Okay, hold.'

Sarah waited, her heart started to beat faster, until a voice came on the line.

'It's Ange. There is no response.'

'Can you keep trying? And can you send me the phone number? If you get through to them before I do, please stress to them to wait for me. It's really important.'

Her stomach felt tight.

She quickly glanced behind her. Sam was gone and his front door was shut. It didn't matter; she hurried off.

She hoped that her instinct wouldn't be right, but this was a worrying lead. Anxiety should have been building up inside her, but instead, she flipped that old, familiar switch in her brain, turned off her emotions and became a cold machine.

CHAPTER 7
DAY 3

Sam looked at the Falcon stamp—it was so detailed like it was tattooed on his hand—and wondered if the promise of what went with it would come true. Not quite fame and fortune—well, not yet anyway. He had lied to the policewoman because he thought it would have been weird to say he had the club stamp before he went to the club. It would have invited questions, like where and when he got it from, that he didn't want to answer.

Mitch was walking down the stairs. He stopped and stretched. 'Who was at the door?'

'Just some woman collecting for charity,' Sam lied. *Mitch doesn't need to be reminded of his friend's passing, especially the depressing way it happened.*

'Pity. I hoped it was the food I ordered. It should be here soon. Food, talk, get ready and go. It's going to be an epic night.'

'You really think so?'

'Yes. We're going to be okay. Did you get some sleep? You're going to need all your energy, little brother.'

'Actually, the door woke me up,' Sam lied again. 'I want to go back to bed so I can really be fresh.'

'Alright, lazy teenager. I'll save you some food.' As Sam passed him on the stairs, he smiled at his brother. *He really doesn't have a care in the world. For his sake, I have to make sure I am not a Debbie Downer about all of this.* 'Tonight at this club, don't worry about hanging out with me. Just do your thing and have fun.'

As Sam lay on his bed, he replayed the events from earlier in his head. He didn't want to miss any vital piece of information, any tell that might help them. He closed his eyes. If sleep came, that would be a bonus. But until it did, he kept thinking.

There was a loud clang, and the shutter to the warehouse door closed. 'Don't worry, we can speak freely here. I guess you have some questions for me and I have instructions for you.' Those are the exact words that Mr White spoke. He didn't give them his name, so they gave him that one when they were alone and discussing the events that had happened while heading back to return the bikes.

Sam asked what the Stitchin was.

While Mitch simultaneously asked who he was.

'Good questions, boys, or should I say, gentlemen. Yes, I prefer gentlemen and I will use that term. Who I am doesn't matter. I am just a facilitator. You could kill me or I can just drop dead and it won't matter.'

Mitch looked at Sam. 'If you mess with or hurt my brother, I will.'

Mr White's expression didn't change. 'You will see me again on and off throughout your journey. I will pop up when necessary to brief you on an upcoming task. Not all challenges, mind you. I try to get a sequence going and have someone from the current mission put you on course for the next. But I will try and see you more often than others. As I alluded to, in the grand scheme of things, who I am is the least interesting thing. Now, for the other question, that is the question. What is the Stitchin? What isn't the Stitchin? It is good and it is bad. It is everything and it is nothing. It is life and it is death.'

Sam kept his eyes shut and gently massaged his temples as he contemplated the riddle. To him, it made sense the more he thought about it. He smiled as he remembered Mitch just grunting, then demanding a response. 'That means nothing to us. Are you responsible for the lines on our legs? What are they? What did you do to us?'

Sam butted in. 'Yes, what did you do to us? One moment we wake up in a totally different location to where we were and have these marks. How did you knock us out and move us?'

'Details, details. I am responsible for nothing. As I said, I am here to facilitate your journey. Those lines on your legs represent the beginning of your journey. It means you have been chosen. Forget everything you knew. Suspend belief. Your lives are to change forever.'

'You're not making any sense,' Mitch snarled.

Sam placed his hand lightly on his brother's shoulder. 'Be cool, remember.' Then he stared at Mr White. 'But I do want to know the details. I don't like strange things happening to me without my consent.'

'Okay. Here's the elevator pitch; maybe that will pacify you.' Mr White stared at Mitch as he spoke and emphasised the word *you*. 'An elite secret membership;

fourteen challenges to be completed and a million-pound gift for each of you at the end. See, Messrs Yates, you will be compensated for any minor inconveniences. Shall I give you the details and rules now?'

Mitch nodded.

I was about to challenge him about those minor inconveniences because he'd avoided answering and they were anything but minor. Before I could find the words Mr White had started talking.

'The Stitchin is an organisation that you never speak of. Never say its name and never mention it to anyone. It transcends any company, government and monarchy; trust me. Like any group, we need new members. Now, because no one knows we exist, one cannot simply ask to join. It is an honour if one is selected, such that one cannot turn it down.' At this point, he held his hand up. 'Now usually, the person or persons in front of me ask why they were selected. And I say I'm not on selections, but I'm told the candidates work it out for themselves eventually. Shall I go on?'

I said yes. Mitch was quiet.

'Great. You will be given a series of fourteen challenges or missions or tasks: you know the sort of thing, to complete. They do get harder as the process goes on but for clever, resourceful gentlemen such as yourselves, I can't see any issues. And the good news is, you've already completed one. You passed last night's initiation; you have the mark. You're going to love the next one. I'm seriously a little bit jealous.'

'Last night was you, this Stitchin, testing us? But we didn't do anything; we didn't complete any task,' Mitch said.

Again the words I wanted to use didn't come to mind. It was not a minor inconvenience to me, being trapped and suffocated to the point of blacking out. But I missed my chance to speak up. He opened his eyes and repeatedly banged his clenched fists on to the bed. He then counted to ten in his head and then continued to fourteen before stopping. He closed his eyes and continued contemplating.

'That's the beauty of it; it's nothing really taxing. You gentlemen obviously impressed with your abilities to handle all those dead people. The Stitchin rest their souls. Find a way out and not get caught.'

'Were we in that warehouse? How can it be so different now?'

'I presume so. I presume you solved the puzzle. I don't know the ins and outs of your missions, as I said I am here to give you the rules and set you on your way. Look, whatever you were meant to do, you did. You got the stitch. That brings me to my next point. After the challenges, you will be marked. This is done as a group set after a few completed tasks; it is your membership stamp. It doesn't hurt, and with time, becomes barely visible. The first one is bigger; the others are smaller. It can be hidden with swimwear or underwear. Just no naked modelling or a porn career for you. It's up to you what you want to tell any bedfellows; just avoid the truth. Small price to pay for membership to this omnipotent group and a million pounds, no?'

'Well, I guess now we know the origins of the line, it's not that bad,' Mitch responded.

'The last instruction. Once you're in, which you both are, you're in. There is no opting out or leaving or telling anyone. This is for life. You understand what I am saying? Same goes for the tasks; you must complete them. Failure to do so means you are out, and as I just said, out is not a life option. Don't look so shocked, gentlemen. You won't fail.'

'But we never asked for this, never wanted to be part of this. You, I mean this organisation, initiated us and now we can't go back or stop. Now, we are being threatened with death. We will just go to the police.'

'Didn't you ask for this, Samuel? People are never started on this journey unless they want to be.' Mr White addressed him, as he was the one who had spoken, but he stared at Mitch. Sam figured he was playing some sort of game with them, trying to psyche them out. 'The Stitchin owns the police, media, everyone. To go to them would just be a waste of life.'

'I'll do it and I'll play by all your rules, but leave Sam out of this. He should just continue with his life as it is—college, then university.'

'He will still be able to do those things; it's actually encouraged that members carry on with their activities of daily life. But he now carries the first stitch; he is in. It is all or erasure.'

'Be cool, Mitch. If you are in this I want to be too. We can help each other, we'll be in this together.' *I tried to motion to him that we could talk about it later but Mitch didn't see me.*

'To put your minds at ease, I have the brief for your next task. All you have to do is go to a nightclub and have fun. I will give you a stamp, which will get you in for free, get you into the VIP section and get you free drinks all night. See, it is not all doom and gloom; there is fun to be had. When you make it all the way to being a full member, you will see that being part of the Stitchin will change your lives for the better.'

'What's the catch? Sam is too young to go to a club.'

'Think of it as a birthday treat from the Stitchin. Everyone needs a rite of passage when they turn seventeen. With the stamp, there will be no questions asked. Go out and enjoy yourselves. Now hold out your hands.'

Sam held out his hand first. Mr White held his phone over the dorsal side. He felt a warm glow the phone was moved. He brought his left hand in front of his face to examine it. He wasn't bothered about what the stamp was. He was more in awe of how it got on the back of his hand. The phone hadn't physically touched him. It wasn't like a conventional stamp. He had never seen anything like it before. Mr White must have thought he was looking at the image.

'It's a Falcon. You gentlemen will be going to the Falcon Club. I'm sure you've heard of it, given how prestigious it is. Your hand, Señor Yates.'

He did the same to Mitch, who traced over the Falcon logo with the fingers on his right hand. He looked at Mitch who seemed to know the club. He was into clubbing.

'This is goodbye from me. Remember, never speak of the Stitchin to anyone, complete your fourteen challenges and be part of the most special thing ever. Fail either of these and it will result in death. Now get your bikes back. I've had them refuelled for you. Go home and be at the Falcon tonight from midnight. As you are in this together, you are both judged together. If one of you fails, the two of you will have the same fate.'

Obviously, the death part freaked me out, and presumably it freaked out Mitch too. But having answers, even though they were vague, was better than nothing. The one part that stuck in my mind was when Mr White said that the candidates work out for themselves why they were chosen. From what I know of elite organisations, via television and the Internet, selection is usually heavily influenced by whether your parents were members. Our parents were important. What if they had signed us up for this when I became of age? They would have only done so if they knew we could have completed it. We will be okay. Plus if the Stitchin is all powerful, we could use it to find out what happened to Mum and Dad.

Sam opened his eyes blinked and shut them. These final thoughts relaxed him and he eventually fell asleep.

A black SUV, with darkened windows showed up at their house. The driver said he was there to take them to the club. En route, they sat in the back of the car in silence. They gave each other the occasional look but there was an unsaid rule between them to not speak. They did not trust the chauffeur. Mitch eventually broke the silence and stated, 'We will walk the last part. Pull up here; we want to get some fresh air.'

When they were out of earshot from the driver and vehicle, Sam spoke first. 'I think this is part of some bigger plan; maybe one involving Mum and Dad.'

'I don't think any of us wanted this for you. I—and I'm sure, they—just wanted you to have a normal life. Not this, whatever it actually is.'

'But I am involved, and I can't get out of it.'

'There is always a way. Let's play it by ear and if it starts getting dangerous, I will find a way to get you out of this. I promise, Sam, I won't let any harm come to you.'

'I'm not some weak little boy; I want to help you. After all, we are in this together. With the two of us, we can get it done. We'll get the million pounds each and then everything will be how it used to be.'

'Yeah, we are unstoppable, I have your back and I know you have mine but listen, I'll do the heavy lifting.'

They walked to the front of the queue and—passing all the dressed-up people felt good. The women were made up and the men were all pumped. Sam thought the clothes he chose to wear—a white shirt and grey trousers that were part of his college uniform—didn't make him stand out. Sam compared himself to his brother. *Mitch looks the part. He's used to this; he's a clubber. He carries himself with confidence.* Sam recalled their conversation to give himself strength for whatever the next thirteen challenges had in store for them.

Everything Mr White told them had been correct; once the bouncers were shown the Falcon stamp, they were ushered in. They didn't have to pay but were escorted to the VIP section. It was a large space, with its own bar and staff outnumbering the guests. It had its own DJ playing different music to the main club, which wasn't too loud so the people in the section could talk if they wanted to. They had their own waitress bringing them drinks. Mitch kept disappearing out of the VIP section; he told Sam that in any club, you had to mingle with everyone, that those people in the VIP section were usually the most boring. Each time he returned he would bring a new woman, or a group of women, into the private section. The women would then be introduced to Sam and he would make small talk. Sam knew what his brother was doing; he was hardly being subtle. As the night went on, the drinks kept flowing and as he started to get merrier he found the random chatting with women easier.

As the night wore on, Mitch was away on one of his 'fit women reconnaissance' missions, Sam noticed a woman already in their part of the club. She was staring at him and he smiled at her. She had short brown hair and—from what he could tell—large blue eyes. Her body looked very athletic in the little black dress she was wearing; there was no fat on her. She started to walk over to him. He quickly looked around but couldn't see his brother around anywhere. This wasn't a setup. The alcohol was giving him confidence, plus he had made enough pleasantries throughout the night to be able to fake a conversation. He decided to meet her halfway.

'Hello, do you come here often?'

'Hi. Has that line worked on any of the numerous women you have been chatting to all night?'

He blushed. 'I'm Sam.'

'That's not much of a codename. How old are you?'

'Erm, twenty-five. What do you mean codename?'

She laughed. 'You're not twenty-five; you're far too innocent. I mean it just sounds like a real name. I thought we didn't bother using our real identities?' She held his hand and turned it over so they could both see his stamp. Then she showed him her own matching one.

He quickly concluded that she was part of the Stitchin too. This was a sobering thought, he knew he needed to act cool and find out as much as he possibly could. He looked around to see if there was anything to hold on to, something to stop him swaying. 'So how many have you done?'

'Naughty, naughty Sam. That's a very personal question. Intimate,' she purred in his ear.

'Sorry.'

'I'm just teasing you. I don't want to talk shop, I want to have some fun with someone who can empathise with my situation. Then you find out my magic number in bed. Full-on naked fun, any positions we want without hiding our legs from one another or keeping our clothes on. We won't need to do the silly little stranger dance and come up with random excuses: I used to self-harm, I lost loved ones, I was in an accident...'

'Aren't you breaking the rules by speaking to me?'

'I've not mentioned the forbidden word, so, no.'

'Speaking of forbidden words, if you aren't going to tell me your real name, what is your codename?'

She leant in, to whisper in his ear again but before she spoke she gently bit his earlobe. 'They call me The Assassin.'

CHAPTER 8
DAY 3

With night-time setting in, the darkness accentuated the blinks of colour. The flashing blue and orange lights from the police and the recovery vehicles gave the place an unnatural aura. Sarah leant against a tree, watching and assessing the scene from her viewpoint. She had taken a back seat for the moment because if she pushed, she ran the risk of the recovery being suspended until tomorrow. The team had brought the wrong Spectacle Lift. First, it wasn't able to reach the fully submerged vehicle, and second, it didn't have the power required to raise the Range Rover. When Sarah arrived onsite, nothing was happening.

They were waiting for the Heavy Spectacle Lift to arrive. Once she had found out that the wrong recovery vehicle had been despatched, arrived and was obviously unsuitable, she was very annoyed. She demanded from Duncan, the man apparently running the show, why they hadn't got the right one there in the first place. He was testy back to her, and now the two were giving each other a wide berth. She stayed against her tree, while he had spent the past three hours stomping around, continually barking orders to people.

The correct lifter was now there and was being set up. The time wasted meant they had lost daylight, which gave Duncan the option to pull the plug and wait for tomorrow. He had been mumbling about doing that, so Sarah stayed away so as not to antagonise him further.

The divers seemed keen to just get it done with, as they had been down to the Rover a couple of times, knew where it was and the lay of the water. They also seemed to be keeping away from Duncan, as they stayed on the boat. Enough time had passed for the news to spread that something exciting was happening. A large crowd had appeared on the opposite side of the lake to where the police were working. The crowds were standing by the water's edge; the area was too large to have been cordoned off.

The group seemed to be mixed with travellers and non-travellers. There was an obvious divide and space between the two communities. The windsurfers were with the non-travellers. *They were probably telling everyone how great they are at windsurfing and all the places they have done it, but they had never come across a car in the water before.* The divers went back into the water this time with the winch from the Heavy Spectacle Lift. There was a growing murmur from the crowd.

'Dudes, remember, you said you would retrieve our camera!' one of the windsurfers shouted.

'You're not going to turn down my umbrella a second time.'

Sarah looked as Dougie held the protection over her head, unaware that it had even started to rain. 'Thank you. How come you are here?'

'Duncan wanted some more warm bodies for crowd control. I'm not sure what he thinks that lot are going to do, but he said he liked to be prepared for anything. I quote, "Cars don't end up at the bottom of a reservoir by accident; usually, it's because it's been involved in crime, probably drugs, so we need to make sure those pikeys don't get to the evidence first.'" He grimaced as he repeated the words.

'What do you think?'

'I can see why he did it, he was initially outnumbered; seems like the whole of the Colwood lot were materialising over there. But now it's late, nearly midnight, and nothing much is happening there isn't a lot of them. Police work is not interesting to the common man.'

He was correct. The crowds were dissipating; the rain that was coming down heavily now was seeing them off. Also, boredom must have set in, as what was happening was not actually interesting. 'They aren't here to pilfer or tamper with evidence. They are uncomfortable with this increased police presence around them and are watching to see what happens. If they had anything to do with the car, they wouldn't be anywhere near here.'

As the numbers thinned out, Sarah spotted a very wet Mikey standing at arm's length from an older man and woman. The man was sheltering the woman with an umbrella, just as Dougie was doing for her. The three of them weren't moving, but just stood staring into the water where the divers had gone in.

'Come with me, PC Barranger.'

She headed over to them, walking quickly to get around the lake, as the young officer kept pace, doing his best to make sure the now heavy downpour didn't affect her. She kept manoeuvring through the departing crowd to get to them.

Mikey spotted her as she approached, shouted 'Gavver alert!' and then walked off.

Sarah decided not to chase him. It was better that he wasn't there. She wanted to speak to the other two. She had already guessed who the man was, as the family resemblance was there. 'I'm a detective, working with the Met, my name is Sarah Silver, and I'm investigating the disappearance of Megan North.'

'Is it true? Is it that boy's car in the water?' The man asked, not taking his eyes off the rig.

'Which boy?'

'The one who was dating my daughter.'

'It's a silver Range Rover, license plate Dent 03.'

The woman seemed unsteady on her feet. The father put his arm around her with his free hand. She pushed it away and regained her composure. She pulled out a cigarette, lit it up and took a long drag. 'What about Megan?' Her voice was very husky, like she smoked sixty cigarettes a day.

'The divers confirmed there wasn't a driver or passenger in the vehicle. All the windows were open, though. There was minimal damage to the car, so it doesn't seem like the Rover made it into Lake Wilson by accident. The divers had time earlier and swept the surrounding part of the lake around the car as best as they could and didn't find anything. We will know more once the car is up.'

She took another drag of her cigarette. 'Thank you. When we heard the car was in the lake, we feared the worst about our poor Megan.'

'What do you know about the car and Megan's involvement with it?'

'She—'

'Ma, don't say anything.' The man spoke.

The woman gave him a silencing look. She was obviously in charge. 'She was dating a young man. They used to drive around in that silver thing. She had been spotted by members of our community driving it herself. Megan was a clever girl, could drive better than any boy.'

'What do you know about Tom Denton and their relationship?' Sarah paused. 'I'm sorry, I didn't catch your name.'

'Carole, Megan is my granddaughter. He seemed nice enough, generous with her. He—'

'Ma.'

'He gave her the car before he passed. Like I said, a generous boy.'

'You never had an issue with the relationship? I thought it was frowned upon to date outside of your community.'

'Yeah, it was. But she told me all about it; we were very close. She didn't tell the menfolk and made me promise not to. Times are changing and if an old bat like me can see that, my son and our kin need to. We need to adapt and find our place in the new world.' Carole stroked the face of her son. 'Michael, she wasn't a bad girl, just fell in love with the wrong person. She never did it to hurt the family, she was just ahead of her time.'

'What will become of our way of life? You more than anyone else harps on about tradition.' He grimaced. 'She, you, should have spoken to me. I would have been able to help. She wouldn't have had to run away.'

'Did she take Tom's death badly?'

'Michael, leave us for a moment. Why don't you and Detective Silver's boy take a walk?'

Dougie spoke up. 'PC Barranger.'

Carole waited for the men to leave them. 'I knew bits, but which teenage girl tells her grandmother everything? I kept the details secret to protect her and the family. If they knew about the boy, they would have done something to him. But they didn't know. It was only when she disappeared that I had to come clean and tell Michael and Mikey what I knew just in case anything helped in finding her.'

'What about her mother? She was the one who reported Megan missing—she must have feared for her daughter to involve us outsiders.'

'She ain't taken the gorger or disappearing news well. She's been unable to leave the house since. Says she needs to be home for when Megan returns. She blames herself and the rest of the household blame her too. It's up to the Ma to the keep the girls under control; she obviously failed by having her daughter run away. Then to find out she was with a gorger—she's too ashamed to show her face.'

'Is that why you all moved away from Colwood?'

'Mikey was there, waiting for her just in case. We heard some news that Megan was up north, so we went to look. It wasn't her. That girl was nothing compared to my Megan. Only a fool could have confused the two.'

'So Tom?'

'I didn't know when it started, otherwise, I would have stopped it. By the time I heard, it was too late; she said she was in love. Then she was damaged. None of our men would have wanted her, so I had to keep it a secret. To protect her reputation and what her Pa thinks about her, I pretended that she was a good girl and that he was a nice boy. I had to tell people she was being progressive in order to be able to show my face. But she betrayed us and he should have stayed away from a young girl who wasn't his kind.' Carole stopped, lit up another cigarette and started to puff away.

'How did you hear?'

'People love to gossip and concern themselves with other people's business.'

'They weren't discreet then?'

'They were seen together. Some boys said they saw her in his car, driving around town. As I said, she was even driving it at times. When Mikey was learning to drive, she made him teach her. He didn't want to—who wants to hang around with their little sister? But he did anyway. That's the sort of person she is; she can make anyone do anything for her. People just gravitate towards her because she is good. When her grandfather died, she would have been about five. She didn't understand what was going on, but she wouldn't leave my side. At night, she would sneak out of her bed and come and sleep with me. She somehow knew she had to look after me and she did. I couldn't be miserable in her presence.'

'Did she have a job?' Sarah wanted to test the waters and see how much the grandmother knew.

'No. She helped her mother keep a good place, cooking and cleaning. Helping out in the community. As I said, everyone liked her. I'm sure you can guess that all the boys wanted her; they would all have married her given the chance. They all watched her, maybe too closely.' Carole let out a massive cackle. 'She changed, though, just before she disappeared.'

'How was she different?'

'She became quiet, withdrawn, secretive. Not in the way she had been, when she was hiding her relationship with the boy, but different, like she had a world of problems on her shoulders. She wasn't her usual bubbly self. Everyone who knew her could tell something was up. I guess finding the boy was too much for her.'

'You mean she saw Tom's body?'

Carole flicked the cigarette on the floor and watched Sarah. 'You don't know, do you? No, she was the one who found him. In his bath, with his wrists slit. Apparently, he did it properly; he went up the arm. She called an ambulance and everything. That is what she told me.'

This surprised Sarah, but the detail Carole seemed to have deliberately thrown in was correct and not public knowledge. 'The police report says it was the boy's mother who found him. It didn't mention her being there.'

'You see, you can't trust the gavvers. Anyway, none of this matters now; all I want is her back. I love and miss her. I am going to trust you; you're like me, I can tell. Been around, driven by a sense of duty, hard as nails. Find her, detective; you are under my protection now. I will let our community know not to touch you and to help you as best as they can.'

'I have a lot more questions. We need to sit down properly. I need a statement from you, Mikey, her father and mother. If you want me to find her, help me so I can try.'

'Not try. Promise me, Sarah Silver, find my Megan and bring her home. You tell her the sins of her past will forgotten, the boy's death has seen to that. She's like a widow now, that's how I can spin it. Pretend they were married. She'll be able to get another man, not the best, that way. It will work out for her.'

'Did you tell her that?' *Sounds like a plan that would make any free-spirited young woman want to run away. Tom's death seems to have been a good thing for them. Did they have a hand in it? It's plausible if Megan did in fact find the body. But why the subterfuge on the report, saying it was the mother who found him?*

'No, I never got a chance to. I only thought about it once she had gone and I was thinking how to make it right. Please bring her back.'

'I can't promise that, but I will promise to do my best.'

Carole coolly stared at Sarah. It was a look that would have caused most to crack. Neither woman was willing to give, but suddenly, Carole broke eye contact and took a step closer to the lake.

The divers popped up and made a series of gestures to the team on the land. The operating crew pressed some buttons and the lifter came to life, making a loud mechanical noise. The motor whirled and the thick chain wound around the barrel as it pulled. The divers swam back to their boat, making space for what lay beneath. As the rain continued to dance on the surface of the lake, something large was about to cause a disruption. Ripples shot out from the chain, the pulley kept yanking, then the eruption occurred. And like Godzilla emerging from the water, the Range Rover broke through the surface.

Carole stopped talking to Sarah and started to run towards the other side of the lake towards the lift. The sight of the older woman breaking off into a run seemed to momentarily stun the group of four, but Michael reacted first and followed her. Dougie looked at Sarah, and if reading her mind, shouted to give himself authority or to be heard over the rain and the machine noises. 'I think you should wait here!' *Nice try, Dougie, but you should have commanded, not suggested,* Sarah thought as she moved to catch up with the Norths.

Water was pouring off and out of the Range Rover, as it was dangled higher and higher. The contrast roof caught the flashing blue and orange lights like a glitterball at the centre of a nightclub. The car hung like a pendulum, gently swaying before being rocked as the crew did their job and swung it around to hover over the ground. They lowered it and physically helped manoeuvre the front wheels to touch the ground. The rear part of the vehicle was soon on the ground. Duncan was directing the team to detach the chains from under the rear bumper, and to attach the towing cables to get the Sport HST on to the Spectacle Lift. Duncan then started to help them.

Obviously, he didn't want to be out this late at night working especially in the rain, which had started to come down heavier. The team members were tired; they had been onsite for double the length of time they should have been. The earlier crowds of travellers who had been shouting abuse about their presence had unsettled them somewhat. Now their boss was interfering and getting in the way. Mistakes were bound to happen.

Someone accidently pressed the boot release. Usually, this would have been done back at the yard, in a controlled environment. It opened slowly, and in the next moment, everything seemed to happen in slow motion. The lights framed everything like flashes of a camera. Every drop of rain seemed identifiable.

With the boot open, water poured out. Duncan turned away from the car with arms outstretched, shouting for everyone to keep away. It didn't work. The officer immediately next to it couldn't take his eyes off the now open boot; he seemed transfixed. Michael dropped to his knees next to the vehicle and started to vomit. As Carole approached, she let out a shriek, covered her eyes with her hands and continued to make a noise that didn't sound human.

Sarah stopped running and walked the last couple of metres to the car. She already knew what they had all seen, she had feared it from the moment she had heard about the car being in the water. Dougie stopped behind her, paralysed.

She moved the wet artificial hair from her face and stared into the boot. The lifeless body of Megan, with her spectacular big blue eyes, stared back at her.

CHAPTER 9
DAY 4

Sam sat on the smooth rock and glanced around; the water looked so inviting. He stood up, dived in the cool refreshing lake and swam towards the waterfall. When he was directly underneath the gushing stream, he floated on his back, looked up and opened his mouth. He guzzled down the quenching water, unable to get enough. But it wasn't enough. Something was wrong; his thirst was insatiable. He licked his lips; they were dry, but how could they be? The only thing that could satisfy him was to be immersed. He let himself sink back into the depth of the water.

It wasn't enough; at some level, he knew his throat felt like sandpaper, and his head hurt. Something else was wrong, but he didn't know what. Subconsciously, he knew he had to wake up. He needed a drink of real water. As he started to wake, he realised he wasn't in his own bed and more importantly, he wasn't alone. He sensed the presence of another person in the bed next to him. This caused him to sit upright.

He forced his eyes open, looked at his bedfellow, felt relieved and relaxed for a second. That was until he noticed the woman also in the room. It was her. *What exactly happened last night before?* She had a towel wrapped around her body, and with another, was drying her hair. She noticed Sam looking at her and smiled at him. 'I would have asked you to join me in the shower, but I just didn't think it was practical.' She laughed and dropped both towels. 'Have you seen my clothes?' Now fully naked, she slinked over to Sam. He looked her up and down momentarily but just stared at the only bit that mattered. They were faded, completely healed and only visible if you really looked. 'There are fourteen, if that is what you are trying work out. It's a complete set, plus I have done over and beyond. You boys don't even count as one; you were just for fun. Shame, we never got to have proper fun.'

'What did you have to do to get them? It looks like you've had them a while.' Sam pointed at her stitches, reaching out a hand like he wanted to touch them.

She contorted her face. 'It was a lifetime ago, but they saved my life. You never forget earning your marks. Maybe when you have a few more under your belt we can talk again. The missions may seem weird but there is a plan. Just trust that you are now part of something great. The diversity in the beginning means you get to truly learn what you are good at, then you can specialise and become an expert and get your codename.' She laughed, not in a mocking manner, but in a humble way. 'I want you to know your current predicament has nothing to do with me. I am just a messenger, but your mission seems simple. Don't over-think it and dwell on what lies beneath. Just follow the instructions and notch up your tally.'

'I'm more confused, what are you talking about? What exactly happened? I can't remember anything after meeting you last night.' Sam glanced over to Mitch, who was still fast asleep. Like him, he was topless, with the sheet covering both their bottom halves. As he began waking up properly, Sam felt awkward, being in bed with his brother and with this naked woman standing there. And he felt weird; not just his head but also his body ached. It wasn't just the bruises from before, there was a new physical discomfort, he had an unusual feeling down below. The more he thought about it, the more aware he became of the sensation. He lifted the sheet and looked down. Nausea immediately punched him in the stomach and he just about managed to lean over the side of the bed as he vomited.

The noise or the movement caused Mitch to stir. 'Naughty boy. Not only have you made a big mess but you've also woken your brother,' The Assassin said. She changed her composure and behaviour, doing a complete three-sixty compared to when Mitch was asleep and they were talking one-on-one.

Sam spat and tried to speak. The shock, the violation and the disgust meant no words came out. He held up a hand to tell her to wait before spitting again. He shut his eyes and tried to compose himself, and he croaked out: 'What have you done to us?'

'What the—' shouted Mitch.

'Mitch, don't move. If you move any further, you will hurt your brother. The tether will only give so far.' She smirked.

Sam fixated on the plastic tube leaving his manhood and feeding into a bag. A similar tube left the bag and was inserted into his brother. Mitch, who had jumped out of bed and started to back away, had caused both tubes to become taut. The bag was suspended in air between the brothers. It was a quarter full with a dark-green liquid. Sam stared at his tube, where he could see droplets of the liquid.

She watched him and followed his eyes. 'See, you should be grateful we stopped you from peeing yourself.' She giggled. 'Now, boys, I would usually be very cross if I was standing here in all my glory and you didn't rise to the occasion. But I guess you can't, so I will let you off. But seriously, I need to know that it's not me, it's you?'

Mitch moved towards her, fists clenched. He barely managed to pass the bed when Sam let out a whelp. The older brother looked at his younger sibling and noticed something red in Sam's catheter. He stood still. Sam held himself and shuffled down the bed so the tether became slack.

'It's blood,' she said as she slowly pulled on her knickers, never breaking eye-contact with the brothers. 'Okay, so here are the rules. First, don't be angry with me. I think this is a waste of two men, me and a hotel room, but it's not my game. I was just sent to tell you the rules. A urinary catheter has been fitted to both of you, feeding into one drainage bag.' She started to get dressed, then pulled out her phone and read from the screen. 'Usually, a catheter is held in place by an inflated balloon. Yours has another feature: metal wings. If you pull on it or try and remove it, it will rip you open. Only Dr Impey can safely remove it. It says the wings are booby-trapped and if removed by anyone other than Dr Impey, you will be ripped open, but in a different way.'

Sam looked at his brother, who had shut his eyes.

'I need to take a piss,' Mitch snarled at her.

'That's what the tube and bag are for, darling. Wee away. You probably want to get to Dr Impey's quickly, because if that bag gets full you really don't want that stuff, whatever it is, going back into your bodies. That's my advice anyway.'

'What is it?' Sam asked her, flabbergasted. He pointed at the bag.

'Honestly, I don't know darling.' He noticed her expression was serious for a moment as she spoke.

'Sam, I can't hold it in.' The part of the tube connected to Mitch turned green, and then the colour shot all the way down the tube and started emptying into the bag.

Sam stared at the bag; his face contorted, and then he looked away. He knew that he felt physically numb down there and emotionally numb. He could only imagine what it was like to have to use that to urinate.

'You've gone coy; I didn't think you were the shy type. Boys, I would like to say it has been a pleasure, but it has actually been really frustrating for me. Dr Impey's address is saved on your phone's map. I sincerely wish you well and hope that we see each other again. Especially you, young Sam. I know the tube makes it look swollen, but I can tell it doesn't need artificial help for that.'

The act of getting ready and dressed was painful, not physical pain but the process. First, they had to forego a shower, which Sam desperately needed given how rough he was feeling. They got to Mitch's clothes first as they got out of the bed on his side to avoid the vomit. He quickly put on his boxers. 'What should I do with this?' He asked holding the tube.

'I guess it should hang down the bottom so gravity helps move the liquid.'

'Yeah, I guess so. This is weird, but look, little brother; it's not dangerous and we aren't in any trouble.'

'We are pissing a green liquid; how can you say it's not dangerous?'

Mitch looked at Sam. 'I feel fine, besides this,' he held the catheter. 'We just go to this doctor and it will all be fine.'

'Wait. If we let it hang freely, it's not really practical for getting around. Most people would get special clothing or tape the bag to themselves. We can't do that, so we need another bag to put this bag in. Thinking about it, it might be easier to put the tube over your underwear and trousers. I'll do the same, then we can put the bag in a bag and hold it in front of us.'

'Why don't we just put on dressing gowns, get a taxi and go to the doctor?'

'We can't walk around this hotel in bathrobes, we don't want to draw attention to ourselves. Whose room is this? Has it been paid for? Will we have to pay extra for my accident? Also, who knows how busy the doctor's office will be? I think we should get dressed in our normal clothes, but definitely get a taxi.'

There was a knock at the door, 'Housekeeping.' Sam looked at Mitch. The knock was repeated, there was a pause and then they heard the sound of the door being unlocked.

'Don't come in!' Mitch shouted. Instinct made him dash towards the door. Sam was paralysed and didn't move at first. That was until he felt a sharp pain in his bladder, blood entered his tube and this broke him free, so he moved with Mitch. He slammed into his brother who was at the door and managed to push it shut as it opened a fraction. 'Sorry, I am changing. Can you come back in an hour?'

'Okay,' the lady on the other side of the door responded.

'We need to get out of here as soon as...' Mitch stopped talking and looked at his brother. 'You're bleeding.'

Sam felt embarrassed and placed his hands over his manhood, 'You moved too quickly. It's okay, it doesn't hurt. Must have been a sudden jolt. We need to move in unison. Maybe once we're dressed, we should tie our legs together, like a three-legged race or something.'

'Sorry, I should have thought more. I just didn't want the maid to come in and see us.'

'It's a stupid idea; it will draw attention to us. I'm fine, Mitch. Let's just go and get this removed.' Sam took a few steps; he felt delicate inside. 'I need to go.'

'Yes, we will; you set the pace.'

'No, I mean, pee. It was the sudden movement, plus I drank a lot yesterday. Can you look away?'

'Sure. When this is removed, we don't have to ever speak about this again.' Mitch picked up the rest of his clothes, turned his back on Sam and started to get dressed.

'This feels so strange. I am not sure I can go; I am bursting to but can't.'

'I know, you think you're going to wet yourself, but you don't. It stings a bit, but you need to go, so go. We can go in the bathroom; you can aim at the toilet. It might help. I wish I wore looser jeans; these ones are so tight I won't be able to do them up.'

'If you weren't such a man-whore, you would have had less tight clothes on, but thanks for trying to take my mind off it. Can we try the toilet idea?' He started to shuffle over to the bathroom.

'You're the one who secured that crazy-nude woman.'

'I can't remember anything after meeting her, can you?' Talking was a good distraction for Sam, so that he wouldn't have to think of the matter at hand.

'I saw you guys talking, so I left you to it. Then next thing I knew, I was waking up to you vomiting, her watching and this thing attached to me.'

Sam held himself and aimed, but nothing happened. 'I guess we were drugged again. Some antibiotics change the colour of your fluids. What do you think they did to us?'

'Neither of us has any scars, and beside this, I don't hurt nor am I sore anywhere. So, nothing too sinister. Maybe they gave us a new party drug to see what the effects are. We're the real-life guinea pigs. Honestly, it's not that bad for a million pounds.'

'That's plausible. Maybe, they are collecting our urine to do all this toxicology on the drug.' Sam felt a sense of relief. The blood in his catheter moved like the mercury in a thermometer and was pushed through with the green urine he was expelling from his body. He was holding the tube; it felt warm. Mesmerised by the colour, he noticed that the green shade was becoming lighter and not just from the lack of blood. By the time he was finished, the bag was nearly full. 'Sorry, I couldn't stop myself. It seems to be clearing from my system. When this is removed, we should drink tonnes of water, pee a lot and just flush this thing from our bodies.'

'Hopefully, we can both hold the next piss in until we get to the doctor. Let's hurry.'

Sam washed his hands and rinsed out his mouth before grabbing his clothes and awkwardly getting dressed. 'Have you got everything?'

'Phone, wallet, keys and my clothes from last night. That's all I had with me.'

'Yeah, me too, plus my watch. I think we're good.'

They held the catheter bag in a black bag that they took from the hotel room; it had kept the hairdryer in it. The tubes were coming out of the waistbands of their jeans and feeding into the bag. Mitch held the bag close to himself so that the tubes wouldn't be so obvious. They shuffled towards the door in unison.

Sam opened the door to check and see if the coast was clear. It was, so they followed the signs to the lifts. They were on floor fourteen, and they knew that the lift had an increased chance of interaction with other people, but they knew it would be more convenient than trying to fumble down the stairs together. He pushed the down button, and as he waited for the lift, his heart started beating faster. He was scared. He had been since he first sat on the motorbike. Then, the fear was mixed with excitement; now, it was dread.

When the lift pinged, they silently went inside. 'That's lucky; it's empty.' Mitch said as he pressed the button for the lobby. They travelled down in silence. There was another ping, to tell them they had arrived at their destination. 'One, two, three, let's go. Remember, small steps. You set the pace and I'll follow.'

They walked out of the lift, and it was immediately apparent that something was wrong in the hotel. There was a maid crying on the sofas in the reception, who was being comforted by another a maid. There were three police officers with the two women. A group of people in different types of hotel uniform—receptionists, porters and managers—were congregating behind the sofa area. An older gentleman, probably the main hotel manager, Sam guessed, was standing away from the rest of the staff. He had a worried look on his face as he talked to an officer and he was gesticulating.

'Just walk, act calm. Don't look anyone in the eye. Sam, come on. No, not that way. Follow the sign to the restaurant. We are just going for breakfast, like any other paying guest. This has nothing to do with us. Just be cool.'

Sam listened as an elderly couple walked past them, whispering, 'I heard they found a dead body. Not a suicide but someone horrifically murdered, and it was just one floor below us, floor fifteen. Oh, just think…'

'Mitch, we need to get out of here now. That woman who was with us, we know nothing about her and have no memories from the night before. I think we need to go. Look, there is another exit over there in the restaurant. No one is next to it. Let's go.'

They headed towards the exit when Sam felt a tap on his shoulder. It was a police officer. Sam watched as the officer sized them up. *He's staring at the bag.* 'Excuse me, gents, you need to stop there, we need to speak to you.'

CHAPTER 10
DAY 4

Sarah pounded the tarmac and it felt good. It gave her the release to vent her anger with the added benefit of getting to know her surroundings. She checked her watch as she briefly paused to have a sip of isotonic water, and she saw that she had clocked nearly ten kilometres. *I'll do another ten and then go to work.* An image of the dead girl flashed in her head, so she sped off, deciding it was easier to keep moving. *In life, you always have to keep moving.* She felt that she covered a lot of ground; did the city centre near her flat, then down to the docklands. It wasn't deliberate; she hadn't mapped out a route or design. Maybe it was instinct that drew her that way. Water usually calmed her, but today, it was disturbing.

As much as she could switch off, some days, it was much harder to do so. Then there were days when she had to open every emotional vent in her body, to feel and give herself the fuel to fight for those who couldn't. Today was one of those days. She felt she had let Megan down, so every cell in her body had to hurt, to feel, to drive her to find the truth and bring justice to the young woman taken way before her time.

This unusual case had taken a turn. It was given to her bizarre manner, and now, it had changed from a missing person to a murder investigation. Her years of experience told her that it was also tied to the Tom Denton suicide, which was a case itself that may or may not be suspicious. She thought it was the former. No official person seemed to care about it or the truth. She could have written anything as the cause of Megan's death and who caused it, and it would have been accepted, filed away and closed. But this girl deserved justice, and Sarah felt it was her duty to make sure she would get justice. No person, especially a young woman, deserved to die like that. She didn't need the autopsy to know Megan would have been aware to some extent of what was happening to her; her wide-open eyes told Sarah that. 'I swear I will get you justice, Megan,' she whispered under her breath as she started to map out in her head what she needed to do. She then changed direction and headed off.

Somehow, she timed it perfectly; and when she arrived at her destination, a familiar face was entering the building. As if by some sixth sense the person must have known that she was being watched as she paused and turned around. Sarah stopped and looked at the other woman, who was staring at her. Sarah mustered the best smile she could, given the current situation and their history; the other woman started to head towards her, with a frown on her face.

Sarah stopped and waited; it seemed like the polite thing to do. She noted that the woman had put on some weight. *I hope it is happy fat and she is comfortable with a significant other. That would make my life easier.* Immediately, one of her hands went to her hair. Judging the other woman made her feel self-conscious, as she realised that she would be looking like a sweaty mess.

She had been through the mills since they last saw each other.

'Sarah, is that really you? You look terrible.'

'Thanks.'

'I didn't mean it like that.' The woman paused, and her face softened. 'I heard what you went through, it sounded really bad. I meant to say, why are you here? Were you looking for me?'

'I was hoping to see you.' Sarah noted a hint of satisfaction cross the other woman's face. 'I heard you worked here and thought by some off chance that I might bump into you.'

'Oh, so this is a professional visit? You never change. But I want you to know that if you do want to talk to someone, I am here. I can listen, be a sounding board. No judgement or opinions. For the sake of your mental health, talk to me.'

'What do you mean?' Sarah asked defensively.

'Do I really need to spell this out? You turned in your own colleagues, partners, because they were dirty, taking bribes. You broke an unwritten rule and then those ex-colleagues and other peers physically took revenge on you for snitching.'

Sarah stared at her.

Her ex-colleague continued. 'I heard you were hospitalised for months, that they beat you to within an inch of your life. They would have killed you but underestimated how tough you are.' She paused to gauge Sarah's reaction. 'Sorry, I am not trying to be insensitive. You know I care for you, I want to help you through the trauma you went through. Let me help you.'

'They made me see a professional counsellor, I'm good. But you can help me by doing what you do best.'

'You're a user: you did it to me before and you want to do it to me again. You played with my emotions as it suited you.'

'I never meant to hurt you. I thought we were friends and when I realised you had feelings for me, I backed off.'

'What was I, an experiment?'

'You were a friend, a good one in a dark time I was going through and things went too far. So it doesn't seem fair to burden these current issues on you.'

'I should be the judge of that.' She turned her back on Sarah and started to head off.

'Her name was Megan North, from the traveller community.' Sarah quickly blurted out to stop the other woman in her tracks. 'She was found in the boot of her boyfriend's car. He apparently committed suicide, and she disappeared a couple of weeks later. Approximately one month ago. The car was pulled from a reservoir last night, the early hours of this morning. I believe she was alive when it went into the water. Given the status of the body, practically perfect from my visual observation, it must have been very recent. This girl needs your help. I need your help.' Sarah started to play her.

'Any pathologist can help you.'

Sarah knew she wanted validation, knew what she had to do. 'We need the best. Mel, you're the only one I trust to do this right. It seems like fate that you are working at the same hospital where my case has turned up.'

'I scanned my emails before I left the house to prepare my day, I did see a report of a drowned girl coming in. The post-mortem is not a priority and is scheduled for a few days' time. But I will see what I can do. I could never say no to you.'

'Thank you, Doctor Sobczyk. You're a legend.'

'You owe me dinner and drinks.'

She came around easily. I guess nothing has changed—quid pro quo. 'Of course.'

'Why don't you come in? Our showers here are pretty good., I have some spare clothes that should fit you. Then you can assist me, if you still remember how.'

I want the information, but this could be awkward. Sarah started to weigh up the options and possible scenarios if she refused. Respite was suddenly provided when her phone started to ring. It was a voicemail, but she pretended to answer a call. 'I was about to do something very important, but understand, I am on my way.'

As she pretended to hang up the call she caught a glimmer of frustration on Dr Sobczyk's face.

'I need to go, but I will join you when I can. Let me give you my number and you can keep me abreast on anything you find, in case I can't get back to you soon. Thank you again.' She placed her hand on Melissa's shoulder. 'It was good to see you again.' She started to jog away.

When she had put enough distance between herself and the hospital, she slowed down to a walk, pulled out her phone and called back the number that had left her a message. It was from Angelique.

'Detective Silver, it is Angelique from Vehicle Recovery or VR. We spoke the other day. I thought you would want to know that I have completed the assessment of the vehicle now that it is out of the lake. The number plate is registered to a Thomas Denton, but it isn't actually associated with the Range Rover, though. According to our database, the two have never been registered together. The vehicle was purchased new and registered to a James Yates over four years ago.'

Angelique paused, maybe waiting for praise, before continuing. 'Mr Yates lives in a house called Pine View, and the address is…'

Sarah already knew, as she had visited the place, but the rest of the message confirmed it. The owner of the car was the Dentons' neighbour. Sarah closed her eyes. She now needed to speak to the neighbour, the actual owner of the car, and not his teenage son. She needed to find out what the autopsy showed. And she needed to go through Megan's possessions, the ones found with her, and search for clues. Sarah opened her eyes with new clarity and bolted off.

In BR-4, an unwashed Sarah paced around the room in her jogging gear. She hadn't bothered to have a shower, instead opting to douse her armpits in water using some paper towels. She navigated the few items meticulously laid out on the floor. *Thank you, Dougie.* There was a piece of paper where the phone found on the deceased should have been. The paper stated that the phone was an iPhone 8 and that it was with Technology Services due to the water damage. *Better add getting the IT guys on our side to the list of things to urgently do, as I doubt that fixing a traveller girl's mobile phone will be a priority.*

She was wearing gloves, more out of habit and respect than to preserve any evidence that would have already been washed away. She picked up the black Gucci shoulder bag. It was empty, as the contents had already been emptied out and itemised on the floor, but Sarah wanted to see if it was real. It had a gold colour chain strap and the flap closure was embossed with a Double G. She turned it over and over and examined the sewing, materials, closures and lining. As far as she could tell, it was real. She estimated it to be worth a couple of grand. There was an interior zipper pocket section that was empty now, but it had a black plastic card and a key in it. They were on a piece of paper next to her foot. She glanced down and saw the silver logo on the black card. It looked like an 'F' written in fancy typography.

She completed her examination of the bag; there were no hidden compartments, nor anything hidden under the lining. Besides the water damage, it was in good condition. Megan had cared for it. On another sheet of paper, there were some designer makeup containers. The Christian Louboutin lipstick was ruined, as was an

Armani foundation. A small glass bottle of Coco Noir by Chanel was intact; Sarah shook it and determined it had perfume in it, but she decided not to open it and smell the fragrance. *Megan liked her labels; the question is how did she get them? As presents or earned; and if the latter, how?*

She put the bottle down and picked up the credit card sized black plastic and key. Besides the embellished 'F' logo, there was nothing on it; no name, no numbers, nor strip for swiping it. *I need to find out if it has touch capabilities. And this key—what does it open? It is too small to be a door key, so it is most likely a locker key. Are the two related to each other?* She turned the piece of metal over in her gloved hands. There was a number on it: 12. The design seemed too fancy, too intricate to be an official key, like one belonging to a school or storage locker. *But then, a personal one wouldn't have a number on it.*

Just as she started to ruminate on the limited information she had been given, her train of thought was broken as her internal phone started to ring. *I wish Doughty hadn't had that re-instated.* It was a number from inside the building, but she did not know who.

'Detective Sarah Silver,' she answered.

'Hi, Sarah, I mean, Detective Silver.'

She could practically feel Dougie blushing. 'Yes, PC Barranger,' she replied, using a stern voice but smirking at the same time.

'Ma'am, I hope my evidence layout was satisfactory. I just wanted to let you know that the deceased's phone is with Tech Services, but they are very busy dealing with collateral from the building collapse. I have tried contacting the actual owner of the Rover, as identified by VR, but to no avail. I will keep trying when I get the chance, but I have been told I need to prioritise dealing with the building incident. I expressed my preference to support you but was told the Megan case was open and shut and you would have it closed by the end of the day. Sorry. But when I do have any spare time, I will check in with you and see if I can help where you need it.'

'Thank you, Dougie; you have been invaluable.' She was glad he couldn't see how red she was, not from embarrassment but anger. Just then, she heard the door open behind her. She didn't turn around to see who it was. She knew already. 'I guess you heard this is a murder case now.'

'Wasn't it always going to be? I mean, they don't let their own mix with outsiders,' Doughty told her, the tone of his voice remaining very neutral. He scanned the evidence on the floor and moved closer to the detective, putting on a pair of gloves as he did so.

Sarah spun around to face him. 'I need more resources to find the murderer, not less.'

He stretched out his hand, and Sarah handed over the black card she was still holding. As she did so, she made a mental note to put the key back that she had left over by the phone. He looked at both sides of the plastic as he spoke. 'We don't have it available. Interrogate her family and find out which one or ones did it and resolve this. There are a lot of other cases for you to be getting on with. It won't be easy to switch you on to our payroll earlier with your new bigger salary, but given how stretched we are for good officers, the budget can handle a week sooner.'

Sarah felt her phone vibrating in the armband where she had it as a music player for her run. She ignored it, but it made her realise that she was still in her running gear and that made her feel self-conscious. She knew she shouldn't have cared, but he was her supervisor, he knew Tanner, and for no apparent reason, he seemed to have done a U-turn. 'You said I had two weeks and could have some junior support.'

'That was for a missing person—'

'She was locked in a car boot and dumped in a lake.' Her interruption came across more sharply than she intended. *Is he testing me or something? I cannot lose my cool.*

His facial expression did not change. '—Which requires lots of evidence trawling. You, better than most of the detectives here, know the stats regarding a murder of this type. Most of the time it is someone known to the victim, usually due to an emotional reason. As I said earlier, I am confident you will find it to be one of her relatives. But you are right; you should have physical support when bringing them in for questioning. Given the other incident, remember to handle them with care. It will probably make them cagier than they usually are.'

Sarah gave him a half-hearted smile in response. Everything Doughty said made sense and was the most likely outcome. *But something about this case doesn't seem right. The family appeared shocked and disturbed when the body was found. Then again, her mother wasn't around, and Mikey did a disappearing act. I couldn't gauge their reaction. I can't be sure—was it them? Surely, Carole would have stopped any retribution. She seemed to be in charge. She didn't seem totally bothered about the whole Tom relationship. But more importantly, why did Tanner care about this, why did he want me to find Megan?*

He smiled back. 'Well done for getting us this far; now just close it off.' He started to head out of the room.

'Thank you, sir, but I haven't done anything yet.' She stretched out her hand and nodded towards his, to take back the card that he hadn't offered to return.

He handed it back. 'Forgot I even had that. The missus, god rest her soul, was always having to remind me where I left my keys. That's why I leave the detective work to you guys.' He laughed as he left.

Sarah's phone started to vibrate again, but she didn't answer it as the commissioner's visit had left her with more questions than she started with, and she zoned out to think it all over.

When she eventually checked it; there were six missed calls from Dr Sobczyk, a couple of voicemails and a text message:

Call me urgently. There is something very strange about the body.

CHAPTER 11
DAY 4

'Are you guests at this hotel?' the policeman enquired. 'When did you arrive and how long are you staying?'

Without missing a beat, Mitch responded, 'We're here for another week, Easter holidays and all that. What is happening? Why are there police here? Is it not safe? I think we need to speak to you with our parents.' He nodded over to the couple that had passed them. 'They will want to hear what is going on. Do we need to change hotels?' He paused, acting freaked out. 'Can we speak in five minutes? I need to pop out and have a pre-breakfast cheeky smoke. We'll be in the restaurant with our folks in a bit.'

'Okay. I will speak to you later. We have a lot of people to get through,' the officer replied.

Mitch ushered Sam towards the door, then outside and into the first taxi waiting in the queue. The car took off after direction from Mitch. They didn't speak.

Sam just thought about what happened. *Mitch made sure no one suspected us being in an expensive hotel by making out that we were part of a normal family and our parents were present. Mr and Mrs grey-nuclear family. Hardly the sort to be involved in anything untoward. We were staying at the hotel, so would be available for questioning anytime. And really, the policeman should have asked anything in front of whom he thought were our parents. The fake father was probably a lawyer; he looked the type. Then Mitch gave us the important out*

116

and maybe a reason why we might be looking shifty—he wanted to smoke. I guess over all these years, through all the times when he has had to lie to authorities, his street-smart sense and skills have been finely tuned. He will get us through this Stitchin, then our lives will be better.

As soon as they arrived at their destination and were out of the car. Mitch burst out, 'I'm desperate to go. I have been since that policeman stopped us and then that bumpy taxi ride just made things worse.'

'Are you sure you can't wait, Mitch? We are just outside the doctor's.' *Here on Harley Street.* Sam felt shocked at the prestigious location. In his opinion, it would have been better if the doctor's clinic had been on some back alley, as he would have obviously been a dodgy practitioner. The saving grace was that the place was close to the hotel.

'I don't think I can control it; everything is just open and it's leaking out.'

'Sure. Shall we go inside so that you won't have to do it on the street?' Sam pressed the buzzer next to the name 'Dr Impey'. There was no voice; the door simply buzzed open.

Mitch closed the door behind them. 'Wait a sec, I'm going to go now. I have to. Sorry.' He held the hairdryer bag down by their knees.

Sam stood with his back to his brother, in an attempt to give him some privacy. If he hadn't had been so scared, he would have also gone when they were stopped back at the hotel.

'Sam, the bag is full, and I can't stop. It's filling up in the tube.' Mitch sounded panicked.

Sam looked down at the clear plastic leaving his body. It was also rising, like some weird green mercury in a thermometer suddenly placed in a hot room. 'Mine too. How much more do you need to do?'

'I've been trying to hold the last bit in, but I just can't. Now, it's full, and I don't know if it is new wee or the same liquid just sloshing around up and down the tube, in and out of me.'

The combination of having his own and his brother's contaminated urine going in and out of his body, the hangover, not eating anything and what their bedfellow had actually been up to at the hotel made Sam feel nauseous. He grabbed the handrail and used it to haul himself up the stairs. 'Let's just go and get this removed.' He stopped leading them up the stairs when he realised that they needed to keep the bag level between them, otherwise, Mitch would get the raw deal. They continued the journey in unison; luckily, the stairs were wide. Unluckily, they had to go to the third floor.

'At least the doctor must be good, to be able to afford digs like this.'

'Or he just does lots of dodgy jobs, like this.'

'If he does anything untoward, I will kill him.' Mitch snarled.

How much more untoward do you want it to get? 'We'll be fine.' Sam lied, as he knocked on the door. There was a buzzing sound, he pushed the door and it opened. They walked into the lobby area. Sam looked around. The room was all white—a white marbled floor, white walls, an unmanned white desk and a white flat-screen monitor and flat keyboard. As Sam took in their surroundings, the door they entered closed behind them. It wasn't a loud slam, just very gentle, and he only noticed because he was turning around scanning the room.

'Sam, come on.' Mitch pointed at a door that had opened to the right of the room. Sam followed his brother. Mitch shuffled directly ahead as much as their tether allowed him to, seeming to take a protective position ahead of his younger brother. 'What the—'

Sam was not sure what Mitch had whispered but as soon as he passed the door and entered the new room, he had the same feeling. This space was the complete opposite of the reception; whereas that had been pristine and minimalist, this was dirty and cluttered. *It looks like one of those drug labs you see on television shows.* There were five doors, not including the one they came from, leading from this room. One had a picture of a rabbit on it, while another had a symbol in a yellow triangle, half a circle in the corner with the other half exploding, whereas one door simply had the number fourteen on it.

The laboratory had people, both male and female, working in it, but none of them looked up from their individual tasks. They were all in skin-tight white body suits with hoods, and their eyes were covered with safety glasses. Looking at them, Sam started to feel claustrophobic. He started to pull at the collar of his shirt so that it wouldn't touch his skin. He just wanted to be out of there, untethered and free.

'Hello.' No one looked up at Mitch as he shouted to get anyone's attention. 'Sam, look, this meth lab is dealing with a green powder. What is that stuff? Someone answer me or I am going to call the police.' Mitch took out his phone, as still no one bothered to stop what they were doing. 'My phone isn't working; it isn't even switching on,' he whispered to Sam.

This pulled Sam out of his anxious state, and he surveyed what they were doing. He recognised some of the equipment and the smells of the solvents being used from his chemistry class. There were Bunsen burners, microscopes, centrifuges, test tubes, ethanol and acids. From what he could tell, Mitch was right—they were distilling a green liquid, evaporating it off and creating a green powder. *Maybe it is the same liquid we have produced in our bodies.* Different benches were doing different things with the green powder; some were making it into capsules, while others were adding a glue-like substance to it and playing with it like putty.

'We don't allow the help to use their phones, and we find it easier to control this policy by just dampening all devices. I am Dr Impey. Now come with me and let me rid you of that inconvenience.'

Sam looked at the man, then at his brother, and then back to the man. He was dressed differently from the others; he was in a well-tailored suit. Whereas 'the help' didn't speak or even look at them, he spoke distinctly and was smiling. He extended his arm and beckoned them over.

'What are they doing? Is that the same stuff—' Sam pointed to the green compound '—that we were drugged with?'

'No. It's an older version, the one you have so kindly tested for us is much newer, more advanced. Safer.' Dr Impey responded in a deadpan way. 'This way.'

Mitch accepted the invitation and led the way; soon, Sam found himself in another room lying down on a gurney as his brother stood with his back to him.

'I don't know how you boys got yourself in this predicament. You're obviously bright boys, hiding the bag like you did, ingenious. But you're naughty, naughty boys, getting yourselves mixed up in this nasty business.' Sam wanted to kick the doctor for his patronising tone and demeanour but just watched him. He saw him take a small device out which looked like a car key fob. 'I am going to deactivate the metal wings so that I can safely remove the catheter. You need to hold very still and be good little boys.'

He moved the fob and hovered it over Sam's bladder and pressed it. Sam continued to watch him at work; the doctor was holding him with one hand and pulling the tube out of him with the other one. He was staring at Sam as he was doing so, seeming to get a perverse pleasure from it. Sam noticed that he wasn't wearing gloves and bit his tongue to stop himself from saying anything, so the violation could just end. He wanted the tube out of him; he broke eye contact and just stared at his brother's back. As the tube was pulled out, he had the sensation that he was going to wet himself. He felt numb down there, which provided the small consolation that he couldn't really feel the doctor's wandering hand.

'All done, you brave little soldier. Now I suggest you drink plenty of water, go help yourself to the cooler over there and then use the toilet as normal. Your pee should return to a normal colour after a couple of excretions. You can take paracetamol or ibuprofen from a pharmacy for any discomfort you might have, but young men like you will heal nicely in no time.'

Sam pulled up his boxers and trousers. He had a million questions that he desperately wanted to ask, but he knew they would have to wait until his brother was freed. Instead, he did as Dr Impey suggested and went to the water tank and downed two cups of water in quick succession. As he started on his third cup, he glanced over and noticed that the doctor was now wearing blue rubber gloves.

After he drank the water, he headed over to the bathroom that had been pointed out to him. He locked himself in the cubicle, closed the toilet lid and sat there trying to compose himself, but the more he thought about everything, the more it made him feel sick, to the point that he felt vomit surging up his throat. Quickly, in one motion, he turned around, got on his knees, opened the lid and threw up. He hugged the toilet bowl as his jaws locked in the open position and the vomit just kept coming out of him.

When he finally finished, he stood up using the walls to support himself and surveyed the mess in the bowl. Instead of flushing it away, he took himself out and started to urinate. It stung slightly, but he didn't care; he needed to be rid of the toxin that had been coursing through his body. He moved his shaft so that the stream washed the vomit from all around the toilet bowl, then, he flushed it while continuing to pee. He looked closely at the fluid; he wasn't sure but he couldn't see any green colour in it. It was quite clear; he strained himself to get every bit of it out. As the last few drops were coming out, he took some toilet paper and blotted it. He examined the sheet; it did not have any green on himself. He stood there and shook himself, feeling relieved for the first time since he discovered the catheter.

When he re-joined Mitch and Dr Impey, he saw them talking. The not-so-good doctor was finished with his brother.

'What was he saying?' asked Sam, wanting answers.

'I'm going to drink some water and flush the drug out of my body.' Mitch moved over to his brother and spoke so only Sam could hear. 'He has told me everything we need to know. I will tell you all once we leave this place. First, I'm going to whizz and then we can go. Don't speak to him or ask him anything. Just trust me.'

Once Mitch had left the room, the doctor sidled up to Sam. He delicately placed his hand on Sam's shoulder and grinned. 'If you need anything, you can come to me. I had a nephew about your age. I can help you with anything at all.'

Sam violently pulled his shoulder away. 'No, you freak.' A line had been crossed; he could not think nor act rationally. Pure anger for everything they had endured was overriding all his emotions.

The doctor moved close to him, and as he spoke, Sam could feel his breath on his face. 'This thing you are involved in, it is not good, I feel sorry for you. Let me help you. I can be a friend, someone to trust, someone who might be able to help you in these difficult times ahead. If you are a good boy, you will find my gratitude invaluable.'

Sam felt revolted, his legs started shaking. 'I will never ask you for anything. You're a pervert and if I'd encountered you under any other circumstance, I would have knocked you on the floor.'

'Oh, I didn't know it turned you on to play like that. If sir desires to be the dominant one, he can.' The doctor laughed and watched him closely.

Sam clenched his fist, his vision became clouded and all he saw was red. The doctor stepped back. Sam was about to pounce, but Mitch returned to the room. 'You ready to go, bro?'

The anger in Sam continued to rise due to everything that had happened—the poisoning, the physical violation, the inappropriate touching, the baiting. He was not ready to go; he needed to hit something, he needed to act to feel better about himself.

He glanced at his reflection in the mirror and imagined a bull staring back. A poor tortured creature that had been taunted and harassed, provoked to get a reaction. It had been chased around the arena with the matador flapping their red cape to antagonise it further. The crowd were jeering and tormenting the beast further.

He leapt forward and punched Dr Impey squarely on the jaw. It felt good. He used his other fist and landed another blow into the doctor's stomach. The doctor was bent over, cradling his belly, when Sam connected a knee to his hands that were protecting his mid-section.

It was at that point that Mitch pulled him off. 'Leave him; he's not worth it.'

'He's a sicko, but that's the least reason why he deserves a pasting. I want answers. What did he put in us? What happened at the hotel? What are they doing here? What are they planning for us?'

'I have the relevant answers; I will tell you outside. Let's go.'

'I like it rough,' said the doctor, 'so I'll let that go. Remember, don't cut off your nose to spite your face; I can be an ally. But if you mess with me again, I'll cut off the said nose.' He was grinning as he spoke.

This time, Mitch punched him. He was obviously stronger than his brother and was more used to fighting, as his first and only strike floored the doctor. Mitch angrily shouted. 'Don't you dare threaten us!'

Dr Impey's composure changed. Before, he was grinning and toying with Sam. Now, without making eye contact with either of them, he spoke from the floor in deadly earnest. 'You boys have no idea what has begun.'

Approximately three hours later, the harbinger's warning kept sounding in Sam's head. *Being in the doctor's office, in the sanctuary of that cubicle, would be good now. So would throwing up again.* All, Sam could do was to continue staring down the barrel of the gun as it was pointed at him. This was the first time he had seen a gun in real life this close. The owner of the gun placed his hand on the top part and pulled backwards. 'What do you have to say?'

CHAPTER 12
DAY 4

A natural break seemed like a good idea, so Sarah stood by the door of the caravan, positioned to step outside if she needed to. It was futile, as her call to Pete Tanner once again went straight to voicemail, so she did not require any privacy. She had been repeatedly trying to contact him since he assigned this task to her, but to no avail. *He'd better not be training for another Ironman triathlon while he has me working a case for him. All he ever does is work and train. He is the fittest man, both physically and mentally, that I have ever seen.*

He was always elusive, even when she was directly reporting to him; daily catchups or constant availability and support were never on hand. He had been a part-time boss at the best of times. He wasn't just in charge of the regional force; he had national responsibilities, and some of his work involved national security.

That was all she knew about it. He was secretive; he had to be. This was his justification for the minimal support he gave her following the Manchester incident, even though he wasn't her manager at that time. To a certain extent, he acted like a strict father, treating her like a daughter he was moulding to take over the family business. Even when they were sleeping together, it wasn't just as lovers; there still remained a master-apprentice dynamic. That is how their relationship was and is. She retrospectively saw it as him teaching her how to cope with feelings and emotions, learning who and how to trust and distrust, and to never, ever fall in love—especially in this business.

Now, she could see the relationship for what it was. Back then, when it was happening and she was younger and less experienced, it wasn't like that. She thought he was perfect, so caring and considerate of her. The physical side was amazing and drew her in like a drug. He built her up as a coach and mentor, and taught her how to see cases differently. He told her he recognised a gift in her and he had to nurture her investigational ability. Over the years that they spent together her feelings for him grew, and she fell in love with him. He was her first and only love.

'No man is worth it, honey,' Carole drawled. 'Forget him and get to work.'

Sarah smiled. 'No man. Just waiting to hear back from the rest of the team. Are you ready to continue?' Carole puffed out some smoke and shook her head. 'Speaking of men, will either of the Michaels join us?'

'They're sorting out the funeral. The men don't know nothing, and I've told you all I know. I knew her better than her Ma; she was like another daughter to me. In some ways, because I wasn't her actual Ma, we were closer.'

'Were she and Mikey close? Could she have possibly told him about Tom?'

'You aren't listening to me; I already said the men and her Ma know nothing.'

'Tell me about the car again.' Sarah sensed that Carole was about to get choked up again, so she tried to move the conversation on. 'You said he gave it to her; do you know if he did this legally? Was there any paperwork?'

'Maybe he did, maybe he didn't, but I ain't seen anything. And come off it, love; what sort of paperwork is a couple of lovesick teenagers going to do?'

'The vehicle is registered to someone else. It might not even have been his to give away. Did she ever mention where he got it from?'

'He was cushty, had lots of money and showered it on her. She never wanted for anything; always had the latest designer togs, proper high-quality jewellery. I know the real bling when I see it. With some of the stuff Megan had, she could've bought ten of those cars.' Carole spoke with a real sense of admiration.

'And she said that they were all presents from him? What did the rest of the family think?'

'She hid the stuff. Girls in our community know they gotta keep things on the downlow. She didn't parade in all her finery around her own gaff. She confided in me, so I let her use this caravan to store her private stuff. I know the temper of her Pa, and we didn't want those nice goods to cause an argument. Only after she disappeared did I tell her Pa about the gorger boy.' The older woman's voice started to give again.

'Can I see the things?'

'Nothing left, she took everything before she disappeared—I, I mean before she was taken from us.' Carole stood up, turned around and grabbed the blanket and cushion she was sitting on. She cradled them momentarily. This exposed a piece of wood that she lifted to reveal a secret compartment. It was about the size of a shoe box and was empty. Sarah felt Carole watching her as she visually scanned the bare compartment. She was about to probe further when the woman snapped while putting her seat back in order. 'No more questions. You ain't gonna bring back my little girl? So don't be wasting our time. If you really want to help, you go and get on with your police work and tell us when you find the man. We'll sort the rest.'

She's getting defensive and deflecting. Is she guilty because she covered for Megan and is now blaming herself, or has she been up to something?

'Just so you know the score, we have started asking around, and this is a tight community. We will find out what happened to our Megan, then there will be hell to pay. Justice will be an eye for an eye.'

There was a knock on the caravan door. Sarah subtly moved one of her hands to her weapon. Carole snapped for the person to come in. It was Rosie; dressed in a black track-suit, her blood-shot eyes quickly darted between the two women, and she walked further into the caravan before speaking to Carole. 'Ma said for you to come and have food with us; she made plenty.' It was clear to Sarah that Rosie had been crying, she didn't even bother to cake her face in make-up. When Carole wasn't looking, she managed to mouth the word 'money' to Sarah before slipping a card into her hand.

'I will let you get to your lunch, but I do need to speak to the rest of the family immediately. This is a murder investigation now, so we will have to bring you all down to the station so we can get formal statements without any interruptions.' Sarah spoke to Carole but made sure to catch Rosie's eye as she finished her statement.

Carole regained her composure and replied with authority. 'Look, you seem like a nice lady; help us but don't get in our way.'

Outside, Sarah looked at the card that was palmed to her. It was a business card belonging to a doctor. She took out her phone and Googled the doctor and his clinic's name; and as she was doing this, it started to ring. It was her pathologist acquaintance, Dr Sobczyk. She cancelled the call and turned the device over. They had been playing phone tag with each other all morning; the doctor had left messages to say to call her back but gave no details of the case. Sarah had tried calling back, not immediately, as she was always in the middle of something else, such as her discussion with Doughty. Then Melissa's phone was turned off, which didn't surprise Sarah given the nature of her work. *Now isn't the time to have that conversation, not in front of the family, and I shouldn't step away, unless Tanner calls.* While Sarah valued the expert opinion of Mel and did want to hear what she had to say, she also didn't want to pander to her every whim. *All those missed calls asking to urgently speak to me, it is just how she is. She loves playing games, especially with me. Demanding— everything is exaggeratedly important. She wouldn't have had time to do the full assessment of Megan's body; I thought she would have been a professional. Maybe it was a mistake to involve her. She's probably trying to ask me out again. She can wait.*

Sarah sat there tightly clenching and unclenching her fists, which were hidden in her pockets. What she really wanted to do was to go over and thump the receptionist, the one who refused to look at her or barely acknowledged her. The only time the woman actually spoke was to say, 'No, it's fine' when Sarah reassured her that she didn't need to keep her company and she could happily wait by herself. She wouldn't have minded if they left her in a room by herself; then, she could have snooped around. She could not wait in the doctor's office as he was seeing a patient there. Nor could she wait in the main reception area, as it would not be good for their reputation to have a policewoman sitting there, as if anyone could tell. Instead, she was put in a random room with an escort, which was grating on Sarah. All attempts at small talk, ranging from the weather to how busy she was, were met with non-committal sounds instead of worded answers. This particular part of the investigation was going nowhere, but all of Sarah's instincts told her something was up.

'Sorry to have kept you. I hope you weren't waiting for long.' He held out a hand to shake hers.

She stood up and accepted. The way he apologised, Sarah knew that he wasn't actually sorry. Far from it. He was well dressed, in an expensive suit. *Money makes him arrogant, but is that all?* 'No worries. Thank you for making the time to see me, doctor.'

'Our practice manager here says you are from the police and want to discuss a patient with me. Can I see your credentials?'

Sarah took out her badge and identification card and handed them over, smiling. 'Here you go.'

'What about the judge or court order?' He responded smugly. 'Detective Silver, you know I can't discuss anything related to my patients without their consent or a legal order.'

'Her name was Megan North.' Sarah closely examined his reaction, and she believed that his pupils dilated slightly. 'She was found dead yesterday, and I am investigating the case. I have the next-of-kin's consent to access the medical records.'

'The name doesn't ring a bell. But I will check for you. Chloe, can you bring a laptop in here, please? What were the circumstances of the poor girl's death?'

'You should know I cannot reveal details of an ongoing investigation with you.'

'Oh, yes, of course. Any loss of life is just so tragic and just upsets me.' His voice sounded higher. *He has lost the confidence he had previously, but people usually do in the presence of the law.* Chloe returned and handed him a laptop. He balanced it open on one arm and proceeded to type with the other. He was doing so in order that Sarah could see the screen. He typed in NORTH when prompted for the surname. 'Is that the correct spelling?'

'Yes.'

Then he typed 'Megan' and hit 'Enter'. Zero patients came up. 'As I thought, no patient or any enquiries to be a patient here from anyone with that name. If you know her birthday, you can put it in, as another way of searching our system.' He moved her fingers over the trackpad and loaded up the search for a patient functionality again, but this time, by inputting the date of birth. He handed over the laptop to Sarah.

She inputted the date, but no patients were found. She passed the laptop back to Chloe, who was lingering and waiting for it. 'Thank you, doctor. Just one thing—when I told you about the victim, why did you say "Poor girl?"'

'Huh?'

'Why not poor woman? Why did you assume she was youngish?'

'Don't know; figure of speech, I guess. If there's nothing else, I had better be getting back to my actual patients. I do hope you find answers.'

'Given the nature of your business, most of your patients would be middle-aged, no? So maybe you might know her and not realise it?' Sarah didn't move out of his way. Instead, she reached inside her coat. 'I just want to make sure. Can you look at this picture and tell me if you recognise this girl? Maybe she used a different name or date of birth.'

He took the picture from her and looked over it, while she looked over him. *That's a nice bruise developing on his face. He seems composed and harder*

134

to read. Is this actually nothing? 'Nope, sorry. Chloe, please show Detective Silver out when she's ready. And make sure to give her a brochure. You never know when you might want some work done,' he said, giving her the once-over.

'Well, thank you for your time, Dr Impey.' Sarah smiled as she thanked him. Her instincts kept nagging her. This man was not telling her the complete truth. *Don't worry, I'll be back with a court order to see your records and whatever else it is that you are up to here.*

As Sarah drove off, she called the other doctor whom she had been meaning to speak to.

'Sarah.' The voice was beamed across the car sound system.

'Finally, Mel. Seems like we kept missing each other.' Sarah tried to sound upbeat and happy to be speaking to Dr Sobczyk.

'I thought you were avoiding me,' Mel laughed. 'I think you should come over. We need to speak in person, and you definitely need to see some things for yourself. The body you wanted me to look at, it's—' there was a long pause, '—unusual, to say the least.'

She better not be wasting my time, playing games. 'What do you mean?'

'You know me—trust my expertise?'

'Yes, of course.' *Here we go; she wants me play to her ego.*

'Well, there were things happening with her body that I have never seen before.'

'Like what?'

'I need to do more tests and investigations, that's why it will be for the best if we speak in person. I want you to see the body for yourself.'

She actually does seem baffled. 'What do you know or can tell me now?'

'She drowned; there was water in her lungs, bloody froth in the airway and water in the stomach, which means she was alive when she went into the water. As you know, this wasn't a natural drowning, so other bodily markers, such as lacerations and abrasions due to drag, aren't present; the boot would have protected her. But the rest of her body seems to be preserved somehow. For example, her eyes are intact and there is minimal shrivelling of the skin. This is definitely journal-worthy.'

'So, she drowned recently and wasn't in the water long?'

'That's what I thought because of the lack of inflation to the corpse. But there seems to be some chemical in her body, one that, as I said, seems to have preserved her organs. If I am right, I am looking at miracle cure level, if this was in a living body the regeneration capabilities could be outstanding. Her kidneys have a sort of green discolouration to them. I am second-guessing myself. I have never seen anything like this before, it seems years ahead of current medicine. Where did she come from?'

'That's what I need to find out. What could cause what you've been describing—some kind of new drug on the scene?'

'I don't know. Could be. Or it could be she has some unique anomalous genetic profile, we need to a lot more investigations. I am waiting for toxicology to come back to me. I've asked a colleague to corroborate what I am seeing. I got to go; we are going to evaluate more of her organs and try to determine what state they are in and what is causing this green hue. Sarah, thank you for bringing this to me.'

Sarah slammed her foot on the brakes, as she was about to hit the car in front of her, which had stopped late at a red light. 'Okay, keep me updated. And thank you.'

She didn't have time to think and digest the information, as she saw that Doughty was calling her. 'Hello, Commissioner.' She sounded a bit too enthusiastic, more than she intended.

'Silver, how's it going? Have you questioned the family, any closer to finding out which one it was?' He spoke in the usual monotone that Sarah had become accustomed to, but this time she noted that there was something ever so off with his voice. 'Where are you? Are you alone?'

'In the car, heading back to the office,' she lied. 'Is something up?'

'Pull over. I need to tell you something. I am not sure if this is going to mean anything to you, but I thought it best that you hear it first-hand.'

Another curve ball into this bizarre case. 'I have parked.'

'As he was your ex-boss and recommended you for your new position, I thought you would want to know. They suspect it was a heart attack; given his age, stressful occupation, and apparent underlying medical conditions. If it is any consolation, Sarah, he died peacefully in his sleep, the way everyone in this profession would want.'

'Please, sir, you can be blunt. What are you talking about?'

'He was found by his cleaner. As I said, no signs of anything suspicious.'

She was confused. 'Who?'

'Pete. Sarah, Pete Tanner is dead.

CHAPTER 13
DAY 4

There was visible sweat on Tony's forehead. He was shuffling around on his seat and was about to get up but couldn't. The two men who had recently appeared on either side of him pushed down each of his shoulders with a heavy hand. 'I don't think Don Luciano wants you going anywhere.' He didn't struggle; there was no way he could break free. The goons behind him made that impossible.

'Do you have a last request?'

Sam's stomach felt like he had left it behind on the top floor of a high-tower while he crashed down to the basement in a fast-moving lift. After his gut flipped, it grumbled and his mind wandered onto thinking about food. He was then hit by a sudden hunger pang. He realised he hadn't eaten anything since they got ready and went to the club yesterday. He looked at his brother who was sitting next to Don Luciano. *He must be hungry too, he's always hungry. Why at a time like this am I thinking about food? Maybe, it was the drug. Don't illegal drugs leave the users famished?*

His thoughts were interrupted as Mitch was being very animated without moving his body. *What is he trying to tell me? Some sort of escape plan.* Sam raised his eyebrows, asking for clarification as he couldn't make out the message. He then looked at Matteo, the man holding the gun, and then at Tony, the man who sat to his own left.

'Please, it wasn't me. I didn't—'

Don Luciano held up his palm, calling for silence. 'Matteo.'

Matteo had a stern expression on his face, he took aim and he squeezed the trigger. Mitch's eyes widened as Sam flew backwards in his seat and fell to the floor.

Don Luciano burst out in a roaring throaty laugh.

'That's gross, Boss. Look at the mess. Even the Kid can't believe it. Get up, Kid, before the excrement seeps out on to the floor.'

'Tony, you have disappointed me. Next time, the gun will be loaded.' As Don Luciano spoke, Matteo stood up, reached across the table and pistol-whipped Tony. Sam stood up. The shock of seeing the person who was sat next to him potentially have his face blown off had caused him to recoil in horror. Then there was the fact that the gunman had very nonchalantly pointed the gun in his own face when he circled the table to find his mark. 'Look what you have made me do in front of our guests. Ace and Kid, I am sorry that family business got in the way of our game. Tony, go away and clean yourself up. Your redemption will begin shortly.'

'No worries, Don Luciano,' Mitch said, speaking for both of them.

'Matteo help Tony get ready. Now that unpleasantness is behind us, I think we should show our guests some proper hospitality. Food.'

With a belly full of really good and authentic Italian-tasting pasta, a couple of cans of full-fat Coke and the mounting tension between Don Luciano and Tony removed, Sam was feeling better. *That is just what I needed; this sense of family is a nice distraction.* He was concentrating on the task at hand, which meant he was not thinking about everything else that had happened these past few days. He flipped; this is how the others had viewed their cards, the corners of the two cards he had been dealt. He thought he saw a pair of queens. The betting had now come around to him. The big blind had been raised. He picked up his hole cards and had another look. Still a pair of queens. He put them down again. He looked at his chips; they were low. Mitch seemed to have the most on the table. He picked up his cards, to look at them again.

He must have been twelve, it was the year before they disappeared, when his father taught him how to play Texas Hold'em. It was a Sunday; he remembered the day because his mother had made one of her traditional roasts. They were good days, with meaningful family time; both his parents promised not to work on Sundays and they didn't. They both worked really hard, with one of them usually spending at least one night away a week. They tried to not overlap the time they were away but couldn't always help it. At the time it wasn't a problem because they had everything they could have wished for. Things Sam thought mattered as a twelve year-old, like the latest technology and clothes, exotic holidays, private school and any extra-curricular activities they wanted. He learnt the hard way that those things meant very little in the grand scheme of things.

Sundays were all about eating well, playing together, and spending quality time together. After they had finished eating, Mitch was helping his mother and Sam was watching Formula 1 with his father. In the breaks, they kept advertising poker, and his father talked with such passion about the game.

'Sam, I have to teach you how to play it. It's more than a game; it's a rite of passage. It's intrigue, it's strategy, it's skill. Seriously, it will prepare you for any boardroom.'

After the race, a pack of cards appeared along with some poker chips. 'Let me teach you the basics. Then we can get your mother and brother involved to make up the numbers.'

His father taught, and Sam listened and practised. The basics were easy enough to understand. What required thinking was evaluating the strength of the two cards you had been dealt, whereas understanding what your opponent held needed a sort of sixth sense, an intuition that built up when playing with more and varied people. And when it came to the betting aspect and the ability to bluff, you became an actor.

Sam wished he had bullets, like Mitch had had earlier. He put down the cards and pushed in his chips in front of the queens. 'All in.' It came out croaky, so he repeated himself, trying to sound more authoritative this time. The man in the seat next to where Tony had been, stared at him and then folded. Mitch smiled at him and folded. Don Luciano was up next. 'Ah, Kid, I really wanted to see the flop.' He was tapping his fingers on his cards, then joined Sam with an all-in bet. The rest of the table immediately quit. Sam turned over his ladies, and the Don turned over a nine and a ten of diamonds.

The flop was dealt and revealed; a three of diamonds, nine of clubs and the Ace of diamonds. *That's going to help Luciano; he's going to get a flush.* To a certain extent, the acting could stop. All the cards were laid on the table, so to speak. The Don smiled. Sam tried to remember all the odds his father had taught him, which would have been more important if he had to bet. *It is about 50:50.* Sam wanted to look away but he couldn't; the turn was dealt, it was a queen. His heart started beating faster in excitement. Don Luciano stood up angrily, cursing in Italian. Sam noted the red of the river card first, then everyone congratulating the Don. Sam just stared at the pointed diamond shape on the last card. 'Better luck next time, Kid.' Luciano told him as he scooped over all the money.

'Well played, Sam, but you were unlucky. Don Luciano, this seems like a good time for us to go. We've had a long night and day. Could we just settle up, if that is okay with you?' Mitch interjected.

Sam felt relieved. While he wanted to win, the moment the last card turned out to be a diamond and he saw the look on the Don's face, he knew that was the better outcome. *It's not like losing cost me anything; the buy-in had been free, and this way I get to keep my kneecaps.* The thought of going home and just trying to relax given everything that had happened seemed perfect. Plus, he wanted to see if they still had the poker chips that his dad had used to teach him.

'Of course, of course. I like you boys and trust you. I mean, you must be special to have brought that package from the Doctor to me. I was to give you something in return. But I was let down, as you saw, so now, I must ask a favour. You must go yourselves and get what the Doctor wanted from me. Don't worry; I will send a man to help you.'

Sam sat in the backseat wishing he was being driven home. Instead, they were on their way to another 'ridiculous Stitchin task.' Mitch had told him when they were about to get in the car and were out of earshot of all the Italians, 'I couldn't say no. Sorry, he's just not the sort of person you say no to.' *Mitch has really taken to the Don, and I think the feeling is mutual. The way they addressed each other and their mannerisms together. I guess my older brother needs a surrogate father. I have always had him, but he's had no one.*

What else did he say? 'I already told you that that Impey bloke gave me a package and told us to deliver it here. Well, the second instruction was to collect payment from them. He didn't say what it was, but he hinted to me that we had to do whatever it took to get the payment. He did say he was told to tell us that the delivery and getting the payment were two separate tasks. Look, if we do this, we'll be a third of the way completing their stupid games.'

Tony, the driver, nervously glanced at him using the rear-view mirror, and when he saw Sam looking back, he quickly looked away. *That's the other thing—why have they given him to us? It's like they deliberately want us to fail or are setting us up to do so.* He noticed Mitch was also keeping an eye on the driver. He had actually turned in his front passenger seat, so he was angled towards the chauffeur. Sam wasn't sure how, but Mitch must have sensed his unease or realised that his little brother was looking at him.

'You okay there, bro?'

Sam responded with a nod of his head and whatever he could muster for a smile.

'Good. What's your story? How's your face?' Mitch asked of the fallen Italian.

This should be interesting, Sam thought as he listened intently.

'I mean, it is not every day that your boss threatens to kill you in front of some strangers. Come on, what exactly did you do, Tony?'

Tony kept his eyes on the road and softly spoke. 'It was all a misunderstanding. All in the past.'

I wonder if he ever had confidence, or has he been broken? Sam wondered. *They, the Don and his cronies, didn't seem to be part of the Stitchin; the vibe with them seemed different. Much more crime lords, not secret organisations. But who knows if all of this will break us?*

Mitch was not having it. 'Must have been a big misunderstanding. Look, we need to know what we are getting ourselves into. We don't want you to betray your boss, but what can you tell us about Dr Impey? How well do you guys know him? Do you work with him often?'

'Never heard of him.'

'He tested some drug on us,' Mitch continued. 'We need to know everything you know about him.'

'You need to ask the Don. I honestly do not know this man. We are expanding our business, lots more new associates, new opportunities. That is why our little mix-up happened. You're brothers. You know how complicated family life gets. What you saw in the restaurant is our way of resolving our problems. By tomorrow, it will all be forgotten. I am sure you two would forgive each other, whatever the issue. As you know—or will come to know— nothing can't be cleared up between blood.'

Sam stared at Mitch, who turned to look back at him, and then asked. 'Is he your brother?'

Tony pulled a face, but instead of answering he announced that they had arrived at their destination.

'I was told to drop you off here and not stick around.' He pointed to a house on the secluded road that he had brought them to. 'Not doing as I am told is what got me in trouble, so you are on your own. I've probably told you too much already. I've done my part and have helped you by bringing you here and providing the equipment you need it's in a black bag in the boot. Good luck.'

They got out of the car. Sam was staring at the house while Mitch was already at the boot, taking the bag out of it. The moment he had shut the boot, the black Alfa Romeo sped off.

'Mitch, what's in the bag?'

'Nothing heavy—I mean, serious.'

'I don't like being left in the dark—'

'I'm not. Luciano only told me; I don't know why. I told you what I could before we got in the car. I couldn't say anything in front of Tony, as I didn't know what he knew.'

'The same thing happened at the doctor's. I was out of the room and you were given our next "mission". This is my life too.' Sam sounded exasperated.

'Sorry, bro. Let's talk about this at home. This isn't the place. Come on, let's get this done.'

'I know. I just hate all of it. So it's just another delivery then?' Sam looked at Mitch, and his older brother's face fell. Somehow, he knew that the easy jobs were over, that this was not going to be simple.

The strap of the black bag was slung around Sam's shoulder, and he was holding the contents. His surroundings were disorganised and full of junk. Not that he had much room to move around, but he had to be careful not to knock anything over. He had been given the easier of the tasks and Mitch had taken the more dangerous one to protect him. But he didn't like it; he hated being in a confined space. Suddenly, he resented his brother. Why did he get to make all the decisions? But his brother didn't know where he was or about his newly acquired claustrophobia. His thoughts drifted towards worrying for his brother, which overrode his own feelings. What Mitch was doing was crazy.

Sam carefully crouched down. *Just ignore how cramped it is in here and how hot it is. Just think of this place for what it is. It is totally different from that other place.* He looked around and saw the garden furniture, stacked not very neatly—the lawnmower and other garden tools, and the bags of compost and the BBQ coal. He played with the equipment from the bag, making sure he knew how to use it. He held it to his eye and looked through it. The part he viewed from magnified the distance nicely; he scanned the area. He found the house they had been brought to. He was in the garden shed of the house. The garden was square and neat. He had to hide somewhere and needed to see the back of the house to complete the part he had been assigned to do. He didn't like it; his brother had told him to just do it, and he had to.

'Samuel, I don't know exactly what is going to happen,' he'd said. 'Just make sure you do it; we need to do this. When you have done it, just run and go home; don't worry about me.'

The bi-fold doors enabled him to be a voyeur and see everything in the family kitchen. He scanned around, and then Mitch came into view in the window of one of the bedrooms on the first floor. He was looking out the window into the garden and Sam presumed he was looking for him. His brother was so visually clear; it was like he was standing right in front of him instead of being as far away as he was. Mitch looked baffled, then disappeared out of sight. He reappeared at the window of another bedroom. Sam kept thinking about the conversation in the car and what Tony had said. 'Nothing that can't be cleared up between blood.' The words angered him; he hated the fact that he was being side-lined.

Everything that had happened to him; both physically and mentally.

The violations.

The not knowing.

He placed his gloved finger on the trigger when Mitch stood dead centre. His brother hadn't told him to do this. He paused for a moment. This was off mission, he would be betraying the person he loved the most in the world. But it had to be done, there was a feeling within him pushing him to do it.

Sam shot.

CHAPTER 14
DAY 4

Sarah wasn't really a bath sort of person. They took too much time to get ready compared to the efficiency of just jumping into a shower. Then there was something about lying there stewing in your own filth that she never liked. She only tended to have one when she was ill, but right now she felt like one. She tested the water, which felt ready, and downed the rest of the wine she was drinking, which meant she'd finished the whole bottle. She slipped out of the robe she was wearing and slunk into the water. As she fully immersed herself, she didn't care that some water sploshed out over the floor. The hot water on her bald head was comforting. Whenever her skin was liberated, it thanked her by no longer screaming out to be itched; and the rash subsided without being fed by the irritation from sweat and contact.

It was soothing; the whole bath was. She continued submerging her head until the back of it rested on the metal of the bath. Looking at the spotlight on the ceiling through the water gave it a halo effect. Bubbles escaped from her nose as she lay there thinking. *I wonder what it is like to drown.*

Even through the water, she heard the bathroom door open, and her heart started to race. Before she could react, a shadow and then a distorted face appeared over the tub. She stayed submerged in the water and turned over so that she was face down in it. She felt the weight of the man on top of her, as he climbed into the bath and laid on her. *This is it.* Everything she had been feeling, she now had to release. She felt him grip her shoulders tightly. She couldn't move and his thumbs started pressing into her neck.

Then suddenly, he released her, changing the position of his hands and starting to massage her, concentrating on her shoulders and neck, allowing her to pop her head up to breathe. When this started to become a bit cumbersome, she sat up in the bath and he moved to sit behind her, continuing to massage her.

'Silver, you're so tense.' Tanner said.

'Perks of the job, I guess.'

'You never let it get to you. You have to switch off your emotions, turn your heart to stone. Don't feel, take that state of consciousness and channel it into the work.'

'Can't we have a night off, Pete?'

'That's the other thing. In this business, you never get a time off. You always have to be on, just learn to control that elephant in you. Like I've said, if that isn't for you, become a teacher, marry an accountant, move to the suburbs and pop out two point four children.'

She turned around and started to kiss him, and he responded. 'I want to wash your hair now, you have such lovely hair.' He worked the shampoo into her wet hair and started lathing it up as he massaged her head too. 'You have the gift, the ability to truly see a situation for what it is. Meaning you have the potential to be a great detective. The world needs investigators like you, to solve the wrongs. Don't get distracted by getting involved; that will weaken the gift.' *He can't be swayed; he is the most focused person I have ever met.*

While she usually hung on to every word Pete Tanner told her, she had heard his apprentice spiel enough. His massages had relaxed her and she just wanted to go to bed with him, not talk and debate. They had been in this quasi-relationship state for about a month; and while they had physically done stuff together, he had always refused to go all the way with her. He said he had to be sure, given their age gap, professional relationship, and his general unavailability, both physically and mentally. This just made her want him more. Sitting in the bath together, both naked, feeling him against her just made her desperate for him.

He stopped washing her hair. 'So, what's the answer?'

'I don't want normal, I want this.' She guessed the answer.

He moved his hands from her head and started to caress her body. Then he whispered to her, 'Shall we move to the bedroom?'

She barely heard him as she was physically distracted and started to enter the throes of ecstasy. He stood up in the bath, she turned to face him, and she was pleased to visually admire his whole hard body. Before she could do anything, he stepped out and held out a hand to help her out. She gratefully took his hand, hoping that tonight would be the night, and followed him as he led her to the cubicle shower. After a quick wash down and some more fondling in the shower, they headed out of the bathroom.

Sarah woke in the early hours of the morning, feeling fully satisfied. She barely had any sleep, but the night had been amazing. Post-shower, she had finally got what she wanted multiple times and wasn't disappointed. Maybe it was the month-long waiting and foreplay; his touch, his experience, his dominance was so much better than she had imagined them to be. She stretched out her arm to touch him. Now that she had had her first few doses of him, she needed more.

When she couldn't feel him, she lifted her head, blinked a couple of times and strained her eyes to look for him. He wasn't in the bed next to her. She scanned the room; he wasn't in the bedroom. She got out of bed and wandered over to the window. She looked out of the penthouse view. She could make out the city lights, all twinkling away at her. In the daytime, you could clearly see Manchester city-centre and the countryside, the best of both worlds.

I know he likes using the gym and pool early in the morning before the other residents can get in there, but would he really have any energy left for a workout? What if it wasn't as good for him and he didn't have a good time? No, he was enjoying himself. Does he regret it?

She moved over to a chair that was next to the window, where he had neatly folded and placed her clothes. She put on her underwear only, opting not to get fully dressed. As she stood outside the master bedroom, she noticed a dim light coming from under the door of the second bedroom, the one he used as his study. She walked over to the door and ever-so-gently pushed down on the handle and moved the door, entering the room. She saw him sitting, fully naked, engrossed in the material displayed on the three screens in front of him. The glow from the screens showed on his face that he was mesmerised by the information.

'Pete,' she said quietly, knowing she had to let him know of her presence but not really wanting to disturb him. As she got closer, she could make out a crest on one of the documents. It was a half-lion and half-fish, golden with wings on a blue background. This was surrounded by a portcullis, a red rose and green leaf with five petals in a repeating pattern. At the bottom, it read, 'Regnum Defende'.

'You're not ready for this. If you stay the path, I will teach you; you will be some day.' He responded as all the screens suddenly went dark. He swivelled the chair around to face her and beckoned her over. She could see he was ready for her again, so she pulled off her knickers and sat astride him.

Sarah lifted her head out of the water and spat out the water she had started to ingest. *He'll be disappointed by the fact that I keep reminiscing about him.* Tanner had taught her not to be emotional or at least to control her feelings and turn them on when you needed that drive. But since she heard the news about him, she could not get her mind off him. She grabbed the shower gel that was on the side of the bath and flung it against the mirror above the bathroom sink. As it broke, she didn't feel any better; the anger inside her didn't subside and if she let it, it could very easily take over.

It had been like that all day. After Doughty had first told her the news, all she could do was think about Tanner. There is no way that man could have had a heart attack. *He was so physically in shape that the mere idea is ludicrous. Anyone who knows him would know that. And it couldn't have been a pre-existing condition; he'd never mentioned any underlying conditions. If he'd had one it would have been picked up and monitored in all the medical screenings he'd had to go through. It just doesn't add up. What did Doughty say? 'No signs of anything suspicious, which obviously means whoever killed him covered their tracks. When something like this, the death of a high-profile chief officer, one with connections to the secret service, is so neat, it never is the case.* She told Doughty all of this, and he seemed to just try and pacify her by saying it would be investigated properly and she shouldn't worry about it.

When she ended the call, she turned the car around and proceeded to drive up to Manchester. Sarah drove for twenty minutes before pulling over and banging her fists on the steering wheel and just screaming inside the car. *I can't go back there. I will let the official investigation play out and then decide; that's what he would have done.* She started to drive around randomly to clear her head and calm down.

She reached an area that looked familiar and then recognised the restaurant where she had met the young bartender from one of her first nights in the area. They had hooked up, and it was good. *I don't feel like being alone, I could do with some of that now.* She didn't believe in luck, just cold hard facts and empirical evidence. But as she was looking at the restaurant, the same guy came out of it. Without thinking, she honked the horn. He noticed her and walked over to the car that she had pulled over.

He seemed a bit out of sorts at first, but as he got closer and seemed to realise who she was, he seemed to cheer up a little. 'You've changed your hair; I almost didn't recognise you.'

Oh yeah, when I met him, I was wearing a more seductive wig, not my formal work one. Very observant, though. 'I am glad that I'm not that forgettable. I needed to change it, have a more professional look. I started my receptionist job at the bank. Do you like it?'

He hesitated. 'Yeah, it looks nice.'

Of course he preferred the other look, not this mumsy one. 'Do you want a lift?'

'I do want to, but I need to get home and sort out some family stuff.' He sounded flustered.

Is he playing hard to get? Maybe he needs some alcohol to loosen him up. 'And a lift will get you there quicker.'

He smiled. 'I thought you were speaking code. And wanted a repeat of the other night.'

There is the cheeky chap. 'To be honest, I was. But I am staying with a friend and don't have that hotel room, so you're safe with me.' *I can't let someone unvetted in my actual place.*

He walked around to the passenger side and got in. 'Thanks. Since, we last hooked up, I mean, spent that amazing night together, I've not been having a good time.'

'Sorry to hear about it. Do you want to talk about it?' *He probably has a girlfriend, and she either found out about us or our night made him realise he shouldn't be with her. If he really wanted to know what a bad time looks like, he should try walking an hour in my shoes.*

Sarah stared at her face in the shattered mirror. The pieces of her scarred skull reminded her of a truly messed up jigsaw puzzle. The distorted reflection that looked back seemed to be judging and taunting her. *You were too aggressive with that young man; I think you scared him. Look what you did to him.*

'No, Silver, I wasn't. He wanted to, needed to as much as I did. He suggested pulling over and going into that alleyway.' She spat back at the reflection.

You used him as a piece of meat, pawing at him. You just wanted that fleeting intimacy so you wouldn't think about Pete for a while. But look what happened, look at the cost to the man.

'He had issues; it was nothing to do with me. He said it himself, he wasn't having a good time since our night together. Our time gave him clarity. Probably, he was guilty about cheating on some girlfriend.'

You didn't let him talk. You pulled over as soon as he was in the car and you found a secluded spot. You hitched up your skirt and pulled down your knickers.

'He wanted it, too. He was hard.'

Then why did he go floppy before he even got close? You rushed the poor chap; he didn't even take his jeans off. You just unzipped him and pulled him out from his underwear. Hardly sexy, was it? Were you trying to replicate the time with Pete in the alleyway?

'It wasn't like that. His mind wasn't on the job, he stopped me from undressing him. He wasn't into it.'

Maybe it was the hair. You should have changed the wig to the slutty version of yourself.

'He said he had been stressed and had sustained an injury. He was a good guy. I will check in on him to make sure he is alright. He gave me his number, I'll let him see if he can work out his issues himself before trying to help. That will give me time to sort out everything I have going on.'

What else was he going to say? I've never seen anyone leg it away so fast. He must have felt as dirty as you did. After he ran off, he probably jumped in a bath just like you did. Washed the whole experience off himself.

'Thank you for the pep talk, Sarah Silver, I needed that. Now I have a murder to go solve. After I get justice for Megan, I will find out the truth about Tanner and do right by him if I need to.'

Sarah sat in her car aghast at the scene playing out in front of her. In her whole career, in fact, in her whole life, she had never heard of something like this happening. And she just knew it wasn't an accident. It was related to her investigation. Everything was.

Someone is cleaning house. Which means this investigation is big. Tanner got me involved in something so powerful it cost him his life, cost two young adults their lives, and is now responsible for this.

Still, she tried in vain again to get through on her phone but it was futile. She knew it would be, but she still had to try. She was behind the cordoned-off area and could only watch the emergency services at work. In this situation, they were in charge. Her badge brought her some extra information about what was happening, but not much more than it would have brought to a civilian. Part of the makeshift blockade was removed and one of the fire engines moved off. Suddenly, her passenger door opened, and a man got in her car and sat down. It took a few seconds for her to register who it was, as she was concentrating on the damaged building ahead, taking in the destruction unfolding ahead of her.

'What are you doing here, Silver?'

He stinks of smoke. 'Just following up on my case, sir. I wanted to speak to Pathology.'

'What about?'

'I used to work with one of the pathologists. She was doing the autopsy on Megan North. She called me and asked me to come and see her. Sir, what are you doing here?'

'Oh god, did you know the pathologist well?'

'Not really.' Sarah lied and then turned her head, to really look at Doughty. She knew what he was about to tell her. While looking at him she could hear Mel's words in her head. 'I've never seen anything like this, miracle cure level, regeneration capabilities.'

Is this what everyone is dying for? What is it and where did it come from?

He didn't make eye contact. Instead, he kept his head straight, looking out at the hospital building that had been on fire. 'That's good. Well, not good, but it could be worse. Especially with the other recent news that you have been burdened with.' He spoke softly, his loud voice was muffled with a new raspy tone, and he stumbled with his words.

Is his throat damaged through smoke inhalation?

'The fire started in the morgue, and both pathologists are presumed dead.

CHAPTER 15
DAY 4

Sam had been running hard for twenty minutes. He had just wanted to get away from that house and everything that had just happened. The terrible gnawing feeling was not dissipating. The equipment in the bag kept slapping against him as he ran. He didn't mind; he felt he deserved pain. Before he knew it, he was in a field. He didn't know the area or how to get home from here. His legs ached, his lungs burned and he had to stop. He came to a halt next to a large tree, bent over next to it and threw up. Vomit spewed from his mouth. *I'm never drinking again.* He wanted to stop but couldn't, the pasta and Coke had all come out, and now, it was bile and the lining of his stomach. He placed his hand on the tree to support himself while he expelled the demons of the murder.

When it finished, after what seemed like an eternity, his throat burned, and he felt extremely weak. He moved around to the other side of the tree and sank down to the ground. He didn't have the energy to move away but to a greater degree he wanted to smell the sick—he felt he deserved to be punished. He took the bag off, placed it on the ground next to him and leant against the tree. He placed both hands on his head and tried to calm himself by attempting to regulate his breathing. As he moved his hands away, he noticed a hooded figure approaching him. There was something about the way he moved that seemed familiar. The man sat down next to him and pulled his hood down.

Sam groggily managed to look at the man properly. 'Dad?'

'Samuel, it's good to see you again.'

He wanted to cry; he was suddenly overwhelmed with a million questions to ask. Instead, he reached out to touch his father, but the man moved his hand away. 'Dad, it's been a while. Why now?'

'You need me. You know I always visit when you get like this.'

Sam looked at him. He hadn't aged a day since he had disappeared. His face was still kind. He knew he could open up to his father. 'I do. I've done something really bad.'

'I know, that's why I am here. Look, I am sorry, everything that happened is our fault. We should have never left you boys. If things could have been different, we would have made different choices. But I am here now, for you. Talk to me.'

'I killed—'

'Shh, you did what you had to do in order to survive. It's okay. He wasn't important, just a means to an end.'

Sam broke eye contact. He felt relieved. This version of his father always knew what he was thinking and always said the right thing. 'You aren't angry with me?'

'No, of course not. I mean, you didn't really do anything; your brother made the decisions.'

'But I allowed it to happen—'

'Mitchell killed the dog; you just shot some pictures of it. Look, son, it was just a dog. It looked old to me, like it was on its last legs. It was probably time for it to be put down.'

'I feel so bad for what we did—I thought I would be feeling worse, I should go to the police. Turn us in.' Sam sounded despondent.

'You were—and maybe you still are—intoxicated by a foreign chemical. Perhaps it inhibits your sense of right and wrong, so you can play their game. Maybe it is some sort of super serum—one to make you physically stronger and emotionally withdrawn.'

'Do you think?' Sam questioned, partly knowing the answer.

'Yes. Now, what about your brother? Do you think he got out okay? You need to go and check on him. He needs you more than you know. You're the strong one. Help him.'

'I am not. Mitch has his life together. I can't sleep properly and have this sense of impending doom hanging over me.' This felt good for Sam—getting everything he wanted to off his chest.

'You boys have raised yourselves for the past four years. Obviously, there have been some hiccups along the way, but only a proper man would have been able to do that. You're stronger than you think.'

'If I were strong, we wouldn't be talking, would we?'

'No. I guess it is time I left. One last thing— remember to delete any pictures you took that have Mitch in them. You don't want to incriminate him. I know you were feeling angry towards your brother but sort it out between yourselves.'

'I was just practising using the camera. I didn't want to make a mistake when having to photograph the actual event.' Sam heard the lie in his voice. 'Okay, I was feeling something, I don't know what, towards Mitch. But I won't use the pictures against him.'

'I know, you were just venting,' Dad said as he pointed at the bag.

'I'm not crazy, am I? I haven't spoken to you in over a year. Not even after the car.'

'No, you just needed a sounding board. Maybe if you let me back in, we can talk more and get you back to sleeping properly.'

'Dad, will you ever come back?'

'I'm always here.' The imaginary figure pointed at Sam's heart before vanishing before him, disappearing as easily as he had joined his son.

Sam blinked a couple of times as a sense of comfort washed over him. He smiled and picked up the bag. He pulled out the camera and switched it on to the viewing mode. The first pictures he had shot were just of Mitch in the upstairs bedroom. Pictures he had explicitly been told not to take. Then his brother disappeared and re-emerged in the family kitchen. Sam had captured that too. He had zoomed in and taken photos of Mitch topping the water bowl up with fresh water and adding poison to it.

The vial of deadly liquid had been in the camera bag. It was green, along with the note to be left behind. Both of these items had worried Sam. He sensed that Mitch had thoughts similar to his own, but neither of them said anything. *What did the evil doctor say—we were the guinea pigs for a newer version of the compound. Maybe that was an old one, or maybe it can kill an animal but not a human.*

Mitch disappeared and came back with the family pet; the dog wasn't barking at him, nor was it treating him like a stranger. The two seemed to be playing with each other; Mitch was stroking it and the dog was wagging its tail. In the pictures, it could have been the owner and the animal playing. Sam deleted all these pictures. The next ones made him feel uneasy—the images that had run through his head as he threw up. They were the visual reminders of the dog drinking from the bowl, and then almost instantly the animal lying on the floor, never to move again. Mitch was in the next pictures, standing over the dog, placing the note. Sam deleted those ones, then left the ones where it was just the dead animal, with a piece of printed white paper next to it. In the pictures, you couldn't make out what the note said; it was too far away. But Sam remembered: 'Next time, it will be the kids.'

The plan was for Mitch to join him, and then they would wait for the family to return home and capture their reaction to the dead pooch. As soon as Mitch had placed the piece on paper, he poured the remaining water from the bowl down the sink, before he darted off. Then the family entered the kitchen. *He must have heard then coming back.* Sam studied the pictures he had taken; his brother wasn't in them. They seemed to tell a story; the youngest child had run over to the dog, he was fussing the animal, but it didn't move. He presumed it was the middle child, based on heights, who picked up the paper. The pictures showed her running her fingers under the words, mouthing the words. Her mother grabbed the paper from her and seemed to be screaming, then guarding the children and pulling them away from the dog. The father just seemed to turn paler and dropped to his knees. The eldest child just seemed to be pointing at everyone and everything; the dad, the mum, the note, the dog. Then a finger seemed to point in the direction of the shed. That was the last picture Sam took; he gathered his things and took off. As he did so all he could think, as he wiped away a tear. *It was not just a dog; it was a living being. I won't kill for them again.*

Sam looked at his brother, who was staring back at him. Each of them was sitting on their own sofa. Sam didn't know who was more relieved to see the other one. When he got back home, Mitch had been waiting for him. They had hugged, confirmed one another was okay and got away without any trouble, but that was it. Now, they silently faced off against each other. Sam had questions but thought he should let his brother lead. The silence felt good, and being home was peaceful, but that couldn't last because of the other thing that was waiting for them when he got in.

'Hey, Kid, why don't you go and get some sleep? You look knackered. It can wait until tomorrow.'

Sam smiled. 'Please, that nickname can't stay.'

'I don't know; it's not every day that a mafia king-pin gives you an affectionate pet name.'

'That's okay to say when you are called Ace.' It came out sounding more bitter than Sam had intended. 'So, Ace, you had a lucky escape, but what if that family had caught you?'

'Nothing. The upper-middle class white folks probably hadn't paid their cocaine bill. We've grown up surrounded by people like that. In fact, I would have been invited to have some tea with them.' Mitch looked at Sam, who didn't seem amused. 'Look, I heard them. I had plenty of time to hide and when they were distracted, easily slipped out. No fingerprints, because of the gloves in the bag, or anything linking us to them. You didn't get spotted, did you?'

Sam got all defensive. 'No, of course not. I took the pictures, as instructed, then left.'

'What took you so long getting back here?'

He caught an accusatory tone in Mitch's voice. 'I got lost. My phone hasn't had any battery since the club. And where were you?'

'You could have charged it at the restaurant like I did. Anyway, it doesn't matter.'

'Seriously, what took you so long getting back here?' Sam asked.

'I was looking for you then had to show my face at work.'

Sam noticed Mitch seemed a bit sheepish, like he was lying. 'Look, it's not every day that you witness the murder of an innocent animal. I was a bit disorientated.'

'Doing it wasn't easy, believe me.' Mitch didn't look at his brother as he spoke. 'But better that than the consequences; remember what Mr White told us.'

'What consequences?' Sam felt, once again, that his brother was keeping information from him.

'About once we're in we have to do what they say. I don't like this, but I think we need to just get on with it.'

Sam stood up. 'I think we should go to the police. End this. Who knows what they are going to ask next?'

'The family didn't call the police. I hid near the front garden waiting for you. No one came. They are bad people.'

'What would you have done if you were asked to poison the kids?'

'Obviously, I wouldn't have done that,' Mitch stood up as he replied and matched Sam's tone.

'Why don't we just go, like run away to another country? It's not like we have any ties here.'

'What if they return, and what about your education and prospects? I promised myself I would make sure you had a good life.'

Sam was angry now. 'Do you think that is what this is? I mean, what is it with that green stuff? It is the same stuff or some derivative that was in our bodies. Seemed pretty lethal to the dog. It's hardly a safe life.'

'I don't know. Look, I need some fresh air; I am going out. Take a shower, have some sleep and we can talk tomorrow when we are both chilled.'

'What about that?' Sam pointed at the package that was addressed to both of them and had been waiting for him since he got home.

'Leave it; it can wait. I need a break. And no police or anything silly, okay?' Mitch was halfway out of the house, grabbing his stuff. Sam just watched him. 'Remember, Mr White said it is an honour for us to join them. We just continue as we are and everything will be fine.'

How can he be so relaxed about all of this? 'Yeah, go sort out your head, and we can talk more later.' *Maybe some time alone, he can really think about this.* The moment the door was shut and he was alone, Sam kicked the sofa his brother had been sitting on and started to curse. He grabbed the package and threw it in to the fireplace. As it smacked into the brick, he heard a definite crack. *Good serves them and their stupid tasks right.* His insolence didn't last long, as he realised that if he had broken something they needed, they could be in big trouble.

He picked up the package, handled it with great care and opened it. There was a tablet in it that had a crack running across the screen. *Maybe it was already like that or maybe it happened when it was being delivered.* Sam switched it on and felt a great sense of relief when it powered up. He examined the tablet further; it was unbranded and didn't look like any he had seen before.

Maybe it is just a cheap knock-off. Besides the crack, the only things he could see was a thumbnail titled 'Task 6.'

There was no homepage or settings that he could see or find. He touched the Task 6 icon and a video started to play. It was Mr White—he was dressed the same as when they met him in real-life, but he was seated. *There's something about the room he is in.* 'Hello again, gentlemen, now remove the SD card from the camera and place it into the reader on this device.' The video stopped itself, Mr White's face seemed to be staring at Sam, daring him to defy them.

Sam popped the card out of the camera and placed it in the tablet. Automatically, the pictures were transferred to the tablet and then uploaded to a cloud. Sam didn't have to do anything; it just happened. *Good job I'd already deleted the photos that incriminated us! Should I wait for Mitch before resuming the video?*

The decision was taken away from him, Mr White unfroze and continued. 'Thank you for your help. Now you have done a few tasks and are getting to know us, we want you to know that we already think of you as valued members of our organisation. Know that there is method to our madness, an order to what may seem chaotic, but ultimately you're on the winning side.'

What does any of that mean? Sam didn't have any time to contemplate what he had just heard as Mr White disappeared, and a more sinister clip took over. It reminded him of one of those music videos where the artist held a piece of paper with a word or two on it. There was no sound, no people in it, just a series of instructions. One of those instructions ordered him to immediately get a pen, saying he had ten seconds to do so. The countdown that appeared made him rush off to do so; but he must have taken longer. By the time he got one, he just caught the next slide, which was an address he had to write down, before it moved on. *I'll just watch it again.* As it continued, he started to feel cold, he dropped the pen, and the hand holding the device started to shake as what he had feared came true.

He wasn't sure how long he sat there, numb, but the initial shock had passed and he thought he should re-watch the video to make sure he understood it properly. He went to play it again but it had gone, disappeared off the device. Sam wasn't sure what to do. *Maybe this will somehow be better after I have had some sleep.* He went upstairs, didn't bother getting undressed and just sort of fell into bed.

'Sam, Samuel, get up.'

It took him a while to realise his name was being called and he was being shaken. His eyes still felt too heavy for him to open them. He barely managed to mutter a word. 'What?'

'I need to see your leg.' Mitch spoke with urgency. 'I've been marked; I now have five marks on me. It's like a tally score. Five of their stupid Stitches...'

Sam stopped listening. He didn't need to look. The mild tingling he felt where the first line had been cut into him already told him that he, too, had been marked.

Somehow, once again, without his knowledge, he had been violated.

Stitched up.

CHAPTER 16
DAY 5

'How well do you know Alistair Doughty?'

'I have only been working in his team for a few months, but from our interactions I think he is great. Plus, everyone in the force says they couldn't want a more fair, better boss. So you'll be absolutely fine, I don't think you'll want for a better man in charge.' Barranger eagerly relayed the information. 'I mean no one would expect someone of his rank to go onsite and take charge in the instance of that fire last night, but he did, just rolled up his sleeves and got on with it.'

Sarah stared at the young officer. He meant and believed every word he was saying to her. 'Fires just don't break out in hospitals. It must have been arson.'

'I heard it was an accident, human error, but not deliberate arson. I was at the station earlier; some of the guys were talking about it. They said it was all the fault of one of the lead pathologists, Darius Walton. Apparently, he always smoked in the building and was a drug user. They said anyone morbid enough to do that job often had multiple addictions. They assumed he must have been high or something and hadn't taken the proper precautions around all the flammable chemicals that they used in the department, so he unwittingly started a fire. That's why it was localised in that department; once it started to spread, the hospital fire suppression system kicked in, so thankfully, there no patient loss of life.'

'Did they say what they were basing their theory on?'

'I just got snippets. It's all hearsay at the moment, we will need the proper investigation to be conducted before drawing proper conclusions. Their speculation was based on a nurse witness and previous complaints made against the guy. He was about to be placed on a disciplinary action.' He paused and looked at her. 'Wait, you don't think he started it deliberately?'

'Go on, walk me through it.'

'After all, it destroyed his whole department, all his records. In effect, he covered his tracks in case there were instances of malpractice. And he took his own life in the process. Guilt. Not sure if he meant to kill his colleague, or if that was an accident. Maybe she had information on him. How did I do?'

'Impressive deductions. Lots of speculation based on the limited information you have heard, but it is a possible scenario. What other ones can you visualise?' *You have a keen mind. Maybe, if I didn't know everything that I do, I would have drawn the same conclusions.*

'Pure accident. A patient. Someone else, perhaps someone with a grievance. Environmental or technical problem. Something going on between Darius and the female pathologist, I didn't get her name—'

'Mel.'

'Yeah, something between him and Mel.'

He's getting closer. 'What do you mean?'

'Maybe they either knew something about the other one, like she knew he had done a bad job and had reported him, hence the upcoming disciplinary action. Or they were having an affair, and one of them tried to end it and the other killed that one and then took his or her own life. Crime of passion. Just seems unusual that they were the only two people to die. At least no patients died.'

'It could be.' *But it is highly unlikely because she liked women.* 'Why kill each other? What if someone killed them because of the affair, like a jealous ex or current partner, or—'

'—they both knew something that the said person didn't want either of them talking about.'

Exactly, Dougie. A little bit of help and you got there. 'Hmm, that is interesting. You can't rule out anything out. What were they working on?'

'I don't know, the guys at the station never mentioned it. Aren't these cases usually the most obvious cause? Darius did it for some reason. I mean just think about the work they do, examining dead bodies and dissecting them. The sort of person who enjoys that work must have some underlying issues.'

They were doing the autopsy on Megan North, the body that was also conveniently destroyed. A body that held many unusual secrets. But it is best that you don't get further involved, as this case doesn't seem to be working out well for anyone who gets too involved.

'Just remember to envision every possible scenario and outcome, then use the evidence to rule out each one. In nine out of ten cases it is usually the most likely outcome, the common one everyone sees. But deducing and proving the ominous one out of ten is what makes a good detective. I think there is hope for you yet.' Sarah smiled at him.

Megan is the key to all of this, so I need to find out what happened to her. Solve the murder of Megan North and everything else will become clear.

Chloe appeared and was definitely perkier than on her previous visit. She was a like a totally different person. Sarah knew she would be, and that's why she brought the strapping PC Dougie Barranger with her. She had tasked him to distract the receptionist and keep her busy. Running interference was part of this job, so she justified her actions as continuing to help train him. Sarah excused herself under the pretence of needing the bathroom and headed straight to the doctor's office. The door was locked, but she made short work of that barrier. As Sarah slipped inside Dr Impey's sanctuary, she knew she wouldn't have long and if she didn't find something useful that she could use against him, she would get herself into serious trouble.

The wall had three framed landscape pictures on it and she peeked behind each one. They didn't appear to be concealing anything. She yanked the drawer on the metal cabinet labelled M–S; it opened and she searched for the surname North. *Nothing. He wouldn't have used her real name after I tipped my hand, and he wouldn't keep anything important out in the open.*

Sarah quickly made her way to his desk and tapped the keyboard to wake the computer, but it was locked.

She typed in a few of the most common passwords but to no avail. *That was always going to be a long shot.* The top of the desk was very minimalist, and there was nothing there that could help her, no printed calendar to look at nor papers to rifle through. Next, she tried the desk drawers, which were locked. Sarah picked the locks and pulled open the top drawer.

It seemed to have personal possessions in it: a fidget spinner; a few pictures, which she scanned and discarded; a letter from KWL, the pharmaceutical company; some sort of alumni invitation; and a tattered version of 'The War of the Worlds.' The next drawer had scholarly textbooks: one on plastic surgery and another on ethics. The last drawer had patient files. She pulled out a handful of the brown folders and started to scan the information in the first one. It was for a woman who had had breast augmentation surgery. Her age, weight and the pictures of her chest meant Sarah could rule her out as not being Megan.

She used the file to learn how to scan the other ones for pieces of information relevant to her. She went through the next few folders, which all proved to be futile. She got on the floor and reached inside the drawers and started to feel under them for anything hidden away. As she started doing this for the top drawer, she stopped and pulled out one of the framed pictures that had been niggling at her.

She had disregarded the pictures previously as they seemed to be the doctor with friends or family. But something had been triggered in her detective mind. She stared at the picture; the doctor was a teenager in it, a good twenty years younger. He seemed happy; it was a casual picture. The girl posing with him seemed a bit younger.

She's not his girlfriend or a romantic interest; he doesn't swing that way. And he doesn't seem the type to want to retain a keepsake of some ex, even if he did experiment in the past. She must mean something to him, though. Sarah stared harder at the picture. *There is a slight resemblance between them. Is she related to him, a relative, a sibling? But why do I know her?*

Her thought process was interrupted as she heard voices at the door. She put the picture down and slammed the drawer shut before rushing back to the centre of the room. His chair was still moving as he entered the room. She tried to stand between him and the desk, so that he wouldn't notice. 'Hello, Dr Impey.'

'What are you doing in here? You shouldn't be in here.' He seemed flustered and was gesturing with his hands a lot as he spoke.

'Waiting to speak to you, of course. Your office door was open. I didn't think you would mind me waiting for you.' She smiled, trying to be as disarming as possible. *I would fare better with Barranger present to distract him too.*

'Patient confidentiality.'

'There are no patients in here.'

'What do you want, detective? Do you have that court order? I am very busy.' His arrogance started to return.

'So am I, doctor. Therefore, I will keep this quick, I have a few more follow-up questions for you.' She watched him as he rolled his eyes. 'Are you close to your family?'

He seemed surprised by her question. 'Yes, of course.'

'That's good. Would family members introduce you to their partners or at least show you a picture of someone they are dating?' *I hope I'm right, it is a bit tenuous, but my gut is telling me so.* 'I guess even if, say, a nephew was too busy to keep in touch with his uncle, his Mum would keep her brother updated, in a close family.'

He moved away from the door and headed towards his desk to sit, breaking eye contact.

'I ask you again. Tell me everything you know about Megan North.'

He looked down at the drawers but didn't touch them. 'I don't know her. Anyway, I must go. I have patients to see.'

His behaviour told Sarah her suspicion was correct. The woman in the picture, his sister, was Tom's Mum. 'She was dating your nephew, Thomas Denton.'

She sipped the eighteen-year-old Jameson—wine just wasn't cutting it anymore—while sitting at her desk that she had set up at home. Sarah spoke to herself out loud, using herself as her own sounding board. 'Why am I involved in this? Tanner knows—knew—about my internal affairs expertise. He knew I am capable of bringing down an entire department. That's the only thing that makes sense. They are dirty here and now I have to fix it, bring Alistair and his co-conspirators to justice. On the other hand we have Dr Impey who was Tom's uncle. He could have known Megan through his nephew. But then again was Tom keeping her a secret? The doctor seems to be of a dubious nature but is that enough to link him to this? A doctor involved in cosmetic surgery and a dead body infused with a new chemical in it—one which from Mel's initial assessment could be very interesting in that market. Is that the missing link? The doctor has connections to big pharma. Is he connected to Doughty, though?'

She stood up and took a gulp of the whiskey, finished off the contents of her glass, before pouring herself another generous amount. Her phone bleeped. She looked at the text message. It was from the police IT specialist, telling her to check her emails. *Those geeks really don't like speaking to people, but I need to form a relationship with anyone who can help me with this investigation.*

'Hello, Iain speaking.' A thick Scottish accent answered her call.

'Sorry for calling outside of office hours, but given your text, I assumed you were still working.'

'Yes, ma'am. I sent you an email.'

She put the phone on speaker mode, placed it on the desk and opened her emails. 'What is it, Iain?'

'I have managed to recover some videos from Megan North's phone. They don't seem relevant to me. Erm …

they are more of a personal, intimate nature, but I knew you wanted to see anything recovered, so I sent them to you.'

'Okay. Thanks. Is there anything else you can get from the phone?'

'It must have taken on a lot of water damage; I can't guarantee that I will be able to get anything else. But I am doing my best to recover what I can. Don't worry; if there is anything else, I will get it. Commissioner Doughty has ordered it to be a priority.'

Sarah opened the email and saw three video files attached. She played the first one. 'What was that about Doughty?'

'He asked me to prioritise the recovery of any data from the phone and share anything with you immediately. He said it was important to you,' Iain enthused.

The first video was of Megan and Tom having sex. She clicked the second video, checking to see who was copied into the email. Doughty was. This video seemed to be more of the same. *He's right; this seems useless. Is that why I am seeing it? Why is Doughty appearing to be helpful now?* 'Do you know why you were able to recover these videos?'

'I think they were favourited and protected by a password, so they were saved in a different part of the phone memory, which I was able to save.'

'I see. Many thanks. Given the intimate nature of these videos and anything else you might get, can you send anything else you get from the phone, no matter what it is, just to me? Save the girl's dignity and all.' *It's worth a shot, but who knows where Iain's loyalties lie?* 'Speak soon, Iain. Bye.' She hung up, not waiting for his response.

The third video was another sex tape. She unmuted the sound, now that she was off the phone, in case there were any audible clues. This video appeared to be filmed in Tom's bedroom. It was taken from one angle; the phone was propped up against something. The other videos were like that too, no third party involved. The locations of the videos were different, though. Both of them knew they were being filmed, as they would both look at where the phone was and attempt to make 'sexy' faces and poses. They didn't chat, just made regular moans and groans. They reassured each other and both said they loved the other.

Sarah kept watching the videos one after the other, searching for anything that could help her, all the while drinking her whiskey. The intimacy made her think of Tanner. *What was it he said? 'This isn't a priority for the department, for anyone really, but it is for me.' Was that a clue? He mentioned the department—was he trying to tell me that the department is somehow involved?* She tried to replay the conversation in her head as best as she could remember it. *Something about my new boss.* Something on the video distracted her. *Hold on; what's that?* She tilted her head to follow the subjects in the video. She got up and moved her face, which was at a 45-degree angle, closer to the screen. She paused the video and attempted to zoom in. The quality of the video meant that as she zoomed in, it became distorted. *'Greasing the wheel'—that's not how Tanner speaks—he wouldn't use that language. Doughty, are you involved in this?*

She sat back and rewound the bit of the video she was looking at. It wasn't zoomed in; it was just normal. She stared as Tom thrust himself into Megan, who howled in ecstasy and repositioned herself. Sarah paused the video and touched the screen.

She stroked Tom on his upper outer thigh. Her heart started beating faster.

She felt scared and exhilarated. 'You poor boy.' Again moving her face closer to the screen, her mouth opened and she started to count.

I don't want to set you up. No, it wasn't that; I don't want to stitch you up. She gently traced her finger constantly over the area of him while saying aloud, 'I don't want to stitch you up.'

Sarah pulled away from the computer, her fingertips tapping her temples in utter disbelief, as she continued staring at the image on her screen. Now that she had noticed the marks, they seemed obvious. She repeated the words. 'I don't want to stitch you up.'

Suddenly, she noted the reflection of a man approaching her chair, but before she could turn around or defend herself, she felt the stab of a needle piercing her neck. She tried to reach an arm upwards towards the assailant, but she couldn't move it. She felt woozy and disorientated.

As she slumped back in her chair, she whispered the words: 'Stitchin, we meet again.'

CHAPTER 17
DAY 6

Sam crossed the street and paced up Honeywell Road for the sixth time. Initially, he did so to see if anything would jog his memory, but that proved futile, so now, he was doing it to kill time. Mitch was at home waiting for him to call with the instructions.

He had lied about the situation with his brother and hadn't explained that he had broken the device and not fully captured their next mission. Given Mitchell's reaction to the cold-hard reality that these people were violating their bodies whenever they wanted to, he also decided not to disclose the true nature of the current task, mainly because he wanted to protect his older brother for once and take the burden away from him. He seemed truly disturbed by the latest markings. But he had a niggling feeling about Mitch that the abandonment and responsibility thrust upon him had made him angry and that part of him was enjoying the darker side of this.

Pacing the street was giving him peace and quiet to think, but no solution came to him. *First problem first— how am I going to find this woman? I'm pretty sure the house number was even— eighteen maybe.* He stopped at the house across the road opposite number eighteen and looked at it, willing it to help him in some way. *Can I do it by myself and leave my brother out of it? This could be a one-man job. But does that abide by their rules? What if he then ends up a task short and they give him something worse?* His head started to hurt as he tried thinking through the problem and rationalising it. *She must be a bad person, must have done something wrong.*

'Excuse me,' a female voice politely said as she passed by him.

He moved and looked up as he did so. She was on her phone, paying him zero attention, but he recognised her face. It was her, his target. *Which house had she come out of?* He watched her as she headed towards a taxi that had just pulled up. *If I don't do something, I'll lose her.* Sam moved towards the taxi and got in just after her.

'You my pool?' he asked.

'No, sorry, sir. This is an exclusive ride for Jenny. I just this minute confirmed it with her.'

'Are you heading towards the Falcon Club?' It was the only place he could think of.

'No, sir, we aren't going that way, we're going to The Hangout. And Miss Jenny paid for this ride by herself.'

'No. I'm sorry. My cab must be coming soon. Sorry again,' Sam apologised profusely as he got out of the car, glancing at the sat nav display on his way out.

'No worries, young man,' the woman said as he shut the door behind him.

Damn, she seems like a nice person. I'm going to need the big guns for this. He took out his phone as the taxi pulled off and booked his own. Then he called Mitch and left him a voice note telling him to meet him at the bar The Hangout and dress to impress.

In the booth, Sam was nursing his second Coke when his brother arrived. He placed the camera on the table before sitting down opposite him.

'Whose beer is that?' he asked, pointing at the bottle on the table.

'Yours. I ordered it when I got here to try and look inconspicuous and not seem like a Billy No-Mates.'

Mitch took a swig and grimaced. 'It's warm.'

'Yeah, I've been here for over forty-five minutes. And so has your two o'clock, the pretty-looking woman. I think she has been stood up. You should go and keep her company.'

'What are you talking about?'

'Okay, hear me out. We need to take some pictures of her; that's our next task.' He lowered his voice to a whisper. 'As we torture her.'

Mitch mouthed the word 'What?' back at him.

'We need photos of her being tortured.'

'What sort of torture?'

'I don't know. They didn't go into details. But I've been thinking you would only torture people if you want to extract information from them or if you were using it to coerce someone else. They never said to ask her anything, so it must be the latter. It's like the dog: they are getting these pictures, then probably blackmailing people for money. The dog people and this woman have expensive houses.'

'And you're okay with that?'

'No, of course not. Like I said, they didn't say what we had to do, just get pictures of her being tortured. And that's where I had an idea.'

'You have a look on your face that tells me I am not going to like this.'

'It is better than the alternative. I hate myself for what we did to that dog. Whatever its owners did, the animal didn't deserve that. Bro, I feel so guilty. I promised myself that I wouldn't hurt anything or anyone for them again.'

Mitch interjected. 'You didn't do anything—I did. Please don't think about it and especially don't blame yourself.'

'I've been thinking about our situation. If we're clever we can get through this without actually harming anyone. Their rules are vague enough that they are open to interpretation. We can outsmart them. Save our souls.'

'Who said I want my soul saved or deserve it to be. Look let's talk about this later, but I want you to know that if we have to do anything nefarious, I will do it. Your hands can be kept clean of blood—that's the way I want it. So, what's your plan?'

Somehow, I am going to save both of us, I promise you that. 'This is what I was thinking. You're so great with the ladies—you could seduce her, have a bit of fun, bondage and everything, and get some pictures, which we'll use.' Sam blushed as he spoke.

Mitch seemed agitated. 'I knew you were going to say something like that. I just knew it from the moment I got here and you said I should go sit with her. It's not that easy. I can't just go over and turn it on.'

'What do you want to do then—go and restrain that random woman over there and torture her? How can we torture her?'

'Mutilate her, you know, cut off the tip of a finger.' He paused. 'Judging by your facial expression, I can see you're not keen on that. What about waterboarding, that wouldn't leave any permanent damage—well, not physical.'

Sam slapped his hand across his forehead. 'Mitch. How do you know this? You can't be serious?'

'Films. And obviously, I'm not being serious. After everything that has happened to me, to us, having something shoved up there, I am not sure I physically can, you know. I already tried. I wanted to make sure it all still works, but it felt raw and sore. Maybe torture should be the way to go. Let's get this over with.' He stood up and walked to the bar before Sam could ask the questions running through his head.

Sam watched him as he spoke to the bar person. The man placed two shot glasses in front of him and poured tequila in them. Sam didn't have to worry about having to drink one, as Mitch downed both shots at the bar himself. The barman then gave him a bottle of beer. His brother didn't come back to their table. He went over to the woman.

It was too far away for Sam to hear the conversation and given his position, he had to keep looking over his shoulder. *It would be too creepy to move to the seat opposite and directly watch them. I'll just leave Mitch to it. Was he serious about the torture?* He ordered himself another Coke using the table's QR code. Even though he had a fake ID on him, it was much easier to do it this way and not run the risk of being challenged at the bar. *I guess it must be going well, as Mitch hasn't been sent packing yet.* He quickly glanced over his shoulder. The two of them looked locked in an animated conversation and she was grinning. *This might actually work.*

The barman arrived and placed his drink in front of him, so he picked up the camera to move it out of the way and started to play it. There were no pictures in the memory, as he had earlier transferred and deleted the ones from the house. He tried to take 'arty' pictures of his drink, changing the settings to black and white, zooming in and capturing the bubbles. He switched from playing with the camera to playing around on his phone. A few drinks later, after playing on his phone for a bit, he continued playing with the camera. He pointed it and starting shooting pictures straight ahead of him, and started slowly turning his body and hands, while taking more and more pictures towards where his brother sat. The images suddenly became blurry. He stopped taking pictures and looked up.

Mitch was heading towards him with his hand stretched out in front of the camera. 'What are you doing?' Before Sam had a chance to answer, his brother continued talking. 'Look, it doesn't matter. She wants to go back to hers and have a drink. We're going to get a taxi; follow us in a bit. I'll text you the location once I know it. When I get there, I'll make sure you can get into the house.'

'How?'

'I don't know yet. I'll make it easy for you to get in without her knowing, like leave the front door open, or a window, or something.'

'Okay. And remember, you need to get her to do some kinky role-play, so that in a picture, it will look like she is in danger, without actually hurting her.'

Sam arrived at the house on Honeywell Road. It was none of the ones he had thought it was earlier. *I am seriously not cut out for this. I couldn't even remember the house right. We need to do this together.* The front of the house was visible from the road, so he wasn't afforded any privacy. Even though it was darker than when he was earlier on the road, he felt uneasy. *I need to do this quickly. Anyone passing by could potentially see me and call the police.* He turned around and scanned the road. It seemed clear. He moved closer to the windows on the ground floor, looking for the one Mitch texted that he had left open. He looked into the room from the outside, feeling like a Peeping Tom. The lights were on, but no one was present. One of the windows was left very slightly open. He checked to see if anyone was nearby and then pulled the window. It opened out towards him without any resistance. He moved to the side of the breach, lifted his leg into the house—*another boundary being broken*—and climbed inside.

There were two empty glasses and a wine bottle on a table in the middle of the room. Sam made his way quickly through the room, grabbing in the bag to get the camera. He paused at the bottom of the stairs. He heard two voices: it wasn't really talking, more whispering and mumblings, interspersed with sounds of stolen affection. One seemed like that of his brother, as best as he could tell, but he couldn't make it out clearly. He crept up the stairs as quietly as he could, listening on his way to see if he could gauge any clues. At the top of the landing, one door was open. That was the one the noises were coming from. He was standing to the side outside the bedroom door, trying to work out what was going on. Then suddenly, the door burst fully open.

The flight instinct in Sam took hold, and he moved back towards the stairs. A topless Mitch stood at the door. 'There you are. What took you so long? Never mind.' He ushered his brother towards the bedroom. 'She's in the bathroom getting ready. I said I was going to get more drinks. Quickly, go hide and get ready with the camera: she seems up for anything, she's definitely on a mission to get revenge on whoever stood her up.'

Sam nodded in acknowledgment and hurried into the room. On the messed-up bed, a formal-looking business suit was laid out. He continued to look around the room and saw a built-in wardrobe. He slid open one of the doors that had shelves and drawers. He tried the other side that had her dresses and some other clothes hanging. He pushed them aside and squeezed himself inside. He left the door open a sliver so he could see what was happening and listen out for his cue. He saw the en suite door open and the woman emerge with a towel wrapped around herself. She walked over to the bed and picked up the clothes. She had a look of doubt on her face, stopped and walked over to the closet.

She stood in front of the door. Sam shuffled himself as far back as he could, but there was barely any room. He tried not to breathe or make a sound. Through the gap, he saw her lift her hand towards the handle. He felt like he was about to wet himself. She placed her hand on the door.

It's all over now; she's going to find me. Still, I won't hurt her.

He moved the closest dress to cover his face. But the door didn't open. Instead, the gap was suddenly closed. Then the other side opened. He sat as still as he could. He could see her side profile clearly as she stood in the lit room. She opened a drawer and pulled out some knickers. She held them up and then threw them back down before rummaging for another pair. He watched as she smiled and then dropped her towel to put on the lingerie. He quickly looked down. The door slid shut and he was left undetected, in darkness. He listened; she seemed to be getting dressed. Then Mitch came back into the room, and he could hear them talking.

'There you are, hunky.'

'That looks so sexy.'

'As you like a woman in authority, you will call me boss.'

This is going to get seriously awkward. He started to play with the camera, to distract himself. He couldn't take pictures given his environment, so he starting to scroll through the ones he had taken earlier and deleting them. *I guess we will have to upload the 'proper' ones later; best to get rid of the history.*

'You're so kinky.'

'Chocolate sauce.'

'I have an idea.'

Gross, gross, gross. 'What?' Sam whispered the words as the photographic story unfolding in front of him broke him from the here and now. He hadn't meant to have spoken out aloud, but he was caught off-guard. He zoomed in on one picture. It was the mirror, but something in the reflection had grabbed his attention. As the magnification increased, the quality dropped. He stared at the closeup, turning the camera around and pulling it closer to his face. *It is her, I'm sure of it. What was she doing there? It can't be a coincidence. This is bad, really bad.*

The door opened. Mitch stood there with his finger over his lips and he motioned for his brother to come out. All the while, he was speaking loudly to the woman. She was tied up with her hands behind her back, while she sat on the chair in the room. Mitch motioned for Sam to snap away. She was blindfolded, and her wet hair looked scraggy and added to the effect. Sam took pictures as his brother spoke. 'You're a bad woman, always bossing me around. Now, I have kidnapped you and I am going to make you pay.'

'Security will be here soon, and then I will punish you.' she purred.

Mitch walked over to her, kissed her, then shoved her tights in her mouth. Sam waited for him to be out of shot, and then took more pictures. Mitch then placed a piece of paper on her lap that said HELP on it written with lipstick. He then took a bottle of chocolate sauce from the nightstand and squirted it over one side of her face. He then turned to Sam and mouthed black and white. Sam understood and changed the settings and took some colourless pictures. Mitch looked pleased with himself and motioned to Sam to leave, then he started to lick the sauce off her. She seemed to be enjoying the experience.

Sam shuffled out of the room and made his way down the stairs. Even though they had successfully completed this task, he was disheartened.

This is bad. Surely, Mitchell will be safe, though.

But he had to warn his brother that he needed to get out of there quickly. That woman was in serious danger. He had seen it in the picture; she was going to be killed.

He had seen how it would be done. The grainy picture he had been looking at from the bar where they had all been was that of their old companion, The Assassin.

CHAPTER 18
DAY 6

Sarah believed she was lying down but couldn't be sure. Her eyelids felt so heavy, but she had to try to open them, as she needed to find out where she was. She only managed a blink at best. She couldn't see anything. After multiple attempts, all she could make out was a bright light and a shadowy figure holding a knife. She wasn't sure what was real or if it were just some trick her mind was playing, as it didn't have the visual information required to fill in the gaps. She made another attempt but couldn't. She just surrendered to the drug and went back to sleep.

Oh, Tanner, why couldn't you have been direct with me, told me everything I needed to know? You were always obsessed with this mysterious organisation and made me aware of it, but that was over five years ago. Damn you, you should have warned me properly, given me the appropriate heads-up, so I could have protected myself befittingly. It was not currently at the front of my mind, so how was I to get your little clue straightaway?

Was I stupid for not always thinking about it? But if I let it occupy my every thought, then I would have become like you. And you did bloody stitch me up. If you'd told me, I would have been on guard, more so than I usually am. From everything you said and I learnt, they are above the law. They are renegades, they are dangerous, they are the type of group that can destroy a part of a hospital, to have you killed and make it look like an accident. They are the sort to leave me unconscious somewhere. Thank you very much.

Find Megan North, because she would have been able to tell me about Tom Denton—she might have known something about his involvement in the system. Was she involved? Did she have any marks? Did they create the mysterious green substance found in her body? If so, for what purpose, what does it do? Why ask her and not Tom? Because he was dead, quickly disposed of.

He is the third person I have seen with the tally—the stitches. He had seven, so he was pretty involved—he must have had some information. We could have found out more about the Stitchin than we knew before. That's the connection, that's why you wanted me to find her. But she's dead, Tom's dead, you're dead and I guess I am about to join you all soon. No I won't.

Sarah's eyes flickered open. She shut them again, as there was that bright light directly above her. As she became more aware of her surroundings, even with her eyes shut, she could not ignore the pain in her chest. It felt like someone had punched her hard on her left breast. She lifted her right arm to examine herself, but it only moved a couple of inches, as some strap around her wrist prevented her. She snapped her eyes open and lifted her head to survey herself.

She was in a blue surgical robe that was open at the front, and underneath the robe, she was naked, apart from the bandages wrapped around her chest and her knickers, which she noted were the ones she was wearing before the abduction. Both her arms and legs were restrained with straps attached to her wrists and ankles, respectively, and the gurney she was on, which was angled slightly. As she put her head back down, it felt cold, and she realised her wig had also been removed. Through all her toughness, the years that had made her hard and impenetrable like her metallic namesake, she couldn't help but feel exposed and completely vulnerable.

She heard the footsteps and twisted her head to see who was there but couldn't see anyone. She recognised the fragrance, L'Eau d'Issey, though; he wore too much of it. There was a humming noise and the bed started to tilt downwards more. He walked around, holding the controller, and stood facing her as she became nearly fully upright. 'At last you're awake, Detective Sarah Silver.'

'What have you done to me?' She wanted to sound calm and reserved but didn't come across as such.

'You have very nice breasts, you know. That is one of my areas of expertise, so I can say that with some conviction. And look, don't worry, you'll heal very nicely, there will be a scar, but it will fade so it's barely visible.' He stroked her head. 'But you're used to scars. My poor, poor Sarah; what happened? Tell me everything.'

His touch sent a shiver down her spine. 'What did you do to me?'

'Just a little insurance policy. You were asking too many questions earlier, linking me to my nephew, so I need to make sure I can control you. Look, this is a good thing, babes; you don't want to get involved, but now you have a reason not to. The information you want will only lead to your demise.'

'What sort of insurance policy?'

'I placed a device in your chest, just under your left breast. I have the partner device and every two hours, I have to input a code into it to stop it from sending a signal, like a phone call, to your device and blowing you up. There is not a lot of explosive in yours, but enough to take out your heart, given its proximity, and kill you. Look—I am a great surgeon; you can go on and live a long, healthy life if you just listen to me. Don't look at me like that; we're like best friends now.'

'You're a psychopath, Dr Impey. Why didn't you just kill me? You should have killed me, because when I am free, I am going to kill you.'

She watched in disgust as he just laughed at her. 'That's the beauty of this. If you kill me, I don't input the code that only I know, and you die. If you try and force the code from me, I will tell you the wrong one— you input it and you die. You try and remove the implant, you die. You don't do what I say, or do something I don't like—you guessed it—you die. Now I know what you're thinking; what happens at night-time when I am asleep, or if I am doing something, which means I won't be able to input the code? I can switch it off for two cycles.'

'Actually, I was thinking, is this what you did to your nephew? Mutilated his body, controlled him, got him to do whatever you wanted from him. I know you didn't do this to Megan, as she was drowned alive. That young woman— girl—would have suffered with her last breath. Now did you kill her? My gut tells me you didn't, but you were involved in it. You know something, you might think it is insignificant but under the right light, it can mean more. Tell me everything.'

He stared at her blankly; she guessed he was assessing her.

'Unless you did them both and I got you all wrong, and you're a murderous lunatic. Tell me, doctor, who murdered Tom? We both know that wasn't a suicide. And who murdered Megan? I can protect you.'

'You can't even protect yourself. I took you off my own back, and it was easy. I did it to stop you digging around and getting us both into trouble. My nephew Tom fell in love with that tramp. She didn't love him back, so he killed himself. I did meet her once. She worked at that strip joint, Desire. She wanted me to fix her co-worker's titties up for a discount; she said she'll bring me lots of business and wanted a cut. She was a scammer and a grifter. I said no, I have enough affluent clients. That's all there was to our encounter. You saw my office and its location—why would I have needed her pikey associates and pennies?'

'If you're lying, I will find out and bring you to justice.'

'There's that sass of yours. And that's the reason I didn't just kill you. You're going to work for me now.

It's always good to have someone from the police in your back pocket.'

'Go to hell.'

He wriggled the device in front of her face, taunting her. 'You'll be there before me.'

As he toyed with her, she finally got the read on him that she had wanted since their first encounter. Now she knew what she had to do. 'I guess I have no choice.' She tried to sound as resigned as she could. 'But first, answer some questions for me.'

'That's not how this works. I give you an instruction or ask you something and you do as I say.'

'Sorry. I didn't mean any disrespect. I just need to know the truth, then I will be yours.'

He looked at her, uncertain about this three-hundred-sixty degree turn.

'I am sure that after our first encounter, you did your research on me, so you know what I've been through. You've seen my scars and surely understand that I don't want to be part of an organisation that threw me away. You understand that I want out.'

'Oh, Sarah, look at you. Poor baby. We need time to build our relationship. I don't believe for a minute you will just change your mind just like that. When that is in place, yes, I can offer some titbits of information.'

'Just like that?' she scoffed. 'I hate them, look at my head, they beat me to death. I am only in this for revenge, it's why I came back, to keep my enemies close. I need money. If I am going to betray the force, I want good money. I want them to pay for what they've done to me. Then I'll be gone. I want to be in the Maldives, sipping cocktails, with random tourists serving my needs. I am in for the right amount. I am sure you can spare it. Think how much more you can get with an inside woman.' She spoke with a desperation in her voice.

'Okay, you can ask me one question, a show of good faith.'

She knew he was toying with her but had to try anyway. 'I want to know who I am getting involved with. Tell me about the Stitchin.'

She watched as the expression on his face totally changed and the blood seemed to drain from his face as he turned even paler. He looked all around him and then walked towards her. He hesitated. His scent was stronger, it made her gag. She could now feel his breath on her, his mouth was next to her ear and he whispered in her ear. The words were quiet and rushed, and she closed her eyes to better hear what he was saying in this agitated state. He kept going, not pausing to catch his breath, all said in a hushed tone. When he was eventually done, he stood back from her. She thought he seemed relieved.

'If it's such a big secret, why do they brand their members in such an obvious way?

'You easily identify yourself as a member in an emergency with the marks. It is their heritage and goes back to the founding. To insert their control device. They aren't given a second look by a lay person, they are barely noticeable after a while if you aren't looking for them. Who knows? And now never mention the "S" word again.'

'Can I have some water, please?' She lowered her head and broke eye contact as she made her request. She maintained the docile pose as he returned with a plastic cup with a straw sticking out of it. He held it to her lips, and she took a slow sip. 'Thank you, doctor.'

He moved the cup away and placed it on the side. 'I am going to release you now. Remember, no funny business.' He paused and took the device out of his pocket. 'You have thirty minutes before I need to input the code. If you do anything I don't like, it will be the end of you.'

'Yes, sir, I am yours.' She spoke quietly, appearing beaten and resigned to her new fate.

He leaned in and kissed her bald head. She didn't react. 'Good girl, remember what I told you. If you are to survive you need to do everything I tell you.' He slowly undid the buckle and then loosened the strap around her left wrist. She left her arm where it was, even though she could now pull it free. He continued to undo the remaining restraints, teasing her with new limited freedom. Sarah dropped to the floor, but Dr Impey caught her, so she didn't fall. Her hands went naturally to his shoulders as she steadied herself. She looked at him, and before he had a chance to react to her changed demeanour, she kneed him as hard as she could in the groin.

'I am no one's puppet.' She delivered a swift additional knee to his midsection as he was now doubled over. 'I would rather die than serve you.' She then hit him with both her fists balled in his back. As he fell to the floor, she kicked him. She leapt down on him, rummaged through his pocket and took the device. She couldn't help but look at it, momentarily forgetting her training to secure her assailant. She caught his hand just before it connected with her face, managing to deflect the blow and not taking its full force. As she did so, he wriggled around and managed to flip her. She found herself underneath him as he pulled out a scalpel.

'You dumb woman.' He spat out the words vehemently. 'You won't be killed by the implant; I will just do it now.' He tried to drive the blade straight down into her face.

She had only one hand free, as the other was trapped under him. She managed to grab his wrist and stopped the tip about an inch from her face. Given her position, she knew she wouldn't be able to hold him off for long, so she darted her face away while giving him another knee to the groin. This one lacked the full force of the first one due to her position.

He started to fight back, and they ended up rolling around the floor, each struggling for an advantage as they grappled against each other. Suddenly, he stopped resisting.

Sarah pulled away and saw the scalpel sticking out of his abdomen, surrounded by an expanding red splotch. She backed off more and stood up, watching as he groped at the blood on his shirt, looking at it and his hands in disbelief. He looked up at her. His expression was a look of total vulnerability.

'I'll see you in hell soon.' He spoke quietly as his strength was leaving him. Then with a final burst of energy, he pulled out the blade and drew it across his neck. Blood shot out from the wound in his belly and then from the slit on his neck as he slumped to the ground.

She rushed over to him and checked his wrist pulse. He was dead and with him, any chance she had of stopping the ticking timebomb inside her. She sought out the device, which she had dropped in the scuffle. When she found it, it showed that she had six minutes of life left.

She prised the scalpel from the doctor's dead body and hovered it by her chest. She cut the bandage off, and just below her left breast, there was a sewn-up incision. *I know where to find the device—I guess my best chance is to try and remove it.* She took the controller for the surgical bed and started lowering it back down to a horizontal position. She lay on her side and lifted her breast up and was about to cut the stitches when she noticed something on the wall. She stared at the device, which she had placed on the bed next to her.

Four minutes left.

Sarah jumped up, grabbed the box from the wall and went back to the bed. She sat cross-legged with the box in front of her. Her heart was racing as she opened the latches to the defibrillator. The machine had an audio option, which she switched on as she teared open the pads. The female robot spoke instructions about pad placement and not requiring additional gel as they were pre-lubricated. She plugged the leads into the unit. *Stand clear, analysing now, stand clear.* She lay down with her finger hovering over the shock button. *Normal rhythm detected. Call 999.* The failsafe in the machine wouldn't allow it to deliver the shock in the absence of an abnormal heartbeat. She had less than two minutes left now.

She took the scalpel again but this time, she jumped off the bed, cut off the shirt from the doctor, placed the pads on his chest and started the machine again.

Charging, charging.

She watched desperately as the indicator showed the machine powering up, unsure if her idea would even work.

Twenty seconds left.

Stand clear and push the shock button.

Sarah ripped the defibrillator pads from his chest and slammed them on hers. Ten seconds left.

'Please be kind.'

She pushed the shock button with such urgency and hope.

Shocking.

CHAPTER 19
DAY 7

The clock on the wall showed the time as 18:14. Sam grabbed at his brother's arm. 'Mitchell don't; please stop,' Sam pleaded as he tried to break the grip his brother had around their latest mission's throat. 'This isn't you; you're better than this.'

Mitch wouldn't relent.

Sam wanted to remind him about playing the game on their own terms without hurting anyone but knew what Mitch was doing was personal. This man had just tried to kill them. *I have to make him stop.* Sam stopped trying and was taken aback. He felt like he was floating above his body and looking down on the situation unfolding below him. He was watching Mitch strangling this stranger, then suddenly he had a flashback to his brother being strangled.

His brother was younger, maybe his own age, and the place looked familiar, but he couldn't quite make it out. Mitch was being choked out—his brother's face was turning red, but Sam couldn't see that of the assailant. It gave him a weird feeling over his body, he felt he shouldn't be looking at this. His voyeur position was that at a door which was slightly ajar. He wanted to turn away but couldn't.

The door handle, he recognised it.

He wanted to say something but when he opened his mouth, nothing would come out. The strangler was now shouting at Mitch. He knew the voice, but it sounded distorted. He had to go in and rescue his brother, but he couldn't move.

Then the realisation hit him that they were back in their own house; Mitch was being strangled in the study. Sam wasn't allowed in that room, that is why the little boy was frozen to the spot, scared to speak out. The voice that usually provided comfort to him was making ugly sounds.

What was James, their father, doing?

Why was he shouting and strangling his eldest son? What had that been about, and why had Mitch never mentioned it? I thought he and Dad had a great relationship? He never hit or raised his hand or voice at me. It couldn't have been anything serious, just awkward teenage and young adult growing pains.

Who I am kidding? That was a different level, not parenting.

Before he could dwell on that incident, his mind flitted to his own strangulation incident from the previous day. It was different from what he witnessed happening to his brother and to what Mitch was dishing out. It wasn't menacing, more playful. After seeing the pictures of the woman, who called herself The Assassin, he didn't know what to do. Was she coming to finish off the woman, or them, or was she just in town for a few days and was just hanging out?

Deep down, he knew the last option was improbable but he had to hope. He looked around for her but couldn't find her outside the house so he headed back to the bar to see what he could find out: any CCTV, footage of whom she was talking to, if she left something behind, anything. It was approaching closing time by the time he got there. He was about to try to go inside when he was stopped.

Out of the shadows, her voice spoke. 'Took you long enough to get back, stud.'

Before he knew it, she was pressed against him, cupping his face with her hands and planting a kiss on his mouth. He didn't get a chance to respond as she pulled away, linked her arm in his and led them off. He didn't know what to do or say, so he just let himself be led away. She was snuggling into him; it felt very couply.

'Where are we going?' he managed to stutter.

'Shh.'

Next, they were down an alleyway. He didn't want to resist and wasn't even sure if he could. Somehow, he found himself pressed against a wall, with a dumpster shielding them from the main road.

'I want to help you, so just listen.' He opened his mouth to respond. But before he could say anything, she placed her hands around his throat, though she didn't exert pressure. 'That's not listening.'

He nodded.

'Just stay the course. Do what they tell you and before you know it, your initiation will be over. Then it'll be like an extremely well-paid job. It's better than being in the rat-race, it's more interesting.'

'A job?'

'Yeah, think of it like Uber. They send out assignments based on your particular skill set and you pick and choose if you want to do it. Obviously, the compensation offered for each one helps you decide. I mean, I took up one in Manchester the other day as it was easy, but I didn't have to because of the location. Sometimes, you get a red category, which is one that you have to do, but that's it. Do the tasks that you want, get paid, and just do the ones they tell you to, and then, when "The Cleanse" happens, we'll be on top, the survivors.' Now, she did start to squeeze. 'And if anyone ever asks, this conversation never happened. I've already said too much.'

In one smooth and swift motion, he dropped his arms by his side, lifted them up between hers and extended them outwards as hard as he could, breaking her hold on him.

Her expression changed, a glint of anger dashing across it, before switching back to how it was previously. 'That's good. You should always stick up for yourself. But you need to understand who your true enemy is. If you're in this, these people—us—we are now your family. We aren't the ones to fight.'

'What was that green stuff they put in us?'

'Honestly, I don't know. I don't think they would harm you, you're an asset in development.'

'But it has messed with me. I don't feel like myself emotionally and I can't stand it. The old me would never have done the stuff they are making me do. They have stripped away my humanity and made me emotionless.'

'So they are helping you.' She smiled.

'Don't.'

'Who knows. Maybe they were testing something to make future members more…' She paused. 'Make them less inhibited. I have to go now.'

'Wait, what's "The Cleanse?"'

'So many questions. It's the future. When you're ready and have proven yourself, you'll be told. Look, my take on all of this and your predicament is that we are soldiers in an upcoming war. We each have a role to play, a duty to perform, and that is why I do what I do. Some you win and some you lose, but in the grand scheme of things play to be a winner in the bigger picture.'

'If you aren't my enemy or on a mission, what are you doing here?'

'I shouldn't be here. Usually, I don't care. But after we first met, your innocence reminded me of my own missed youth. I was about your age when I was initiated, so I know what you're going through. Before you, I heard rumours of someone who was about to hit the halfway mark; he must have been slightly older than you. Then, he just quit, and I mean he quit life. Some say the eighth mission is the hardest, it is really when they truly test your resolve and if you have what it takes. I am reaching out to you, so that you won't make a mistake and turn away from this opportunity.'

'Has anyone ever left?'

'Once you're in, you won't want to leave.' She placed her hand on his leg, on top of the area where the marks were. 'Bye for now. I'll make sure our paths cross again in the future and I'll be sure to help you feel again.' She gave him a little peck on the cheek before disappearing into the shadows.

It was 18:16 when Mitch finally broke his hold on the man, Jack, pulling Sam back into the present. 'Get it out of us.'

Jack coughed and rubbed his neck. 'It doesn't work like that. If I could still control the devices, I would have killed you both already. Damn it, I would have killed everyone with one of those things implanted in their legs.'

Sam looked at the middle-aged man. *He's probably slightly younger than Dad would have been if he were still alive. Definitely a little rounder. Would Dad still have been in shape as he got older? Would he have needed glasses or had grey hair like this man? Was he involved in the Stitchin?* 'Bro, let's give Mr. Dixon here some time to think about. After all, he knows we're just the messengers, and he'll have to answer to powers way above us.' He motioned for Mitch to follow him outside the room. 'We're not your enemy—just think about it.' He closed the door behind them.

'He was about to crack,' Mitch snapped back. 'Why did you stop me?'

This reminded Sam of when they entered this man's house and threatened him. After the initial unpleasantries of barging into his home, which involved a bit of pushing and shoving, they were in his living room. There was a large clock on the wall, which kept catching Sam's eye, he preferred to look at that, the time was 17:14, than looking at the reaction of the Jack as he was shown the pictures they had taken earlier.

The family in distress that he had captured on film earlier turned out to be that of Jack's brother, his sister-in-law, niece, nephews, and of course, the deceased family pet. The next set of pictures the man had to view was that of his mistress being 'tortured'. The pictures seemed to abate his initial anger. As he looked at them, he slumped down on the sofa, mentioning the names of the people caught in the stills, then he muttered, 'What did you do to the dog, man? If you touch those children… Jenny, no. If you hurt her, I know bad people; they will do you over. If you've harmed her—'

'Who do you think sent us?' Mitch spat back at him. 'We were sent here to pass the message on and get your agreement. If you don't comply, your family or lady friend will be hurt or even killed. You know them—they order, and someone will carry out what they want. So far, they killed the dog and hurt your female friend, so you know they are serious. Only you can stop them and save everyone.'

'I have done so much for them; I can't believe they think they can treat me like this. I deserve respect. Why have they even sent you two?'

'No offence taken there, man. We don't want to be here; just agree and we can all get on with our lives.'

'You don't know what they're asking me to do. I just don't think I can. It will be easier to just kill myself.'

It was 18:18 when they left the room. *Did Mitch even listen to this guy? He's disgruntled with the organisation.* 'I stopped you because he reminded me of Dad. Hear me out; what if Dad didn't run off with some other woman and Mum went looking for him to bring him back? It never made sense, why neither of them never came back. What if our parents were involved in the Stitchin and that's why they aren't here? Think about it—why were we initiated into this—why us? Then think about the fact that people just don't disappear. What if they've gone into hiding because they didn't do what they were ordered to do?'

'Sam, they're dead to us. If they were involved in this organisation and didn't do what they were ordered to, they would have been killed. If they just ran off to avoid the Stitchin, why didn't they take us with them? And if that is the case, then they are dead to me, like they should be to you. You don't remember them like I do; they were so vanilla. They weren't involved in the Stitchin. They were bored with their mundane lives; James went off with his mistress, and Mum had her own fella on the side and went off with him.'

'They wouldn't have left the house then and all their belongings. Surely, they would have gotten a divorce.'

'Sam, they didn't want us! They abandoned us.'

'What if it wasn't their fault and they couldn't help it? Didn't you hear what he said about his marriage? Jack was into the Stitchin, then they pushed him too far, or he's been doing it for too long and now wants out.'

'Trust me; they weren't Stitchin, just regular losers.'

'I know you were older and knew them better than I did, their faults and their anger. I remember a time when Dad was choking you. What was that about?'

Mitch paused. 'I don't know, I can't remember. When?'

'It was in his study, you must have been my age. I doubt it is something you would forget.'

'We fought a few times, when I found out he was cheating on us. Look, let's get back to our ward.'

There is something he's not telling me. What is he hiding?

As Sam's hand was on the door handle and he was about to re-enter the room, he thought back to what Jack had said and ultimately done to them. His mind desperately racing for clues. After he 'threatened' to kill himself, he stood up. It was 17:44 and Mitch was right by Jack's side.

'Don't worry, boy, I'm not going to harm myself.' He walked over to a cabinet in the room and opened it, taking out and holding up a bottle before putting it down and selecting another. 'Port?' He didn't wait for an answer and just poured three glasses; he downed his own one before topping it up again and then bringing over the drinks he poured for Sam and Mitch. 'I was their technology guy, I built things for them. I am sure I'm not their only one, just one of the many, so they don't need me and they could just get another minion to do their bidding. At first, I did it because the work was so interesting. I was using raw materials they provided that were years ahead of their time—they still are.' He paused to top up his drink again.

Mitch took a sip of his drink. 'What sort of things?'

Jack slapped his own hands around his head. 'In the beginning, it was going so well. It was challenging; the tech given to me was so advanced. I pushed myself hard because I had to learn, I wanted to. I did it; I made breakthroughs for them.' He gulped his drink down. 'This went on for years, but it came at a cost. The secrecy, the lies, the stress. It killed my marriage, I took a mistress, Jenny. I had to. She brought me back to life. It's peaks and troughs with my marriage and mistress now; it works. My life is good and I have enough money. I don't need to take more jobs, not even red ones. I have earned the prestige to do as I please.'

Mitch topped up his own drink and that of the flushed man. 'What did you make?'

'Ah, yes, my contribution to the world.' He pulled out a small oval shaped fob. 'I made a tracker, nothing like the world has ever seen. It can be implanted in a person—it can brand a person's flesh, and if necessary, it can explode and deliver a fatal blow.' Sam moved his hand to where the Stitchin marks were and noticed that Mitchell was doing the same. 'You shouldn't have messed with Jenny and my family; it's not personal.' Jack pointed the device at them and pressed it.

Sam gasped.

Mitch turned to look at him and then shouted out, 'No!' before jumping up and lunging towards Jack.

Jack looked astonished, moving his eyes from them and back to the device in his hand. He pressed it repeatedly, before Mitch reached him and knocked it out of his hand.

Jack slumped to the floor and spoke quietly in disbelief. 'It doesn't work—they changed it.'

Before he could utter another word, Mitchell had his hands around his throat and was throttling him, screaming. 'What have you done? I'm going to kill you.'

As they went back into the room at 18:20, Sam held Mitch back. 'Let's try and reason with him, the enemy of my enemy and all that.' Jack was now swigging directly from the port bottle. Sam noted that it looked like he had been crying; he wasn't sure if it was from the strangling or the situation. 'They updated the implant, so you can't control it or them. And now, they are forcing you to do something else. They forced us to, but we never hurt your female friend; those pictures were staged.'

'Sam, stop talking. We can't trust him.'

'It's over.' Said Jack. 'You can both get lost. Go away, little monkeys, and tell them I'll do it. You've won, and they've won. I'll do it. But before you go, always remember that what happens next is on you too. I already hate myself, but you two need to understand that the consequences of what you are forcing me to do will all be your fault. I hope you can live with yourselves.'

CHAPTER 20
DAY 6

Shocking.

Sarah was flung backwards, her body lifted off the ground and she went flying across the room. The physical sensation was like being kicked in the chest but for her she hadn't really thought about the consequences, so did not anticipate the aftermath of pressing the defibrillator. Her head unceremoniously smacked into the bed frame and she slumped down on to the floor.

She sat there dazed and saw the body of the dead doctor—she wished she could take flight, charged with electricity from the machine, point her hands down at his body and zap him with blue bolts of lightning from the charge. But it was nothing like that and she could only sit there stunned, with pain searing all over her body.

'I'm alive,' she murmured, when she finally became lucid. 'It worked, I managed to stop whatever you put in me, the electrical current disabled it. But for how long?' She started to assess herself and noticed she was bleeding from where he had sewn her up. She tried to stand up but stumbled.

'Come on Silver,' she shouted at herself. She sat there—focused on her breathing and trying to calm herself and get some strength back. After a while she grabbed at the bed and used it to pull herself up. Following their altercation the room was messed up, she scanned it looking for sterile surgical equipment. Eventually she found what she was looking for, she took the new scalpel out of the package, stood in front of the mirror and started to cut open the remaining stitches, those that hadn't ripped open from the defibrillation.

DAY 7

She quickly assessed the young man standing at the door of her latest sanctuary. He seemed scruffier than most of the others. *Was he too tired and overworked, or was he trying too hard to fit in?* She held the gun to the viewfinder and opened the door, angling the weapon so that it remained trained on him. The open space between them was just big enough for her to accept the delivery. He gave her the items, she thanked him and she closed and locked the door while watching him disappear from view. Sarah placed the items on the floor and backed away from them with both hands on the gun aimed and trained should anyone enter. She made her way to the living room and glanced at the television screen; it showed the live stream of the lobby and the reception. She waited to see the delivery guy leave the building. It was not perfect security by any means, but it gave her some comfort. *Am I being too paranoid?* This had become her normal over the course of the day. Just hide out and order everything she needed; which included new clothes, food, pharmacy supplies and ice—lots of ice.

She made her way back to the delivery and slunk down to the floor, where she opened the pizza box and ripped off a slice and started to gobble it down. After devouring two slices, she unscrewed the Pepsi cap, not caring as it fizzed out over her hand and the floor, and she pressed the bottle to her mouth and guzzled down the liquid. She then started on her third slice, and as another piece of pepperoni went down, she felt a burning in her chest.

It's the pizza and pop; it's just indigestion. My heart is fine, just slow down, Sarah.

She chucked what remained of the slice back into the box and took a sip of drink. She placed the bottle on the floor and used it as a crutch to help herself to get off the floor. She got to her feet, she let go of the bottle and placed her hand over her chest. She used her other arm and rested it against the wall to stabilise herself. She closed her eyes and slowly breathed in and out. The discomfort in her chest seemed to stabilise a bit, but now, she felt something unusual on her hand. She opened her eyes and looked down at the grey T-shirt she was wearing and her fingers. Her fingers had a sheen of red on them, and the T-shirt had a growing red spot of blood.

Sarah bent down, grabbed the gun and headed towards the main bathroom. On her way there she glanced at the television screen, to see if anything was happening at the lobby. It just showed the concierge at his desk. She smiled as she surveyed the mess in the once immaculate apartment. This place was fancier than Tanner's had been, and knowing what she did to it gave her a sense of perverse pleasure. *As I'm off to see my friend, I might as well top him up.* She stopped in the equally disturbed kitchen and grabbed two bags of ice out of the freezer. She tore them open as she entered the cold room and tipped both bags into the bath. 'There you go, Dr Impey.'

She looked down at the lifeless, naked body in the tub. Her eyes lingered on his Stitchin markings; she had never seen a completed set. Tanner had told her they went up to fourteen, and here was the proof. 'I see your marks are barely visible, I guess you got them many years ago.' She dipped her finger in the freezing bathwater, flicked an ice-cube floating on the surface out of the way and touched his tally marks. *I wonder what they would feel like on an alive body.* She left her finger to linger on the other one, the one that was out of place. 'Then there's the one you gave yourself.'

She picked up the black box she had left on the bathroom sink. The box itself was the size of an expensive watch box. It was heavier than it looked, made out of some kind of metal. 'While it would have been nice if your lovely penthouse had information I could have used, this will make do as a consolation prize.' She shook the box that she had found hidden with a gun. 'The question is whom to trust with it, and of course, your body, because we both know you can't stay in there forever.'

She opened the box and looked at the two devices inside. They were not quite identical; the original one looked like an older model, whereas the one she had put in there looked newer but was definitely part of the same family.

'I guess you removed your keep-you-honest explosive tracker yourself ages ago, just like you made me cut myself open and remove the gift you implanted in me.'

She snapped the box closed, took off his blood-stained T-shirt that she was wearing and looked in the mirror. 'My bandages need changing. Shame you aren't alive to help me.' She laughed as she started to delicately cut away at the old dressing, making sure not to touch the part directly in contact with the wound. 'That's not the only reason I wished you weren't dead; I would have relished the chance to really make you pay for what you did to me. Shocking myself hurt, it hurt like hell. It still smarts, and who knows if there is any long-term damage to my heart?'

She cleaned the surrounding area with saline solution and started to unpack the new bandages to apply them to herself. 'At least it stopped whatever you put in me. I'm not going to lie, doctor, it was not pleasant cutting myself open, then having to dig around in myself and pull the damn thing out.' She examined her newly bandaged self in the mirror, turning from side-to-side. 'It was like extracting a bullet. I have had that done to me before, but I didn't have to do it myself. Yes, it is a shame that you took the coward's way out.'

She stripped off her remaining clothes and headed into the separate shower cubicle where she took the hose from its holder and washed from her stomach downwards. When she was done and had dried herself off, she dressed in the new clothes she bought herself and had delivered expressly from his online account. His details were all saved on his home computer; all she had to do for groceries and clothes was click and wait. This suited her current needs, because she had gone dark. She hadn't been back at her place, so there was no trace of where she was. She didn't use her phone or cards.

While the computer was good for her shopping needs, it didn't seem to have anything of interest to her investigations: Megan and the Stitchin. For both of those, she just had the bits of information the doctor had given her, before dying, to work from. 'I am going to leave this safe haven soon because it won't take anyone long to work out that you are missing and connecting us. I am not sure if I will see you again, Impey, but I will make sure that every inch of your body is examined and violated before your corpse is placed somewhere unmarked and no one knows where you are. I am going to find the truth and expose all of this, so your whole life would have been utterly pointless. Now it's time to rest and then I am off to see an old friend, and let's hope for his sake that he has never laid eyes on you or even heard your name.'

DAY 8

She had been at it for just over an hour. This had allowed her to do a superficial search. After all, this was a house, and she needed a lot more time to conduct a thorough search. She couldn't access the computer—it was heavily protected and was beyond her technical know-how. She did find a Glock 17M in the desk of the study where the computer was. The books and papers in that room turned up nothing. In the master bedroom, she found a hidden compartment behind the wardrobe; there was a thousand pounds in cash, a Taser X26, and a Heckler & Koch G36. However, she didn't find anything that could link the owner to either of her investigations.

You just wouldn't leave anything incriminating around your house; even Impey didn't do that, and I know he was involved in the Stitchin. Most likely, if he is involved, he has another location where he would keep the goodies. But then, wouldn't you want it or need it close at hand? She massaged her temples. *I haven't had a chance to look properly; I need to get behind the walls and under the floorboards, but I doubt I have the time to do that. There is one way to know for sure; but if I cross that line, even if it is confirmed or not, there will be no coming back from it.*

She closed her eyes and pictured Megan's face, Tom's face, Mel's face, Tanner's face and even Impey's face, and then took the taser out of her pocket, checked that it worked, and headed towards the front door.

Sarah spoke to herself as she got into position. 'So much for Detective Sarah Silver. This is the end of my career. How my ex-colleagues, those left alive, will relish in the irony. The holier-than-thou detective who couldn't be coerced with kick-backs and bribes couldn't even last a week in London. She thought she was above the law and got her comeuppance. This isn't just a simple break and enter like before; this will be assault with a fireman on an officer. Plus I will have the retribution from the unreported self-defence accidental death to deal with. If it's all over for me I am going to expose the Stitchin and their collaborators as best as I can.'

Or die trying.

She waited by the door, deciding she would have to act as soon as he entered the house, because the moment a light was switched on, it would be apparent that the place had been disturbed. She needed the element of surprise, otherwise, her plan might get the better of her. She moved to the right-hand side so that she could tackle the situation head-on. *I would be too vulnerable; a frontal assault would be to my disadvantage.* She moved to the left-hand side. *This would be a better place to attack from behind, but if the door is opened fully, I could get trapped behind it.* She moved and sat on the second step facing the door. *I might lose my bottle if I have to speak first.* She unscrewed the hallway light and took up a new position in the study, standing in the doorway of the room and the hallway. One step back and she was hidden from being visible from the front door, but close enough to attack swiftly. *I hope I can do this precisely, with minimal damage, but whatever happens, this is the end of my career.*

A flash of light shone through the glass arch at the top of the door. *This is it.* She checked the Glock in her waistband, having swapped Paul's pistol for the superior gun, and stood back with the taser poised in her hand. The beam of light went out and she heard a car door shut. She switched the taser to her other hand and wiped her sweaty right palm across the new black T-shirt she was wearing, careful to avoid her injury. She switched the weapon back and listened carefully to the footsteps on the gravel path.

Seems like only one; the search didn't indicate that anyone besides him lived here for quite a while. No sounds of chatting. She heard him at the front door, key entering the lock. *He's hardly a stealthy man but definitely a fighter.*

The door opened, and she heard the click of the light switch attempting to illuminate the area. *It's now or never.* She moved out of position and quick as flash was upon him. Taking him by surprise she rammed the taser in his chest and pressed the button.

She stared down at him in the seat she had bound him to using duct tape, as he started to come to. She had gagged him, but his rage was apparent. He didn't need words to express how he was feeling as he became aware of his situation.

She watched as he looked over at the desk. 'I guess you're wondering about this.' She pulled out the Glock but didn't aim or threaten him with it. He tried to respond but couldn't. 'I need a knife; I'll be right back in a second.'

She went to the kitchen, grabbed the sharpest looking knife she could find and returned to the study. He was wriggling around in the chair but he was too well restrained. 'Look, sir, I am sorry about all of this, but I

226

need to know if I can trust you.' She held up the knife and walked over to him. 'I guess this would have been easier to do when you were unconscious, but I didn't have time. You barely stayed down long enough for me to restrain you. Now, I am going to take the tape off your mouth so we can talk. As we're in this nice, big, detached house with a front drive and everything, I am sure no one will hear if you shout out. I trust you won't do anything stupid.' She ripped off the tape.

'Damn it Silver, what the devil are you playing at? You're finished; you'll go down for this.' He spat the words out.

Anger is good; if he were guilty, he would be calmer. But then again, they are all great actors. 'I will tell you everything. I just need to check something first.' She grabbed at his trousers to make it taut and pierced it with the knife.

He started to squirm around and try to break free. 'What are you doing? You're crazy. Get off me. Let me go!'

'Sit still; do you want me to accidentally cut you? This will just take a second.' She continued to hack away at the fabric. Her heart was pounding. *I hope he can't hear it.* 'Sorry about your suit.' When the tear was big enough, she ripped off the trousers and looked at his exposed leg.

I thought he would have been hairier. He was wearing Y-fronts. *I would have guessed that.* The area she wanted to see was exposed. All her focus now came back to the task at hand, and her pupils dilated as she took it all in. Still, she yanked his underwear up at the side and placed her hand on him. He tensed up, she ran her fingers over the top of his leg, rubbing it, even going under his underwear, feeling it all. 'Oh my god.' She started to laugh.

'Get off me, woman. You really have lost it.'

His bark seemed to pull her out of her hysteria. Sarah got up and stepped away from him. She withdrew the Glock and placed both hands on it, sliding back the barrel to the chamber. She pointed it at his head, and then down to his exposed leg and then at his groin. 'Alistair, tell me everything you know about the Stitchin.'

CHAPTER 21
DAY 8

Sam looked at his reflection. This was the first time he was wearing a tuxedo and it made him feel like James Bond. He turned to the side and pulled his hands up to his chest, with both index fingers pointing up to make a gun. He pouted and posed. Behind him, he heard his brother snigger. Before he could defend himself, Mitch cut in, 'Don't worry, I just did the same thing myself. See, it's not all doom and gloom.'

Sam responded with a smile. *Just because they dress us nicely doesn't mean they are going to be nice. If the last mission taught us anything, it is that they aren't nice to their own.* 'It has been one hell of a crazy week.' He never mentioned his interaction with The Assassin to his brother. Everything was happening so fast he never got around to it, which meant he never told Mitch that this mission, their eighth one, could be the making or breaking of them.

'We're about half-way through all this. Who knows what they are going to throw at us. Just be careful and let's keep our wits about us.' Sam dropped his voice to a whisper. 'Remember we do this on our terms, in a humane way. We outsmart them so as not to harm or hurt anything.'

'It's all happening so fast. We will reflect and make amends, I promise, but we have to put ourselves first and do whatever it takes. This is about our survival.' Mitch replied. 'Don't look at me like that. I hate myself too but I am just looking out for us. For you.'

They walked over to the reception desk; two people sat there with their backs to them. Sam guessed that one was a man and the other was a woman, based purely on their body shapes and the way the clothes fitted them. They were wearing matching fluorescent yellow blazers, the colour of a high-vis jacket, but not cheap looking; these were tailored, high-quality clothes. As Sam approached the desk, both receptionists simultaneously spun around to face them. Sam was taken aback. Both wore masks, the same bright yellow as their clothes, with a mesh design, so their skin and features weren't visible.

They both stood simultaneously in their matching suits. The yellow material, including gloves, covered all their flesh. Mitch caught Sam's eye and seemed as bewildered as he was. The one whose body appeared male spoke in a distorted robotic sounding voice. 'Mitchell Yates, please head to the lift on my left.' His left arm raised and pointed to a door that slid open. 'Samuel Yates, please head to the lift on the right.' The female receptionist raised her right arm, pointing to the wall, where a door opened directly opposite the other one. 'Gentlemen, please go into your designated lifts.'

'We stay together. Sam, come with me,' Mitch stated.

The female spoke in her robotic voice. It had the same metallic reverberation as the male one but was more feminine. 'Please, Samuel to the right, Mitchell to the left.'

Sam looked at his brother, whom he sensed was about to kick off. 'Mitch, it's okay. We'll take our own elevators. I'm sure we'll help each other in this task, just like in all the others. Let's just get this over with.' *I have to be brave.*

Sam stepped into the lift, then turned to see Mitch in his own one. As the doors closed, they smiled at each other. Alone in the elevator, he remembered the warning and his heart started beating fast. He closed his eyes to try and calm himself. When he reopened them he noticed that there were no buttons, nothing to push, nor any writing or instructions. Like the building they had entered, it was all glass, too sleek-looking and ultra-modern. He felt the movement hurtling him skywards but couldn't tell how high up he was when it finally stopped at the destination. The doors opened and ahead of him it was pitch-black.

He gulped and took a seat backwards, so his back was against the wall of the lift. He didn't want to step out into the darkness. It reminded him too much of when he got initiated into all of this.

A male robotic voice spoke from the darkness. Sam was too anxious to even try and work out if it was the same person from downstairs. 'Please step forward. Dinner has been prepared for you. Just walk in a straight line and you shall come to a chair. Sit. There is a table in front of the chair, where a luxury three-course meal will be served to you. It is in the dark to enhance the culinary experience and to awaken your senses. Dining in the dark is very trendy at the moment. Please take your seat, now.'

Sam didn't move. *Just a dinner, yeah, right. If it is food, Satan only knows what they are going to feed me. Will Mitch be eating with me?* He took a small step forward.

The voice from the darkened place spoke. 'Ten.' There was a pause. 'Nine.' It was a countdown. 'Eight.' *I guess I don't want to see what happens if it gets to zero.* Sam took a proper step and walked forward, into the absolute midnight.

The light from the lift disappeared. As he walked onwards attempting to reach the chair, he felt dizzy and unsteady on his feet. He wanted to get down on to the floor and crawl but didn't. *Are the lights about to come on and a bunch of weirdos jump out with a big Stitchin surprise?* His steps were made even more unsteady in the borrowed designer shoes that had been delivered along with the tuxedo. Reaching the seat was somewhat a relief.

'There is a rule that must be complied with. All courses must be finished. Now, enjoy.'

He looked around, trying to pinpoint the source of the sound and to see if that bright yellow could be seen. It couldn't. *It's probably speakers.*

'Mitchell, are you in here?'

There was silence. He tapped the table in front of him, searching for the cutlery. When he found some, he had to search for the plate in front of him. In this blind state, he had to try and eat whatever was served. He moved his face down, closer to the table, but it didn't help in being able to see anything. *Is that smell vinegar or fish?* He tried poking around the plate with the knife and fork he was holding. When he managed to get something on his fork, he popped it into his mouth. It was cold and had a sharp taste, making him screw up his face as he chewed it. He thought he recognised it. *Is that a cucumber, or some sort of pickled gherkin?*

He scraped along where he thought the plate was, until he found some more food. As he pulled the utensil to himself, a big chunk of something went into his wide-open mouth with some sort of lumpy sauce. *It's sort of like hummus in consistency without the taste. But what's the main thing? It's sort of slimy. Chewy.* Rubbery. He stopped chewing and ran his tongue over it. *Is that a sucker? Is this some sort of tentacle?* He spat it out.

He probed around with his hands, looking for a drink, something to wash out his mouth. Eventually, he found something. *It's some sort of jug, but I can't find a glass, or would I even be able to pour it?* He picked it up and drank directly from it. It was just water. He greedily guzzled it down. *I guess hands are the only way to eat everything. Screw them and having any manners.* He rummaged on his plate, grabbed the tentacle thing and dipped it on the sauces, then scooped up anything else he found on the plate. He squished it all together and shoved it defiantly in his mouth. He chewed it, and as liquid dribbled from his full mouth, he wiped it on his sleeve. He swallowed bits when he could and tried to ignore the gagging.

He chugged from the jug to wash it all down and to clear out his mouth. When he was done, he slammed the jug down harder than he had intended. *Take that and bring it on.* The table pulled away from him; he wasn't actually sure if the table was moving or if it was his chair. There were mechanical sounds of things shuffling around, and then they stopped.

'The main course is served.'

His eyes had now adjusted to his pitch-black surroundings, and when the disorientation queasiness had passed, he yelled again. 'Mitch!'

There was silence.

I know how to play their game. He reached down, searching for the plate. He found a knife; it felt different from the previous one, but he didn't bother with it. Instead, he went straight for the food. He found some baton-like rectangles, picked one up and took a bite. It was crunchy but didn't have a discernible taste. *Some bland vegetable, but why it is making me so thirsty?* He sought out the jug but couldn't find it, and instead, he came across a wine glass. He knocked it and it should have spilt over, but it didn't. After accidently bashing the glass on his teeth, he tasted the liquid. *I guess it's as red as its room temperature.* He wanted to spit it out. He wasn't used to drinking wine; he didn't like the earthy smell, the sour taste and the full-bodied consistency of this drink. He gobbled down the rest of the thirst-inducing batons, washed down with a mouthful of the drink. He was not sure what either was.

Next, what he found was hot. He poked it with his finger; it felt squishy. He picked it up and bit into it. *It's some sort of meat.* He couldn't tear off a piece easily and had to really bite down. *It's very fleshy.* He started to chew the piece in his mouth. He tasted the juice—it was familiar, a sort of metallic taste. *It's blood.* He stopped chewing, trying to work out what to do next. *It's fine; it's just a blue steak.* He chomped down, swallowed and continued tearing away at the hunk of meat in his hand. *It's just a rare piece of beef. But it doesn't taste like beef, but then again, I have never had it this rare. It's just mooing. The French eat this all the time. So do the Spanish.* If he stopped, he wouldn't have been able to continue, so he powered on. He had to; it was the only way he knew he would be able to finish it.

The chair-table switch happened again. 'Last course, dessert. Some say it's the best.' The voice distortion made everything spoken seem eery and not humorous or endearing. The plate he found was smaller than that for the main course, but he felt many different consistencies on it. A powdery substance, *icing sugar*; a gelatinous-like block, *jelly*; and a thick but squishy thing, *mousse*. He had learnt that it was better to just try to 'down it', so he took the block, used it to pick up the powder and popped it all in his mouth. The granules were sweet with a citrus hint, but on the opposite end, the jelly had a sour taste. He chewed it; there was something inside, something that seemed out of place. *An edible ball with a bitter centre.* He gulped it down, thankful to no longer have it in his mouth and wiped his mouth, leaving his arm there just in case. *Nearly done, then it's over.* As he brought the 'mousse' closer to his mouth, there was a smell that he hadn't noticed before. It was pungent, like blue cheese. It had a mousse-like texture, so he didn't need to chew. He swallowed it. *Sort of tastes like nuts, but old ones.* He grabbed the rest of it and ate it. When he thought he had eaten everything, he stood up, wanting to vomit.

'Am I done? Have I eaten everything? Have I passed?'

'Dinner is completed,' the voice answered.

It can't have been that easy.

'Have I passed?' he urgently demanded but couldn't wait for the response. He doubled over and started to throw up. Once he started, he couldn't stop; he vomited out everything he had just consumed.

'The first part of the evening is over. Now for the second part. Take off all of your clothes. All of them. When you are done, enter the elevator.'

When he had finished hurling, he stood up and wiped his hands that were now covered in vomit over the jacket. *It would be good to have a day not being drugged, poisoned with drink and food so I don't end up spewing my guts out. Anyway, I play their game my way. If I have to take it off, I might as well.* Once his hands felt cleaner, he discarded the garment. He whipped off the cummerbund and bowtie, chucking them to the floor, and he walked away from the mess that he could only smell.

His throat burned. *Why do they want me to be naked? Is it because I threw up?* He fumbled as he tried to undo the dress shirt in the darkness. *Screw this.* He ripped it off and used it to wipe his face. He slipped off the shoes, becoming shorter. When he started to take off his trousers, he felt vulnerable, standing there in his underwear. *What are they going to have me do or do to me?* He paused, then slowly shuffled towards where he thought the lift would be. He waited. He had no idea how much time has passed; to him, it felt like ages.

Then the countdown restarted. 'Ten.' Placing his right hand inside the pants, he covered himself up. 'Nine.' Then he took the underwear off using his left hand. 'Eight.' Once they had fallen to the floor and he was completely naked, a streak of light appeared at his seven o'clock. 'Seven.' It was the lift opening. He used his left hand to also cover himself. 'Six.' He tried to see what was in the room, but the light didn't illuminate it and show him anything. 'Five.' He moved his naked self towards the lift. 'Four.' He stepped in the cubicle of light. 'Three.' He wasn't sure if it was being stark-bollock-naked, being back in that lift, or having just purged his entire insides that gave him the terrible gut-wrenching feeling that was washing over him.

The lift hurtled him upwards, fast. It felt a lot quicker than last time. He moved his left hand to the glass wall to stabilise himself. *This isn't the same lift. It's smaller, as the distance to the wall is shorter.* He briefly took in his surroundings. *It's some sort of glass; well, it feels like glass, and it's small. I can't really move around.* He started to sweat. He felt he couldn't breathe through his nose anymore, he opened his mouth gasping to desperately take in air. The view changed from the grey, mechanical workings of the lift to the night sky. *It's taken me outside.* He felt dizzy and wanted to drop to the floor but couldn't, as there was no room. *It's more like a coffin.* He continued trying to take in oxygen, and then let out a blood-curdling scream as the coffin tilted forward.

He placed both hands in front of himself, not bothering to try to maintain any sort of dignity. It was the only thing he could do to try to stop the sense of falling that overcame him. He continued screaming, shouting out curses and demanding to be let out of the glass coffin that had now suspended his naked body, practically fully horizontal at the top of a skyscraper. He stopped due to the pain in his throat, which was already raw from vomiting.

They aren't going to kill me; it's just another test. I hope whatever Mitch is going through it is it not as bad as what they are putting me through. Be safe, Mitch. Maybe I should have warned him, but then he would have been worrying about me. I need to get through this so I can find my brother and help him. Just be brave.

He tried to rationalise what was happening, to pull himself together, but he didn't have long to think, as he was soon distracted by the wetness he felt on his leg. He looked down and saw water; his prison had started to fill up with water. It felt weird, though, as there was a pressure and movement that didn't feel right.

Water was rapidly filling the coffin. He had to push against the glass to manoeuvre his face out of the water. *What is it? How much can they throw at us?* There was that pressure again. It was on his back, and then he felt it on his leg.

Something is in here with me.

He looked down, trying to see what it was, but now, it was harder to position his face out of the water. It felt rough, like something scratching him. Then where his hands were, a network of white lines appeared as the glass appeared to be cracking where he was pressing on it. He let go as all the whole box seemed to be full of water.

As he flailed around, his legs were kicking around as best as they could, and suddenly, he saw a snake pop its head from between his legs, baring its fangs. He screamed uncontrollably even though he was submerged in water and no one could hear him. It was all he could do.

CHAPTER 22
DAY 9

The grandfather clock in the study chimed in the new day. If out of respect for the timepiece Doughty waited for the twelve dongs to stop before rasping out. 'Huh? What are you talking about? What stitching?'

Sarah looked at him. He genuinely seemed taken back. *He hasn't heard that word before, or he would have acted differently. Then there was the fact that there were no marks on his leg.* She moved the gun so that it was no longer trained on him. 'I'm sorry. I had to know. Let me explain everything to you and then you can decide what you want to do with me.'

'Untie me first.'

Best not to, in case he slips up, but I'd better get his sympathy quickly. She lifted up her top so he could see her bandage. 'Just over a day ago, I was assaulted in my apartment. Dr Paul Impey—' *he doesn't seem to know that name,* '—drugged me and implanted a device here inside me. He did it because he wanted to control me. He was paranoid because I was getting too close to finding out something about his nephew Tom Denton. He was the man who was dating Megan; he died in a suspicious suicide and he had seven marks on his leg. The doctor wanted to stop me investigating further and making the link to the organisation he worked for. He thought he would get in trouble with them if it was through him I found out about them. He wanted to stop my investigation and have the additional benefit of having

240

me in his back pocket. He didn't know that Tanner had already told me about this organisation years ago. When Paul Impey found out I knew about them he freaked out, he became genuinely worried. Tanner must have found out about Tom's involvement, that's why he wanted me to find Megan. To find answers, facts, anything I could on them. They are the Stitchin.'

'Who? Sarah, listen to yourself doctors and devices and organisations. Look what you have done to me, your superior, someone who could have been an ally. This isn't normal behaviour. Let me help you, get you help.' She noted a calmer, pleading tone in his voice.

'The Stitchin, no "g", are an organisation that Pete Tanner became aware of over ten years ago. He brought me in to his confidence regarding them about five years ago. They have infiltrated multiple companies, military units, governments; they have their own agenda. We never got close to finding out what their endgame is or how far their reach goes.'

'Come on, you know better than to listen to conspiracy theories.'

'Tanner was obsessed with them. You know the man; it wouldn't have been nothing. He said when he had the right proof and found people he could trust, he would have exposed them. I believe he must have been close, he must have uncovered something and that's why he was killed.'

'If what you are saying is even remotely true I owe it to Pete and our friendship to listen. You have my attention but you are skating on very thin ice.'

'As I said, somehow, he knew Tom Denton was an initiate.' She started to pace around the room as she said her theories out loud. 'He died—maybe suicide, or maybe he was killed—I haven't figured that out yet. He was quickly disposed of, so no evidence was left behind to find, apart from his girlfriend, Megan. That's who Tanner wanted me to find: she must have known something, or would have been able to point me in the right direction of where to look. But she was murdered.' Sarah paused. 'And there was something unusual with her body. That's what Melissa, the pathologist, said— things had happened to Megan's body that she hadn't seen before, some unknown substance that changed her organs. Melissa needed to do further tests, but then, she was murdered, her colleague was murdered and all the physical evidence was conveniently destroyed.'

'You're telling me that this Stitchin did all of that? They started the fire at the hospital and murdered the two pathologists? We found a suicide note at the house of Darius Walton—he confessed to what he planning, said it was due to malpractice. So you are saying they planted that evidence?'

'Yes. It all makes sense now; they are cleaning up something, covering their tracks. I don't know much, just that they are a ruthless organisation that needs to be brought down. Impey told me before he died to think of them as the government to every other government across the world, only nobody knows they exist. He said they had interests in everything: from pharmaceuticals, which is where he fitted in, to technology, finance, agriculture, and weapons—literally everything.'

'Sarah, I can't believe an organisation like this exists and has been operating under the radar. It's unbelievable.'

'Tanner was on to them; they exist. They mark their members with a series of tally marks cut into the upper left leg; some sort of initiation and control.' She turned away from him. 'That's why I had to check your leg. I am sorry. Impey also told me that they embedded a device underneath the skin where those marks are, which can kill a person.'

'What sort of device?'

'I don't know. This was new information to me. The good doctor removed his own one. I removed something similar that he put in me. We need someone with the technical know-how to examine them, but the person has to be discreet, someone we can trust absolutely. That will give us proof.'

'What about this doctor? I want to speak to him, get him on record.'

'There was an altercation as I attempted to escape. He got injured and when he realised I had the upper hand, he killed himself instead of allowing himself to be taken. If he had been taken and entered into the system he knew they would get to him. I cleaned up, leaving no trace behind. Dragged his dead-arse body to his private underground parking. He had already disabled all of the security cameras because he didn't want evidence he had kidnapped me. I shoved him in his Telsa, lucky I could stash him in that as I would have pictured him more as a Porsche man, and drove to his home, which was programmed in the car. He's currently in an ice bath in his apartment. I've been hiding out there for the past day. I searched the place and couldn't find anything to prove any of this, apart from the device that was implanted in his leg. He had removed it and put it in a box. So, I removed mine, after disabling it, too. Those and his body, which bears the stitches, are your evidence.'

'Open my computer.'

'What for?'

'I want to show you something. You asked me to hear you out, which I have done.'

'I already tried accessing it but couldn't get past your protection.'

'The password is h&%N@Mc{. Go into my emails and look under the folder with your name.'

Sarah did as instructed. There was one email in the folder that was from Tanner. She read it. It was about her transfer to his division.

'You said you trusted him; as you can see, he trusted me.'

She re-read the line: 'I trust you, Al; look after Sarah. She will probably drive you crazy, but she isn't as tough as she appears.'

'Now untie me and let's work this out.'

She picked up the knife she had used to cut his trousers and cut his restraints. 'I'm sorry, but I had no choice. I needed you to hear me out.'

She didn't take her eyes off him.

He stood up and just walked past her. 'Do you want a drink? I have a good Scotch from Christmas.' He walked out of the room, not waiting for her response.

She listened as he went upstairs. *I trust you, Al.* She started to tidy up the study while she waited for him to return. It wasn't long until he walked back in the room, dressed in a tracksuit. He was carrying two glasses and an unopened bottle of fancy-looking whiskey. *He's deliberately exaggerating the gesture of opening the glass bottle for the first time, in the way he broke the seal, for my benefit.* He poured two glasses and handed her one. She accepted it.

'What do you want to happen next, Sarah?' He sipped his drink.

She mirrored his actions and took a sip. 'I guess we need to secure—'

Before she could react, he was on her; he had her in a sleeper hold.

'Don't fight it.'

He's so strong.

'I'm going to help you.'

I trusted you.

'Don't resist.'

How could you?

A strong, sharp smell rushed up her nostrils and caused her to jerk awake. The ammonia stench brought tears to her eyes, through them she assessed the situation. Doughty had reversed their roles; she was now secured in the same chair she had tied him to. He was hovering the smelling salts under her nose.

'How could you?' she demanded.

'Can you blame me? You could have just come to me and asked for help, laid out your evidence and your case. Instead you held me hostage and came up with some fantastical conspiracy. I think you need help, which I'm going to give. I have a colleague here who I want you to speak to. This is off the record for now.' He stood aside and Sarah saw the woman standing behind him. 'I invited her here discreetly, to talk to you, to help. Give me Impey's address and I will check that out. I am giving you the benefit of the doubt by checking out your story, but if you try anything funny with Dr Walters, it will be the last thing you do.'

'Hello Sarah, my name is Michelle. Alistair told me the details of how we're here in these unusual circumstances. I am here to listen to you.'

'Okay, I'll speak to your psychiatrist, but what if she deems me to not be crazy?' Sarah watched as Doughty didn't answer he just raised his eyebrows.

Surely, if he were that smart, he would have known that given the Manchester investigation and its consequences that I had to suffer for uncovering the truth, I had to go through extensive psychoanalysis. If I want to fake a positive result in my favour, I can. This psychoanalysis isn't going to work.

Sarah slunk down further on the sofa, doing her best to be as inconspicuous as possible, but given her environment, that was hard to do. She was surrounded by men, and given recent events she had had her fill of that gender. As she assessed each of them, she hated them all. *Desperate sickos. Pathetic losers, exerting what little power they have over women.* They weren't paying her any attention; she was the least interesting person in the room to them. They were mesmerised by the display occurring in front of them.

If only Doughty's shrink could see me now, she would have a field day. Good job the Walters woman was clueless and I was able to run rings around her, but I can do without weekly chats with her.

A loud cracking sound roused Sarah back to the here and now. She looked at the riding crop that had been lashed on the table, then up at its owner.

'Mistress Anushka, queen of the whip, will see you now. Should we wait for your man before we get going?'

'No, it's just me, and I want to talk to you. I'll pay for your time.'

Anushka pulled the curtains around the booth. 'Whatever your wishes are, we fulfil them here at Desire.'

'Sit, have a break.'

'The boss said you requested me and would pay well,' Anushka purred.

Sarah slipped over two hundred pounds across the table. *Thank you, Dr Impey.* 'Is this enough? I don't need your services; I need information. I asked to see someone who was friends with Megan. Megan North.'

Sarah noticed how Anushka changed, her composure went from that of a flirty professional on the game to a woman who was distraught. 'That poor girl; she was a good sort.'

'You heard what happened to her? How?'

Anushka quickly scooped up the money. 'Who are you?'

'My name is Sarah, I'm the policewoman investigating what happened to your friend. I want to make sure the same thing doesn't happen to any other girls.'

'Was it to do with this place? I always said she was too nice to work here. You go see Marc. He works the door and security. Tell him Nush sent you. He'll know if she ever got mixed up with a punter.' She stood up and was about to open the curtains.

'Thank you, Anushka.' Sarah stood as well. 'How do you know what happened to Megan? That information isn't public.'

'I heard it from Bea. How she found out, you gotta ask her yourself because I don't speak other people's business. Sarah, you seem too nice to be working as a policewoman.' With those parting words, she pursed her lips, turned back into the professional and sauntered off.

Sarah just sat there thinking. The hostess came over to her, asking her what she wanted. 'Can I get the bucket of beers? Also, can you tell me if Bea is working today?'

'She's in later, honey. I'll be right back with those drinks.' She winked and did the walk-off too, not quite at the same level as Anushka, but she tried.

Marc didn't need the two bottles of beers he had already polished off to be forthcoming. He had been happily chatting away to Sarah once she name-dropped the Mistress and identified herself. He saw them as peers. They had been sitting in the security office for the past thirty minutes as he looked for any archive footage of Megan.

'I don't think we're going to find anything. She didn't mix with the clientele here; she did her job, and that was it. Given her background, she knew how to handle herself and people didn't mess with her.'

'Was she open about her background then?' Sarah took two bottles of beer from the bucket, opened them, handed one to Marc and took one for herself.

He knocked the bottles together before taking a gulp. 'Yeah, she wore her heritage as a badge of honour. We all loved her stories. I mean, you never get to hear about gypsies and some of the stuff she came out with. The sca—' He paused. 'Wheeling and dealing, culture and fighting. When the customers found out she was a gypo, she became the forbidden fruit. The exotic, I mean, none of them had ever interacted with a woman from that community, let alone see her norks. Yeah, of course, sometimes the men would get fresh with the girls, but my team looks after our babes. No touching, no verbal abuse, no sex, no nothing that the girls don't want. Pay well to watch a dance, on stage or private, and that's it.'

'What about a boyfriend?'

'She had one; she talked about him. Wait, wait, wait.' He jumped up from his seat. 'The boyfriend came here once. It's not allowed; it's one of our main rules. The girls have to seem available even though the punters can't ever have them. Need to fuel the illusion. Yeah, so the boyfriend picked her up after a shift once. I remember having to remind her of the rules. It never happened again.'

'What happened with the boyfriend?'

'He met her at the "secret" staff entrance, which is separate from the customer one. We have cameras on it, for the safety of the girls. Let me find it for you.' He tapped a monitor. 'Bea has arrived. You should be able to have a quick chat with her before she starts.'

'Thanks, Marc. I'll be right back. Help yourself to more beer.'

She looked at the empty bottles. *He didn't have to take me so literally. I guess the free booze is one of the perks of the job—that and spending time with all these young, interesting women. Who knew Bea would be so interesting? I mean, damn, I was not expecting any of that.* Sarah tapped her temples as she started to think.

'You're back. I found that tape. I need to have a wee, just hit play.' He tried to motion towards the button, which ended up as him pointing to everything in the room.

'I'll figure it out. Hey, Marc, did any of the other girls ever have anyone pick them up—Bea, for instance?'

'No that's against the rules,' he slurred. He gave her a thumbs-up as he staggered out of the room.

Sarah walked over to the screen that was paused and hit the play button. The video showed a door. She put the volume up, but all that could be heard was static. *This CCTV has no sound.* Megan walked out of the door. *She looks her same alluring self.* A man appeared from off-screen. The position he came from meant his face wasn't shown and the camera just picked up the back of his head. Megan looked annoyed as he approached her.

Something is wrong with this. I've seen enough video footages of Tom. He's moving differently here; it's not the back of his head. It is not Tom. They appeared to be arguing. *Sound would have been good. Why does the guy seem so familiar?*

Megan was very animated as she spoke. The guy held his hands up, trying to diffuse the argument. He turned slightly, not enough to show his whole face but a bit of his side profile. *I know him.* Sarah felt a knot in her stomach. *It can't be.* Megan and the man embraced. Looks like they had made up, they were kissing. He turned around and had his arm around her shoulder. Megan had a smile on her face. He was also smiling. They walked off together.

Sarah wiped her hand across her forehead: she re-wound the video and paused it on the best shot of his face It was a face she knew intimately, once from spending the whole night together, and the other time after 'accidently' bumping into him, though at that time, he had been unable to perform.

251

How are you involved in this? Have you been playing me?

She stared at the man on the screen, grabbed the nearest bottle of beer and threw it against the wall. It smashed.

'Damn you, Mitch!'

CHAPTER 23
DAY 9

Death by snakebite? Drowning? Falling from a skyscraper? In the split second, he couldn't decide which would be worse.

He looked at the blurred lights in the distance, then at a nearby tall building—at the top it had a digital time display: 00:02. He focused on the blue numbers and tried to calm himself to stop taking on water. *What if Mitchell is in the same situation as I, on the opposite side of this building? It can't end like this.*

Sam jammed his knee up as hard as he could—given the limited space and the fact that he was submerged in water—into the glass. It cracked and water started gushing out of the hole he had made. He put his feet and hands in the four corners as best as he could and pushed his body back. The snake—or part of it—must have been near his back because when he moved himself against the back of the glass coffin, it slithered in the water to be in front of his body. The force of the water pouring out caused the glass next to the hole to shatter and grow. Glass, water and the snake went hurtling down towards the ground.

He hung on, spitting out the water in his mouth. The cold air smacked his naked wet body. He pressed himself even harder into the back wall. Even though he was now exposed to the howling wind, he distinctly heard the glass crack behind him.

The whole capsule jolted backwards, reversing the mechanism that had propelled it horizontally. Soon, he was upright and able to stand, and he moved an inch away from the back wall but stayed close to it as the sides protected him from the cold wind. Being this high up with nothing in front of him except shards of glass around the edges made him feel dizzy. Suddenly, he became aware of a pain from his right knee, the one that had connected with the glass. He looked down and saw that it was bleeding. He ignored it as he became aware of a sensation that he hadn't felt before. It was so unusual, weird. *It's like someone is poking my skin from the inside.*

He touched his left leg, where the vibe was coming from, then three half-inch lines appeared seared on his skin, joining next to the tally mark of the five that were already there.

The first 'stitch' was bigger and had its own stitches. It must have been where they implanted the device. It is now 'healed' and looks just like the others. And that device is making the other marks. Eight in all. What…

Before he could finish his thought, the damaged glass pod tilted backwards, and the floor slid away in the same movement. This caught Sam off-guard. He didn't have a chance to grab hold of anything—not that there was anything to grab.

As quick as a flash, he was sent hurtling down a chute, sliding in a fast descent, unable to stop.

DAY 10

The beaten, bloody young man didn't move. His eyes were shut, and he remained motionless as he was prodded. 'Get up. Wake up.' There was still no response. He glanced at the time, 07:51. Sam placed a hand on the chest of the body, hoping to find his beating heart.

What have I done? I promised myself to not do exactly what I have done. I hate what I've become. Damn them. How can I ever make any of this right?

Eventually, he found movement, and a sense of relief gushed over him. It couldn't erase the past hour, but it helped somewhat. He grabbed some duct tape and bound the man's wrists together, then did the same to his ankles. He then gagged his mouth and dragged the body over to the bed. He contemplated trying to pick up the body and placing it on the bed, but that would take too much effort and he was already behind schedule. Instead, he took out the syringe he had been given. Sam took the safety off and held the needle by the man's arm. It will just knock him out for a few hours, no permanent damage. *I can't do this, I can't trust them, he's innocent.* Sam took the safety cap and was about to place it back on the needle when the body moved. Sam was taken aback. The man opened his eyes; his pupils were dilated, and it was obvious that he was wild with rage.

Sam rushed out of the house, ignoring the smarting of his knee injury that the fight had exacerbated from the other night, and jumped into the waiting car. It sped off even before he had a chance to close the door properly.

'Are you okay? What happened in there? You took a long time.' Asked Mitch.

'Yes, I'm fine,' he snapped back. 'Like everything they tell us to do, it wasn't straightforward. He fought back, but it's okay, I'm okay. Thanks for checking in. We'll get through this.' Sam started to play with the radio stations on the car stereo, pretending to look for something better to listen to.

I don't feel like myself. With every task we do, it seems like I am losing my identity, who I am. What a joke; I don't even know that. I feel abused and beaten. Five minutes ago, I physically lashed out at a stranger. I've never even had a fight in school. But I had to release all this rage, all this resentment that has built up in me. I can justify it, that it was my task to borrow his identity. I had to do it to get my number nine. A simple task compared to the previous one, yes, but he surprised me and threw the first punch. But instead of just using that syringe that they gave me, I fought back, fought hard, and beat him unconscious.

Mitch lowered the volume using the controls on the steering wheel. 'I think that green drug they put in us has affected us in ways we don't fully comprehend yet. It has made me more detached from the world. I care about you but nothing else. I would like to think that before I wasn't as cold-hearted and selfish as I am now. So, if it's done that to me, it must have really messed with you. Maybe that's why you did what you did.'

Sam felt relieved hearing this validation and having his brother confirm what he had thought. 'Do you think we will ever go back to ourselves again? Can we give away the money to make all this right?'

'Maybe some of it. But remember we're doing this to make our lives better. Look, Samuel, I know we briefly discussed what happened the other night, but I think we need to talk about it a bit more.'

Sam noticed his brother used his full name, something he rarely did, but ignored the fact. 'You got buried alive, and I got drowned while being suspended from the top of a skyscraper. I don't think either of us wants to relive the events.'

'It seriously messed with my head, not being able to help you. I know it must have done the same to you. That's why I think we need to properly discuss it.'

'Mitch, now isn't the time. We've got to concentrate on the second half of this double challenge. Part one was easy; let's take that win, do part two and talk later.' *To be honest, I don't want to think or talk about that night again. It broke me.* He could sense his brother looking at him.

'What happened to the bloke just now when you injected him? Did he go out cold?'

'Yes, out like a light,' Sam instantly responded, hoping his brother wouldn't see through his lie. 'How are we doing for time?'

If Mitch noticed, he didn't say anything. 'I've made it back up. I'll get you to your first day of work on time, if not early.'

'Great,' Sam sarcastically retorted. *Don't be a brat; he has the harder part of this.* 'Are you ready?' He looked at his brother dressed in all black, then glanced over at the black bag chucked on the back seat. *While I had to go and steal someone's identity, all he had to do was go collect a bag from Don Luciano—albeit a bag with a gun in it, which he'll have to use. How is he going to get away with this? What have we let ourselves in for?*

'You should see the disguise they have given me to wear. While it is obviously a rubber mask, because of the identity of who the actual politician is and his real blubbery, rubbery face it's a good match. There's a accompanying wig and some sort of voice distorter too,' Mitch said through a smile. 'Don't worry, little brother, I'll be fine. I will do my part, cause a big distraction and diversion, so you can do your bit.'

His voice wavered as he said that; he's worried, but he is trying to hide it from me. 'I'll be fine. We could give away half the money and still have a million pounds between us. What do you want to spend it on?' He wanted to try and ground his brother back into the endgame, hoping it would give him the confidence to carry out his task.

'You will finish your A levels, then go off to university. We can pay for a top one in the States and leave all of this behind us,' Mitch said confidently.

We'll never be able to leave this; it will never be over. Doesn't he get that? 'Sounds great. What will you do?'

'Open a motorbike repair shop, wherever you end up. Ride the open roads when you're studying and getting on with your life, but always be close by so that we can be there for each other.'

'Thank you. I wouldn't have it any other way.' *He's changed since the other night too.*

'We're a few roads away. It's best that I don't get any closer. You'll have to walk the rest of the way.' Mitch started to park the car. He opened his door and stepped out but spoke before closing it. 'Don't worry about me. I will be in and out. You do the same. Oh, the Don sent me a little something for you, too; it's in the back. I'll give you some privacy to get ready.'

Sam stared at his face in the mirror as he washed his hands. While it was his face, it didn't belong to him. For the past two hours, people had been calling him a different name: 'Loni'. He had easily assimilated Loni, and he didn't even have to change his appearance to make it believable. After all, he had Loni's passport and the identification badge that the company had sent him. His namesake had unruly brown hair, but everyone assumed he had had a nice smart haircut for his new job. They were both white males, of similar age. He wore a Prada suit courtesy of Don Luciano, which meant he was smart and presentable. Everyone he had encountered just bought into the lie without any questions.

He dried his hands and was about to walk out of the restroom when he remembered his glasses that he had left by the washbasin. He put on the Prada frames with the non-prescription glass lenses and left the room. He headed to his first appointment, but as he walked across the lobby, he looked at the six clocks showing the time across the world—here it was 10:50—then he stared down at the proudly emblazoned logo and name of the bank on the floor.

The security guard, the same one who had let him in in the morning, greeted him again. 'How's it going, Loni? Hope everyone here has been making you feel welcome.'

'Yes, they've all been great.' And they had. The real Loni had interviewed with senior management and the head of human resources at the central office, while the person showing him the ropes was more middle management, and an assistant human resources personnel who worked in the office did his induction. There wasn't a need to blag why he might have seemed different to the 'original' person interviewed over six months ago. Every time the name was mentioned, he couldn't help but think back to when he broke into Loni's flat-share and found him sleeping. All he had to do was inject him with the unknown substance and take his passport and identification badge, which had already been sent out to him. He hesitated because he was scared it might kill him. While he was deliberating, Loni woke up.

Loni looked scared and held his hands up in resignation. But something inside Sam had kicked in, and he lashed out. Loni didn't fight back. Sam laid into him, dragging him out of bed and just started beating him. He had snapped. All his anger, all the hatred he had built up since starting these tasks, all the revenge he wanted, he unleashed on this innocent person who was basically in the wrong place at the wrong time. It was only after the bloodied Loni appeared lifeless that he stopped.

Thinking back to that face on the ground and remembering what he had done made him grimace. *I should have just injected him from the start.* He thought back to after the beating, when he cried, cried at what he had done and become. He tried to redeem himself by just incapacitating Loni with duct tape, but then, he woke up again. Even then, he couldn't inject him. He hit him again. *What if he wakes up and breaks free and notifies the authorities? We will get caught. Maybe, that is what we deserve. Just to end all of this.*

Sam swallowed hard, shook his head, walked into his empty three-sided cubicle and logged into the computer, using the details they had given him earlier. He looked at Loni's diary; the couple due in at eleven o'clock were late. A fellow bank employee walked in; she was wearing a nametag and had her ID card clipped to the waist band of her skirt.

'Hello, I am Megha.' She stretched out her hand. 'Just wanted to welcome you and let you know that some of us are going for a few drinks after work, and you should come. We can't do a team lunch as we have to stagger the times we eat, so we thought drinks would be a nice mixer. We're a really friendly bunch; you're going to love it here.' He smiled at her and nodded, and was then saved by his appointment arriving. 'Great; I'll chat with you later.' She didn't even give him a chance to speak.

After what is going to go down, you all are going to need lots of drinks.

The couple sat down and introduced themselves as Catherine and Josh. She did most of the talking for them. Sam ran through the mortgage application questionnaire and just filled in the responses as they gave them.

They were in their mid-twenties. He is punching based on looks, but I guess the fact that as a dentist, the fact he earns a lot makes up for any shortcomings. Plus, this private bank is one that his family uses, and they are paying the deposit for them. Why am I being so mean about them? Seriously what have I become? Is it jealousy? They have a simple, normal life, one that society dictates we should all strive for. One that is definitely not on the cards for me.

The whole process felt quite monotonous, and he noticed that he was repeating the questions. *I can rule out mortgage advisor as a future career.* When he got to the section about wills, he didn't ask them about it; he answered for them. He ticked that they already had one and wanted to place it in a bank safe deposit box.

'All of that looks good. I just have to photocopy your documents. There's a more private room where you can wait. I'll take you there.'

He led them to the room, waiting for the system to update with the information he had just entered. When he had settled them in with tea and water, he could act on the plan he had been tasked to do. 'Just wait here and

I'll be right back.' He then went to the duty manager, Aaron, to the get the pass to enter the safety deposit box room. Aaron smiled, checked his iPad and just handed it over. Sam was walking away with the swipe card and a post-it note with a code on it when Aaron called his name.

'Loni, just a moment.'

He stood with his back to Aaron, quickly glancing at his watch. *Damn it.* Sam eventually turned to face the manager as his heart started to beat faster, knowing what was about to come, and he mustered a smile. 'Yes boss?' Aaron was tapping away at his device.

'I just wanted to say, great cross-selling. Well done. Now, try to get them to use our recommended solicitors. We can always sell more.'

'Sure thing.' He walked off feeling relieved. *He's very friendly but has no idea. Just doing the day to day, the mundane. Poor guy.* He stood right at the centre of the logo in the lobby when the front door burst open.

Sam stared at the assailant dressed in black. He wore a rubber mask and was brandishing a gun. The aggressor pointed the weapon at the security guard, then into the air and fired it.

CHAPTER 24
DAY 10

Sarah checked her phone again; still no response from either her voicemail or text message. *I can't message him again. Ultimately, I don't want him to know I am on to him if he's playing me. If he isn't, I need to keep it casual. I don't want to scare him off until I know. I picked the restaurant that night, which was even before I was on the Megan case. There was no way he picked me because of my profession; he doesn't even know what I do or my real name. Surely, it's just a small world. Damn it.* She thumped her fists on the steering wheel. She didn't have a chance to replay their encounters in her head again, which she had been doing since she clocked him on the surveillance, because her own stakeout just kicked off—her woman left Desire.

Sarah watched as Bea got in an Uber at just after two in the morning. She switched on her car engine and waited until the taxi pulled away, and she started to follow. *I have to analyse this lead. Mitch—if that is his name—will have to wait.* As she drove, she thought about her interaction with the stripper and why she was now following the mark.

'Hi Bea, can we talk? Anushka and Marc said you may be able to help me.'

'Sure thing, sweetie, but we gotta do it while I get ready, as I'm running late for my act,' Bea replied as she stripped off her day-wear.

'Go for it; nothing I haven't seen about six times already tonight. I'm a private investigator, hired by the club, to make sure all you women are safe. I need to make sure no customers are hassling or endangering any of the workers given recent events.'

She paused. 'Have they?'

'That's what I'm here to find out.'

'If you find out anything, make sure you let us know, so we can watch our backs.' She started to shave her armpits.

'Is there anyone you're afraid of? Do you remember anyone who may have had a reason to hurt Megan, or someone who's infatuated with her?'

'She loved the attention, guess she didn't get much of it growing up, but no freakos from here. I've worked a few places and as joints go this one ain't bad. If a punter gets fresh or too handsy, security are all over them.'

'Were you and Megan close?'

'No. I mean, I liked her and all, it's just that we didn't hang out outside of work—their kind aren't meant to, are they? But then she didn't play by those rules. What was your question again?'

She does like to chat, occupational hazard. 'How did you find out about what happened to her?'

'Mikey told me.'

'Her brother?'

'Yeah. I … er … bumped into him, and he mentioned it.'

'When was this? How did you know each other?'

'Megan introduced us once. Guess I am just good with faces. Babes, do me a favour—go to my locker and get me the silver glitter spray. Here's the key.' Bea handed it to her. 'Number three.'

It was the same type of locker key found among Megan's possessions. 'Sure. I guess Megan's locker was given to someone else when she stopped working here. What happened to her things when she passed?'

'Dunno; Marc will know. Her stuff was probably given to the other girls. Guessing she would have just kept makeup and things in there like the rest of us. Nowt special.'

The locker was big enough to fit an airplane-sized cabin carry-on. Bea's was messy; Sarah wanted to rummage through it but knew she was being watched. She took out the spray, which was at the front and passed it over.

'Cheers. I need to go on now. Remember, babes, let me know if you find out anything.' Bea lingered like she wanted to say something but blew Sarah a kiss and strutted off.

What did you want to tell me, Bea? Don't worry, I'll find out in a bit.

Bea's taxi pulled over without any indication in front of a very conspicuous building. It was too late for Sarah to stop behind it, so she continued on ahead and stopped when she could. She adjusted the mirror and saw Bea getting out of the car. The driver waited, watched his passenger go inside the flashing neon lit eyesore, and then drove off. Sarah got out of her car and walked over to the building. The 24-hour gym did not seem very upmarket. She noted when she had just driven past that it wasn't glass-fronted, so she didn't bother to approach it with much caution after quickly glancing around for any cameras. The front door required a code to be inputted. She quickly looked up the chain of gyms and searched forums for a code for this one. The first one, she found on a chat forum, didn't work when she tried it. She was about to enter the next one when the door opened. She seized the opportunity and held the door. A random guy left. She bowed her head, let him go and then went inside.

Given my attire and lack of gym items, if challenged, I won't last long without blowing my cover. If I go to the ladies' locker room first, maybe I can find some stuff to help me blend in. Though at this time of night it shouldn't be busy unless this is a front.

She very carefully opened the door and walked in. There was a small corridor that had a large laundry basket with a few used towels in it. As she walked past it, towards the end where there was a cut-away door, she heard a voice. She paused, recognising it as Bea's. When the second person in the conversation spoke, she felt flushed and her suspicion was confirmed.

'Wait, grab that 'Cleaning in progress' floor sign and stick it outside. Then lock the door so that we 'won't be disturbed. I'll re-check the stalls.'

'Sure, baby. But it's late; no one comes to the gym at this time, especially no woman.'

Sarah heard the sound of high heels on tiles and knew she didn't have long.

She lay still under the damp towels, after climbing in the basket, as the clacking sound got louder and went past her twice. She concentrated on listening.

'Done, hun.'

'Now tell me again exactly what happened.'

'The club hired someone, some woman, to investigate what happened to your sister. Something about them doing due diligence. It's kind of sweet of them, if you ask me. I got pally with her. She gonna tell me if she finds out anything and I'll tell you.'

'You sure she wasn't gavver—police? What was her name?'

'Hmm… She didn't say. She was pretty, won't have been police. She said the club hired her. I'll ask around when I next go back in. Marc will know for sure and tell me.'

'What does she look like?'

'Red head, slim body, probably used to be a girl like me once—'

'Ginger? Not brunette?'

'Definitely, a stripper-red colour.'

'Okay, okay. Doesn't sound like that gavver woman. They wouldn't even know Megs worked there.'

'Mikey, babes, calm down. You have an important night; concentrate on that. If stripper PI finds out anything, you'll be the first to know. Our poor Megan— who did she get herself caught up with?'

'Meet me after the fight; I'll need you. I will need to destress and celebrate properly; feel how big my balls are now.'

Sarah heard sounds of kissing and groping. 'Of course, I want you in me so badly. You're such a tease with your pre-match abstinence. Please be careful and don't get hurt.'

'It frustrates the hell out of me, which means I'm going to kill the other guy. Then we will do it all night. I'll come to your place once I've demolished him.'

'Yes, baby. Sure you don't want me to come and watch you in action? Afterwards, we can do it at the funfair, on your ride. Hall Park isn't far away; I'll get an Uber and be discreet.'

'Not this again. You know you can't; women don't go to these events. How are you going to explain being the only female there? When I got enough money, we'll take a trip away somewhere.'

'I thought you got a lot from your sister? There were thousands in her locker. And the other stuff in there; we can flog it?'

'Stop, don't act like a typical gorger girl. Don't question me, otherwise, there is no future for us.'

'Sorry, Mikey. I'm just as frustrated as you are. It'll be good once we can have sex again.'

There were more slurping sounds before the clacking sound started up again, getting louder and then passing by. As the door closed behind Bea, Sarah lay still. Mikey sounded like he was next to her as he muttered, 'Dumb cow.' Then she felt something on top of her.

She listened some more and then heard him leaving the changing room. She removed the towels from on top of her, including the wet towel he had added. As she got to the door, she heard him speaking to another man. She didn't recognise his voice.

'You ready, brother? We got big bucks riding on you.'

'I am spoiling for a fight. He's dead.'

'Good man, good man.'

She let them have a head start and wasn't exactly following. Given how empty the roads were at this time of night, 03:24, it would have been a dead giveaway. His male companion was driving recklessly, *probably under the influence*, in the direction of Hall Park, according to Sarah's sat nav.

What was in the locker, Mikey? You're going to need my help if this has anything to do with the Stitchin; you're in it way over your head and you don't even know it.

She pulled over down a side street, a few roads away from the park. There was earnest silence in the air, as she got out of her car and began walking up the residential road. The houses were nice, not like on the Denton's road level of expensive, but it was a rich area.

I guess any properties near a common or park would be worth a fair few bob. I wonder what the owners would think if they only knew what was about to take place?

She peeped around the corner to make sure it was clear before proceeding. As she approached the common, she could see the outline of the funfair in the distance. She kept to the shadows and headed towards the metal enclosure; even though everything was dark and quiet, she felt there was definitely something in the air. The night seemed somewhat charged.

She watched from behind a tree: the normal entrance into the funfair was manned by a guy wearing a security armband. Mikey and his mate went in. A while later, a couple of other blokes were let in. The men were arriving discreetly; they weren't being loud or drawing attention to themselves. She needed to find another way in, so she headed towards the opposite side to the men. When clearly out of sight, she approached the security fence. *Teenagers sneak into these places all the time. It should be easy enough.*

There was a crowd control barrier that was easy enough for her to jump over. Now she had to penetrate the metal panels which were twice as high as she was. Each one was clipped together next to its neighbour twice and was set in place by a heavy-duty-looking black stand. She started pulling at a panel and kicking the stand to see how secure it was. *The mesh is too close; I'm not going to be able to climb over this by myself. I'm going to have to try to go under.* She moved around, looking for a gap that looked bigger, until she came across a large puddle between two stands. *I guess this is it.* She turned her face to the side and lay down as flat as she could in the puddle and pushed her body in the

271

muddy grass to take as much give as possible and started to scooch herself along the ground.

Once inside, wet and covered in mud, with a series of decent scratches, she started looking around. The rides, usually abuzz with flashing lights and blaring music as they try to grab attention, seemed meek, all powered down and dim. In what she guessed to be the centre of the fair was the red and yellow big top: she knew that's where they would be. She approached it from the back, got on the ground again and snuck under.

Lifting the tent was like opening a curtain to a VIP party: suddenly, there was noise, atmosphere and action. Luckily, where she had entered put her under the bleachers. She stayed there hidden away, watching through the cracks in the tiers. The seats weren't occupied, and the group of men, about forty, were all standing around the centre. They were split into two factions, each cheering for their respective champion. Sarah had entered in mid-fight: the guys were bare-chested and bare-knuckled and were slinging throws at each other. They seemed similar in build to each other.

This is brutal, compared to gloved professional boxing, it is vicious, animalistic. These men are in it to inflict pain on the other. They don't care about rules.

The man on her right then landed a clean right hook on his opponent, who spewed blood from his mouth, possibly a tooth, as he went down.

One side of the crowd cheered and backslapped each other as the referee raised the arm of the man standing as the victor. The other side carried off their fallen fighter and dumped him on the bench to lie down.

The referee motioned for silence: 'Now, we have our main event, the match you've come to see. The King of the Kales, Henry Wood, the tenth of his name, versus the Dazzler himself, Mikey North, the Fourth.'

Sarah watched as both sides parted, and their fighters emerged as the referee-cum-announcer kept spewing on. She heard words about give up or not being able to get up. Both men wore jeans with their torsos out; Mikey was a powerhouse and was definitely bigger than his opponent—*so much for weight class*—but Henry seemed a bit taller and was pure muscle. They fist-bumped one another before taking a defensive stance and starting to dance around, looking for an opportunity to strike. That didn't last long as Mikey hurtled his whole body into Henry, receiving numerous precision blows to his right kidney but they didn't seem to faze him. Up close, Mikey began his onslaught.

Sarah snuck out the same way she entered. *Hopefully, you boys are going to give me enough time.* She knew everyone would be watching the fight, as this was the main event, so she ran around freely, looking. She ignored the stinging from where she scraped herself entering the place and worked on a hunch. In this unfamiliar setting, she was slowed down. It took her longer than she would have wanted to eventually find it: she stopped in front of the attraction she had been searching for. *Thank you, little referee man.*

She took out her tools and picked the lock to the cabin of the funfair ride the Dazzler. Inside, she closed the door behind her. The name 'North' was painted on the back; she was in the right place. The control booth seemed bigger than it looked from the outside. There was another door that led on to the ride, a desk that had the ride controls, and a chair for the controller to sit. Mikey had strewn his clothes all over, along with take-away food boxes, and wedged under the desk was a Louis Vuitton Keepall. She placed it on the chair and was about to open it when the door burst open.

She looked up and stared at Mikey. He seemed surprised to find her there. He looked at her through one menacing eye; the other was swollen shut. *He's not going to listen to me, to any rational argument, with all that testosterone pumping through him.* She reached for her gun, but it wasn't there. *Damn it, I must have lost it on my way in.* She grabbed the bag, slammed the controls on the desk in front of her, kicked the chair towards him and ran out the other door.

As she made it to the metal platform of the ride, it suddenly burst into life with the lights on and music playing. She had to duck as a metal arm holding a carriage came towards her. She glanced back towards the booth; he was not inside. The speed had started to pick up and as she tried to get off the platform, another arm came darting towards her. It caught her off-guard, and she had to roll on the floor to avoid getting smacked down by it. She couldn't roll off to the side though, as the carriages were too low to the ground. She crouched up and as she did so, saw Mikey's legs: he was also on the platform, and he was moving fast towards her.

He knows the pattern of the ride; I can't stay here for long.

As the next carriage whizzed past, she jumped on it. He tried to grab her but wasn't quick enough. Now, the carriage started to individually spin all the way around while also being spun around the metal arm. She caught a few glances of him as she was getting tossed around unsupported in the carriage while holding on to the bag.

I've got to make my move and time this right.

She waited until the carriage was facing outward and jumped when the stairs to the platform were visible. She managed to clear the ride and land on the surrounding grass. The landing winded her and she inelegantly continued to roll. She didn't have time to catch her breath as a hand clamped around her throat. Mikey hoisted her up in the air. She kneed him in his right kidney, and he dropped her.

The lights and noise had attracted those remaining spectators over; given that it was Mikey's home turf, she presumed they were his mates.

The men formed a sort of circle blockade around them. She looked around; there was nowhere that she could make a run for it.

Mikey stood up now, staring at her; he got into his fighting stance and hurtled towards her.

CHAPTER 25
DAY 10

Almost instantaneously, everyone dropped to the floor, locking their hands behind their head, looking away from the 'robber.' Sam remained standing; it was just him and the masked assailant who were upright. He glanced at the time, 12:05, they were on time. They were facing each other. Sam couldn't tell where the other person was looking, as the mask covered their eyes. Part of him wanted to laugh at the ridiculousness of the situation. The intruder was wearing a rubber Halloween mask of their 'clown' of the current deputy Prime Minister, Morris Ronson. He even wore a blond wig, representing the straw mess that Ronson sported, but his body was that of a much younger man. The fake-Morris swept the gun around but never pointed it at Sam.

There was a tug on his trouser leg, 'Loni, get down.'

Sam looked down and saw Aaron. He complied.

'Just do what he says; we aren't paid enough to be heroes. They have so much insurance cover; the policy is to not risk doing anything,' Aaron whispered.

'Quiet. All the alarms have been disabled, so I have fifteen minutes. Nobody try anything funny or you will not get out of this alive!' shouted Morris. His voice was unrecognisable; it had a robotic reverberation.

The similarity of the voice to that of the receptionists from the other day sent a shiver down Sam's spine. He noticed a black disk on Morris's Adam's apple with black straps going around his neck. It was noticeable when he lifted his head up and the mask rode up a little.

'Now who is in charge here?' Morris said as he finished locking the door and started making his way around the lobby, chucking grip ties at every individual. 'Secure the person immediately next to you.' He stopped at the security guard and handcuffed him himself. 'Get up.' He pushed the guard to walk in front of him, as a human shield. 'We are all heading to the vault. Everyone, get up.' He pushed his shield towards Sam and took out a knife. 'Turn around,' he glanced at Loni's name badge and cut him loose, chucking a black sack on the floor in front of him. 'You stay here and empty the tills. No funny business, otherwise, your girlfriend here will get it.' He looked towards the manager. 'Give him the keys, except for the ones to the vault.' He shot the gun again.

It was aimed past the manager's head. Sam noted the look of fear on his face and felt sorry for the man. *I wonder if he messed himself.* 'Boss?'

'Just do what he says, Loni.' Aaron replied, chucking over a set of keys.

Once they had all disappeared through the door heading to the vault, Sam picked up the iPad from the floor and headed through another door, the one towards the safety deposit boxes. He used the passcode given to him earlier to get through the main door. Once in the room, he looked towards the door where the camera was. The light on it wasn't flashing; it had also been disabled when the power had been cut. Sam whipped out Aaron's iPad, tapped the security box icon, and then the search functionality. He entered the name Paul Impey.

Two box numbers came up: 4347 and 9010. He mopped his brow with his suit sleeve.

'Paul, they never told me you had two boxes—which one am I meant to get?' He stood there speaking out aloud, momentarily stuck. 'Hold on; they never told me because they never knew. You're as slippery as that snake. Guess you ended up like it too. Middle-age must be the expiry date for Stitchin members. You, Jack— presumably they don't offer a support program and demons eventually catch-up with you. But maybe, with your help and whatever secrets you've stashed away in that second box, I won't get that far. Now, do I have enough of the stuff to get both open?'

He pressed 4347 on the iPad and scanned the silver surfaces in front of him. A red light started flashing to his left.

'I really hope this is some sort of insurance policy you had and not just pictures of young men you fantasised about.'

He inserted the manager's master key into the slot and took out a black travel-sized deodorant-looking bottle from the sack. He took off the lid and covered his mouth and nose then put the nozzle close to the customer key slot and sprayed it. He didn't use the entire canister, as instructed.

'I hope this works.'

He looked at the slot. Nothing happened.

He shook the canister, trying to gauge how much of the liquid was left. He was about to spray some more when, out of the keyhole, a black plastic-like substance oozed out and instantly solidified. There wasn't much there to get a grip on; he had to pinch it with the tip of his finger and thumb. He turned both the manager's and the makeshift keys, and the former turned easily, but the latter was harder to turn, but it did eventually, much to his relief. 'Thanks.' He grabbed the black box from inside and placed it on the floor. He fumbled as he rushed to open it; and when he eventually managed to, he found a brown sealed envelope.

'Damn it; this is what they wanted. It is not the contents of your other box.'

He has a security box in the bank; access it, make sure no one knows what you have done. You need to secure some confidential information. It will just be some papers; they will be sealed. Do not open them; we will know, and your time with us will end abruptly.

He closed the black box, picked it up and put it back into the hole in the wall. He locked 4347 so as to leave no trace behind and went over to 9010. He shook the canister and sprayed the entire remaining contents on the lock, while using the master key on the other one. He hadn't judged it properly, and there was a larger grip on the customer key, which made it easier to open than 4347. He took the black box out and put it on the floor. He opened it; inside was another sealed brown envelope. It was the same as the one from the other security box. 'What the hell?' He stood up totally bewildered, uncertain about what to do. As he was glancing around, he saw Catherine at the door, peaking in through the window; she stood open-mouthed, gaping at him.

How much did she see?

Sam rushed over to the door and opened it; she was by herself. 'Where's your fiancé?'

'Loni, what's going on? What are you doing?' she asked, looking perplexed.

He ushered her into the room. The black security box was open on the floor, with locker 9010 open. 'What are you doing here?' he asked.

'We were waiting for you, then heard two bangs. Josh said it sounded like gunshots, so he went to investigate. He told me to wait. But I got scared, so I went looking for him but got lost. Then I saw you through the door. What's happening?'

'Nothing, just a drill. Go back to the room and wait; I'll be there in a second.'

'I can't find the room or Josh. You shouldn't do drills when customers are in the bank. We have lunch plans and need to get going.'

'This isn't a high street bank; guess you'll need to get used to private banks once you're married.' *Hopefully that will shut her up.* He started putting everything back, carefully making sure he didn't leave a trace behind. *I just hope she doesn't blab that she found me in here. I could always inject her.* He searched his inside jacket pocket and checked that the syringe that was meant originally for Loni was still in there.

'What's in the envelopes and that bag?' She pointed at them. 'You know what? It's okay. I'm going to find Josh.'

'This part of the assessment is over; I can come with you.' He glanced around to make sure he had everything, that both black inner boxes were back in their shells, and that the outer silver doors were closed and locked. The two envelopes and the iPad were in the black bag. *I still need to attempt to empty the tills. Maybe I can use her as a helper.* She looked flustered and kept pulling on the door, totally ignoring the exit button to push. 'What's the matter?' he asked. 'I said there is nothing to worry about.'

He watched her as she paused longer than seemed necessary. 'I just don't like being trapped. All we wanted was to get our mortgage; now I'm stuck in a room.'

'All you need to do is press that button to release the door.' *Should I ask her to not mention she saw me in here, say I wasn't meant to be seen, as part of my training? Or would that draw unnecessary attention to the situation?*

He didn't have time to decide as she was already out of the door. 'Wait.' She was hurrying down the corridor and then entered the door to the main lobby. *She can find it when I don't want her to.* Before he pushed the doors and joined her, he took out the two envelopes. *I don't know which is which. Even if I did, who knows which was the right box?* He folded both of them and tucked them down his waistband at his back, covering them with his suit jacket. He looked at his watch— 12:25. *I'm behind schedule.* Catherine was banging on the front doors. She turned to face Sam. He noticed her mobile in her hand.

'I've called the police. Something is going on here that isn't right. Where is everyone else? And why were you acting shifty with those safe deposit boxes? You can't just keep members of the public locked up.'

'It's a role play, a crisis scenario. You need to cancel the police, otherwise, you will get arrested for wasting police time.' *I can just tell her afterwards that I didn't want her to panic, that's why I've been telling her it's a fake situation.* 'Look, my part is to fill up this bag with certain things: some items from the security boxes and now, money from the tills.' He ran over to the door where the tills were, opened it and used the keys to open a drawer. He started shoving money into the bag. 'You can help me; I need to empty the money. I'm behind because you distracted me. Everyone else is in the vault, including the other customers. I guess that is where Josh is; they will be back soon. Then you guys can go.'

At that instant, the door that everyone had left through opened, and Aaron entered with his hands in the air, followed by the security guard who was still handcuffed and the masked Morris brandishing his gun. 'You!' he shouted, pointing at Sam. 'Bring that bag over to me!'

Catherine shrieked. 'Where is Josh?'

'Ma'am, please calm down. Everyone is safe; they're all in the vault,' Aaron whispered from the floor.

'But he wasn't with everyone else; he was with me and then went off.' She started waving her arms about and moved towards the Morris thief. Sam tried to intervene by coming out of the till area and chucking over the bag, hoping that Ronson would quickly just get out of there.

'I want my fiancé and to leave this place now.' She stood right in front of the assailant.

'Miss, calm down, please,' Aaron pleaded.

'I've called the police, I know my rights, you can't keep us here against our will.' She started to cry. 'I'm scared, I just want to go—' She lunged towards the main door. Ronson moved to intercept her and they ended up in what looked like an awkward embrace.

There was a loud bang. The gun went off.

Sam watched it all as if it were happening in slow motion. Her momentum carried her through and she landed on him, then both of them dropped to the floor with her lying on top of him. He pushed her body off himself, dropped the gun, and had his hands up by his head. He was screaming, but Sam couldn't hear anything; it all seemed to be happening in silence.

Morris knelt by the bleeding woman, trying to shake her awake. Aaron was suddenly holding—albeit very shakily—the gun, pointing it at the masked robber. The security guard was shouting.

Sam's hearing came back as he heard the gun being haphazardly emptied into his accomplice. The masked Morris-Ronson slumped down dead.

Sam dropped to his knees; he wanted to scream out his brother's name, but nothing came out apart from a sob and then a whisper, 'Mitchell.'

Sam dejectedly stared at the fancy expensive, antique clock on the wall, 16:07. He felt removed from his own body; the whole situation was so surreal. *Turn your emotions off, don't think about earlier. Don't feel anything.*

'Well, come on lad, show me yours; I've shown you mine.'

From his peripheral vision, he noticed the man pulling up his trousers and re-doing his belt. He seemed as much as a buffoon in real life as he did on the news. Sam stood up, shaking as he did so. He felt completely raw, empty. He lifted the left corner of the blazer, dragged up his shirt and pulled down his trousers and underwear so his Stitchin marks were visible. The man pointed a stumpy digit towards the marks and counted aloud.

'Eight. Excellent, excellent. Sit, dear boy, sit. It reminds me of my Eton days, all boys' private club, doing our bit for the world. You going to go to Oxford? If you say Cantab, we won't be friends.' He paused for effect. 'Hahaha, I'm just joshing with you, lad; those marks, when you get them all, will mean we're family. And don't ever let anyone say I'm the crazy uncle; I'm more like a fun big brother.'

His words made Sam shudder; he had to stop him talking. 'It will be eleven soon. This delivery to you, Mr Ronson, is my eleventh task.' *My voice sounds different.*

'Please call me Morris. That's splendid, and what a jolly task for you. Eight was definitely the hardest for me. That's really where they test your resolve, to see if you have what it takes; it's a personal one. The other deliveries—espionage, theft and dare I say it, murder—are easy.' Sam noticed that he ruffled his already straggly hair as he said 'murder.'

'Well, I guess you have people to do that for you now?' Sam pretended to laugh and picked up his bottle of beer from the table. His hand was visibly shaking, he moved his other hand to the bottle and moved it to his mouth to take a swig.

'Who knows? You may be correct. Perhaps your swan song will be to kill that nonce in charge for me. Then I can finally become Prime Minister.' Morris Ronson laughed. 'Sure you don't want to try this Tignanello?' He swallowed a large mouthful of it from his glass.

Sam wasn't sure if he was being serious. 'Last time I drank red wine, I threw up.'

'Dear boy, it was probably cheap nasty stuff. One sec.' He stopped talking and rummaged around in his jacket pocket. He pulled out a second phone that was vibrating; his first was already on the table next to his glass of wine. Sam watched as the real Deputy Prime Minister's pupils dilated in response to what he was reading. He chugged his glass of wine. 'This is a bit awkward, young fellow.'

This whole day has been one awkward mess. If I only stop to think about it I'll either scream and shout or curl up in a ball on the floor.

'I need to check that delivery you have for me. Now. You haven't looked at it, have you?'

'No, of course not,' Sam responded instantaneously. *I never got a chance to even try and look at the contents, too much going on, what with all the people getting killed to bring this to you.* He felt angry, and stood up, aggressively. 'You know what? I will try some of that wine.'

Morris Ronson clicked his fingers, and another wine glass was brought over. 'Wait here,' he told the waiter. 'I need to check something with this young man, see if anything is wrong, though I'm sure it won't be.' He raised an eyebrow towards Sam as he spoke. 'However, if it is, then I am going to leave and you're going to kill him. No hard feelings, buddy. You know how it is.' The waiter pulled out a gun and pointed it at Sam.

Having a gun pointed at him now, didn't bother him. *I never opened it but I have no idea which envelope to give you. What if I give you the wrong one?* Sam reached behind him.

'Hands where I can see them,' the waiter snarled.

'I don't have a weapon; I am reaching to get the document,' he snarled back.

Morris indicated that Sam should continue.

He felt both envelopes. His finger kept brushing between the two. *Screw this.* He pulled one out and handed it over.

Morris greedily accepted it. He took the phone that had given him the instructions and switched what looked like the flash on and passed it over the seal. He held it up, then pulled it closer to his face. 'This isn't for your eyes,' he barked at the waiter, who kept his gun trained on Sam but moved away from the table. He then opened the envelope, keeping the contents close to his face. He moved the paper to his side, making sure the back was facing Sam and the waiter.

Sam looked at him; he seemed to go paler, and his eyes were once again wild.

Morris slumped down into his chair. 'Well, that's interesting.' The jovial tone he previously had was gone. 'Have that glass of wine. Everyone should at least try decent wine once in their life.'

CHAPTER 26
DAY 10

Sarah held the ice pack to her face. The cold felt good against the heat of her skin. She watched from her seat as the two men appeared to argue. She looked down at her watch—07:32—they had been at it for over half an hour. The younger of the Mikeys, the one who had gifted her the injury, obviously didn't like what he was being told. She knew he still wanted to fight; the animal in him wasn't finished with her, especially after she had landed some blows on him. They probably didn't hurt him as much as her face was smarting, but his pride had certainly taken a hit. Being smacked on the knee and falling to the ground in front of his mates were what would have smarted more, then having your father arrive, stop the fight, send everyone home like you were a teenager who just got busted for having an unsanctioned gathering. Yep, no doubt about it, Mikey was ready to kill her. Luckily Mikey Senior stopped him, but how long she was protected was anyone's guess. It did seem like she was on borrowed time.

She glanced around again, mapping out potential escape routes. She was back in the big top, sitting on a seat right in the centre, where Wood and North had previously fought. She looked over to the father and son, who were standing right in front of the main entrance. She couldn't hear what they were saying; she could only read their body language. Junior was respectful to his father, but judging by the way he glanced over at her, his clenched fists, and flashes of anger across his face, she could tell he was fighting all his instincts to come over and try to pulverise her. *He wants to try and finish what he started earlier.*

Senior, on the other hand, while he no longer had the physical strength of his son, obviously once did. Now, he had a mature presence. *He's trying to rationalise what harming a police officer would entail. Or maybe he remembers the pass I was afforded by his mother and doesn't want to defy her. Or he wants to know the truth about what happened to his daughter. While the brother is trying to subvert the truth, he knows something. I guess my chance to find out is now or never.*

She stood up.

'Sit back down,' Mikey Senior barked at her.

Sarah did as instructed not because he demanded it of her but because as she got up, she was a little unsteady and knew she needed more recovery time. The two men continued their verbal joust for a couple more minutes, then Mikey Junior grabbed two additional chairs, dragged them to where Sarah was sitting and sat on them. He stared at her wide-eyed, then his look changed.

What's he playing at? It's like he's backing down.

'Remember to whom you are speaking, our culture and that we are still mourning my sister, and my dad's baby girl.'

He is pleading with me; he doesn't want their father to know about all of Megan's activities, and I guess, his own. 'As I have from the beginning, all I want to do is find out what happened to Megan.'

Mikey Senior sat in the extra chair. 'Well, tell us what happened. I am all ears. I want to know everything.'

Sarah thought she caught Mikey Junior shake his head left to right ever so subtly, as if saying no. 'The investigation is still ongoing; I still have a few outstanding questions that I need answers to. That's why I am here. You tell me what you know and I will do the same. We all want the same outcome. It's time to help each other.'

'Watch yourself, girly. After what happened to Megan's body when in your people's care, you have no damn right to even say her name. I have a good mind to burn down all of you.' Sarah looked at the broken father as he spoke. The many gold chains around his neck now jangled as the wearer was shaking. 'If we hadn't lost many good people—my kin—in that building collapse, all manner of hurt would have been unleashed on you police.'

'I don't blame you. It's tragic; what you have been through, no one should have had to go through that. I heard that you all went down to the hospital demanding retribution and causing quite a scene. I get it, believe me, I want you to have justice. But do it the legal way, sue the hospital and the trust. You don't want to get yourselves arrested. I know money won't even start to compensate for your loss, but the truth might. It could help you get some closure and start the mourning process. Let me get it for you.'

Mikey Senior stood up, grabbed the chair he was sitting on and bashed it into the ground. 'I thought I could deal with this, but I can't,' he said as he got up and walked away.

Sarah could do nothing but watch as her temporary defender left.

She turned her attention to the son, who was also watching the older man leave.

He spoke without looking at her. 'Let's talk. I don't want Pops knowing what Megan was really like. Let him have his idealistic memory of her and I will answer what I know. But this is between us, no recording or reporting it and letting it get back to my people. When justice, as you call it, needs to be served, you let us know and we deal with it in our own way, without the courts. Do we have a deal?'

'We have a deal,' she replied. *If it is the Stitchin, the legal system won't be an option.*

'What did Bea tell you? I presume, with your new hairdo, you were this private investigator at Desire earlier?'

The adrenaline has left his body, and seeing his father broken means just maybe, he's ready to help me. I just need to gain his trust.

'It's a wig. I was shot in the head by a man, a turncoat, who got off on hurting women. The injury, surgery and scar tissue meant my hair can't grow back, so now, I wear wigs. Guess it makes going undercover easier. Because of what I've been through I have a duty, a vocation, to make sure men don't get away with hurting women. I will bring them to justice.' He was now looking at her. 'I found out your sister worked at the club. I went to find out what I could. I thought the women would open up to me more if they thought I was hired by the management.'

'How did you find out about tonight and end up here?'

'I worked out that you were seeing Bea, so I followed her to the gym, then I followed you.'

'That silly woman; she doesn't get secrecy.' He seemed exasperated.

'She never said anything. The security guard mentioned seeing her outside of work with someone who fit your description. I worked out the rest, being a detective and all. You're quite distinctive.'

'Who is this pervert? Is it that Marc bloke? He always seems to take too much of an interest in Bea and all the women.' He paused and look lost in thought. 'It was him, he must have hurt Megan.'

'That is a possibility, that is why I need to investigate and find out who had a motive and opportunity. After, my initial assessment I think he just saw it as his role to look out for the girls. He didn't seem creepy; trust me, I can tell. But I haven't ruled him out; I haven't ruled anyone out.'

I can't tell him about the Stitchin. That will endanger him and the traveller community, and as Doughty pointed out, it is a story that won't be easy to swallow, especially given their trust issues.

'What do you think I know? What do you want from me?'

I need to tell him half of it, not enough to get him embroiled in all of this. 'The only way I can find out what truly happened to Megan is to follow the clues. To a certain extent, she led a different life to the one she presented at home. I believe it is something, someone in that double life that caused her life to be ended far too soon. The boyfriend—' she paused, to see his reaction, '—is dead. I can't ask him. My current theory is he got her involved with the wrong people.'

He knows something; since I mentioned Tom, he stopped looking at me.

'Any personal items, a diary, letters, a phone will give me something to interrogate.' She lowered her voice. 'What's in the Louis Vuitton bag? I presume it was Megan's, which she kept at the club, and when she passed, Bea gave it to you. Mikey, help me find your sister's killer. Tell me, what was in that bag?'

She watched him as he now glanced at the bag, which had been deposited on its own front row seat. He stood up. 'If there was something, anything, to lead me to what happened to her, I would have sorted all of this. There is nothing, no clues.'

'I see things differently from most people. What seems like nothing to a normal person is a piece of a jigsaw to me.'

'It was Megan's though, right? It now belongs to her family. It's not going to some police station. You can look but not take anything.' He walked over to the bag, picked it up and tossed it over to Sarah.

She stood up, mainly to assess her strength, placed the bag where she was sitting and opened it. *He alluded to this.* She rummaged through it; it was a bag full of cash. She took out a couple of wads and flicked through them, all twenties, nothing seemed to be hidden between them. She poured all the money out on to the floor, held up the bag and examined it. There were no extra pockets or hidden compartments. She turned it inside out. There was nothing.

'See—nothing.'

'Was that all that was in there? Nothing else?'

'There were some clothes, expensive ones, according to Bea. She took them to sell them, because it would be weird for her to wear them.'

'Message her and tell her to put everything from Megan's bag in a separate carrier bag. Tell her to wear gloves as she does so. We'll have to meet her and I'll collect it from her.'

He seemed to eye her suspiciously before complying. 'Did you drive here? My lift is long gone. You can drop me off.'

When his phone was back in his pocket, Sarah continued her line of questioning. 'How much money is here?'

He paused before responding. 'Twenty thousand.' He came over and started to pack it all back into the bag. 'Shall we go? I should have been there hours ago.'

'Sure.' *What is he playing at, why the sudden U-turn?* She led him back the way she came in, hoping to find her gun; and as they walked, she continued her line of questioning. 'Where did it come from?' *There was more; he's spent some of it. It's brand-new money, not notes that have been in circulation. Not the sort of money the clientele from Desire would be shoving down her G-string.*

'She earned it from that place, or from him.'

'Tom?'

Mikey spat to the floor before answering. 'Yeah.'

'Besides him, did she ever mention any other men to you, or Bea, or any of her other friends?'

He scowled at the detective. 'She wasn't a slag. She had one boyfriend from outside the community. She wasn't working her way through every gorger out there. What are you asking?'

'Like I said, I must investigate every possible avenue. Tell me what you know about Tom?'

'Nothing to tell, never met him.' His tone was defensive.

They reached the perimeter. She looked for where she entered and saw her gun, half buried in some mud on the other side. She went back under, and he pulled the fence up to make it easier for her. 'How did you find out about him?'

'Megan wasn't being discreet. I caught her out in a lie once. At times, she tried to act better than her kin and folk—smarter, like she had all the answers. From when she was little, you could tell she wanted a different

295

lifestyle.' He moved to the side, where the two fences were connected. He lifted one out of the concrete slab and came through before replacing it. 'I o'erheard her talking one time to Rosemary about a gorger boy, getting her pal to lie and cover for her. I followed her that same day. She went to Desire. I didn't know what sort of place it was. I didn't go in that first night; I just thought it was a nightclub. It was about a week later, when she had snuck out and wasn't at home, that I went back there. I went inside. She wasn't there; that is when I met Bea. I used her to get information about Megan. She got soft for me.'

Sarah didn't react.

'You gotta understand that it is different for men and women folk in our community. We won't put up with damaged goods or disgrace to our family reputation.'

Who is he trying to convince? Sarah bit her bottom lip to stop herself from answering back and risking him withdrawing his sudden confession.

'Bea told me Megan had a rich fella, but he never went there. Boyfriends weren't allowed. Then she told me to stop going there as she wanted to date me, and she would tell me anything she could about Megan.'

'What did Bea find out? What did she tell you?'

'Nothing really. Just said Megan was happy.'

She tossed him the car keys as they now stood by her vehicle. 'But—'

'You're like a bloodhound.' He got inside and started the engine.

'After everything you've said and implied about honour and family, I just can't believe you would let it go. You needed to see it for yourself.'

He stared at her. 'I tried asking her about it. I tried to be understanding. But she didn't know I had changed; my outlook in life had started to change. She thought I was the same big brother she grew up with. She never said anything. She was more secretive. She now had her own wheels. I followed her to the Land Rover once. Funny enough, I taught her to drive. When her feet could reach the pedals, she wanted to drive, but I didn't want her totalling my car, so I taught her.'

He drove off. There were a lot of vehicles on the road now as people were starting to get about their day. He didn't like just sitting there in a traffic jam and just continued talking. 'Like I said, she was strong-willed. She would have got some boy to teach her. I thought she might as well be taught proper. She 'hid' it in a supermarket carpark or down by the docks; it was never anywhere near the family or the community. She would use it to go to work, to other bars and clubs, and to his house.'

Sarah looked at him; he wasn't looking at her, just staring out at the road ahead, driving more aggressively than needed. She fingered her weapon. 'What happened?'

'I saw them together. He wasn't one of us; I doubt that he could have taken care of her in a fight. Fight off other men. He just had money, but nothing else. I told her so; we got into an argument. I wanted her to see that once he got what he wanted and after the novelty wore off, he would ditch her. Then no one from our community would even give her a second look. Gorger culture is to mess around and not settle young. Her life would have been over.'

'How did Megan react?'

He didn't answer instead he changed the subject. 'Tell me about the man who shot you?' Sarah knew what he was doing but they had come so far. She sensed she was getting close. And decided to talk to him. She told him about Manchester and they made small talk. He was driving around not really heading anywhere. This pattern of small talk and driving continued for hours.

Then he went back to their conversation, when he was ready.

'She didn't like hearing the truth. Megan didn't like hearing what she was doing to her family. She defended him and ran off mid-argument. I was so angry with her. I went to wait for her at his place, but then, something snapped, and I decided to have words with him.'

Sarah clocked his driving; now, he was barely paying attention to the traffic lights.

'The place seemed empty,' he continued, 'so I decided to go in and see what all their money looked like. I didn't do anything wrong, and the back door was open. I was mistaken. When inside, I heard voices. I couldn't make out what they were saying. I went upstairs. That's when I met her man for the first and only time.'

'What did you do?'

They were now in a town, right in the centre withing some shopping district. He looked around and saw a spot and in a sudden movement slammed the car into an empty space. It was parked nearly perfectly if not in an inelegant manoeuvre. Sarah's passenger side was next to the kerb; she glanced out and saw they were in front on an electronics shop.

His hands were twitching as he held the wheel, his body seemed, to her, to be jerking in his seat. He looked at Sarah. 'I didn't do anything. When I walked into that house, I was planning on hurting him, maybe even killing him. But honestly, it wasn't me. He was already in the bath; his wrists were slashed. He … he looked at me and gasped out Megan's name.'

'He was still alive; didn't you help?' Her eyes flickered to the left, out the window, and she saw the faces of various actors, sports stars, and strangers staring at them from the multiple television screens displayed in the store front.

He used her distracted state and jumped out the car. He started to bang his fists on top of the vehicle. She got out and stood across from him. 'I didn't know what to do and I knew I—we—would somehow be blamed. Then I heard the front door open. It was Megan; she was calling his name as she entered the house. I went into his bedroom and the window was open. Outside, I saw a man just about to scale over their wall and leave their property.'

'Who?'

'No idea—'

'We'll get you to a sketch artist,' Sarah cut in. *He looks terrible, he needed to confess, the colour is now draining from his face.*

He pointed at Sarah, the colour and his anger visibly returning to him. She turned around, following his gaze. She looked at the window—all the screens were showing breaking news. She was stunned as she stared hard at the information—a man wearing the mask of the deputy prime minister tried to rob a bank and was shot dead.

Mikey pointed at the robber's actual face, that was splashed across the screens. 'It's him, the man I saw in the garden, the one who must have killed Megan's man. That's him.'

CHAPTER 27
DAY 10

The clock in the bank showed the time as 12:40 for London. Sam dropped to his knees. He wanted to scream out his brother's name, but nothing came out apart from a sob and then a whispered, 'Mitchell.'

'I had to. Loni, you saw it; he was going to kill us all. He already killed an innocent woman. I had to defend us; he was crazy. You'll back me up, right?' Aaron pleaded. 'Get the keys, uncuff Grant. No, phone for an ambulance and the police. Quickly now.'

Sam got up, reached into his pocket, and walked over to Aaron, who was crouching over the two bodies. He took out the syringe, unsheathed the needle, and continued his approach from behind. Sam was about to stab the manager in the neck and plunge the liquid into his system, hoping it would kill him. But just as he was about to do so, Aaron pulled off the rubber mask from the dead man. Sam looked down at the face on the floor: the body's eyes were wide open, it was as if they were staring at him, piercing through his very soul. His mouth was covered with blood; it was obvious that he died in a lot of pain.

He thought about the stranger, the dead man whom he had encountered when he came off his bike; before that, everything was different. That dead body seemed to be a harbinger. From the time he laid eyes on that body, their world was thrown into further chaos, and they were thrust onto this bizarre journey. He then had a flash of Loni's bloody face.

It's not over yet.

Sam put the syringe back in his pocket. 'I need some fresh air.' He walked over to the main door and started to unlock it. At this point, the rest of the staff and customers emerged from the vault. As he worked on getting the door open, he heard Josh shouting his fiancée's name. Police were by the entrance. He raised his hands in the air and spoke totally detached from the world. 'I work here. The robber was shot dead by the manager. A customer was also shot.'

'Step back and keep your hands in the air.'

It was a couple of hours before he was allowed to go outside and get some air. He had to return to give his statement properly, but they decided that everyone needed respite. As he walked down the steps to the building, he noticed the car that had dropped him off earlier. It was parked down one of the side streets, waiting. He headed over to it, opened the passenger door and climbed in. He looked at the driver's seat and burst out crying.

The car drove off.

'What's the matter? Are you hurt?'

'For a moment I thought, I thought you were dead.' Sam reached over and touched his brother's hand, which was on the steering wheel. 'You were meant to be my accomplice; I thought it was you under the mask.'

'I'm fine, I've been waiting in the car all this time. I swapped places with Tony. What happened in there?' Mitch asked.

'He was shot dead. Don Luciano's man was killed by the bank manager. He shot some woman and then was killed. It's all gone wrong.'

'After I dropped you off, I got a call from the Don telling me to let Tony go in the bank in my place. He wanted stuff stolen, and said as I was only going in to be a distraction for you to complete the mission, it would be better to let Tony go in and be the distraction, plus fill his pockets. But I made him promise before he did anything to make sure you got what you needed and to help you. Did you get the papers?'

'Yes, but—'

'Well, we've done our task. Next, all we need to do is deliver the papers to someone at a bar. The location is in the sat nav; we're about twenty minutes away. I'll go in with you to make sure all is good. Then I suppose I better go see the Don and explain about Tony. We don't want those guys on our case. Whatever happened in the bank, you did your part, and nothing that happened was your fault. Right?'

Your fault. At those words, Sam jolted awake. The Eurostar also jolted. Sam looked at the electronic display—the time showed it was 19:15. He then looked at his brother who sat opposite him and by all appearances was fast asleep. After the shock of finding out his brother was alive, he had been feeling anger and resentment. The whole thing was just a few hours ago, but the fact that he couldn't sleep because the events kept playing in his head told him he really needed to sort out his feelings. Outside, it was dark. *We must be in the tunnel.*

He glanced around. The carriage was about three-quarters full, mainly with families given that it was still the Easter holidays. No one was paying them attention.

'Mitch.'

There was no response. Sam got up and headed to the restroom. He locked the door. He briefly looked at himself but found it was a stranger that stared back at him in the mirror. *I don't recognise myself anymore.* He splashed some cold water on his face before putting down the toilet seat and sat down, then he reached around and pulled out the second envelope from his waistband. He briefly held it in his hands before ripping the package open.

Inside was a single sheet of A4 paper. He took it out and stared at it, turned it over and then back. One side was blank, but the other had something on it. As he looked at the content, he caught a glimpse of his reflection in the mirror and the bewildered look on his own face. It reminded him of the Deputy Prime Minister's face when he also examined the contents of the envelope Sam had given him. That, too, had only one sheet of paper in it.

They can't have been mixed up; if so, I would be dead.

Sam spoke to himself in a hushed tone. 'And Morris Ronson's paper seemed to be what he was expecting. Maybe, it wasn't quite what he wanted, as it did seem to initially shock him given his body language and mannerisms. Then he started mumbling. Now, what was he saying? 'Sands' and 'blood', two words that don't really go together. Sands, blood, sands, blood, sands. Then I tried your wine as you were working out how to achieve your orders. What did you say to me?' Sam replayed the conversation in his head.

'You must take me for a right *quockerwodger*.'

'I don't know what that means.'

'Puppet, dear boy. But let me tell you this. Everything I do is because I want to. Speaking of puppets, it looks like I have the bloody good job of informing you about your next job. Now, where did you say that brother of yours is again?'

'He had to return the car and stuff.'

'Well, it looks like it's for both of you. You're going on a little trip, a chance to lie low in case there is any heat from your early escapades.'

'What sort of trip?'

'Paris. You're going to Paris. I'll sort passports and tickets, but I will need a picture of your brother to do that. Then all you have to do is get on the Eurostar, sit back, and then it's amusement time.'

'That's it, that's the mission?'

'Well, no, you'll have to deliver a little something.'

'Obviously. What is it this time—drugs or guns?'

'I don't know. All you did was deliver the location and the name of the recipient to me. As for what it is, I guess somewhere en route, that will become clear. We are all tiny parts in a well-oiled machine.'

Sam suddenly bolted upright. 'Blood on his hands—he was muttering about blood on his hands.'

He took another look at the piece of paper in his hand. It was a series of letters and numbers that meant absolutely nothing to him. Weirdly, while it made no sense, he could see there was some sort of pattern to it. *I will crack you.* He folded the piece of paper and stuffed it in his wallet, then discarded the envelope after making sure nothing else was in it. He then flushed the toilet and washed his hands in case anyone was waiting outside. He headed back to his seat. Mitch was awake and was talking to someone, who was sitting where he had been.

'What is he doing here?' Sam said under his breath. He sat next to the man, to trap him in. 'Still alive then. So what's going on here?'

Jack looked at Sam. 'Ah, Tweedledee. I was wondering where you were.'

'Don't push me, man. Remember, I know where your brother and mistress live,' Mitch interjected.

Jack appeared unconcerned and started to address Sam. 'As I was telling your brother, I was sent here to deliver my finished product to you. Look over there in the luggage rack. See that large grey Samsonite suitcase at the bottom. It belongs to you guys now.'

'What are we meant to do with it?' Mitch asked.

'What's in it?' Sam asked at the same time.

Sam noticed a wry grin flash across Jack's face. 'So many questions. They don't like one person to have too much information. They're worried someone will put all the pieces together.' He pulled out a white envelope and chucked it down on the table towards Mitch. 'You know who else works like this, keeping the information restricted to certain cells, not knowing who else is in the organisation.' The bitterness crept back in the voice, just like how he spoke to them when they first encountered each other. 'In fact, not knowing what the master plan is and just blindly following orders like a good foot soldier. Terrorists.'

'Shouldn't we work together then and help each other? We aren't your enemy; this organisation is.' Sam looked at his brother as he spoke, hoping for support, but Mitch was reading their instructions.

'You opened it,' the older brother asked Jack.

'You are to deliver the suitcase to a hotel near the Gare du Nord. The Hotel Paris Terminus Nord. There is a conference taking place there; just check the bag in with the attendees' luggage,' he answered, making no attempt to hide his indiscretion. 'I needed to know. It's not like I wouldn't have found out later anyway. Even though they control the news, I am sure I would have read some lame excuse, some contrived accident.'

'What's in the suitcase?' Sam asked again.

'I am not meant to tell you. Like I said, they don't want any of us to have all the pieces of the puzzles. But I want you to know. Remember, I never wanted to make it, I wanted out, but you forced my hand. I told you that what happens next will be on you. You don't know the little pleasure it has given me when I sat down here and found out it was you two who will be the deliverers; it's poetic justice. I have completed my part and have now handed it over, so my jobs are done. I am out of it now. What happens next is all on both of you.'

'What is it?' Sam knew the device master was toying with them. In the pit of his stomach, he had a bad feeling; he knew what it was. He just prayed he was wrong. Everything leading up to this moment was telling him he wasn't.

Blood on his hands. Serious consequences.
Terrorists.

The silence was penetrated by an announcement, first in French and then in English. It was telling the passengers that they would shortly be arriving at the Gare du Nord and to not forget their personal belongings.

'Oh, the irony.' Jack looked at Mitch, then at Sam. 'An explosive, an incendiary device, a bomb.'

Sam closed his eyes as his worst fears were confirmed. As he reopened them, Jack was slowly mouthing the word 'Boom!' as he pulled his hands apart and spread his fingers to act out an explosion.

Mitch looked around and then knocked Jack's hands. 'Why did you have to tell us that? You're not absolving the blame by putting it on us.' He spat out the words quickly. 'You made it, so whatever happens is your fault. It's your skills. We might have to deliver it, but we were never meant to know what it was. This is nothing to do with us.'

'Ignorance is bliss. Your brother wanted to know, so I answered. It's up to you boys what you do next. Deliver it and kill many, or don't and then they will send someone to kill you.'

Sam wasn't listening. His elbows were on the table and his hands were on his face.

Jack stood up to leave. 'The explosive yield is high. They really want the person dead. Collateral damage will take out the whole room. I looked up which conference is taking place at the hotel. It's just a bunch of scientists.'

Sam passively swivelled his legs into the aisle to let him pass. As Jack passed him, he grabbed his jacket. 'How do we stop it?'

The device master looked down at him with a certain pity in his eyes. 'You can't. I couldn't, even if I wanted to. I'm walking across the platform and getting a train back to London. In one hour, the bomb is going off. Where it does is up to you. When it does, you want to be as far away as possible, otherwise, well, you can guess. And I want, you,' he paused and looked at Mitch too, 'you both, to survive, so you can live with the guilt, like I will have to.'

Sam's hand fell away. Jack adjusted his coat and walked away, heading in the direction opposite where he had indicated that the package for them was. The rest of the passengers seemed to take this as their cue and the herd followed the leader. Sam and Mitch remained seated, looking at each other in disbelief.

The train screeched into the station and another announcement boomed out for everyone to disembark. 'What are we going to do?' Sam asked his brother, who was just staring out the window, at the people getting off the train.

'I will complete the mission. I want you to get out of here. Go and catch the next Eurostar home. He said he is heading back. I bet there is one leaving shortly. Make sure you're on it. Avoid him; he's not worth it. And just don't look back.'

'I'm not leaving you, but that's not the point. I don't think we should do this.'

'Well, what are we going to do? We can't leave it here; this station is rammed and full of families. For all their faults, they aren't going to want to draw attention to themselves. If I just take it to the place, it's bound to be more discreet. Who knows, maybe someone else will pick it up, know how to disarm it and take it on to wherever it is meant to go next.'

'You don't really believe that.' Sam wasn't sure if his brother heard him or deliberately chose to ignore him; he presumed the latter. Mitch had already stood up and was walking over to the case. Sam rushed to join him as he proceeded to exit the train.

'Get out of here, Sam. You did the heavy lifting infiltrating the bank and then dealing with everything that went down there. Let me do this one.'

'But Mitch, it's a bomb, it's going to kill people,' Sam whispered.

'If I go now, I can get it in place and have enough time to get out of there. If I waste time and we try to come up with some sort of plan, which will mean our own downfall, I won't be able to escape the blast zone. Let me go and do this for us.'

'What about the innocent people?'

'I can't think about them. I wish it wasn't like this, believe me. But it's us or them.'

'But Mitch—'

'Sam, it's on me. You have nothing to feel guilty about, it's all me doing this one. Look, Jack is getting on that train. Get on it too, buy a ticket on the train.' Sam found himself being escorted onto the train by his brother. 'Promise me you will stay on it. If you don't, I will wait for it to depart and that will mean I won't have enough time to escape. Is that what you want?'

'No.'

'Okay, so promise me.'

'Okay. Just go.' Sam boarded the return Eurostar. He looked at Mitch from the door, who was standing still on the platform, with the suitcase next to him. 'Go.' Sam made his way further onto the train and looked for a seat. He sat in the first one he could find that was empty. Only when he was seated and looked out the window did he see Mitch leave. Sam started tapping his legs with his fingers.

I can't, I can't just sit here.

He stood up. Then sat back down again. 'No.' He jumped up and battled his way off the train from the now constant stream of passengers boarding. When he finally made his way back onto the platform, his brother was long gone. He looked for the closest exit and headed out the station. Once outside, he looked around and asked the first person who stopped close to him. 'Excuse me, do you know the way to the Hotel Paris Terminus Nord?'

The first two people ignored him; the third stopped and listened, and responded in broken English. 'Go through the station. Other exit. Nord. Nord,' while pointing her finger back towards the station.

'Thank you,' Sam called back, as he had already turned and started to make his way back into the station. He stood in the middle of the central concourse, looking for a sign. There were too many exits. And he didn't have time to go the wrong way again. There was an information bureau, with a couple in front of him. He stood behind them, while the customer at the booth, an American, was asking the way to the Louvre.

'Do you know where the Hotel Paris Terminus Nord is?' he asked the couple in the queue.

They looked at him and then at each other. Then one of them pointed to the exit immediately to his left. The American was still talking; Sam was feeling impatient and pushed through the door. There was a large red bear statue outside. He was standing next to it, about to ask someone else where to go. When he looked up and saw the hotel, it was on the other side of the road. He assessed the traffic from his bear position. It was zooming along, without letting up. He couldn't run across. He scanned the road looking for the official place to cross the road.

Suddenly, there was a bang. A smoke plume, dust, glass and screams all exploded from across the road, from where the hotel was. Sam didn't realise it at first but the blast had lifted him off his feet, then he felt it when it sent him hurtling against the base of the statue.

CHAPTER 28
DAY 11

Sarah sat in the darkened room, waiting. She wanted to shut her eyes and catch some much-needed sleep. The night before was Fight Night, followed by the driving around and getting the confession from Mikey, after which she headed straight to work to follow up the leads, but then got put on terror threat level work and had to graft all through the night. She hadn't slept.

She touched her bruise and thought how far she and Mikey had come since he first gave that to her. He never admitted it to her, but she could tell that finding Tom with his wrists slashed, knowing that someone did it to him and not being able to tell anyone about it really messed with his head.

Or was it that he planned to kill Tom, but when faced with the reality of death, got scared of how close he came and the real consequences?

As she waited, she replayed the recent conversations and events of the previous day and the morning that led her to this moment in her head.

I am getting closer to the truth; I can feel it.

A shell-shocked Mikey had got back in the car and started the engine. *I had no choice but to join him.* He pulled off, he didn't even check if it was safe to do so, and started driving and talking.

'The man is dead. He killed her boyfriend—I just thought it was some rich, posh-person business. Rich people are the dodgiest crooks out of everyone. Their scams are always large scale.'

He was talking fast, was he guilty for his inaction?

'Part of me thought maybe his folks might have ordered it because of Megan being his girlfriend. But that would be too far for Lord and Lady Twat. I hid in the bedroom when Megan found the body in the bath. She was screaming it was all her fault. I was not sure what she meant by that. I should have just asked her but I couldn't admit I was there.'

He ran a red light.

'I was searching for that man, to no avail, he said. 'You don't know how much I tried to find him and now he shows up dead on the news. I wanted to put the screws on him and find out what happened. Then Megan disappeared, I never thought he was involved. It was only when you came here filling my head with that stuff about her man getting involved in something suss. I am so stupid, I should have linked all this together earlier.'

'There is no reason or at the time evidence for you to have made the link. There still might not be, I need to work it out.' *I said to try and make him feel better, reassure him.*

'We can't find out anything from a dead man; I guess that is your job. You now do your "detectiving" and find out what happened if you must. Remember what I said to you at the beginning: all of this is between us, you don't go around mentioning this, reporting it in your little files. Megan's reputation must be protected. I don't want to get dragged into going on record or have anything I have told you broadcast. If you do find out anything else, you let me know and let us administer our own justice: an eye for an eye. Lastly, all the money, the compensation from the car and what you people did to her is ours.' He stopped talking and pulled up outside a block of flats.

Bea was waiting outside. She gave me the best death stare she could manage, then made a beeline for Mikey and wrapped her arms around him, kissing his face and asking about the fight. She whispered in his ear.

'Just show her the stuff,' Mikey ordered.

Bea sauntered over to me and handed over a bag that she had been carrying over her shoulder. 'It's all in there, her clothes. That's all that was in there.'

I opened the bag and rummaged through it. Pulling out a piece at a time, examining it and handing to Bea to hold. The integrity of the evidence was long gone and we were not going down an official route now. It was just designer clothes: various pieces, including lingerie, which caused Mikey to look away. 'What's this?' *I asked as I pulled out the clear glass tube, which was empty.*

'She had her eau de parfum in it, Coco Noir. Doesn't really look like a nice perfume dispenser, if you ask me.'

I took off the lid and sniffed the jar; it smelt of an aroma I didn't recognise. So I let Bea sniff it. 'Are you sure this is that scent?'

'Yes, babes, I introduced her to the scent. I used to wear it.'

'I'll be in touch.' *I got in her car and drove off.*

Back at the police station in BR-4 I was waiting for the Megan evidence to be brought back. The day was coming to a close and the few staff around were busy, my case wasn't a priority. *I didn't engage with them as I wanted to keep a low profile. As I waited I read the information about the bank robber.*

Before his death, he was known to the police, as a 'known associate of mafia connections.' *Then I hypothesised,* 'Tom Denton was a potential Stitchin recruit, initiated by his uncle. They killed Tom midway through his initiation. Did he fail or do something wrong? They used Tony Marino. He then potentially killed Megan, because she was involved or knew something. Or had taken something, the green drug, that she shouldn't have. Tony then broke into a bank, attempting to steal money, and got himself shot dead. It's that last bit that seems too sloppy, too exposed, not what we know of them. They don't need to steal money from a bank. Was he on his way out of the organisation, and that was his retirement plan? Or was he there to get something else?'

There was a knock at the door, and the evidence duty officer brought in a sealed bag. Once he had left the room, *I took out the bottle of Coco Noir. Shook the bottle, which I remembered about when Bea said its name.* Because the bottle was black, you couldn't see what was actually in it. If Megan decanted the original into the dispenser, was something else in here?

I opened the bottle; the smell that had lingered in the dispenser wasn't present in this bottle. I emptied the

317

evidence bag and poured a little of the contents into it. The fluid in the bag was a green liquid.

This is it; what did Mel say? 'Some sort of chemical in her body that preserved her organs and gave her kidneys a green discolouration to them.' Then when Mel tried to have this liquid analysed she was killed, the sample destroyed, and no trace of it was left behind.

I held the bag up to the light and looked at the emerald sheen coming from it. It was when this sample entered the system—that's when everything was annihilated: Megan, the laboratory, the people who knew about it. Is this what everyone is dying for?

There was a cough from the door. *I palmed the Coco Noir bottle before turning around.* 'What happened to you and what's that?' Alistair pointed at the green liquid.

'We have a lot to catch up on, Commissioner. As for this, I don't know. From what I can tell, the Stitchin are wiping out all knowledge of it. At first, I thought it was a new drug that they had produced, but now, I'm uncertain. Sir, you need to have this analysed, but it needs to be done in secret. It can't go on the network for cross-analysis, because when the hospital guys tried that, well, you know what happened to them.' *I handed the bag over to him.*

'Have you seen the news?'

'More on the bank incident?'

'No, Paris. A bomb—the information is trickling in. We are going to raise our own terror threat level. I need to go now and meet with COBRA. I want you with me, your help, your analytical skills. This is national security and has to be priority. Join me.'

'Yes, sir, of course.' *I followed him out of the room.*

As we walked he examined the bag. 'Is this all of it?'

'Yes.' *I lied.*

'It is not much to work on. I am not sure if any lab will be able to work with a sample this small. But I will try for you, on the downlow. Also, as you mentioned it, the man at the bank wasn't related to your Stitchin; he didn't have the marks. I discreetly looked at the body myself. I'm sure you've read his file by now. He has mafia connections, not mysterious organisations. Now clear your mind on that and help us on this terror threat.'

I didn't return to BR-4 until over twelve hours later, and by then my mind was fried. Dougie was waiting for me. 'I have that information you wanted.' He passed me a piece of paper. 'I am not sure if this is still relevant; I actually had it ready a while back but you hadn't been in, hope you've been okay.' He looked at my face as he spoke.

I had to stop myself from placing my hand on my chest, where the real pain was. 'Don't worry about me, I am fine. This I did while training.' *I smiled at him and took the piece of paper.* 'Thank you; let's catch up properly later.'

'Yes, ma'am.' He took the cue and left.

I opened the piece of paper. It had details on James Yates, the registered owner of the car in the lake. I already knew he was the Dentons' neighbour and had asked Dougie to provide background information on him days ago that I had nearly forgotten about.

I scanned what little information there was, then got to the family section. He has a wife and two sons: a Mitchell and a Samuel. When I saw that name, it all came together.

Sarah was brought back to the present as the light in the room she sat in was switched on. It was pitch-black outside; it was nearly the end of the day. She wasn't sure if she had fallen asleep or not. The man who turned it on didn't notice her at first. When he did, he jumped back, startled.

'Hello, Mitchell Yates.' Sarah beamed at him, tapping her gun, which was on her lap. It wasn't pointed at him.

He closed the door. 'You.' He stumbled the word out. 'What are you doing here? I've had a long, crazy day and I don't have time for whatever this is. Explain yourself.'

'Put your hands in the air where I can see them. My real name is Detective Sarah Silver, but I have a feeling you already know that. Now I have some questions for you, and I want the truth.'

She watched him as his pupils dilated. He complied; she walked over to him and patted him down for any weapons.

'This seems like a very elaborate way to cop a feel, pardon the pun. Seriously, what do you want?'

She stepped away. 'Drop your trousers.'

'Are you for real? Is this some sort of sick joke?'

She trained her gun on Mitch. 'I think you know what I'm looking for.'

He banged his hands on his head. 'You're involved in this. You've played me.'

'Funny, that was what I was going to say.' She stared back at him.

He pulled down his trousers and part of his underwear and revealed his markings.

'Twelve, and they look relatively fresh. You're still a trainee?' *He never had any marks when we first met; I would have noticed. Or was I his first mission?*

'Yours?'

'I don't have any.' She exposed her skin where the markings should have been. 'I am a detective investigating your future employer. I plan to bring them and everything they've been doing to light. Now you're going to help me.'

He covered himself up again and sat on the bed. 'One thing I have learned from them is that members always identify themselves to each other; it's like some sort of ritual. A badge of honour. If you are who you say you are, will you help us?'

She dragged the chair she had been sitting on over to the bed. She kept enough distance between them in case of a surprise attack, but it was close enough for her to look into his eyes. 'I don't trust you yet. Answer some questions for me and we'll take it from there.'

'Anything, but if you're legit you have to promise to help us. Please.'

'Let's start from the beginning. When we first met at that restaurant, was I a mission, someone to sleep with and pump for information or keep tabs on?'

'No. I slept with you because you are hot and gave off the vibe that you wanted me to. At that time, I wasn't even involved with them. That happened shortly after we met.'

'And that second time when we bumped into each other and you didn't perform, what was that about then?' There was no scolding in her voice; the way she spoke was very factual.

'You were outside my work. I was feeling down and wanted some companionship. It had nothing to do with them. I shouldn't have tried to be intimate; beforehand, they had a catheter shoved up me, that's why I couldn't. I wanted to see if it still worked but when it came to it I was still sore and mentally I was feeling terrible at being their minion.'

I just wanted a cuddle too, to briefly forget Pete. 'Okay, who lives in this house and how well did they know your neighbour, Tom?' She watched as he paused; he was thinking. 'You know he was Stitchin too, but he didn't make it as far as you.'

'My brother, Sam, lives here with me. Please swear whatever happens you will help him and keep him safe. He's innocent. He didn't know Tom or have anything to do with him. Everything bad that has happened, I did them all. He just delivered packages here and there. We had to. Look, both our parents left four years ago. Just upped and went. He was thirteen, I was twenty-one. We couldn't tell anyone as he would have been taken away and put into care. To the outside world, we had to pretend that everything was good. We haven't really interacted with anyone. The Dentons never bothered us, and we kept away so that it appeared like there were no problems at home. We had money to last a while, then I took multiple jobs to pay for everything. We sold off the most expensive things we could, when we needed to. I advertised our car for sale maybe six months ago. Tom bought it. He paid cash. That was my last interaction with him.'

'The Silver Range Rover, registered to a James Yates?'

'Yes, it was my Dad's. It's not like he was around to use it. After he left, I used to drive it, but then, we needed the money more, so I sold it.'

'What about his girlfriend; did you ever meet her?'

This question was met with a long pause. Mitch stood up and walked over to the window. 'I am going to answer you honestly because I want you to help my brother—to—help us. But I want you to know that I am not proud of this. I did meet her; it was only a few times though, both really short and slightly peculiar.'

'Go on.'

'The first time, I was paid to meet her and do stuff. Erm ... that sounds wrong; hear me out. I presume Tom's parents didn't like her, given her background and all, so they got someone to pay both me and her money to kiss and make out. I wouldn't usually participate in anyone's sick games, but I needed the money and it was easy. I didn't realise what would happen. They told me where to meet her, that she would reciprocate, everything. I presume they took some pictures and showed him. I guess they wanted to split them up and it would be more effective if she cheated with someone he knew. But it backfired big time.'

'What do you mean?'

'It was shortly after we did that, that he ... he took his own life.' His voice trembled.

She could tell it cut him up. She wanted to go over to him and console him, but something held her back. Then she watched as he just sank down to the floor and started to cry. He was trying to muffle the sounds, which meant his body was shaking. This time, she let go; she could feel what he was feeling.

She put her gun on the bed and laid down on the floor behind him. She wrapped her arms around him in a warm hug to comfort him. She spoke soothingly to him to calm him down. She wanted to tell herself that she was doing so because she needed him lucid to answer more questions and tell her details about each and every stitch. But that would have been a lie. She knew broken, damaged people; maybe that is what first drew her to him, and this time, she didn't feel like being the cold-hearted detective. She embraced and nurtured him to try and regain some of her own humanity.

CHAPTER 29
DAY 12
Part I

'Was I imagining things, or did you have a woman in your room last night?' Sam whispered to his brother, as the blacked-out car drove them to their destination.

Mitch looked at the black divider that gave them privacy from the driver, whom they never saw even when they got in the vehicle. 'It was that Manc woman I hooked up with a while back.'

Sitting still was making his bruised back feel even more sore, so he was irritable, plus guilt was eating away at him like a parasite. 'When did you even have time to arrange a hookup?'

Is he not bothered about what we did in Paris? I wanted to talk to him about it, and about what I had to do as a consequence but he was busy entertaining a woman all night.

His voice lowered that Sam could barely hear him. 'Turns out she is Old Bill, she sought me out, but I'll tell you the rest at the club.'

Sam didn't speak these words he just practised them in his head. 'Mitchell I am sorry. I can't live with myself and what we've done from the dog to Paris. And deep down I know you want to do the right thing too. Why else were you speaking to a policewoman? So I have done it for us. I have told the police about Jack and where he will be. They can arrest him, the Don, and we can turn ourselves in. It is time we right all the wrong we have done.' Just saying these words to himself and knowing their role in all of this was coming to an end so they could start making an amends for their sins made him feel mildly better.

I just need to tell Mitch. He hesitated. 'Argh … the horrible Falcon. Given what happened to us last time we went there, and the fact that this is the penultimate act, it is not going to be a simple case of chaperoning and then introducing Jack Dixon to Don Luciano. Mitch, don't try and protect me, what will happen will be.'

Mitch continued speaking in a hushed tone. 'We'll be okay; the Don likes us. He didn't care about Tony. To be honest, I think he wanted him dead. The Italians aren't even part of the…' Mitch drew an 'S' in the air.

'How do you know that?'

'He told me he's a goon for hire. Given his connections, he is paid to carry out some unfavourable tasks; he doesn't even know the employer. It is some legacy thing handed down to him by his father. He'll have our backs; he is a man of honour.'

'That's interesting. But it's the other one I am more concerned about. You know what a slippery bugger he is. Given what he created, what it did, I can't see him complying with us.' *And I want him there for the police to get him.*

'His mistress is already at the club. That should entice him to join. Look, there he is, waiting.' The car slowed down outside Jack's house, where he stood waiting on the kerb. 'See, he is playing ball, they have him in line. Soon, this will be all over for us.'

The last part is true, this will all be over and we can try and get back our humanity. I think being full Stitchin members would have been a very dangerous and deadly path for us and we wouldn't have been able to live with ourselves. I am doing this for us.

Jack pushed his way into the car. He was dressed smartly, as were they all in order to get into the club. He reeked of alcohol and looked at both brothers and smiled. 'You made it. I'm actually glad to see you.' He didn't bother slurring out the words quietly. 'We're the same now...' He awkwardly pointed between the three of them. 'Murderers.'

'You're drunk,' Mitch cut in. 'Maybe you need to think before speaking and save this conversation for later.'

'Speaking of drinks, isn't there a bar in here?' Jack banged on the divider. 'Where's the champagne?'

There was no response.

Sam spoke. 'We'll be there soon, and then you can have all the alcohol you want.'

'Don't you want to get smashed too? Erase the memory of what *we* did?'

'Listen, Sam didn't have anything to do with your creation. I delivered it. He's innocent; he tried to stop me, so his hands are clean,' Mitch interjected. 'Anyway, why are you suddenly so moral, with a conscience now? I bet you have done unspeakable things in your past. You wouldn't have got to where you are without getting your hands dirty.'

'Don't lecture me, boy.'

Sam stopped listening to the argument, as they were coming up to the club. It wasn't that that had distracted him: a woman who was literally dressed to kill made her way to the front of the queue. She flashed the back of her hand at the bouncer and the security rope was dropped so the female assassin could make her way in.

CHAPTER 30
DAY 12

Part I

Sarah stared out the back window as the unmarked van drove them to their destination. Being part of the special task force Doughty set up meant she had to go. She was not sure if he truly wanted her help or if he wanted to keep her close by given her recent actions. She had to completely disavow that it had anything to do with her ongoing investigation and more to do with her wanting to help and be a team player.

Commissioner Doughty barked his orders to the team. 'This club, the Falcon, has mob ties. That is not our concern; we are to go in undercover and apprehend this man.' He handed out the picture. 'Jack Dixon. We believe he has vital information regarding what happened in Paris. We got an anonymous tip off that he would be here, the caller knew things about Paris which isn't public knowledge, so we are treating this as a serious lead. If Dixon is there we need to apprehend and extract him. The fact that he is on our turf; I can't stress enough what is at stake here.'

Sarah smiled at Dougie, whom she could tell was extremely pumped for this opportunity. *I don't care what they say; this is all tied together. Megan frequented the Falcon Club; she had their membership card on her. She was potentially killed by Tony, who killed Tom. He broke in the bank for some reason. He is associated with the people who own this club. This club where we need to seize a man, Jack Dixon, who has potential answers about the Paris bombing. Which means the Stitchin was involved in the Paris bombing.*

'Someone was really making a statement, killing a bunch of academics. Usually, terrorist attacks are more random, getting as many people from the general population as possible. This seems a lot more deliberate. I can understand why the French authorities want to speak to him so desperately. It will be interesting to see what this man has to say,' PC Barranger stated.

'I see Silver's smarts are rubbing off on you. Keep your eyes and ears open, while we are there to get him. It will only serve us well to see if he is meeting anyone or who his associates are.' Doughty took out his phone and started to read a message.

That's exactly the point it wasn't standard terrorism, it was for a purpose. It has the Stitchin written all over it. Why can't the Commissioner see this?

'That was from DGSE, thanking us for the update and offering assistance, they are on their way. We don't have time to wait for them so we're going ahead but they will be here for questioning. I don't want the French secret service running God knows what on our soil if we mess this up.' Doughty paused before continuing, 'Even though it happened on French soil and French nationals made up the majority of those murdered due to the hotel staff, it was an international scientific conference, with many countries, including our own, losing people. This thing is going to get very complicated politically.'

'The keynote speakers were Canadian, as well as French and English. There were high numbers of Swedish, Spanish, and Saudi Arabian delegates.' Dougie read off a sheet. 'Just over twenty of the academics and five hotel workers were killed, and a further fifteen people are in hospital with serious injuries. The death toll is expected to rise. Sorry day for geneticists—'

'What was that?' Sarah interrupted him.

'ESHG, the scientific meeting. European Society of Human Genetics mainly attended by geneticists…'

Sarah stopped listening to him. She continued staring out the window, thinking. *How could I miss it? I was looking for the missing link, and it has been staring me in the face all this time. It all goes back to their green liquid; that's the connection. She thought of the Coco Noir bottle and the secret substance it held and how she had stashed it away safely. I bet it has something to do with genetics. Genes. That is why they wiped out people with knowledge in that field, or maybe it was a specific person, and the rest were collateral damage.*

The van had stopped opposite from the club, and she caught a glimpse of Mikey Junior embracing the bouncer, who she thought looked like he came from the traveller community too. Mikey entered the club, followed by three friends.

What the hell is he doing here?

CHAPTER 29

Part II

The club seems a lot busier this time. Maybe it's because we're not in the private room. In front of them was a sea of clubbers, dancing with their arms thrown in the air. The music was banging. Sam recognised the song: *4 minutes* by Madonna with Justin Timberlake and Timbaland. It was an old one but currently playing as a new super club remix.

'I'm outta time, and all I got is four minutes.'

Jack stood next to him and on the man's other side was Mitch. Jack seemed to be looking around; it was soon obvious that he had been looking for the bar. As soon as he spotted it, he made a beeline for it. Mitch went with him. Sam wanted to grab his brother and warn him of the upcoming raid but he stayed where he was, scanning the crowd, looking for her. *I need to speak to her and find out what she's doing here and warn her.*

He thought he saw her. He moved from his spot and started to work his way through the crowd. The gyrating dancers didn't move out of the way; they didn't want to give up the space they had secured for themselves. Sam felt the heat and sweat from the clubbers; it was making him feel claustrophobic. His heart was pounding, he felt hot, and wearing a shirt wasn't helping. It started to stick to him. As he tried to battle his way through the party, he was getting all sorts of knocks and bangs from the horde. It felt like they were swallowing him up. He looked up to the ceiling. A strobe light caught him right in the face, dazzling him. He felt someone prodding his back and leading him out of there. It brought him back into the moment.

It was her.

She escorted him off the dancefloor. Walking with her was easy. The previous resistance of navigating the pack had gone. They seemed to clear a way out for her, as she definitely gave off a 'move out of my way' vibe.

When they were off the dancefloor and away to the side, they both asked the other, 'What are you doing here?'

'You shouldn't be here, Samuel.'

'What do you mean? Why are you here?' he asked her.

'I have business here.' She pulled out her phone and showed him the first part of her instruction.

'The London cell has been lost. Eliminate all of them. Falcon Club today at 23:00.' He read it out aloud in utter disbelief.

'This wasn't an optional task for me. It was an order. You can't be here; it is all about to go down. You need to get out of here.'

'Well, don't waste time, give me a sign, tell me how you wanna roll.'

'The police are coming, you need to get out of here. They will arrest everyone and clean it up that way. Let me find my brother and tell him what is going to happen. We were sent here to do a task, our thirteenth one. We are about to complete it and then pay for everything bad we have done. I won't mention you. Run.' He stared into her eyes as he spoke.

'What have you done?' she asked while shaking her head. 'Sweetheart, take care of yourself.' She gave him a peck on his cheek and he watched as she vanished back into the crowd.

Sam moved back to where Mitch had left him, on a raised section that was not part of the main dancefloor. He figured he would have a better view from there, and he wouldn't have to be in the thick of it. From there, he was looking all around, trying to find his brother. He noticed that nearly directly opposite him but separated by the sea of dancers, the booth was occupied. Where it had been empty, he could now see Don Luciano drinking with a beautiful woman, flanked by Matteo, the Don's henchman who had pistol-whipped Tony at the poker game, and someone else whom he didn't recognise. Sam was distracted by a sudden commotion on the dance floor—he saw Mitch pushing people away from Jack who was double-parked, holding two drinks, and having trouble navigating the dancers. They were heading towards the Don and his private booth.

He then noticed to his three o'clock the detective woman, Sarah Silver, who had been at his door enquiring about Tom, the travellers, and Megan North. She was staring at Mitch. Sam made his way on the dancefloor and started pushing towards his brother. He stopped moving when he noticed a red laser dot on his chest. He looked around and saw a man pointing a gun at him.

'Time is waiting, we only got four minutes to save the world.'

CHAPTER 30

Part II

Sarah didn't like the place. It was too crowded, there were too many civilians. She looked back for Doughty to suggest they call it off and wait outside either for their mark to enter or leave the club. The music was too loud for her liking it was blaring out but the clubbers seemed to be lapping it up. In unison, they all had their arms in the air, as something she didn't recognise played.

'I'm outta time and all I got is four minutes.'

Doughty and the three other officers had spread out, in the search pattern, and were working their way through the crowd. Now, as well as seeking the bomber lead, she was scanning the crowd, looking for the travellers. 'I need to speak to Mikey and find out what he's doing here and warn him that a lot is about to go down and he needs to not be here when it does,' she muttered to herself.

Sarah thought she saw him. She moved from her spot and swished her way through the mass. The throng didn't move out of her way; they were too busy rubbing up against each other, trying to copulate. As she brushed against them, she could feel the heat and perspiration radiating from the mob. It was making her feel annoyed. Her heart was thumping; she felt weary, and wearing her gun in the holster made her feel a bit paranoid, given the close proximity of the general public to it. She shoved her way through the gathering, using her elbows to shove people out of her way as necessary. A man stood on her foot. She resisted the urge to punch him, by staring up at the ceiling. She was scanning the upper layout of the place. Then someone prodded her in the back, pushing her in a certain direction. She swivelled around and came face to face with Mikey.

He pushed past everyone and led them off the main arena. He was like a bouncer and just bulldozed his way through the crowd; she no longer had to push them herself. The clubbers parted to make a path for them. He was not someone they wanted to cross; it was some unwritten rule, some weird club etiquette. When they were off the dancefloor and away to the side, they simultaneously demanded of the other, 'What are you doing here?'

'Do not get in my way, Silver.'

'What do you mean? Why are you here?' she asked him.

He pulled out his phone and showed her some photos. 'These men are the colleagues of that bloke Tony. We're here to see if they were involved in what happened to Megan. Pat works the door here and recognised the man from the news as being a subordinate to picture man. You should not be here. This isn't a time for talking or police.'

'Well, don't waste time, give me a sign, tell me how you wanna roll.'

'Don't do this, let me handle it, trust me one more time. Something else is going on here, something big, and you really don't want to be caught up in it. I won't be able to protect you,' she pleaded with him.

'You're not bad for a gavver. Remember, whatever happens, make sure Megan's honour is never questioned.' He grabbed her hand and put it against his mouth and gave it a peck. His behaviour surprised her and momentarily disorientated her. She could only watch as he disappeared back into the pack.

Sarah went back to her search position. The private booths had started to fill out. The one in the centre had an older gentleman and a young woman sipping champagne. It was cordoned off and had two men wearing headsets close by. There was a bit of a scuffle on the dancefloor. In the middle of that she clocked the mark. She was about to press her ear to speak to her team, when she noticed he was with Mitch. She paused and watched. They were heading towards the centre booth.

She then clocked Mikey. He was thumping his arm in the air, pointing towards the centre booth. She scanned around and saw that his two mates had seen his signal and were heading there too. Then she noticed that Doughty was in the booth to the left. He had his weapon drawn. It was lowered but was out. She looked on as Alistair watched Jack Dixon being escorted by Mitch towards the booths.

'Time is waiting, we only got four minutes to save the world.'

CHAPTER 29

Part III

Sam's heart was racing. In those few seconds, he worried that the laser light was acting like a homing beacon for a weapon. Its sight was trained exactly where his heart was. He looked at his chest and the target, and then up at the man. It was obvious that he was going to shoot him. Sam raised his hands in the air and shouted, 'No!'

Without warning, two splodges of red exploded on the man's own chest. They seemed to grow at an exponential rate, and he disappeared from Sam's view along with the target that had been on his own chest. He grabbed at his own torso, as if looking for a wound, but there was nothing.

He scoured the club and saw the female assassin standing in the middle of the dancefloor with her gun raised and pointed at where the man who was about to shoot him once stood. She glanced at Sam; her face was different, as the softness she demonstrated with him in the past had gone.

The clubbers started screaming at the sight of a gun and a dead body. Everyone started darting about.

'The road to hell is paved with good intentions.'

Most people were scrambling around on the floor. Glasses were smashed. Sam looked at the giant wall of screens that had been showing music videos. There was a splattering of blood across them. He looked for his brother, who seemed unhurt and was signalling to Don

Luciano where Jack was The latter was flailing around on the floor. The female detective was pushing forward and was heading towards his brother. He couldn't see his saviour. There seemed to be another man gunned down, someone he didn't recognise, who had a guy seeing to him who was holding up a police badge of some sort. It was utter carnage. He needed to get his brother.

Then he saw another man. He looked young and he had some sort of weapon. It didn't look like a gun but whatever it was, it was pointed towards his brother. Sam called out to Mitch, but over the music, screams and shouts, he couldn't be heard. He pushed on, trying to get to his brother.

All of a sudden, there was a new commotion where the Don was; Matteo, his number one, was on the floor. Luciano grabbed the woman he was with and flung her out in front of himself like a human shield, then fell to the floor himself.

A big, stocky man who looked like a traveller to Sam with the back and sides of his hair shaved off and the remaining hair slicked with tons of gel, torpedoed himself through Mitch and Jack. The latter had been trying to stand up but was now floored again. He then turned around and hurled himself at the female detective. Another of his kin, Sam presumed, was now in the Don's booth. He caught the woman and pushed her to the side.

That's when Sam saw her again. In a fluid motion, she had kicked the knees of the Don's other man, and they appeared to wrestle a bit. She took him down easily;

with a series of precision elbows and knees and tactical moves, he was floored and disarmed.

While she did so, another traveller knocked her to the ground from behind. He stood over her with a knife in his hand. It looked like he was going to plunge it down into her chest. Sam jumped up and down on the spot, waving his arms in the air, shouting. The diversion, while not amazing, caught the traveller's attention long enough for The Assassin to get her bearings. She regained her psyche, pointed her gun at the man's head and fired. His body toppled on where she would have been, but before it had the chance to fall on her, she slid out.

'We only got four minutes to save the world, no hesitating.'

Sam looked around and saw that Jack was now getting up, looking all around him. Now, more clubbers had vacated his area, as that was the main section where people were falling left, right and centre. He was able to scramble away. He joined a group of people heading towards an exit. The young man whom Sam had spotted earlier grabbed the bomb-maker by his shoulder and shoved his plastic toy-looking weapon in Jack's face. He then pointed it around at everyone in a defensive stance. His hand remained on the slippery man's shoulder as he attempted to herd him out of the exit.

Then suddenly, Sam couldn't see his hand or him. The Assassin reloaded her gun, continued walking, and was a mere couple of metres away from Jack when she fired three times: once in the head and twice in the chest.

'Tick tock tick tock tick tock'.

CHAPTER 30

Part III

Sarah grabbed her gun without taking her eyes off her boss and Jack. Doughty's voice abruptly came into her ear through the comms. 'Everyone, I have eyes on the mark. He is heading towards the middle booth, where Don Luciano is sitting. We're at the back of the club; converge on my position. Get him out of here alive without any incident.'

She noticed that one of Luciano's men had clocked him and his weapon. The man had started to shout and pulled out his own gun. She was too far away to do anything, so she leapt onto the dancefloor and headed towards them all, while she also tapped her ear. 'Doughty, look out!'

It was too late. She followed the sequence of events. The bodyguard shot Doughty, who had been too busy watching their own target. She could no longer see Alistair; he had gone down. The clubbers around her started to scream at the sight of her gun and presumably, some had been close to where the Commissioner had gone down. Everyone started darting about.

'The road to hell is paved with good intentions.'

In the chaos, nearly all the clubbers were kneeling down and were pushing and shoving each other to get out. Sarah noted that Mitch was pulling and tugging at Jack, who was cowering on the floor. The traveller men hadn't dropped to the ground and were rushing to the middle booth. One of the other officers was next to

343

Doughty and was administering CPR. Dougie had spotted where Jack was and she saw that he had pulled out his taser. She was trying to triage the situation and work out whom to save, considering her own agenda. Everything was happening so fast. She decided to get to Jack and get him out of there.

Sarah tried to assume command and instruct the team what to do, but the comms were out. She tried to call out to Dougie, but over the din, couldn't be heard. She was now close enough to take the shot. She aimed at and shot the man who had taken out Doughty on his right shoulder, the one who was holding a gun. She shouted, 'Secure the weapon!' hoping that one of her team might hear her, lip-read her or know what they should do. This was in vain, as it looked like the Don was going for the weapon himself.

Mikey was in the Don's booth now. He seemed to pick the female companion of the elderly Italian up and put her to the side. Sarah then felt the weight of a man land on her before she had a chance to react or even register the threat. He was swearing at her, calling her 'police scum'. Sarah was on the floor with him on top of her. She had dropped her gun when he surprised her. She kneed him in the balls and punched him in the face. As she was about to flip positions with him, she momentarily turned to the side and saw a limited rotated view of the booth. The Don now had the weapon of the man she had shot. He aimed and fired it multiple times at Mikey. She wasn't sure if it was the older man's aim, or the close distance between the two, but Mikey slammed into the Don as he fell.

Her assailant was no longer attacking her. She saw that Mitch had pulled him off and was punching him in the face. She then noticed that his younger brother, Samuel, was also here. He was jumping up and down.

'We only got four minutes to save the world, no hesitating.'

She looked around and saw that Dougie had secured the witness and was leading him out of the club. He was being cautious, clearing the area and protecting his mark. She thought how far he had come and felt proud of him. She wanted to check on Mitch and Mikey and Doughty but knew she had to go and help Dougie. That man he held was the priority of her department and for bringing down the Stitchin. Dougie briefly caught her eye; they looked at each other and she caught a glimpse of the smile he flashed at her.

He mouthed, 'Are you alright?' then his head shattered in a red explosion, and his body dropped to the ground.

'Tick tock, tick tock, tick tock.'

CHAPTER 29

Part IV

'Mitchell, come on, we have to get out of here. Jack is dead; it's a total blood bath in here. Let's go.' Sam pulled his brother off the man he was pounding. His brother seemed totally disorientated; he got it. He wasn't even sure what happened himself. Everything was going down was so fast; people were trying to kill him, each other, he wasn't exactly sure who was on what side, or what side he was on.

This is all my fault. I tried to do the right thing and now look what has happened. We need to go to the authorities and explain everything.

Only two things were clear in his mind: The Assassin had saved his life, and now he and his brother had to get out of there and go and make this right. Sam looked around: she had dropped her weapon and was already blending in with everyone else, making for the exit. Mitch's fists were bloodied.

'Sam, are you okay? I've been looking for you.' He gave his younger brother a hug. He recoiled slightly as he saw someone over his brother's shoulder. 'Don Luciano.' Mitch ran over to the middle booth and jumped up. He tried to peel the hulking mass covering the older man off of him. 'Sam, come and help me.'

He reluctantly went over and helped his brother. 'Who is this?'

'Dunno, some gypsy. They were in here going for the Italians.'

'Is he dead? Mitch, the police are also in here.'

'I hope he is. Yeah, I clocked them too. Don't worry we will get out of here in a minute.' They had managed to get him off Don Luciano. 'Don, Don Luciano,' Mitch said as he shook the body. 'He's gone.'

Matteo reached up with his good hand. 'Behind this booth, follow the corridor and take the back exit.'

'We'll help you to come with us,' Mitch told him.

'I can't leave the boss.' Matteo teared up as he spoke. 'And I have to make whoever did this pay. Pass me the gun.'

Sam didn't move, but Mitch prised it from Luciano's hand and gave it to Matteo. 'We'll help you later, if you need it.' He looked at his brother. 'Let's go.' He stood up and ushered his younger brother towards the escape route they were told about.

'What was that about?' Sam asked in the secluded corridor, away from the mayhem in front of the club.

'Let's get out of here, then talk,' Mitch responded.

Sam pushed ahead of his brother, frustrated, and slammed the emergency exit, which set off the alarm. It led to an alleyway behind the club. The car that had brought them to the place was waiting. The back door was open, and the engine was running. Sam looked at Mitch, who shrugged his shoulders and motioned for him to get in.

'Are you here for us?' Sam spoke to the black glass immediately as he got inside the vehicle. 'Is anyone else coming? Shouldn't we wait for—'

Mitch was right behind him and closed the door behind him with a sense of urgency. 'Who else should we wait for?'

Before Sam could answer, there was a hissing sound. He watched as the back of the car filled with a white smoke. He pulled on the door closest to him, attempting to open it. It didn't budge. The car started to drive off, as Sam bashed on the door and window, feeling weak and tired.

CHAPTER 30

Part IV

Sarah looked for the shooter. In that instance, they had also taken down Jack Dixon. Her lead who was also the international intelligence on the Paris bombing was dead. Sarah shot her gun in the air twice and looked around at the people left in the club. Given the low light, loud music, and disoriented crowd, unless you had been looking specifically at a person, it was hard to determine who had done what. The numbers had thinned out slightly, and there were empty sections, but given that the place was at capacity or over about four minutes ago, it was still a tumultuous situation. In one such area, the perfect place for someone to have killed Dougie and the witness was a gun.

Mitch was being picked off his traveller combatant by his brother. The centre booth had multiple bodies; she couldn't tell who was alive or dead, but it didn't seem like anyone there was currently physically capable of firing a gun. Doughty was out of it, and the officer looking after him was doing just that. Then there was a woman. Sarah had clocked her before and assumed she was a clubber. She was scrambling to get out with everyone else, but there was something about her body language that didn't seem right and that caught Sarah's attention.

She headed towards the woman, who seemed to sense her presence and turned around before Sarah got to her. They faced each other for a few seconds, before the woman spotted Sarah's gun and started shrieking, 'She's got a gun, she's got a gun!'

'I'm with the police,' Sarah reassured as she held it up in a non-hostile way.

In a split second, the woman flew through the air with leg outstretched towards Sarah. The flying drop kickout would have floored and unarmed the detective if she weren't anticipating it. She turned to the side, catching the leg mid-flight, spun around holding the assailant and flung her down on the floor as hard as she could. 'The blood-splatter pattern all over your body gave you away, plus you have the face of a total psycho.'

Sarah dropped on top of her, landing an elbow in her mid-section.

She straddled her, and the woman tried to fight back using her legs to grab the detective's head or torso, but to no avail. Silver then shoved her gun directly in the woman's face; her hand steady. 'Give me a reason to use this, please.' The woman didn't resist. Instead, she held her hands up together. Sarah pulled out a pair of handcuffs and restrained the unknown woman.

She stood up, looking down at her second-rate prize, when something told her to turn around. The man she had shot—the Don's henchman—was standing. He had a gun pointed at her, albeit with his weaker hand. She was deliberating what to do, what risk she should take, when the officer who was keeping vigil over the Commissioner took Doughty's gun and shot the Italian.

More of her team had entered the club, they would soon bring order and medical assistance to those who needed it. Sarah decided to not stick around and to leave with the handcuffed woman, and as she led her out, they walked past the body of Dougie.

Sarah whispered in the woman's ear, 'If I find out you did that, I will kill you.' Outside, she looked at all the emergency vehicles arriving. *Who can I trust? Even if there was someone, I don't want to restrict how I deal with this woman.* 'Where did you park?'

'RS 5 Coupe, dark silver, round the corner.'

It was the first words her prisoner had said to her. It told her she didn't want to be entered into the system. When she got to the car, Sarah secured her in the back with cuffs both on the hands and around the legs and strapped her in, then she drove the car off.

'You seem like a professional,' Sarah said, 'Therefore, I am not going to beat around the bush. Tell me what deal you want to tell me everything I want to know. Bear in mind that if it is not reasonable, I will torture the information from you.' As she spoke, she looked at the woman's face in the rear-view mirror.

A slight smile flashed across her face. 'Pete Tanner told me you would avenge his death, before he pleaded for his life.'

Sarah was about to slam the brakes, get her gun and shoot the woman dead, when out of nowhere, another vehicle smashed into the side of the Audi. The Coupe flipped over on its side and continued rolling.

CHAPTER 31
DAY 13

'Sam, Sam.'

Hearing Mitch call his name roused him. He wanted to rub his eyes and wipe his nose and mouth as he felt snot and saliva around them, but he couldn't raise his arm by more than a centimetre. He started banging his arms up and down quickly in an attempt to free them, while he kept blinking, trying to waken himself.

'Are you hurt?'

Sam still couldn't quite open his eyes. *Every time, with these people, they do something to me, knock me out, and I find myself waking in some precarious situation.* Unable to move his arms he felt more trapped than all the previous times he had woken from their other interferences. While his mouth wasn't covered the restraints made him feel suffocated. Not being able to wipe his nose and mouth and having his own secretions just ran down his face was torturous. He rattled his shoulders and legs and those bits of his body that he could move.

'What do you want?'

'Is your brother still sleeping? This isn't the time for rest. Remember, a stitch in time saves nine.'

I know that voice.

'Don't touch him,' Mitch snarled.

Sam burst awake. The face, the one that didn't particularly haunt him but consumed his thoughts from time to time, was right in front of his. The space invader

352

was far too close. Sam could smell his breath and feel it on his skin. It made him feel nauseous.

'Good, you're awake,' he said, moving away from Sam.

Now that the man was out of his face, Sam had a chance to look around. Sitting down right in front of him, with a strap around each wrist that bound him to his chair, was Mitch. He looked at his own predicament. He was in the mirror situation, installed on a seat and bound at the wrists. He tried to stand, to see if the chair would move, but it didn't budge. The man walked between the two chairs, temporarily stopping the brothers from being able to look at each other.

Mr White, as they named him, held up hands so that each brother could just see a palm. 'Congratulations on getting this far; truly remarkable. When I first saw you both, I never doubted it; you're both special. So here we are, on your fourteenth and last mission. For every person who joins us, their journey is unique to them. You two have shared a similar path in getting here, so it seems right that your final challenge is the same.'

'Why are we tied up like this?' Mitch hissed at him. Sam heard the annoyance in his brother's voice. He wished Mr White would move so that they could make eye contact and at least pull faces at the weird bloke spouting nonsensical drivel at them.

'To free yourself is quite simple. All you need to do is press one little button, built into the arm of your chair. Push it, and your bonds are released, and you get your final mark and become one of us. You will get a bank account with one million pounds deposited in it for you to spend as you like. Then as a Stitchin member, you become one of the elite. Your life will change for the better.'

'What's the catch? There is always something with you, with them,' Sam asked.

'No catch. Just that once the button is enabled, you might want to press yours quickly and first. The one tiny, teeny, weeny, small point is that only one of you can push his button. Once pushed, the device in the other one's leg will deliver a lethal poison, explosion, electric current or something along those lines. You get the drift—the other will die.'

'What?' Sam asked in disbelief.

'To be clear, if Samuel presses his button, he will be freed and will complete the initiation, and Mitchell will die. If Mitchell presses his button, he will be freed and will complete the initiation, and Samuel will die.' Mr White stopped talking with his authoritarian tone and lowered his voice. 'Sorry, they're not my rules.'

'We won't do it!' Mitch shouted. 'You can't make us.'

Mr White's voice returned to its previous volume. 'If neither button is pushed within an hour, both your devices will expire and you'll both be killed. It's one or none.'

'That will be a waste of two potential assets. You've lost many members recently, you need us.' Sam was clutching at straws, trying desperately to use the knowledge he had gained to try and help them.

'We're actively recruiting globally, it's a fast process. I'll be honest initiating you both at once has been cumbersome. So one of you screw over the over or console each other for eternity in hell.'

'We'd rather do that than keep playing your games. We won't be responsible for killing the other,' Sam stated.

'That is your choice.' Mr White reached into his white jacket with a white gloved hand, took out a remote control and pressed the button. On both chairs, part of the right armrest slid open, exposing the kill switch.

'Tell us about the Cleanse,' Sam blurted out to stall for time.

Mr White stopped, surprised. 'Where did you hear that from?'

'Let us go and we'll tell you.'

Mr White regained his composure. 'Seems like the good Dr Impey has been a bit more naughty than we first thought. Never mind.' He then reached into the other side of his jacket and took out an hourglass, placed it overturned on the floor and stepped towards the door. 'You know how it works. Goodbye, and hopefully, I will have the pleasure of seeing one of you in the future. May the Stitchin help you find your way.' The door closed behind him as he left the room.

'Come back here, you need both of us alive. We will be good assets,' Sam shouted.

Mitch was shaking his head looking perplexed. 'What have I done? Sam, listen to me; when that timer is halfway through, I want you to push the button on your chair,' he said, with a deadly earnest expression and a clear voice.

'What? No. I can't do that. You press *your* button.' Sam stared at his brother, with tears in eyes. He couldn't maintain eye contact and had to look away. He looked around the room. It reminded him of that warehouse down by the docks, where all of this began for them. He then glanced down at the hourglass. The sand seemed to be gushing from the top to the bottom.

'Sam, Samuel, look at me. I want you to press your button.' Sam looked back at his brother; Mitch's eyes seemed glazed over. 'Look, this is all my fault. I got us into this, so it is only right that I get us out of it.'

'No, we were both there for most of the tasks; it is both our fault,' Sam tried to rationalise with him. 'You never forced me to do anything; it was them and their sick games. I mucked up the last task. I called the police anonymously to let them know bomber Jack would be at the club. Once they grabbed him my plan was to turn ourselves over to them too. I betrayed you.'

'You only did what any normal person would have. If only it had worked out as you planned you might have saved us from me. This is all on me.'

'Mitch, stop saying that. I went along with it all.'

You don't get it. That's not what I am talking about. I...' he cleared his throat. 'I signed us up to the Stitchin.'

'You did what?' Sam choked out the words.

'You know Tom Denton? Some people approached me and paid me to make out with his girlfriend, Megan. They paid her too. I thought it was his parents trying to split them up, given her traveller heritage. The night we kissed, outside a club she worked at, I learnt it wasn't the parents after all. Megan told me about these marks Tom was getting on his skin, as some sort of initiation. He was involved in some big money-making scheme; that is how she described it. That morning, as I was getting home, I bumped into Tom. I guess before he had had a chance to see the evidence of what Megan and I had been up to, I asked him about it. He was reluctant to tell me at first, but I guess he figured he owed me given that we used to be friends and the things he bought from me cheaply; and in his words, I had the same background and credentials. He told me to contact his uncle, Dr Impey, and he gave me his uncle's contact details. I did, and I signed us up.' Mitch looked away from his brother as he spoke. He was fidgeting in his chair as he confessed. 'All the Stitchin evil that happened to you is because of me. I got us involved in this; I didn't really know what I was getting us involved in, but it is my fault. I was meant to look after you, to be your big brother, but instead, I got you embroiled in this. I am culpable for having you subjected to surgical violation, blackmailing, beating people and sentencing people to death. So push the button; I deserve it.'

In Sam's head, he had flashbacks of being made to crawl through the tight enclosed pitch-black space, the tingling sensation in his penis and the stinging feeling when he had to pass that green urine, the creepy doctor touching him, The Assassin who had saved his life, staring down the barrel of a gun, beating Loni to a pulp and the massive dust plume that sent him flying through the air from the explosion, and the people they killed. He didn't realise it, but as these thoughts raced through his head, he was subconsciously tracing over the outline on the button with his index finger.

'When I walked into that Paris hotel with the bomb, I knew what I was doing. There were families in the lobby; I remember seeing a mother holding a little baby while the father was playing with the toddler. As I looked for the conference, I saw a young woman who worked there and was showing off to a co-worker an engagement ring she had just been given. During the dinner break, when I planted the bomb, all the scientists were congregating. I heard them discussing with each other how they were curing diseases in children. And I just blew up all those people, blasted them to death. I should die too; I have killed people or am responsible for the death of many. I can't live with myself anymore, with what I have done.'

Sam's memory flitted back to the bank, when he thought it was Mitch behind the mask, when he briefly thought his brother was the robber and had been shot dead. He had felt so empty, like he'd wanted to die too. Mitch had been a surrogate father to him when their own parents had abandoned him; he couldn't harm him. He looked down and saw where his finger was; he quickly pulled it back.

He was crying now. 'I can't, Mitch. Press your button, please. When I thought you died at the bank, I wanted to die too. I won't be able to cope without you. I can't do this without you.'

Mitch had started to cry, while he continued to squirm in the chair. 'When I was placed in my glass coffin and it was filled with soil, there is something I've never told you. There was a screen in it and I could see everything happening to you. That was my greatest fear; it wasn't about what was happening to me but not being able to help you. But you were incredible, dealing with that height, the snake and the water. It showed me you'll be fine without me, that you can handle anything. You are so much stronger than you give yourself credit for. Sam, you'll have a million pounds, you'll be eighteen next year, and the world will be your oyster.'

'No,' said Sam. 'You gave up the past four years of your life to look after me, and you can't give up the rest of your life for me. You're only twenty-five. Take the money and disappear. I want you to push your button; honestly, I don't mind.' The sand in the timer looked like it was over halfway through. 'You have to do it soon; there is no point in both of us dying, and there is no way I will press my button. If you press yours, you can avenge me. You mentioned this policewoman; you can use her and find out about them and bring them down. That's a reason for you to live. Please push the button and avenge me, otherwise we will both die in vain.'

'No, Sam, it's not going to happen. Listen, we never got a chance to talk about her. Her name is Sarah Silver. Find her; she will help you if you need it when I am not here. She knows about them; she was investigating them already. She knows bits of our story but not all of it. I never told her all the details of what we had to do. She promised me she would get you out of this. Now press the button.' He grunted somewhat as he continued to stir.

'I can't. Just like you say you can't, what makes you think I can? I am going to shut my eyes, so you don't have to look at me. Just do it, please, Mitchell.'

'I am not the man you think I am. I am not a good person. After Tom died, Megan contacted me, saying it was our fault, that he committed suicide after what we did. Did I feel guilty? No. Instead, I slept with her a few times. She seemed distraught and wanted the comfort, but I did it just for sex. One night, she came to me for help; it was the night she disappeared. She seemed desperate, but her state and the way she was acting put me off. I didn't even invite her into the house. We just talked on the driveway. What sort of bloke does that? I just used her when she was vulnerable. She wanted to sell the Range Rover back to me; she said her family had found out about us, and she needed the money. As we talked, she thought she saw her brother drive past, confirming her suspicions. She hid in the boot; that's how paranoid she was. I didn't help her. See how bad I am?'

Sam opened his eyes, looked at his brother and glanced down at the hourglass. Time was very nearly up; there was just a little bit left in the top section. *It is all going to be over soon.*

He was about to say something, but Mitch continued talking. 'I just came inside the house, thinking nothing more of it, thinking it was just a gypsy scam at play. Later that night, I looked out the front for the car, but it had gone. I thought she'd got bored and just driven off. But the other night, Sarah told me they found her body still in the boot of the car, which had been dumped in the lake. I guessed her family had driven by, seen the car and taken it, and then did that to her. But it was my fault. I shouldn't have slept with her when she was so distressed. I could have helped her. I should have invited her into the house. I should have made sure she had managed to get out of the boot. That's another death on my hands. I deserve this.' He stopped fidgeting, as he had managed to free himself. He suddenly stood up.

'Mitch don't do this. Please sit back down and press the button on your chair. Honestly I want you to.' Sam was crying, as was Mitch. 'Get away from my chair. Call Mr White in here, tell him we'll do whatever they want. They have won.'

'I love you, little brother.' As he said this, Sam could only watch as his brother moved next to him and he stroked the face of his little brother, placing his hand on Sam's forehead and kissing it before he pressed the button on Sam's chair.

The moment he pressed it, the restraints that had held Sam down dropped off. Sam stood and grabbed Mitch who would have fallen to the ground. He hugged his brother, who was lifeless, and carefully laid him on the ground. He tried CPR on him, from what he had seen on television, but nothing happened. Unlike on television, there was no miraculous coughing and then awakening. There was nothing; his eyes remained closed, and he wasn't breathing.

'Wake up, damn you. Please.' Sam choked out the last word.

Sam sat on the floor cradling Mitch's head in his lap while carefully stroking his hair. 'Mitch, I love you; please don't go. You were the best big brother ever. None of this is your fault; honestly, it isn't you.' He looked helplessly around. He saw the chair Mitch had been sitting on. He reached over to the button on it and without hesitation, he pressed it. He felt a tingling where his stitches were and he closed his eyes.

CHAPTER 32
DAY 13

Sarah had been drifting in and out of consciousness since the crash. Immediately after it happened, she fought to stay awake as people were trying to get them out of the car. She was trying to warn them about her companion and the need to keep her restrained. Then as they pulled her out of the Audi, she realised that they weren't medical rescuers or fire fighters. As it was straight after the collision, it was too soon to be official help. She was too weak to resist them. During her lucid moments, she figured out that they were not good Samaritans but professionals. They extracted her and the other woman. She didn't know whom they wanted, but she could guess who sent them. She was aware of being restrained and transferred to another vehicle.

During the journey, she passed out and had no idea how long they travelled or where they ended up. She had moments when she briefly woke up, but they weren't long enough for her to fully assess the situation. Now, she was starting to properly come to and she became aware that the right side of her body was hurting. She thought her right arm was broken. That was the least of her pressing concerns, because as she became more alert, she realised where she was.

Sarah looked all around her and then started pushing against her enclosure. It seemed like some toughened glass—it was cold, solid, see-through and boxed her in. She was stood upright, it confined her not giving her

363

much room to manoeuvre, and she couldn't bend down if she wanted to. It was the size of a coffin. Anything that could have been used as a tool to assist her had already been taken off her. She couldn't get a strong swing, but she punched the glass with her left hand as hard as she could. It was her weaker hand, but her right one was too painful. It had no effect except to make her knuckles hurt. She was clenching her fist and then extending her fingers, contemplating whether to try again or not. Then she noticed that there was water at the bottom and that it was rising.

A short and stocky man, dressed in white from head to toe, entered the room. 'Hello, Detective Silver.'

She just stared at him.

'Not feeling talkative? That's okay. You can just listen, then in the end, there is only one question you need to answer.' He spoke firmly.

She hated him already. *Is that an earpiece? Is he getting instructions from someone? He doesn't sound natural.*

'You know who we are, so we can skip a few steps. We need new recruits at a more senior level. That's where we think you and we will be a good fit.'

The water was up to her knees now.

'What I don't know is what the purpose of this Stitchin is,' she said.

'Do you really want to waste your limited time on questions? You're a clever woman; you can tell me what you think.' He gave an exaggerated look at the water level.

'This Stitchin thinks it is better than everyone else, some sort of elite club, controlling many different things, from new technology to the manipulation of genes. It's about power and control. You want to wipe out the unworthy; you're some sort of population cult with only the chosen selected members surviving.' She spat out her theory.

He burst out laughing and pointed at her. 'You've been reading too many of the wrong science-fiction novels. It is the complete opposite: we are all about preserving life; we're here to ensure the survival of everyone.'

'Well, that's a lie.'

'You don't have time to debate the semantics of our methods. You have a choice to make: stop your investigation, join us and pledge an allegiance to us. Help us with our mission. Once your loyalty has been proven, you will advance and find out the answers to the questions you seek. And don't think about betraying us: if you pretend to join us and double-cross us, your sister, her husband, your nieces and everyone you've come in contact with whom you even remotely like will be killed.' The water was up to her waist now. 'I have to go; my colleague will help you if you decide to take us up on our kind offer. I hope to see and work with you in the future. We have a saying that I want you to remember, as it seems fitting for your current predicament: A stitch in time saves nine.'

The man in white left the room and a figure dressed in fluorescent yellow clothes from head to toe entered the room. Sarah glanced at the matching shirt, trousers, blazer and shoes but focused on the mask he wore. It was the same colour but had a mesh pattern to it; she couldn't make out any of his features. He moved awkwardly and stood directly in front of her water-filling glass prison.

She clenched her fist and struck the glass as hard as she could. *Once the water gets any higher, my punches will be less effective; not that they are having much effect now.* She kept hitting the glass wall, staring at the man, unable to tell if he was watching her or if he cared what she was doing. Her hand started to bleed. The water was up to her chest now; punching would no longer work. She stretched out and tried pushing the top off. It didn't budge. The water was up to her neck; it felt cold on her skin and bit into her bleeding fist.

'What's your deal?' she shouted at the yellow statue outside the box.

There was no response.

The water was up to her mouth now; she tiptoed and started to gulp in air. There was no way out of this; this was the end. *I have failed. I let down Tanner, Mitch and his brother, Megan, Dougie, Doughty if he is still alive, everyone.* She pushed herself to the top of the upright casket, the only part with air left in it, and took her last breath, as the water filled the last remaining space.

'You know that silver is malleable; you can bend it without breaking it.' Those words were from Tanner when she asked for his advice about the Manchester problem; now she kept hearing him say them to her. 'Be malleable.'

I can't let this be the end, not like this. They need to be brought to justice, and the truth has to come out.

She screamed to the man that she agreed, but as she was already submerged in water, no words came out, just the remaining air from her lungs. She tried to make eye contact with where his eyes should be, nodding her head as best as she could.

Poor Megan, drowning in a trapped space—what a horrible way to die. Unable to breathe, helpless to fight back, seeing your life flash before your eyes, being forced to ingest and inhale liquid until you met your watery grave. I didn't find out the truth about what happened to you. I let you down. Now, our fates are the same.

In her last moment, she gave the thumbs-up signal just before she lost consciousness and her life.

The yellow man punched the glass right at the centre, and it broke with his single strike. Water gushed out. She coughed out water once her mouth and nose had been liberated from the water. He opened his fist once his punch had smashed through the glass wall; he gripped the side, effortlessly ripped out the whole front glass panel and discarded it to the side. Sarah fell on him; she was coughing more water out and would have collapsed on the floor if he hadn't been holding her.

She had to know; she attempted to grab his face mask with her bleeding left hand. Before she could touch it, he secured her wrist with his right hand. She darted her right hand, ignoring the immense pain that moving it caused her, and pulled off the mask. She stared in utter disbelief at what was under the mask. He dropped her, turned and left the room.

She spat out more water and then picked up her wet self from the ground and stood up. It hurt, but she pushed through the pain and limped towards the exit. The door was metal and heavy-duty; she had to push it open with her left shoulder. It led to a long, narrow corridor that at first reminded her of a hotel, with doors similar to the one she had come through, evenly spaced opposite and down the length of the hall. It wasn't decorated or furnished like a hotel; there was a lot of metal, and the place was giving off a sterile vibe.

She noticed two doors three down from where she was that were open and hobbled towards them. She felt unsteady on her feet. She looked in the first one: in it were two chairs, set up to face each other. They had restraints around the arm rests, and one chair had the straps cleanly open while the other looked like someone managed to force them open. Besides that, the room was empty. The room next door had medical equipment. It looked like someone had recently been treated there. She noticed her female adversary's shirt from the club in the room: but the woman wasn't there.

She continued down the corridor, there were signs and instructions, but she couldn't read them as they were in the Cyrillic alphabet. At the end, there was a staircase. She could either go up or down. In these instances, she knew the logical choice was to go down, get to the street level and escape. But her instinct told her to go up. She climbed two flights of stairs and burst out of a door at the top. A blast of cold air hit her. It stung her wet clothes that clung to her body, and instantly, her suspicions were confirmed. She crossed the deck while grabbing the railing. She looked down at the water. It looked deep, like they were far out to sea.

She scanned the ship as best she could from the stern to the bow. It seemed large. She likened it to a decommissioned military vessel. She held onto the railing and headed towards the bow. *Maybe I can see something from the front that will tell me where we are heading.* As she approached, she saw a lone man at the very front. He was sitting on the railing like he didn't care if he fell in; he wasn't holding on, it was dangerous and reckless, and he could fall at any moment.

She called out to him but didn't get a response. It was only when she was within touching distance that she recognised him—it was the person she had sworn to protect.

'Sam.'

He turned his head to look at her and answered back, 'Detective Sarah Silver, you're too late. My brother is dead.'

'What happened to him?'

'He sacrificed himself to save me. I tried to kill myself but just got my fourteenth mark instead. Do you want to know something funny? Well, not actually funny, haha, more the dark and twisted variety. Just before he died for me, he told me something, something that made me realise I had killed someone else. I should have been the one to die in that chair. One night, I got home and found our dad's car, his silver Range Rover in our driveway. I knew Mitch had sold it to our next-door neighbour, who seemed to share it with his girlfriend. Once it had been sold, every time I saw that car, it cut deep; it reminded me of everything we had lost. It was cursed: my parents left when we had it, Tom died when he had it. And here it was back on our drive, taunting me; no doubt it would have taunted Mitch if he had seen it.' He was staring out into the abyss of the sea as he spoke. 'It seemed abandoned, no one was in it, so I got the spare keys from our house and took it for a drive. I hadn't even learned to drive when Dad first got it; I always thought that would be the vehicle that I would learn in. It seemed fitting that the prophecy should be fulfilled. Ironic, huh? It was an automatic; it was easy to drive, and the roads were clear at that time of night. It took a few bumps and scratches but all in all, I drove pretty well. I didn't know where to go, I hadn't planned a route, but before I knew it, I found myself at Wilson Lake. Dad and I used to do water sports there. If I couldn't have him, have his car, why should anyone else? I drove it into the lake. I didn't know about her; how was I meant to know she was in the boot? She never made a sound. I didn't know. I've been having sleepless nights since I drove the car into the lake, worried about the consequences of the joy-ride. Oh my god, how little did I really know! If I'd known she was in the boot I wouldn't have been able to live with myself. What did I do? How could I have not realised, not checked the boot?' He drifted forward like he wanted the water to swallow him up.

Sarah understood what he said, what he confessed to doing. But she knew it would take a while to process and deal with the ramifications. However, it couldn't take priority now. She grabbed him and pulled him back onto the deck. 'It was an accident. A terrible turn, but you didn't do it deliberately. It wasn't your fault.'

He was slumped on the ground. 'I can't even feel sorry or mourn her. All I can think about is my brother. You were at the club; I saw you there. You should have helped him then if you really cared.'

Sarah sat on the deck with him. 'I tried, believe me, I tried. There was something special about Mitch; he was a good man. Apparently, I met him by chance, but we were brought together and I wanted to help him. Help you. He told me about what he got you guys involved in; he didn't care about the consequences for himself, he just wanted you to be safe. He made me promise to look after you, to help you, to get you free from all of this. You said he sacrificed himself for you; don't let it be in vain.'

He stood up. 'What are you doing on their boat?'

'They arranged a little car accident for me after the club. I guess something similar happened to bring you here. I woke up in a glass coffin that was filling with water. They wanted me to stop my investigation and pledge my alliance to them.' She stood up to join him.

'I guess you did, hence you're strolling around up here.'

'They killed people I loved, including your brother. Believe me, I truly hate them. But if I didn't agree, I would have died. This way, there is a chance, even if it's a little one, that I can stop them or at least save some lives. Let me help you? Help me. We'll be stronger together. We'll play their game, uncover all their little secrets. And then, when they least expect it, we will exact our revenge and avenge Mitch, Pete, and everyone else they have wronged by bringing them down. Are you with me?' She held out her hand, hoping he would accept it.

'You're right; the best way to destroy something is from the inside.' He took her hand, and then embraced her in a warm hug. Holding her tightly, he whispered in her ear, 'I have already employed your philosophy. When I left the room I was being held in, I went into the room next door to mine. I didn't know what to do. In there was … someone who helped me in the past; she was being treated for a few injuries. She helped me again, she told me how to destroy the ship, inside-out, and then she left. I followed the instructions she gave me to get to the engine room. There was a guard in there. I took him by surprise and injected him with a tranquillizer that they gave me a few days ago and have been carrying with me ever since. I did what she told me and damaged a couple of pistons. They are misaligned, the failsafe is switched off. This ship is going down. I doubt it will stop them and their plans but maybe it will slow them down.'

'What plans?'

'The Cleanse.'

On cue, the ship shook and a loud siren went off.

Sarah pulled away from him. 'We need to get off it.'

'No, I am staying.' Sam smiled. 'Call it redemption.'

Sarah continued steering the lifeboat away from the main ship. She had only just managed to get it in the water when an explosion violently rocked the ship, with a burst of sound and fire emanating from the middle of the vessel. When she first got to the lifeboat, it was obvious that at least two others had already launched. There could have been others throughout the carrier, but these were the ones nearest her position. In reality, she had no idea how many people were on the ship and how many got off. Or if indeed Sam had done enough damage to sink it. From her vantage point it looked like a sturdy behemoth that could take quite a pounding. Suddenly, there was another explosion. It was louder, and the flames lit up the night sky and darkened the water. It illuminated the face of her passenger.

She looked down at Sam and the bruise she had given him with the lifeboat oar to knock him out and drag him with her to their escape. In the position in which he lay and the unusual lights flickering across his face, she saw the similarities between him and his brother.

'I need your help,' she said. 'I have to tell you what your brother told me about your parents. We need to figure out what the green substance they are manufacturing is. I have glimpsed what is beneath the mask of that fluorescent thing, and I need you to tell me about the Cleanse.' She wiped away a tear, then turned on the internal switch within herself. She steeled herself and turned herself back to Silver. She watched from afar as the ship got smaller. 'This is just the beginning of me sinking your organisation, I am going to unmask everyone, and I'm going to bring you all down, Stitchin.'

EPILOGUE
DAY 14

Laurna downed her coffee. It had been a long day and night, it was just past midnight and she knew she wouldn't be sleeping anytime soon. Currently, she watched the man and woman interact, given their history there was tension between them, that much was apparent. But they were giving each other a wide berth which she knew was because what they had both been through with the fight being taken out of them. Laurna couldn't take her eyes off the man, as she watched him shielded by the one-way mirror. He looked so vulnerable, in her head he changed to a younger version of himself: first a twenty-one-year-old, then a thirteen year old, then a toddler. She touched her side of the glass and left her hand there. A buzzer sounded breaking her from trance, she turned to look away from the mirror and saw a red light flashing above the door. She swallowed hard and dabbed at her eyes.

She moved over to the door and spun the hand wheel and stepped back over to the glass wall. Now she was not facing the door or the caller and could continue to watch the two people on the other side of the glass. She did not bother to turn and face her visitor, in her new position she no longer had to deal with pleasantries. 'What is the status of the ship?'

'The fires have been put out, no explosions as the saboteur wanted, no actual damage beyond the cosmetic, the rouse worked well. We are fully battle-ready and can even torpedo their life-boat.'

Laurna turned and looked at the man dressed in white for the first time.

Mr White very briefly made eye contact with her, before looking down. 'Apologies, I didn't mean to speak out of turn.' He stumbled out the words. 'I was just stating the options. I know a plan has been formulated for both Yates brothers.' He briefly stopped talking and thumbed through the files he was holding. He handed her one, and then opened the one he had kept hold of, reading from it. 'Mitchell is physically fine, the anaesthetic delivered to render him to appear dead has been flushed from his system and has left no lasting damage.' He paused and looked at Mitchell on the other side of the glass. 'His psychological profile, indicates he will play ball as a Stitchin member as long as his younger brother is okay.'

Mitchell approached the mirror in his room, coming right up to it, and stared at it. It looked like he was trying to see beyond it, like he knew he was being watched.

Laurna's heart started to beat faster, she hoped Mr White could not tell. 'Walk with me,' she instructed him, mainly to distract him. If it was up to her she would have stayed and looked at Mitchell all day.

He left the room before her and she turned and had a last look. The woman, The Assassin was a loyal Stitchin member. She had instructed herself on numerous occasions, now the killer was next to Mitchell, on their side of the glass talking to him.

Mr White followed her as she walked along the corridor. 'The report indicates it is Samuel that could be an ineffective member as he is playing with nothing to lose, given he thinks his brother is dead. Even pairing him with the detective, who is a total wildcard, means we cannot predict how Sam and Sarah will behave. Hence that comment about the torpedo earlier.' He stopped talking and when she didn't respond he continued, 'I mean no disrespect, Number Thirteen. I never doubt the council. I am just being cautious having so many of you on board this vessel. I have never met a council member in person, let alone have three under my care.'

'A journey of a thousand miles begins will a single stitch,' Laurna interjected.

'A stitch in time,' Mr White responded with a little bow of his head.

'Speak freely I value honest counsel.' She instructed him.

'If we had left Samuel paired with our trusted female member the probability of success in his next mission would have been higher. Sarah Silver is unpredictable and that makes her dangerous to our goal. She hasn't been through the initiation and now she is on a mission; one that seems integral to the next stage.'

'Noted.'

'I can't go any further, Number Thirteen. I am not allowed to enter this part of the ship.' Mr White stopped as she walked past a bulkhead flanked by two fluorescent yellow-clothed guards.

'Speak later.' Laurna didn't turn around to look at him and just continued walking, keeping her head straight so as not to look at the sentinels on either side of her. Passing by them she felt a momentary sense of relief before realising she was on her way to have to sit down with one of their kind. Their leader, in all sense of the word. While they were her subordinates they would definitely break her neck like a twig if Number Fourteen commanded it.

At the end of the metal, sterile hallway was a flight of stairs leading downwards. She headed down, pulling on her collar as she felt she couldn't breathe. It was different from that shortness of breath gasp; it was stifling like there was no oxygen in the air. The ship was cold, but she felt like she was wrapped in a fur coat instead of a one-layer uniform. *Do not show any weakness.* She repositioned how she was holding the envelope that Mr White had handed her earlier, to not have one part look crumpled or show her sweat marks, to give away her trepidation. She steeled herself as the descent plunged her deeper and deeper.

She finally arrived at her location. It felt like she had travelled to the very bottom of the vessel. No one was around, they were not allowed to be here, it was completely shut away from the rest of the ship. She entered the only room in this secluded section. The other two council members were already seated. Number Fourteen was dressed in the same type of clothes as the sentinels, though he was in a fluorescent green. He was not wearing his mask nor had his hood up. Laurna

378

looked at the metal skull and lack of human features on the android.

Number Fourteen spoke in its robotic voice. 'Number Thirteen, sit. Now we can get on to business.'

I outrank you machine, don't ever forget that. She closed the door behind her and moved so she wouldn't be seated with her back to the door.

'It is a pleasure to see you,' Number One said.

The machine's head turned to look at Number One and then turned back. *They lack human emotion and social graces, they weren't built for that, but it is learning.* 'Likewise,' Laurna replied, taking her seat. This was only a half-truth because she couldn't see him, the darkened room plus the large cowl hood he adjourned obscured his face.

'First piece of business, I see you have the results of our latest experiment,' Number One continued.

'Preliminary tests shows the new compound, the green one, offers a decent level of protection, test subjects are immediately fine, however, long-term outcomes are lacking.' Laurna placed the envelope on the table and slid it open to Number Fourteen. 'But I haven't looked at the official analysis yet; do you want the honours?' She knew he lacked the dexterity to open the envelope.

Number Fourteen scraped it along the metal table, using one of his un-gloved hands. *Is he deliberately breaking protocol and exposing himself, to prove he is different from the rest of the machines?* When the report was partially off the table, he grabbed it with his other hand.

'How many of the android units are operational?' she asked.

'There are five, one of which we modelled on a female body type,' Number One answered.

'They do not have the same processing unit as I do,' Number Fourteen interjected.

'As Number Thirteen is aware, we created a super advanced unit to control the others, be more self-aware and have a seat at this table. The mass-produced ones are the soldiers, that will act as instructed. We are completing final testing on the units before we roll-out mass production. Pass the envelope here.'

The android passed the sealed papers to Number One in the same manner as it had received them. 'The central processing unit within my mainframe is one of a kind…'

Laurna stopped listening as the machine listed out technical details about itself. *It wants to be like us, it has been asserting itself as different. A ghost in the machine.*

Number One started to speak. 'Purifying the compound through the human body has given it an eighty-eight point seven percent effective rate against the biological threat—'

Number Fourteen stood up and slammed its fists down on to the table, causing the metal to bend and making a loud clanking noise within the room. 'We now have a defence against their primary weapon, we must attack now while we have the upper-hand.' It seemed to grind its clenched fists deeper into the table. While it could not change the inflections in its voice, the standing and physical actions made it seem like it was angry. 'Their mistake for underestimating us, attack.'

Laurna looked at Number One but still couldn't see his face. Number Fourteen sat down and removed its fists back to its sides acting like the outburst hadn't happened.

The machine continued to speak; now back in its seated position it seemed impassive. 'That will be the response of the other even-number council members, you know how emotional they are, they will demand we go on the offensive.'

'And what about you?' Number One asked.

'I challenged you both now to prepare you for the response of the other council members. I do and always will do what I am programmed to do.'

Laurna looked at the damaged table sitting in the middle of the three of them, and seriously doubted that. 'Very good. I think we need more androids operational before we can attack them and win.'

For the next thirty minutes they discussed and debated the technical challenges they faced in mass producing the machines.

'It is getting late or early, whichever way you look at it. You know protocol dictates that for security reasons the fourteen of us never meet en masse in person and if we do it is not for a long time. We now break, it was nice seeing you both in person.' Number One stated. 'We will bring all points raised to the other council members and vote where necessary. I bid you both farewell for now.'

Both stood up to take their leave, Thirteen nodded her head very slightly in acknowledgement while Fourteen just headed for the door.

'Oh, Number Thirteen can I have another minute of your time.' Number One called to her.

'Sure.' Laurna held back while the machine exited the room. Once it was gone another door which she hadn't even noticed opened behind Number One.

'Come with me.' She followed his instruction and wheelchair, which seemed to move effortlessly, as it passed through the door. She still couldn't make out any of his physical details as his face remained shrouded in darkness and the robe he wore covered his entire body. *I figure he is old and decrepit given he is Number One.* They entered a command centre of a ship, not as big as the main bridge of the vessel they were on but still advanced and impressive. 'Prepare to detach us from the Battlecruiser and head to the co-ordinates I gave you previously. Track the location of Number Fourteen and once he is off this submarine and back on the main ship set off.'

Laurna had no idea that this ship within a ship existed nor that she would be leaving so suddenly. She wanted to return upstairs and continue her rumination before Mr White disturbed her. Number One continued gliding forwards on to another room after he finished giving his orders to his private crew. She followed him. When they were alone he spoke again. 'I sensed your apprehension when Number Fourteen had its outburst. Please speak freely here.'

'It is a machine, programmed by us, it should not be having or playing at having emotional outbursts.' She paused, unable to gauge a reaction from the cloaked figure but decided to continue. 'I think they should be taken off-line, checked for defects, areas prone to malfunction. I do not think one of them should be on the council.' She remembered he opposed the rest of the council members in voting against having the machine as the new Number Fourteen. She hadn't been allowed to vote as it was her first meeting.

Eleven-to-one, they can't all be wrong. What don't I know, am I not seeing?

'That is the problem and why we need to be discrete, as a council member it is afforded the same level of protection and access to all ongoing missions as you and me.' He stopped as a red bulb started to flash and a siren sounded. 'Sit down, this next part gets bumpy.'

Laurna did as he suggested, and listened as heavy clunking sounds, metal bashing noises, and machinery operating rang out. The room shook and the separation was complete. The sensation was similar to the impact of hitting water following zooming down a water slide. The ship settled and sped off, it was so smooth she couldn't even tell they were moving.

'Where are we going?'

Before she knew it, he was next to her. He didn't say anything but somehow she knew he wanted to tell her something. Instinctively she leaned down, so her ear was next to where his mouth should have been. She only guessed because she still couldn't see his features. He whispered the answer to her.

He pulled away and moved to where he had previously been. She wanted to sit down, to take some time to assimilate the astounding information he had just given her. She barely took in what he was now saying.

'I fear we are facing two wars: one our primary mission, which our latest green drug may give us our first real advantage in over a hundred years and a second, of our own making. The rest of the council seems blind to this second point, they accelerated the advancement of the machines. When we were not fully ready and do not have the appropriate safety measures in place. That is why the next mission for the Yates brothers is so important. It is vital that we ensure each one succeeds in their tasks if we are to win both wars.'

She managed to regain some composure. 'Why them?'

'I need new recruits who don't know the whole picture and aren't tainted by other council members.'

Why does he think I care? 'Why are you taking me in your confidence?'

'I believe on the matter of Samuel and Mitchell accomplishing greatness, we are aligned. You want them to survive and do well.'

Does he know? How? 'I oversaw their recruitment but have no further interest in them.'

'You don't have to be coy with me, I have taken you in my inner circle, you don't have to lie. I know they are your sons. Like any good mother, even a Stitchin one, you don't want them to die.'

Laurna was stunned he knew the truth but had to try and act like it didn't bother her. *Damn you James for dying and leaving all of this on me.* She bowed her head in agreement. 'Stitch on.'

'Stitchin be.'

THE STORY CONTINUES
IN
STITCHIN: THE CLEANSE